PRAISE FOR *TURBULENCE*

"A thoughtful exploration of the blurry difference between heroes and villains. Ethical questions are deftly scrutinised in a depth that a comic book or film would struggle to match." *The Sun*

"Basu knows his stuff… he conjures up a vast array of imaginative powers [and] unflinchingly depicts the costly consequences." *SFX Magazine*

"It is, unabashedly, a new style modern superhero novel with a distinctive twist. It is also current, smart, energetic and a sparkling read. Most of all, the frenetic pace is great and the dialogue fizzes with whip-sharp quips and comments. It's funny, it's intelligently witty, it's great. Loved, loved, LOVED it." *SFF World*

"An excellent book, a thoughtful read that throws out questions without any easy answers, that opens up the superhero genre to deeper analysis, and yet is also an incredibly enjoyable superhero story itself." *Fantasy Faction*

"As unpretentious as it is entertaining, as compelling as it is thought-provoking, it establishes once and for all that the novel is as much a home for the superhero tale as film, tv and comics… it's not just an astute and captivating read, but an important one too." *Too Busy Thinking About My Comics*

"A new breed of superhero novel likely to appeal to both classic hero fans as well as fans of contemporary fiction… This is one of those rare superhero stories that is not overshadowed by the powers but is told in the humanity that pulls the superhuman together." *Geek Native*

TURBULENCE

TURBULENCE SAMIT BASU

TITAN BOOKS

TURBULENCE
Print edition ISBN: 9781781161197
E-book ISBN: 9781781161210

Published by Titan Books
A division of Titan Publishing Group Ltd
144 Southwark Street, London SE1 0UP

First US edition: July 2013
10 9 8 7 6 5 4 3 2 1

What did you think of this book?
We love to hear from our readers. Please email us at:
readerfeedback@titanemail.com, or write to us at the above address.

To receive advance information, news, competitions, and exclusive offers online, please sign up for the Titan newsletter on our website.

www.**titan**books.com

TURBULENCE

CHAPTER **ONE**

In 1984, Group Captain Balwant Singh of the Indian Air Force's Western Air Command had dangled his then three-year-old son Vir off the edge of the uppermost tier of the Eiffel Tower in Paris, nearly giving his gentle and hirsute wife, Santosh Kaur, a heart attack in the process. With the mixture of casual confidence and lunacy that is the hallmark of every true fighter pilot, Captain Singh had tossed his son up, caught him in mid-air and held him over the railing for a while, before setting him down safely.

His son's future thus secured, Balwant had turned to shut off his wife's uncanny impersonation of a police siren with the wise words, "Nonsense, foolish woman. See, my tiger is not afraid at all. He is born for the sky, just like me. Vir, say '*Nabha Sparsham Deeptam*'."

Vir had not been in the mood for the Indian Air Force motto at that point, his exact words had been, "MAA!"

All these years later, Vir still remembers that first flight with astonishing clarity: the sudden weightlessness, the deafening sound of his own heart beating, the blur of the world tilting around him, the slow-motion appearance of first the white dome of Sacré Coeur and then a wispy white cloud shaped like Indira Gandhi's hair behind his flailing red Bata Bubble-Gummers shoes. His father had said that moment had shaped his destiny, given him wings.

But his father isn't here now. Flight Lieutenant Vir Singh is all alone in the sky.

And had Balwant Singh not prepared Vir for flight, this day would probably have been a lot more difficult. As he descends from the clouds, his breath steaming from the cold, Vir looks at his shoes, ready to see a new world reveal itself slowly behind them, zooming slowly into focus from high above. Pakistan. North Pakistan. Rawalpindi District. Kahuta. He looks far beyond his shoes, to the ground, where the sprawl of the AQ Khan Research Laboratories complex lies below him like scattered Lego bricks.

Vir stands several hundred feet up in the air above a highly guarded nuclear research centre, the heart of the Pakistani nuclear weapons programme, named after a man most famous for allegedly selling nuclear tech to North Korea, Libya and Iran. Not really the sort of place where Indian Air Force officers are welcome guests. And he hasn't brought his fighter jet, his trusty Jaguar, with him. It's not that he has forgotten it in his hurry to get dressed; he simply doesn't need it any more.

Vir can fly. He stands tall, legs slightly apart, a wingless angel swaying slightly in the wind, rivulets of icy water running down his body. A young man of great presence, of power and dignity, which is only very slightly diminished by a passing migratory bird's recent use of his shoulder as a pit-stop.

The sun is harsh above the clouds, Pakistan is sweltering in the grip of summer, from the microwave that is Lahore to the steamer that is Karachi. Vir is grateful for Rawalpindi District's notoriously unpredictable weather: storm clouds are gathering around him, providing him both a degree of shade and an appropriately dramatic background, given his current circumstances. He's wearing a light-blue grey costume, the closest approximation of sky camouflage that his commanding officer has been able to procure for him. His squadron leader has asked him to put a mask on as well, like Zorro or Spider-Man, but Vir is flouting orders; men who can fly need to feel wind and sky-ice on their faces.

Storms are gathering everywhere in the region. To the west, Taliban and other tribal warlords hold sway over vast tracts of land, and constantly threaten the stability of the nation. Every day, young men blow themselves up near schools, markets and embassies. In the cities, parents complain about insane vegetable prices and worry about sending their children to school.

Halfway across the world, American leaders shiver at the prospect of mad-eyed Taliban fanatics seizing control of Pakistan's nuclear weapons. Washington sends billions of dollars to help Pakistan fight its demons; this money is not used, Pakistani leaders swear, never-ever pinkie swear, for the constant expansion of Pakistan's nuclear arsenal. And yet this arsenal continues to grow, and the Kahuta project is where uranium is enriched. This is where Pakistan's first seventy nuclear weapons came from. This is where thousands of centrifuges spin out missile-ready uranium, and hundreds of scientists design missiles to put it in. Clearly a destination of choice for flying Indian Air Force soldiers with destructive ambitions.

One swift, devastating strike, he has been told. *The sooner the world's nuclear weapons are history, the sooner we can all stop living in fear.* Vir had wanted to start with North Korea, but understood what his squadron leader had explained: the moment a single attack happened, other nuclear sites would be savagely guarded. Some scientist would figure out how to defend buildings against him. When beginning a noble anti-nuclear mission, where better to start than in your own neighbourhood?

It is his moment to shine, to swoop down like an avenging hawk, but Vir hesitates. He takes another look at the roofs of the Kahuta complex and pretends to consider where a good point of entry would be. Then he pulls a satellite phone out of a large waterproof pouch on his belt and makes a call.

"Squadron Leader?"

"Vir! Is it done? We haven't heard a word."

"No. Sir... I think we should reconsider this mission."

"You have your orders."

"But sir, the consequences –"

"– have been computed. Your concerns have been noted. Now carry out your mission, Lieutenant. Don't report until you're done."

The line goes dead.

Vir heaves a deep breath and looks down at the factory again. The mission is simple enough. He flexes his muscles, preparing to let go, to drop like a meteorite.

The phone beeps. Vir takes the call.

"Vir Singh?"

"Sir."

"Can I interest you in buying a new credit card?"

"What?"

"Kidding. Listen. Abort your mission. Fly home."

"Who is this?" It's not the voice of anyone Vir knows. Young, male, Indian, from the accent. Vir hears seventies rock music faintly in the background.

"So, what's the plan, Vir? Bust into the nuke factory, kill a few people, fly out with some uranium? Does that sound smart to you?"

"How did you get this number?"

"On a toilet cubicle wall with 'Call For Good Time' written beside it. What are you, stupid? You're about to make the biggest mistake of your life. Your father was sent to a needless death in an obsolete MiG-21 and now you're about to throw your own life away and start a war in the process. Abort!"

Vir disconnects the call, struggles to process the enormity of the security breach that has clearly happened, and then gives up. He tilts his body and stretches, like a diver getting ready to plunge.

The phone beeps again. Vir ignores it for a few seconds, then takes it out and throws it away.

And then flies down a little, catches it, and takes the call.

"You want to take out Pakistan's nuclear weapons, right?" his mystery caller continues as if there had been no interruption in their conversation. "You want to make things better one step at a time? Make the world a safer place for one and all? Well, going down there and re-enacting *King Kong* isn't going to achieve that. It looks smart – one tiny flying man going in, smashing things, and getting out – but it's not possible. Not in this world, not even with *your* powers. Not even Chuck Norris could have pulled this off in his prime."

"Bruce Lee?" a woman's voice asks in the background.

"Lee's dead. Jesus, don't be ridiculous. Sorry, Vir. But listen, man, this won't cause any real damage. I can tell you where to go. I know where all the nukes are. But now is not the time."

"Pakistan's nuclear weapons are a threat to the entire region," Vir says, distracted by a memory of the day his uncle Kulbhushan had suddenly run out into the streets of Chandigarh wearing nothing but a pair of Argyll socks, loudly proclaiming that insanity ran deep in their family. He shakes his head. Focus. "And the Pakistan government might lose control to the Taliban soon. This is a necessary step. I am acting as an independent individual and not as a representative of any country or army."

"Yes, and you just like to hang out at Indian Air Force secret bases. The booze discount is awesome. The problem, Vir, is that you haven't thought this through. You've been following orders, not using your head."

"I must know who I'm speaking with. Who do you represent?"

"No one. Everyone. Look at you. You're the finest, most powerful human being India's ever produced. A born leader. You're a – and I can't believe I'm saying this out loud – superhero. Meta-human, science hero, post-human, fly-guy, deadly post-nuclear weapon, whatever. Someone who should be setting an example. Who's the greatest Indian leader ever?"

"Gandhi?"

"Our survey says... Gandhi. Ask yourself this. If Gandhi

had your powers, would he be flying around above a Pakistani nuclear site wiping his foggy glasses and trying to start World War Three, or would he be doing something slightly more productive?"

"I'm not –"

"Thinking. I know. The game's changed, Vir. The world's changed. I'm not saying throwing some uranium at Uranus is a bad thing. But some people might not be pleased when they find out. And they will find out. You're currently potentially visible to about seventeen satellites, including the Spacecraft Control guys in Bangalore. Bengaluru. Whatever. No one's really noticed you yet, but that's because they're not looking for you, and mostly they're looking for Taliban soldiers leaping from rock to rock."

"They can't possibly get clear images of me with current technology – sorry, who are you?"

"But there'll be footage of your flight lying around that no one's seen as yet. Not only was doing this by day monumentally dumb, you made the mistake of flying to Kahuta directly from that secret base you've got in Kashmir. People in between will have seen you as well. Bad move. It's not going to take a genius to figure out where you came from."

"You can't be sure that anyone's observed me."

"I've observed you, haven't I? And it's not even my job. You know what things are like. If a pimple explodes unexpectedly in Islamabad, the Pakistani government says an Indian hand squeezed it. We do the same. You want to give them actual evidence of an attack on a nuclear site? You'll go down in history as a prize moron."

"Why should I believe any of this?"

"Don't if you don't want to. Maybe all this is a dream. What did you dream about on the plane from London, Vir? I dreamt of big shiny spaceships and aliens. Maybe that's what you should be thinking of, not pig-headed local missions."

Vir looks at the phone as if it just bit him. When he speaks into it again, his voice is hoarse with rage.

"You don't know what you're getting involved with. You must tell me everything you know immediately. If you're the one who's been trying to stop us, you're in more danger than you can imagine. We will find you."

"You won't have to try very hard. I want to meet you. But if you go into that factory today, you won't come out. You've been sent on a suicide run."

"What?"

"No one in the Air Force top brass knows about your mission, Vir. I've been listening. No Indian military chief in his right mind would have allowed this mission anyway. Whoever sent you here wants you dead. What do you do with a stray superhero? Send him to the place where your enemy keeps his nukes. Either way, someone powerful dies."

Vir struggles for a response and finds nothing. He listens, instead, to his caller, whose voice is getting more and more incoherent.

"The world needs you for more than this, Vir. I could use your help, this is bigger than India or Pakistan. No one could have planned for what happened to us on the plane. There were 403 of us when we started. There aren't now. When this is done, check your mail. Come and meet me in Mumbai. We're going to have to work together."

"I don't believe any of this. I can't abandon my mission

based on what you say."

"Well, you shouldn't have stuck around and talked for so long then. You showed up on the KRL motion detection system a while ago. You're not big enough or giving off a large enough heat signature for them to start throwing missiles at you, but you might want to make a move before they take a much closer look. The Americans will be looking for you by now as well – they've probably told their Pakistani friends you're not one of theirs. Smile and wave, Vir."

"Why didn't you tell me before?"

"Because, in case it wasn't clear enough, I don't want you to waltz into AQ Khan Labs and start a war. But I don't want you to die today, either. Now get out before they come for you. We'll talk later." The phone went silent.

Vir tucks his phone into the case on his belt. He stands in mid-air, in mid-thought, and is tempted to laugh. But then he looks up, to the west, towards the flash of light, towards the shining winged metal falcon hurtling towards him, hears that familiar jet-engine scream, and he knows the time for choices is over. The Fiza'ya has arrived.

The phone beeps again. On auto-pilot, Vir picks it up.

"F-16," his mystery caller says. "Whatever you do, don't fly back to India."

Vir hangs up, and tries to get his still-human mind to figure out a course of immediate action. It's been a month since he discovered he could fly, and he still doesn't know why. But he does know how to start, and he swirls and streaks off, cutting through the air, still marvelling at the beauty of the landscape gradually turning into a blur beneath him.

After that first exhilarating dash, he swoops up, stopping,

surveying the skies. He's been sighted. The F-16A, specially designed for manoeuvrability, has followed his trajectory and is speeding right at him. Vir wonders at the skill of its pilot: it was no mean feat to have spotted him. His appreciation is lessened, though, when he sees a stabbing point of white light coming from under the Viper's left wing. The M61 Vulcan cannon, six-barrelled, self-cooling, high-speed spinning Gatling gun of every pilot's nightmares.

Vir shuts his eyes and speeds north, the world a dull grey roar, the moaning of the jet streaking behind him flattened out, punctuated by the ceaseless hammering of the Vulcan. He hasn't had the opportunity to time himself; he doesn't know how fast he can fly. He does know, though, that the F-16 flies fastest at high altitudes, so he dips sharply, lower and lower, feeling the slap of warmer air. His skin tingles and quivers.

His phone beeps.

Vir shuts his eyes and begs his unknown powers for more. His clothes, not tested at this speed, are beginning to rip and tear. A lucky shot from the Vulcan grazes his back. He knows he's far stronger than normal humans: his squadron leader spent most of one afternoon shooting at him at close range with increasingly heavy firepower to no effect. But he doesn't know exactly what the limits of his resistance are. And he wouldn't have chosen this time, this place or this weapon in his quest for greater understanding.

He's bleeding now, as he takes off again, trailing a thin jet-stream of suspended red droplets.

The phone beeps until Vir reaches a climax of world-ending rage. He slows down, loops, and comes to a shuddering halt, and then drops like a stone. The F-16 slows too, but shoots over his head. Vir takes the call.

"Not a good time," he says.

"You're incredibly fast. Do you know where you are now? You're near Gilgit. That's about 260 kilometres in just more than a minute."

Far ahead, the F-16 goes through a sharp turn, its bubble canopy gleaming in the sun.

"Make this quick," Vir says.

"Just a heads-up. You've killed the Viper, right?"

"Not yet."

"Well, if you don't, the Pakistanis have evidence of an act of war. Listen, he's probably seen you and has good pictures of you. You need to take him out. Think like a pilot. Don't race him. Dance with him. He's a fatty."

"Go to hell," Vir snaps.

The fatty is close now, Vulcan hammering away. Vir flies up, making short, sharp, diagonal dashes, flitting bat-like closer to the F-16 until he can see the pilot, who's chattering excitedly into his mouthpiece as he tries to steer his wobbling craft into position. A burst of speed, and Vir is directly above the Falcon. He drops gently on it, and hangs on. Panicking, the pilot cuts loose. Vir darts aside as the jet roars away, leaving him wobbling and coughing in its slipstream. When the roar has faded somewhat, he puts the phone to his ear.

"That was good advice," he says.

"Hey, no problem. Excellent network on these satellite phones, huh? What is it? Thuraya? Globalstar? My phone usually gets cut off when I walk from my bedroom to my kitchen."

"Focus. What do I do now?"

"Oh, yeah, babbling, sorry. I do that. You should head north.

Don't turn right until you reach Tajikistan. Come back through Nepal or Bhutan. Try not to provoke the Chinese."

"Has he got pictures of me? Is our secret out?"

"I've been trying to jam his communications, but I don't know – something might have got through. Why don't you ask him? He'll probably be back, get him then. He'll have told them about you, but without pictures everyone will assume flying men are American."

True enough, the F-16 is back, and this time it's locked in on Vir. There are two Sidewinder heat-seeking missiles on rail launchers on its wingtips – the pilot launches them both in quick succession and then comes in, cannons blazing.

Vir pauses for a second and looks around, taking in the majesty of the scene. The Karakoram Mountains lie to the north, harsh cliffs and peaks cutting dagger-like shadows. No clouds here: the sun is bright, unrelenting. He breathes in, enjoying the mountain air. And then the missiles reach him. Vir darts aside politely, watches the Sidewinders shoot past, and then races towards the jet.

Afraid now, the pilot swerves sharply. But Vir is faster, he joins the F-16 in flight and together they head for the hills. Ahead of them, the Sidewinders swerve and circle, sensing their target's trajectory. The pilot now sees Vir's face clearly for the first time: this is no small robot spy drone, this is another man, their skins are the same colour. His jaw drops; he stares at Vir with religious awe, unable to persuade his hands to move the controls any longer. Time stops; human and superhuman make eye contact.

"Sorry," Vir says. He streaks upwards as the Sidewinders close in on him and miss, smashing into the F-16's canopy instead.

The blast hits Vir hard, a flying wing from the shattered F-16 hits him even harder. He rolls and tumbles in mid-air, losing all control, and hurtles flailing towards the mountainside, seeing serious pain await him at rainbow's end. Burning debris races with him. His mind begins to drift away in a torrent of fire and wind.

Snapping to attention, he spots in the shadow of a rock-face a dark hole in the centre of a ring of flaming debris, a crack in the mountain: a cave. Using the very last of his strength, he aligns his body to the cave-mouth, swims into the right parabola, and manages to rocket into the darkness just as the broken jet smashes thunderously into the mountainside around him.

Vir slides toboggan-like through the cave, the sudden coolness strangely relaxing even as his body screams with pain. He dimly hears the sound of men shouting. Turning his head as he slides, he sees bearded, robe-clad, gun-wielding men up ahead, in front of a lantern-lit door. He smashes through the door, taking the men with him, on to a metal platform, through a crude iron gate, and suddenly the world is well lit again, and he's back in mid-air inside the mountain, the gunmen falling by his side, screaming. And then he crashes into the cavern floor, slides a little more for good measure and, thankfully, stops.

Flat on his back, breathing raggedly, he takes in the scenery. A huge cavern that's been converted into a bunker. Well-lit, generators humming, crude electrical wiring everywhere. To his right, rows of tables, some covered with guns and ammunition, some with food and supplies, others with computers. Platforms, tunnel openings and ammunition racks line the cavern walls. Sirens wail. Gun-wielding men in boots thunder down metal steps and out of inner caves, shouting.

Vir sighs. To his left, a white-robed man sits unperturbed, typing at a computer. Vir squints and peers at the screen, expecting blueprints, war plans; instead he sees a Facebook homepage. The man rises, turns slowly and looks at Vir. And as Vir sees, through the red and green worms of pain floating across his vision, the man's face, the long salt-and-pepper beard, the deep, sad eyes, the straight, proud nose, the famous white turban, he closes his own eyes and starts laughing uncontrollably as he drifts into unconsciousness.

When he opens his eyes again, there are about thirty AK-47s pointed at his face, and a man is trying, unsuccessfully but passionately, to stab him in the chest with a Gerber Infantry knife. As Vir looks at him, he leaps backwards, muttering sheepishly. Someone has tied his hands and feet together. He snaps the ropes without effort and rises to his feet slowly, looking for the white-robed man. He has disappeared, though there are several lookalikes among the gunmen around him. On a high platform to his left, a few women who look like belly-dancers squeal, giggle and point. Vir realises, suddenly, that he has been naked for a while. His belt, the only surviving article of his clothing, lies around the smoking ruins of his shoes. A sound comes from it. It's his phone, beeping.

One of the gunmen picks up the phone and takes the call. Vir doesn't know whether it's his mysterious new ally or his squadron leader. He snatches the phone from the gunman and puts it to his ear. Static, mostly. Satellite phones are useless indoors, especially burnt ones.

Seeing their protests ignored, the gunmen begin to shoot him; bullets fly off his skin. He was once caught in a hailstorm, this doesn't feel very different. His muscles creak to life, one by one. Acupuncture by AK-47. More people scream, howl, fall to their feet in prayer, throw things; he's not particularly bothered any more.

"We'll talk later," he says into the phone, and crushes it with his fist. He heaves a huge and weary sigh, and stretches, looking curiously at the men emptying their guns in his unyielding flesh. Some have gone to get grenade-launchers; others just stand around uselessly. Something in their faces moves him to pity; their fight was a dark one before, but it is hopeless now.

He politely asks a nearby cowering man for his robe, and gets it. And then he flies off, out of the cavern and into the sky.

CHAPTER **TWO**

"The wonderful thing about Bollywood," Uzma says, gently twirling a strand of her long black hair, "is that everyone in the industry is so nice."

All the other actresses sitting or standing in the crowded Daku Samba Entertainment office lobby look at her with identical expressions of incredulity, wondering whether Uzma is joking, mad, drugged or all of the above. Even Uzma's (current) best friend and Mumbai hostess Saheli feels slightly apprehensive as she nods and smiles beside her.

"You've been lucky," Saheli says. "Most outsiders trying to get a job here have horror stories."

"I've heard a lot of that too," Uzma says. "But you know what? I think it's all made up by people to scare newcomers away. Discourage competition. I think if anyone comes in with the right attitude and the right kind of talent Bollywood's much more warm and welcoming than anything back home. And people who haven't landed an acting gig after spending years here? They should probably just quit."

Saheli flinches and scans the room, half expecting all the other actresses there to fly screaming at Uzma and tear her limb from limb in a frenzy of manicured nails and strategically applied stilettos. But no, they're just sitting there listening to her, and none of the women, several of whom have clearly been auditioning unsuccessfully for at least a decade, even seem angry – though some look extremely depressed.

Uzma does cut a fairly formidable figure: tall, toned, dark, smouldering, impeccably dressed, and a rich Oxford accent to boot – essential for those romantic blockbusters where the hero, in between foiling international terrorist plots in Sydney and dancing in Macau, pauses to play American football for Oxford. But while Saheli has spent most of her life instantly disliking women like Uzma – and, it must be said, Uzma herself, during their days together at St Hilda's – she's becoming accustomed, slowly, to the fact that she's become really fond of Uzma now. Her initial dismay on reading that email about Uzma's planned visit to Mumbai – *Just a week, darling, until I find digs of my own. It is my first time in your city and I haven't seen you in SO long* – disappeared the moment she saw her former classmate step out of the airport.

A pure Bollywood moment: the crowd parted like the Red Sea as Uzma sashayed out, effortlessly performing the Heroine Time-Slowing Effect, her hair unfurling, cascading, shining, a smile of pure delight spreading across her face as she saw Saheli goggling at her. Unmindful of the jaw-dropping eye-popping handbag-flopping effect she had on the crowd, Uzma raced across the tarmac and swept Saheli up in an enthusiastic embrace. Several men in the crowd burst into spontaneous applause. Babies gurgled. Aunties wept joyously. As far as Mumbai was concerned, Uzma Abidi couldn't have made a better entrance.

"Uzma Abidi?" a dishevelled assistant director calls, entering the lobby. "Come in, please."

Uzma is ushered through the door. It shuts, and the large Warhol-style portrait of the leering henchman from Bollywood's most famous epic resumes its gap-toothed observation of the assembled ladies. A disgruntled murmur fills the lobby.

A tiny model-type in a tinier dress taps Saheli on the shoulder and voices everyone's concern: "Who *is* that?"

"Her name's Uzma. She's new in town," Saheli says, wondering exactly when she had signed up to play a supporting character in Uzma's biopic. That Uzma is in Mumbai now, looking to become the next Aishwarya Rai, is mostly Saheli's fault.

Uzma had been exposed to Bollywood a little while growing up in England, mainly videos of blockbusters from the seventies and eighties, a time when Indian men had hairy chests and unrepentant paunches, wore cravats and bell-bottoms and were social chameleons equally at ease in tribal villages surrounded by feather-duster-sporting dancers and in underground lairs full of metal drums, collapsible henchmen and chained virgins.

Saheli had introduced her to the New Bollywood, the in-your-face, slick, Armani-enabled imperial-ambitions, global Bollywood, the dream machine that had spawned hundreds of enterprises like Daku Samba Entertainment. Told her stories of hip, edgy companies with producers flaunting designer eyewear and customised iPhones, swanky offices with intentionally ironic decor and voluptuous receptionists with call-centre New

York accents. Of a new generation of actors who had come from nowhere and were currently staring back at the world through giant screens and YouTube windows everywhere, talking about how they would only shed their clothes if the role demanded it. Of girls from Mexico and Germany, and everywhere else, gathering in Mumbai like tinsel-tinged salmon. Of young, ambitious, world-cinema-educated, genre-blending, fast-talking, next-big-thing directors actually interested in making good films. Uzma had fallen hard, and decided that Bollywood was a bandwagon she had to be on top of, making suggestive hip movements with men twice her age.

"She's fresh, no? And not bad looking," Tiny Model says, trying to add to her air of casually detached interest by pretending to be absorbed in a tabloid whose front page proudly proclaims: Man-tiger monster sighted in Kashmir: Is this the next Monkey-Man? "Does she have, like, connections?"

"No," Saheli replies, surprised to find how proud she sounds. But, yes, in the face of all logic, she's thrilled to bits by what Uzma has achieved in two weeks in Bollywood.

Day One: Uzma arrives from Lucknow, where she has spent two weeks with her great-aunt, who had stayed in India when her sister, Uzma's grandmother, had moved with her husband's family to Lahore in 1947. Unfortunately Uzma's great-aunt's sense of connection with the outside world had also been packed into one of those large aluminium trunks all those years ago, so Uzma is glad to have escaped.

Mumbai takes one quick look at Uzma and clasps her to its sweaty bosom. On their journey from the airport to the nearest local train station, the auto-rickshaw driver bursts into song in Uzma's honour and insists that, as a token of India's generosity, her ride with him costs nothing. He does take half the fare from Saheli, though. On the long three-stage journey to Saheli's home, a flat in Navi Mumbai, Uzma is dismayed to find that the fortress from which she intends to launch her assault on Bollywood is at least two hours' journey away. But her mood is considerably improved when Saheli's parents – who had spent three long years clucking uncomfortably about the clothes they'd seen Uzma wearing in Saheli's photos – see her and fall in love. Saheli is too flabbergasted at the miracle she has recently witnessed – a woman in the crowded ladies' compartment on their local train actually getting up to offer Uzma her seat – to notice that she has been cast as Uzma's sidekick in her own home.

Day Two: Uzma ventures forth to conquer the big, bad world of Bollywood. Her first stop: a coffee shop where she meets Chrisann, a film-journalist friend of Saheli's. Within ten minutes Chrisann, widely known as the snootiest woman in the greater Mumbai area, offers Uzma her complete list of film-people phone numbers and an invitation to the premiere of the new blockbuster *Khatra: Luv In The Time of The Dangerrr* where she will have the opportunity to meet "industry insiders". An hour into this five-minute meeting Chrisann's brother Bruno, a TV producer, turns up, is instantly smitten and asks Uzma if she's interested in becoming a cricket presenter – one of a fast-growing breed of glamorous young women called upon to provide in-depth cricket analysis in skimpy clothing for India's never-ending slew of cricket shows.

Uzma, whose interest in cricket is nonexistent, turns this offer down, but accepts a lift to Bandra for a small, intimate evening at Toto's which turns, in several stages, into a pool party at a

B-list Bollywood star's house, several phone numbers and one inebriated proposal of marriage from a society photographer. Uzma stumbles into Saheli's house at four in the morning smelling of Mumbai, and Saheli's parents laugh nervously but fondly as they let her in.

Days Three to Eight: Saheli and her parents mope forlornly around the house, missing Uzma desperately. Uzma's memories of these days are blurred at best, but from extensive reconstruction Saheli has deduced the following: Uzma drifts from party to meeting to launch to premiere to party, making friends, influencing people. Before she has faced the camera even once, she is featured in two human-interest pieces about the most promising newcomers in the film industry, and in three tabloids as the secret new girlfriend of three separate stars. Seven industry big-wigs "discover" her at various nightspots. She is offered dozens of reality shows and contests, most of which involve singing or speaking in Hindi, neither of which Uzma is really capable of.

She runs out of money on Day Four, and graciously begins to accept film offers. She finds out soon, though, that the enthusiasm that producers, directors and actors feel when they meet her at parties doesn't extend as far as their chequebooks. Using the acumen genetically acquired from her mother, a leading corporate lawyer in London, she soon figures out that the contracts she is being asked to sign involve her a) never working for anyone else and b) sitting and waiting for films that, thanks to the global economic recession, might never be made. She signs up for a few ad shoots instead, becomes the first outsider in the history of the Mumbai entertainment industry to turn a profit within their first week, and spends all her newly acquired riches getting a Sapna Bhavnani haircut.

She makes exciting new friends: Capoeira dancers from Brazil who have come to Bollywood to be instructors, Zen Buddhist monks who moonlight as DJs, Formula One glamour girls from Australia. An A-list star invites her over to his sea-view flat to give her advice, gives her advice all night, and his wife returns from a bag-buying trip to Mauritius and gives her Ethiopian coffee in the morning.

Day Nine: A bleary Uzma returns to Navi Mumbai to take stock. Saheli listens, gaping, as Uzma trots out Bollywood-insider stories about treadmills for dogs and secret liaisons among rival domestic help cliques in Pali Hill. Saheli feels a terrible pang of sorrow when Uzma announces her intention of leaving at the end of the week she'd invited herself for. Saheli's parents are even more stricken: Uzma is the daughter they've always wanted, they tell her. Uzma spends her evening with Saheli's family, turning off her constantly ringing phone after an hour. Saheli's father gives her Instructions Essential for Single Girls in the City. Uzma is surprised when he warns her not to tell any prospective landlords that her parents are from Pakistan.

At midnight, Uzma's parents call from London. They are worried: a few plainclothes policemen have come to their house and asked several questions about Uzma. On being assured that the only danger Uzma faces currently is the prospect of exploding from all the food Saheli's mother is force-feeding her, everyone laughs heartily.

Days Ten to Twelve: Saheli calls in sick and plays trusty sidekick. The dynamic duo's mission: to find Uzma a place to live. They wander up and down Mumbai and find that all available housing is a) too expensive b) too small c) too remote

d) simply not available because Uzma is female, Uzma is Muslim, Uzma is single, Uzma is foreign, Uzma is alone, Uzma is an actress, and you know what they say about struggling actresses. Uzma is dismayed, all the more so because it seems to cause each prospective landlord genuine pain to turn her away. They all assure her of their undying sorrow and regret. They promise to help her find any place but theirs. There are three or four places where they don't run into categories a) to d) but another problem rises, like Godzilla from an iceberg, in each of these places e) it just doesn't feel right.

Day Thirteen: Uzma gets on the phone and makes appointments. She travels all over south and central Mumbai, squired by an enthusiastic army of new friends, and as she passes the city stares and sighs in appreciation. She gets several offers, mostly second or third leads in star-studded "musical romantic action comedy thrillers". Or leads in clearly third-rate movies with leery co-stars and directors.

Saheli expects Uzma to take one of these offers, and is surprised when in the evening she finds Uzma, having spent a certain amount of time thinking intensely, has decided that she doesn't want any role that she hasn't earned. She has not come to Bollywood to be an Item Girl; she wants to be an Actress. Uzma wants to work in Meaningful Cinema, Edgy Multiplex Films – at least until she gets to play the lead opposite Shahrukh Khan. And while she has enjoyed the attention and casual offers, she knows she wants to work with Serious Artists. Therefore Uzma has decided to use her contacts to find auditions, not eye-candy roles. Her first port of call: a new, cutting-edge company named Daku Samba, currently auditioning for the female lead in an Indian reworking of *The Tempest*, a magic–realist noir piece set during the Mumbai floods of 2005.

Day Fourteen:

"Wake up, love. We're done."

Saheli shakes herself awake. Uzma towers above her, looking amused.

"How was it?"

The whole lobby leans forward as Uzma's face clouds over.

"Terrible."

"You're not a very good actress. You're clearly lying."

Uzma smiles, the sun bursts out of the clouds, and all the other actresses are stunned to find they're actually happy for this girl.

The Daku Samba door opens, and Anurag Kashyap, Dark Lord of new-age Bollywood, steps out. Uzma's competitors gasp, quiver in excitement and slip into poses that would fit into Kashyap films, their faces flitting through Moody, Angsty, Tormented, Post-Coital and Wearily Amused, their eyes moist and intense. Kashyap looks at them, shudders imperceptibly and turns to Uzma.

"Well done," he says. "I'm really looking forward to working with you."

Uzma and Saheli float out of the building into the streets of Juhu on a pink cloud of excitement.

As they step out, auto-rickshaws queue up for the privilege of taking the new Queen of Bollywood wherever she wants to go.

Saheli's phone rings. She takes the call, and as she listens the smile slowly fades from her face. When she disconnects and turns to Uzma, she looks worried.

"Your great-aunt called from Lucknow," she says. "The police were over, looking for you."

"That's weird," Uzma says. "It happened when I was there as well."

"Why?"

"I don't know. They probably check on foreigners all the time. When I was there, a couple of policemen took me to the station one day and asked me all sorts of stuff."

"What are you saying? Why didn't you tell me?"

"Mostly because I forgot all about it. There was no trouble, they were very sweet. They just asked me whether anything out of the ordinary had happened to me. One of them said they needed to run some physical tests on me, but I told them I'd rather not, I was completely knackered, and my great-aunt would be worried if I wasn't home soon. The inspector in charge told me not to worry, they'd make up the test results – they were looking for some terrorist who was on my flight from London, but I clearly wasn't their man. Then he dropped me home on this old noisy bike. He was really fit."

"Well, they're looking for you again. Your great-aunt told my mother she gave them a big scolding and told them you'd gone back to England."

"They're lucky she didn't shoot them – there's an ancient gun in the house. Par-nani's a crazy old bird, and she's not scared of anyone. And she's hated the police since the 1940s. Should I be worried?"

"I don't know. Is there anything you've done that you want to tell me about?"

Uzma's phone rings. Smiling an apology at Saheli, she takes the call.

"Uzma Abidi?" a young male voice asks.

"Yeah? Who is this?"

"My name is Aman Sen. I've heard you're facing certain difficulties. I believe I have a solution."

Saheli and the auto driver wait patiently for several minutes as Uzma alternates between the words "Oh?", "Really?", "Yeah?" and "Brilliant!" When Uzma hangs up, she's grinning widely. Silencing with an elegant palm the auto driver's attempts at introducing himself and his soon-to-take-off career as a stunt driver, Uzma turns to Saheli.

"There's a place in Versova. Yari Road. Slightly crazy owner just called. Says he's inherited a big house and doesn't know what to do with it, so he's letting people stay there. He's heard I'm a brilliant actress and wants to help me out, so he's all right with me paying whatever I can afford."

"Sounds like a mass murderer to me," Saheli says.

"Shut up. Yari Road's a good place to live, right?"

"Most of the entertainment industry stays there. You'll be neck-deep in parties."

The auto sputters forth, weaving snake-like through traffic. Uzma leans back in the seat and looks at the garish stickers of actresses on the auto's sides.

"Do you think there'll be some of me one day?"

"Uzma, I need to ask you something."

"Yes, sorry. Have I done anything illegal? No. It's just been a really great trip so far. I've been really lucky."

"You were lucky in college. You were popular in college. But these last two weeks – there's something I'm not getting here. I keep trying to figure it out. Sure, you're hot. But I've lived in this city all my life, and I've known you for four years, and something just doesn't fit. No one has the kind of luck you've been having so far."

"No one you know, you mean. Maybe I'm just... right, I sound like a complete bitch saying this, but maybe I just have a destiny here, yeah? Maybe this was where I was meant to be. Look, I know what you're saying. It's been weird. Not just in Mumbai. People in Lucknow kept trying to invite me into their houses and feed me. It's just been wonderful. You know – you ever have the feeling that you're part of something bigger?"

"Yes, but it never means anything. What are you talking about?"

Uzma stirs uncomfortably. "See, on the flight from London to Delhi – it's about thirteen hours, you know, you've been on it – I had this dream. A really long dream, because I pretty much slept through the entire flight – don't remember a thing after getting on that plane."

"So you slept on the plane. Why are you telling me this?"

"Well, that was really when things got a bit odd. It was this really bizarre dream. I was at a big awards show – like the Oscars, but more Bollywood, you know, lots of dancers and glitter – and I was getting prize after prize after prize, and everyone who was anyone was there and they all loved me and we all went to this smashing party afterwards. And they told me I was the best actress ever and everyone would come see all my films and they would make the world perfect."

"So you had a good dream. But how is this relevant?"

"I don't know. But then I landed in India, and ever since I got here people have just been incredibly good to me. Maybe I'm just – meant for this. Maybe everything's just going to fall into place for once. Maybe this is what happens to some people. You don't know, right? I know it sounds really stupid and vain, and I've been trying not to think about it. But I have this strange feeling that everyone's going to love me and everything's going to be all right."

"Well, I'm happy for you. I suppose this is what it feels like for people when they find out what they're meant for. I wish I knew what I was meant for."

"I can't believe I just told you all this. You must hate me now. I sound like such an ultimate cow."

"No," Saheli says. "I don't hate you. I don't even feel jealous of you, and I really should. It's all very strange. I think you're right. You're going to be a big star."

As the auto whines towards Versova, towards Uzma's next conquest, Saheli looks at her former classmate, now staring out at the sea as the wind caresses her hair, and feels a burst of sadness. That sense of loss every first agent, every first small-time director, every childhood friend, every parent knows. The knowledge that your part in the story is done, that something larger than you is taking place but there's no real room for you in it any more. The slow realisation that you were part of something once, but it's gone now, it's slipped out of your fingers. The star has moved on, and it's time to take a bow and make your exit as gracefully as you can.

CHAPTER **THREE**

Uzma stretches out on her old, creaky four-poster bed and looks out of her window. The sun is setting outside, and her room is bathed in amber light, tiger-striped on her wall through the palm trees just outside her window. The sharp, pungent smell of the sea drifts in; a gentle breeze tinkles through her wind-chime. The breeze is warm and salty but her room stays pleasantly cool. The first thing Uzma noticed about her new home was how pleasant it was for Mumbai, almost as cool as the air-conditioned five-star hotels she has been drifting in and out of for her meetings with the tycoons of Bollywood.

Today is her first day in her Yari Road home. It's an old, somewhat fusty four-storey building – a very strange house for Versova, where most old buildings have been torn down and replaced by large multi-storied housing complexes with gates and guards and fancy names. Uzma has a whole floor to herself: her new landlord has warned her that she might have to share her floor with another tenant, but there's plenty of room – there are three large bedrooms on this level alone. And there hasn't been any talk of rent. To add to this cocktail of delight, her landlord has not shown any definite signs of being a pervert or a werewolf. Only a certain excessive brightness in his eyes and an air of barely concealed amusement at everything around him prevent him from seeming completely ordinary.

Aman Sen is an unremarkable-looking man in his early twenties, medium everything. Most of the men Uzma has had conversations with since arriving in Mumbai have been extremely impressive in one way or another: ambitious, well-groomed, fast-living, ultra-sharp entertainment types in various shades of attractive. There's certainly nothing unattractive about Aman, it must be said, but he's the person whose name everyone at a glamorous Mumbai party forgets within two seconds of hearing it. Following the recently delivered commandments of Saheli's father, Uzma has Not Been Too Friendly with this Spouse-less Landowner, thus cunningly avoiding a Compromising Situation, but she had Aman pegged as eccentric but harmless within two minutes of meeting him. Compared to the sharks she has been swimming with, he is but a goldfish.

Aman shares the first floor of the house with Tia, an effervescent, curvaceous and altogether adorable Bengali woman in her early thirties who swept Uzma up in a huge hug the second they met and has now decided, to Uzma's slight worry, to be her best friend and constant companion. Tia and the other two inhabitants of the house, whom Uzma has not met yet, have only known Aman for two weeks, but already Tia and he are very close – unless Tia walks around in tiny shorts in front of everyone she knows. Uzma is on the second floor, and on the third are the two mysterious entities described to Uzma as the Scientist and Young Bob.

Tia has taken charge of the house: she runs the kitchen, the errands and most of the conversation. The house was probably not built for renting out. There's only one kitchen, a vast hall-like room on the ground floor that has seen cooking on a mass scale once, but now lies mostly unused. The rest of the ground floor is divided between a dining room and a huge and draughty living room where a few very modern sofas, a foosball table and a very large flatscreen TV stand uncomfortably, like jugglers at a funeral.

This is the first time since her arrival in India that Uzma has been alone in a large room for any length of time, and now that she has space to breathe she is surprised to find how much she misses her family. Something about Tia reminds her of her eldest brother Yusuf's wife. Probably the loud and tuneless singing that Uzma can hear drifting upstairs as Tia attacks yet another room somewhere in the house, armed with a duster, a mop, a bucket and a smile.

Uzma's phone is on silent. She has decided not to go out tonight, to spend time with her new housemates. But her housemates don't seem to be particularly social: Aman disappeared into his room hours ago and hasn't emerged yet, and something tells her that the Scientist and Young Bob might not be the most delightful company. Uzma potters around her room for a while, wishing she was better at spending time by herself, when she sees Tia coming down the stairs from the third floor.

"I thought you were downstairs," Uzma calls. "Who's singing?"

"What singing?"

Uzma listens again and finds, to her surprise, that there is indeed no singing.

Tia shrugs. "It's Mumbai, Uzma. There's always some noise somewhere. You bored? Come with me."

They head to the living room and plonk themselves down on the sofas, and Tia tells Uzma the story of her life, of her childhood in Assam and her marriage, at the tender age of twenty, to a tea estate manager from Darjeeling. It hadn't been a very happy marriage: her husband had been handsome but weak-willed, and her in-laws fierce and medieval.

Evening turns slowly into night as Tia speaks lovingly of the green hills near Guwahati and the swift grey waters of the ever-shifting Brahmaputra River, and Uzma listens in wonder, trying very hard to not reveal to Tia that she doesn't really know where Assam is. As she watches Tia's eyes shine, sees her laugh uproariously over the smallest things, she realises that no matter how awful Tia's family had been, for her to abandon that life and come to Mumbai, to live in a house full of strangers younger than her, is a far more difficult journey than any Uzma herself will ever have to make.

"It's not so bad," Tia says. "I'm really happy with this house. Aman's a sweetheart – you'll love him when he gets a bit more comfortable around you – the other two are hilarious, and I have to say I really like you. I'm glad I came to Mumbai."

"You should have come years ago, then."

"I could have – but I couldn't leave my son, could I?"

"You have a son?"

"Yes. Three years old now. You'll love him when you meet him."

"You must miss him terribly."

Tia's smile vanishes completely. "I'm with him, always," she says, rising from the sofa, not meeting Uzma's eyes. "I'll never leave him. Dinner?"

Dinner turns out to be a grilled lobster, sitting red and voluptuous in the kitchen, and Uzma is delighted. "Did you make this? When? How?"

"I'm very efficient," Tia says. "You'll see."

They sit in the dining room in happy silence and devour the lobster. Aman doesn't make an appearance, but as the mighty crustacean's last white, succulent meaty bits are on the verge of vanishing there's a shuffling noise at the door.

"Uzma, meet Balaji Bataodekar, also known as Bob," Tia says as a plump, dark, Elvis-haired boy, not more than fifteen, enters the room warily. He sticks out a pudgy hand, which Uzma shakes with due solemnity. Bob, however, is here on matters far more important than meeting glamorous women from distant lands.

"Can I have some?" he asks, looking meaningfully at the lobster.

Tia glances at him, then at Uzma, and says, "Of course, darling. But not too much, no? It heats up your stomach. There's lots of ice-cream in the fridge."

"I'm sick of ice-cream," Bob says, scooping up the remaining fragments of lobster and shovelling them into his mouth. "Sick of nimbu-pani, sick of mint. I want vada-pav, mutton kolhapuri and pizza. With lots of jalapenos. That's what I want."

There's a huge muffled boom from upstairs.

"The Scientist at work," Bob says.

"Aman told me the soundproofing was finished," Tia says.

"It is," Bob says, and sniggers.

"Can I meet him?" Uzma asks. "Sorry, I've been up really late the last few nights and I'm terribly awake. Can we go up?"

"You should definitely meet him," Bob says.

"I'd rather not," Tia says, covering a forced yawn with a delicate hand. "He hates being disturbed when he's working. I think we should all go to sleep."

Uzma recognises refusals when she sees them, and doesn't push the matter.

An hour later, Uzma is nowhere near sleep; her body has become accustomed to heading out for the second party at around this hour. The coolness that enveloped the house has vanished: it's a hot and muggy night, and aspiring queens of Bollywood do not enjoy sweating under creaky fans. The only sounds to be heard in the house are dull clangs from the third floor. Uzma decides it is time to be social again.

After swiftly and silently climbing the stairs, Uzma finds the third floor's layout is the same as hers. The door of the room directly above hers is open. She sees Bob stretched out on his bed, asleep, his hands clasping his considerable belly. He appears to be in some discomfort; his face is clenched and he's sweating profusely. Not finding anything in this sight to engage her extensively, Uzma turns and walks down the narrow corridor by the stairs to the door behind which lie the Scientist and his Vulcan-like clangs. She knocks, quietly at first, and then loudly, and then, unused to rejection, starts banging on the door, even before she remembers the room has been soundproofed.

After a few minutes, the door opens and Tia comes out, adjusting her clothes.

"What's wrong?" Tia asks.

"Nothing. I couldn't sleep, so I thought I'd come up and hang out with the guys if they were awake. Am I – sorry, I think I'll just go back to bed. Good night."

The door to the Scientist's room is ajar behind Tia, and a bright green light comes out of the room, making Tia's head glow a vaguely sinister green. Uzma flinches a bit when Tia beams at her and her teeth shine fluorescent.

"No, you're not interrupting anything," Tia says with a giggle. "I just like being here and watching him work sometimes. Come in. Make as much noise as you like, you won't disturb him."

Uzma wants to point out that Tia had said, just a while ago, that the Scientist hated being disturbed. Instead, she tiptoes in and observes the Scientist's room with a mixture of awe and incredulity.

The wall between two bedrooms has been knocked down, forming one large hall. The sizeable windows have been shut and covered; a gigantic split air-conditioner hums away on a wall. To Uzma's left is a ceiling-high pile of assorted objects and apparatus: metal sheets, wooden planks, boxes full of screws and bolts and other little thingummies that Uzma cannot name, naked computer motherboards, containers of an incredible variety of shapes, materials and sizes, dozens of tools for cutting, welding and shaping, miscellaneous toys and gadgets, vehicle spare parts, gas cylinders, evil-looking liquids bubbling in flasks that sit on stands, rising out of the debris like lighthouses. A lot of these have been wired, soldered or otherwise melded into nameless machines, each of which is performing its own assigned mysterious task.

The sheer variety of objects is stunning. It would not be

surprising if the entire mass rose and formed a bizarre sentient golem-like creature, the love-child of a laboratory, a witch's cauldron and the bedroom of Leonardo da Vinci as a child. From this mountain of scrap, hundreds of wires trail out across the room, at first in amorously intertwined clusters, but then forming independent streams and tributaries, flowing across an ocean of grease stains, spilt paint and burn smudges, dotted with islands of more clustered junk.

In the centre of the room stands what appears to be a metal statue of a man, with green-glowing wires coiled around it like veins. Beside this stands a thin, short man in his fifties, clad in a frayed white shirt, pyjamas that were white once and big, bug-eye goggles. His head is exceptionally large, and bald except for a few wisps of hair drooping from above his ears in a defeated sort of way.

"Uzma, this is Sundar Narayan. The Scientist," Tia says.

Uzma is surprised when the Scientist does nothing to acknowledge her presence. She's even more surprised when he moves and she sees that his face is completely slack, his mouth hanging open. He's drooling slightly, and his movements, for all their speed and dexterity, are somewhat odd, puppet-like.

Narayan hovers around his growing creation like a moth, prodding, poking, adding wires and circuitry, fingers almost blurring. It's as if he's a sculptor, or a musician playing the most complicated piano in the world. Whatever it is he's building, it's something that's already perfectly designed in his head. Occasionally he darts off to another part of the room, plunges his arm into a heap of assorted junk and emerges holding something shiny, which he then runs to add to his strange masterpiece.

Uzma is irresistibly reminded of a video she'd seen on National Geographic years ago in Oxford, when a visiting uncle from Pakistan had insisted that she stop watching *Friends* and learn something instead – she'd switched channels unwillingly but had soon found herself engrossed in a show about a weaverbird building its nest, creating an elaborate colonial home with just its beak, its incredible skill rendered eerie by the madness of fast-forward TV. Narayan looks more like a token Indian extra in a zombie movie than a bird, but he, too, is constructing something solid and curvy and beautiful out of little bits of detritus the world has no further use for, another wondrous device that seems to follow scientific principles its maker should not be aware of.

"You're taking all of this in very well," Tia says. "The first time I saw him do his thing, I was completely freaked out."

Uzma stares at Narayan in bewilderment, still waiting for some indication that all of this is an elaborate prank, some kind of bizarre household initiation ceremony involving balloons and streamers. As if in response to her searching stare, he turns away from his machines and towards her, his goggles making it impossible to see if he's looking at her. She almost screams when he snores loudly, and his head lolls to one side. Then he swings and sways, a flesh scarecrow, and returns to his tinkering, leaving Uzma breathing in great gulps and shuddering at Tia's reassuring pats.

"Is he... asleep?" Uzma asks, resisting the urge to run.

"Yeah. He does all this stuff in his sleep, and when he wakes up he spends all day in here trying to understand his inventions. I don't think he's got anywhere yet," Tia replies.

"Makes stuff from his dreams? How is that even possible?"

"Well, poets do the same thing, don't they? He says it's something to do with his subconscious working out the engineering problems his everyday mind can't. Id-Design, he calls it."

"So what has he invented so far?"

Tia gestures to Uzma's right and she sees, in the far corner of the Scientist's den, a strange assortment of objects in glass cases on little stands, a small exhibition of the insanity she feels snickering and gurgling in the air around her. There's what looks like a lava lamp, amoeba-like green globules floating in a viscous orange gel, with a sign in front of it that proclaims XONTRIUM EGO SUSPENSION in a child's shaky handwriting. The next case contains what looks like a toy gun, the sort of thing aliens in science-fiction B-movies use when asking you to take them to your leader, it's labelled TACHYON DISLOCATOR. A few other cases contain more devices Uzma cannot understand. Their labels are of no help either, the names written in Sundar's sleep-hand all gibberish, a child's attempt at science-fiction names for the future-tech doodles in his school diary, names as meaningless to Uzma as "iPod" or "Twitter" would have been to her mother in the seventies.

The final case, in the corner of the room, is large and empty. This is clearly where Sundar's statue-with-wires-and-things will go once it is finished. None of this makes any sense. Uzma is suddenly reminded, again, of television, of Adam West *Batman* reruns, of villains with colourful lines and even more colourful costumes, building doomsday devices considerately labelled DOOMSDAY DEVICE so Batman and Robin knew exactly where to go *CRASH*! when dismantling the villain of the week's secret underground lair.

"What is this stuff?"

Tia shrugs. "He doesn't know. He doesn't even know what to call these things until he labels them in his sleep."

"I don't know the first thing about science," Uzma admits, "but this is very *Doctor Who*, yeah? Do a lot of Indian scientists do this?"

"Invent stuff in their sleep that no one understands? Maybe they all do. Maybe Id-Design is really popular among scientists. Who knows?" Tia says.

"I don't know if I can live here. It's not safe."

"Well, if he did something naughty, I'm sure he would marry you afterwards. He's a gentleman."

"Be serious, Tia. How can you share a house with this guy?"

"He's a complete sweetie when he's awake," Tia says. "And you'll barely see him if you don't come up here. The only time Aman ever meets Sundar is in the dining room, when Sundar's eating tomato rice."

Narayan, possibly hearing the magic words in his sleep, lurches towards Tia, and Uzma feels a lot better as she sees her new friend recoil sharply.

"Aman said it was a bad idea for you to meet him for a while," Tia says, regaining her composure. "But listen, don't get scared by all this. It's kind of cool to have a mad inventor living upstairs, no? And he totally looks the part."

Before Uzma can reply, there's a loud banging on the door. Tia opens it.

"Okay, something very strange is happening on TV, and I think you need to see it," Aman says. He's dishevelled, wide-eyed, clearly very excited.

"Stranger than this?" Uzma asks in a voice of ice, gesturing dramatically towards Sundar and his statue.

Aman opens his mouth to speak, chokes on his first word and looks around the room thoughtfully. He registers Tia's amusement, Uzma's indignation, and the intrepid Sundar, currently engaged in pulling a large length of glowing green wire out from under a stuffed one-eyed emperor penguin. Sundar chooses this moment to trip and crash into his pile of raw materials. When he stands up, there's a clothespin attached to his nose.

Aman meets Uzma's gaze squarely and grins.

"Much stranger than this," he says.

Uzma races into the living room just behind Aman. They fling themselves on a sofa, the TV is turned on to DNNTV, India's most trusted, most popular and least modest English news channel.

A very pretty reporter – standard issue, fair, well-ironed hair, early twenties, terrible fake American accent, wearing a blazer in the channel's colours – stands with a heavy DNNTV microphone in front of a large white building that seems to have done something to annoy a mob of about a hundred people, who are all productively occupied hurling bricks, bottles and other handy projectiles at its windows. The red bar on the screen underneath the reporter's face announces that her name is Namrata, and she is in front of the NH Sukumar Hospital in Chennai, Tamil Nadu. A scrolling ticker under the bar also announces that a sweet-shop owner from Amritsar has set a new Guinness World Record for eating sweets, and a former Indian test cricket captain has announced his return to the sport.

"Unparalleled scenes of public frenzy shatter the placid peace of Chennai in this path-breaking global exclusive brought to you exclusively by DesiNow News," the reporter Namrata gushes. "The brutal murder of a young and innocent couple sparked off a fire last night. Tonight, will this fire burn Chennai's heart? We bring you uninterrupted live coverage – after these messages."

"Why are we watching this?" Uzma asks.

"Wait," Aman says, his eyes fixed on the TV.

After a few minutes of educational lingerie advertisements, Namrata returns, and, accompanied by lots of flashy visuals, narrates the tragic story of the Iyers, a young couple, software professionals, who had been savagely attacked by an unknown miscreant while driving towards the NH Sukumar hospital the previous night. Their car had pulled into the hospital driveway with Mr Iyer dead and Mrs Iyer clearly dying – and in labour. She had clung on to life long enough to deliver her baby, and then passed on. Following the birth the hospital had shut its doors to all patients within an hour and turned out most of its staff by dawn. Given the normal length of time Chennai hospitals take to do anything, there was clearly something very strange going on involving the baby Iyer.

"All through today, an unusual collection of politicians and public figures have been gathering inside the hospital behind me," Namrata chirps, making sure to indicate that the massive building behind her, with NH Sukumar Hospital written on it in shining letters, is, in fact, the mysterious hospital to which she alludes. The cameraman zooms in close on Namrata to make sure other reporters wandering around delivering pieces to camera don't mess up the frame. "While other media channels have missed this breaking story, focusing instead on the first match of the new Indian Giga-League Gully Cricket Tournament – watch it live on DesiNow Sports, or online at DesiNowGigaLeague.com – we at DNNTV are here with you because we have confidential sources on the inside and, soon, exclusive footage that will show you what happened inside this hospital today."

"Her accent is slipping," Tia observes.

"That doesn't matter. Look, this is the same girl. She covered the riots in Hyderabad the other day," Aman says.

"What riots?" Uzma asks.

"Bunch of attention-seekers, crackpot Hindus against crackpot Muslims fighting one another to a draw over some non-issue."

"But doesn't that sort of thing happen all the time?" Uzma says.

"Sure. Filler news, but this looked like it was getting bigger. Same girl also did the story that happened ten days ago in Calcutta – bunch of people burning effigies of all four thousand employees of the Cricket Board of India. I think there's a connection."

"You think this reporter's causing these riots, somehow?" Tia asks, languidly stretching out on the sofa.

"No, you do hear about the media setting up stories, but that's not what I think this is. These were all big stories – I don't know what this hospital thing is, but, look, she's a junior reporter, she shouldn't be beating her seniors to scenes of actual violence. She's going to get lots of promotions very soon, or get kicked out on her butt. I think she might know something. Maybe she has an unusually strong nose for news."

"I don't understand," Uzma says. "You think this girl knows beforehand where important news is going to be?"

"Aman, was she on the plane?" Tia asks, sitting up.

Aman nods. "Later," he says, as Uzma turns to him, eyes blazing.

"What plane?" Uzma asks.

"I sat next to her on a flight, not long ago," Aman says. "Look."

Namrata has slipped into the hospital through a back door held open by an exclusive secret inside source.

"I'm the only person inside this hospital – this place of healing now under siege – who isn't a part of the conspiracy that surrounds this mysterious baby Iyer like a fog," she says, blithely ignoring the existence of her cameraman and all the patients and remaining staff in the hospital. "But soon we will find out, together, exactly what is going on. Live and exclusive on DNNTV."

By one of those strange coincidences that often happen on TV news, the people Namrata needs to interview are miraculously waiting around together in a well-lit room, all miked up and ready to be surprised. In swift succession, Namrata names a series of slightly eccentric politicians, mostly small-time guardians of the nation's morals, famous for such things as vandalising stores on such Western Imperialist occasions as Valentine's Day, or beating up girls in pubs or wearing jeans, or random acts of violence towards gay people, Muslims or celebrities who refused to dance at the weddings of party leaders. There are four fat men and a woman named Rosy. It is she who steps forward, possibly not by consensus, because the men wobble angrily in the background.

"We wish to announce formation of new political party that will change world," she says.

"Yes, tell the viewers of DNNTV," trills a thrilled Namrata.

"AKWWEK," Rosy continues, clearly not a fan of concise names. "Avatar Kalki Whole World Ethirkaala Katchi."

"Could you translate that for the viewers of DNNTV?"

"We are forming fully global party of future with benevolent grace of holy tenth Vishnu Avatar Kalki," Rosy explains to a furiously nodding Namrata.

"Do you know who might be responsible for the gruesome murders last night?" Namrata asks, clearly expecting murder-related political intrigue, not gibberish about ruling the world.

"You are not understanding important significance of what I am saying," Rosy says, now irate and puffy. "We are presenting to whole world most holy tenth Avatar of Vishnu, preserver god of Hindu trinity. What I am saying is, Baby Iyer is not only Baby Iyer. Baby Iyer is Baby Kalki, same tenth avatar as mentioned."

"I am knowing – sorry, are you saying this baby is Kalki? How do you know this? Could you show us the baby?" Namrata is gamely fighting both Rosy and growing suspicions of her own insanity.

One of Rosy's fellow AKWWEK party leaders steps up and shoves her aside, like a rhythm guitarist taking over the band partway through a song.

"Myself Muttiah, General Secretary," he growls. "Time has come to clean world of sins, and Baby Kalki will soon grow up to be Full-Power Avatar Kalki and destroy all rascals and rowdies while riding white-winged horse Devadutta. No more of decadence of westernised Kali Yuga, all this McDonald's and IPL cheerleader and reality show promoting sex and obscenity and also vulgarity in tennis and films showing leg and kissing. Time of Satya Yuga is commencing shortly according to Vishnu Purana. AKWWEK will help most divine Avatar Kalki with process of democracy at grass-roots and all-India level, thus allowing Avatar Kalki to become world's first democratically elected god."

"Live and exclusive on DNNTV," Namrata gurgles, eyes almost popping out of her head with excitement, "your first glimpse of the baby that the newly formed AKW – AKWW – Kalki Party claims will one day be the world's first god to win an election!"

"Who is claiming? Who is making claim?" Muttiah isn't pleased. "We are providing hundred percent genuine divine avatar! Soon he will be manufacturing weapons of power and destruction of mass to shock and awe all evil societies in the world, making India glorious superpower! According to holy text, Kalki is scheduled to undertake travelling around Earth with great speed, destroying millions of thief dressed as king in provocative clothing, displaying eight kinds of supreme power! He will lead army of superman against all evil. We are having new dawn of age of miracle and Kalki is most biggest miracle!"

Uzma giggles at this and turns to Aman and Tia, and is surprised to find both of them absolutely riveted to the screen. In fact, Tia has huddled up to Aman now, they're holding hands and completely unaware of it, like two children at a horror movie.

"What's wrong with you people?" Uzma demands. "Don't tell me you believe him!"

Aman and Tia disengage, embarrassed.

"No, of course not," Aman mumbles. "Sorry, every time I

see politicians like this I'm generally afraid for the country. For the world."

On the screen, Namrata is trying to slip past the cordon of AKWWEK politicians to get a global first exclusive sight of the alleged Baby Kalki, ignoring Rosy's protests of "But we are showing Baby Kalki to live rally, not to single channel, sorry."

At a signal from the intrepid reporter, the cameraman ups his game: he's off, treating his viewers to a video game-like live view of his jerky run through the corridors of the hospital, peppered with the occasional flailing limbs of AKWWEK party members trying to block him, until he barges in through a heavily guarded door, and there's just a flash, a smudge of blue, a suggestion of a bright blob on a white bed surrounded by kneeling women in white saris, a hasty zoom, a blurry image of more chubby arms than a baby should have and a blue head that's not human at all, before a burly party member cannons into the cameraman; a wild swing, a patchy white ceiling and then static fills the screen.

So engrossed are Aman and Tia in this that they completely fail to notice Sundar Narayan wander into the room and walk right by Uzma, slumped on her sofa. They don't know he's there until he announces his presence by saying, "Good people, my Tia's unconscious. Can I have another one?"

Aman and Tia both gasp and look at Uzma, but Uzma doesn't waste time asking questions: she springs up from the sofa and runs out of the room, ignoring Narayan's feeble greeting and Aman and Tia's shouts. She runs up the stairs, panting, barges into Narayan's lab and sees, lying on the floor with an ugly bruise on her forehead and a glowing green wire hissing and spitting in her badly burned hand, another Tia.

And when Aman, Tia-from-downstairs and the Scientist catch up with her, she's standing, grim and angry, arms crossed, eyes flashing.

"They're twins," Aman offers weakly.

"Forget it, Aman," Tia says. "It won't work. You might as well tell her, she's nice."

"Who are you people?" Uzma thunders. "And what *the hell* is going on?"

CHAPTER **FOUR**

"You want the short version or the long version?" Aman asks.

"Short."

"We have superpowers."

Uzma scans the room and considers her response, wishing she had taken self-defence classes at school.

"She thinks we are mad," Sundar says.

"Show her," Aman says.

"Don't be scared," Tia says gently, and suddenly there are two Tias where there was one, a second copy stepping smoothly out of her body and moving beside it, as silently and effortlessly as a computer file. They stand, side by side, completely identical, hair, clothes, everything but the expressions on their faces – one smiles, the other looks uncertain.

On the floor behind Uzma, the injured Tia opens her eyes and says, "So, she knows, huh? Told you we wouldn't last a single night."

"Are you all right, Uzma?" Sundar enquires, extracting a chair from his junk-mountain. "Would you like some water? Would you like to sit down?"

Uzma sits down on the floor, her eyes unable to leave the Tias. She gulps a few times, struggling to speak.

"Superpowers," she says eventually.

"I know it sounds stupid," Aman says, "but you did want the short version."

"You've already seen Sundar in action," a Tia says. "Aman, why don't you give her a little display?"

Aman smiles and closes his eyes. Nothing happens. He grins widely after a while and looks at Uzma.

"You've left your phone in your room, haven't you?"

"That's your power? Phone location?" she says.

"No, there's a little more to it than that," says the Tia on the floor behind Uzma and giggles. "He does things with wi-fi. He wishes it were kung fu, but he's got wi-fi. He's a super internet nerd."

"It's a crap power, but it can be useful," Aman says. "Now would you like the long version?"

Uzma stands up.

"No," she says. "I – I've got to go."

"No. Why?" a Tia asks.

"You've got superpowers. That's – great. But I can't afford to get mixed up in whatever it is you're doing."

"But we're all –"

"I won't tell anyone about you. But I'm starting out on my own in this country, and I have plans, and the police – I've got to go, okay? You people are lovely, but I don't want to know any more. Let me leave now, please."

"You're one of us," Aman says.

"Don't be ridiculous." Uzma starts for the door.

"No, really. You have powers as well. We were all on the plane. You had a dream. We all did."

Now Uzma freezes, and her hand involuntarily flies up to her mouth.

"Sit," Sundar says. Uzma finds the chair this time.

"Aman dreamt of aliens," a Tia says. "I dreamt of talking photo albums, all with me in them, but different lives. Bob was in a giant kitchen in the sky, Sundar –"

"I met Edison and da Vinci and a Chinese man no one understood," Sundar says sheepishly.

"And within a few days, strange things started happening," Aman says. "Did the police find you?"

Uzma nods.

"They found all of us. Took us to strange hospitals. Ran tests. Found nothing. Sundar was awake, my brain tested normal – I got into their computers and saw – and all of Tia's copies are perfectly unremarkable on their own."

"Apart from their beauty and grace," Tia puts in.

"Of course," Aman says. "So they let us go. But I heard the calls they made, and I figured I was in big trouble – everyone on BA142 was in big trouble. So – moved to Mumbai, bought this house, and got these guys to join me."

"I don't have a superpower," Uzma says. "The police did come to me in Lucknow, but they were very cool. They said they didn't need to even test me. I'm normal. I – this isn't happening."

"I'll get you some water," a Tia says, striding towards the door.

"A young, beautiful girl with no one to protect her gets

taken to an Indian police station to have tests done on her and walks out unscathed, talking about how cool the police are. That's not normal, Uzma," Aman says.

"I thought everyone in India was just very nice."

Uzma watches, fists clenched, as Aman, Sundar and Tia laugh heartily for several seconds.

Aman then wipes his eyes and says, "I think your power is that people like you and are nice to you. That fits in with your wanting to be an actress. You want to be a star, right? You want people to love you."

"What does that have to do with anything?"

A Tia bursts into the room.

"Aman, we have a problem." The door is open behind her, and hot air rushes into the room. "Bob got hot."

"How?" Aman snaps.

"She let him have some lobster," the Tia says, pointing at the Tia in front of Uzma. "It's a furnace outside, and Bob's groaning."

"Lobster. Jesus. Why?"

"That doesn't matter now, does it?" Tia-near-Uzma says. "I'll fix it. Do we have more ice-cream?"

"Ice-cream won't help," Aman says. "Wait."

He closes his eyes and tilts his head.

"Coconut water, oatmeal, wheat, green vegetables, radish, dal, unripe banana, black pepper, pomegranate, papaya."

"We got nothing," a Tia says. "Should I just feed him some ice?"

"Watermelon, dandelion, yogurt, soya milk," Aman continues. "Or, yeah, ice. Get busy. And for god's sake, close the door behind you."

Two more Tias emerge from the Tia-near-Uzma. Four Tias

run out. Aman and Sundar look pointedly at the Tia behind Uzma, currently engaged in studying her burns.

"I'm staying," she says defiantly. "I want to listen."

"What's wrong with Bob?" Uzma asks.

"Bob's got a slightly weird power," Aman says. "His stomach controls the weather near him."

"So you guys keep his stomach cool and save on air-conditioning?"

"Precisely. But just imagine what this power could mean on a grand scale."

"I was wondering why you knew so much about what he should be fed."

"Oh, I don't, Tia takes care of all that," Aman says. "I Googled it just now."

Sundar clears his throat portentously.

"About what you and Aman were discussing earlier," he says, "we – I – have deduced that the power given to each passenger on the plane is intrinsically linked to whatever he or she desired most in life. That is why Aman said your powers make everyone love you. For us, too, it is true. I was a successful physicist before, a string theorist at the Indian Institute of Science, but as the years passed I found myself moving further and further away from what had first fascinated me about science as a child in Madras – the sense of being an explorer, a voyager into the unknown, an inventor with the power to change the world."

"A mad scientist," Tia says.

"Classic mad scientist," Aman says. "Complete with the need to infodump whenever he's awake, until your sleep schedule is as messed up as his."

Sundar smiles. "I was certainly being driven insane. In fact,

I was so tired of the endless routine of conferences around the world and bitter politicking to publish in journals that I was contemplating giving it all up and retiring to play the mandolin. Then, of course, I went to London to attend a conference – against my will," he says.

He stands, head bowed, in silence.

"And?" Uzma asks after a few seconds.

"He's going under again," Aman says. "You might want to get out of the way."

Sundar's arms swing up, elbows moving like a puppet's, and Uzma stifles a scream. Sundar heads, unseeing, towards his work in progress.

"Should we take this outside? Which is worse, unbearable heat or zombie scientist?" Aman asks.

Uzma drags her chair as far away from Sundar as possible and sits.

"Keep talking," she says.

"My powers let me hook up to anything on a network – computers, phones, satellites, all sorts of stuff," Aman says. "All our powers grow the more we use them, and I'm sure there are lots of applications I haven't even thought up yet. I don't really know how this connects to what I wanted most – I mean, it's not like I didn't have broadband, and more importantly I've never had the slightest clue what I wanted in life. But Sundar's theory is pretty true for me as well."

"How?" Uzma asks. "I don't think I became an actress because I wanted to be loved – but even if we let that go, why do you have powers if you didn't want anything?"

"Well, this is what I figured. Growing up in Delhi – and Delhi's a city of networks, the social kind, and contacts and families – I've always felt left out of things, like I didn't know anything, the right people, the right places. It's not like I lacked anything I ever needed to live a comfortable life, but I've never had the connections I needed to make a difference, to be relevant in any way. I don't know how it was for you growing up in the UK, but here nearly all of us have this huge sense of irrelevance. We'll never change anything. The world will never know us. We grow up thinking hard work and a certain amount of ability are all we need – and then we eventually have to accept that they can only take us so far. I'm not even talking about being famous here – I've never wanted to be famous. But we never feel like we're a part of anything. Nothing to believe in or fight for. I don't know if I'm making sense."

"You're making as much sense as anything else at this point," Uzma says. "Why were you on the plane?"

"I was coming back from New York. I'd gone there with my mother, and she stayed on with an old friend of hers."

"It would have been fun if she'd been on the plane," Tia says.

"Yeah, I would have been married by now," Aman says. "She's supposed to come back in a couple of weeks, actually. I've been trying to persuade her to hang out there for a while. Anyway, this has nothing to do with my powers, Tia's story has a more direct connection."

Uzma looks at Tia, eyebrows raised.

"I have a family," Tia says. "I have a three-year-old son. He and I are sleeping next to each other right now, at home. At least I hope we are. I grew up in Assam –"

"I know that."

"Oh, she told you. Sorry, I was here. I don't know how much

she told you, but if she told you anything you probably know I was very unhappy. My in-laws were horrible, and I used to dream about having many other lives, going to an office instead of sitting at home all day, being a teacher, being a dancer, an actress, a cricketer – anything else. I talked my husband's family into letting me go to work, but it was so difficult to manage the house, the work, the baby – and then I found out my husband was having an affair. I ran away – I had this online friend, a Brazilian journalist in London who said he was in love with me, so I went. But then it turns out he wasn't really serious, and I missed my son so much – I came back. On that flight."

"And they took you back?"

Tia nods. "Yes, but things were really difficult, of course. And I wasn't really mad at my husband – I just wanted a life of my own, you know? I've often wished I could be several people. Travel, live several lives, learn so many things. This power is amazing. Your power is lovely too. I can't imagine how it must feel, knowing everyone likes you."

"I'm still not convinced that's because I have superpowers. It's not a very nice thing to think," Uzma says. She turns to Aman again. "Well, now that you've told me this, what do you want? What's the plan?"

"We want to form a real-world Justice League – of India," Aman says.

"I'm British. My parents are Pakistani," Uzma replies.

"I know. I was kidding."

"Well, stop. Why did you bring me here? How did you find me?"

"Finding you was easy enough. Powers."

"I don't get it."

"My powers are more than a free internet connection. The whole cyber-security thing – it doesn't really apply to me. I can go backstage on any site. Nobody asks me for passwords. If your computer or phone is on, and connected, I can see everything on it. I just have to ask nicely."

"You have really creepy powers, don't you?"

"I haven't been reading your email, if that's what you're worrying about. But, yes, when I found out what was going on I went to the British Airways system and took out the list of people who were on that flight. Wiped information from credit card records, visa agencies, everything I could think of. And then I poked around in a lot of other places. And I wasn't the only one. The police didn't just come after us. They were sent after everyone on that flight. Someone found out what happened. I'm just – faster at getting numbers, jumping from system to system. I've been learning."

"You messed with my records?"

"Don't get mad at him," Tia says. "The truth is, we're all in danger. A lot of the people on that flight are dead or missing. He's been trying to get in touch with everyone. I know we seem like a bunch of clowns, but people like us are disappearing. Or dying, like the Iyers we just saw on TV. It makes sense to get together, then, doesn't it?"

Aman and Tia wait as Uzma digests this.

"Plainclothes policemen went to my parents' house," she says finally, her hands shaking slightly. "Are they in danger?"

"I don't know. I don't think so," Aman says. "They know you didn't leave India, and they don't know where you are, so I don't think there's any immediate threat. The people who visited your parents weren't policemen, anyway – probably private detectives hired to find out if you'd left the country. Whoever's looking for us can't afford to go public – they don't want the British authorities looking for them. The Brits don't know about this yet. No one on that flight was allowed to leave the country after the investigations kicked in, which was two days after we reached Delhi. Twenty-four people were on transfer flights or left India within a day. Someone hunted them down. Killed each and every one of them. All over the world, from Hong Kong to Toronto."

"What should I do? Should I warn my parents? Should they talk to the police?" Uzma asks.

"I really think it's best we lie low as much as possible for now," Aman says. "We really don't want them – whoever they are – to know where you live. If this news explodes all over the world – and I could make that happen – it hurts them, but it doesn't help us. I've pretty much changed all the data they had on anyone on that plane. I did this as soon as I found out people were dying. Right now, a lot of the information on the passengers on the flight has been changed to Britney Spears lyrics. There are multiple lists floating around, mostly with fake addresses, dead people, criminals. But someone must have printed hard copies of the original list at some point. Now they're not keeping anything online, or on computers at all. They've also switched phones."

"Hang on. 'They'?"

"Whoever 'they' are, they're not the government," Aman explains. "This operation's being run by a few people, probably Indian, high up enough in the military or the government to arm-twist other people into organising a large police operation, but it's all very hush-hush. The police thought they were looking for terrorists who were carrying some sort of biological weapon. Lots of people are lying to lots of other people. And there are limits to how much I can find out – sometimes, I just don't know where to look.

"There were a few politicians, a few government officials and a couple of Air Force officers on the flight. Of the 403 people on the plane, at least a hundred were cleared by the tests – they couldn't find anything abnormal about them. I've been attacking their records fairly consistently wherever I can find them, so it's safe to assume they've simply lost track of a lot of these people. A few of the others are fairly rich, some are famous – they might have bought their way out of trouble, or they haven't been attacked because they're well-protected, or because it would bring more attention than they're ready for now. But the rest of us won't get off that easy."

"What about the people who weren't cleared by the tests? What was wrong with them?"

"Maybe their powers were visible. I don't know. Also, the ones who got cleared were all Indian – except you and a few other people of South Asian descent, all of whom were visiting family here. All the other British people, all the passengers from other countries – all gone. They've been taken away. There's not been any outcry in the press abroad, so there must have been some kind of cover story. High-level officials, nothing put down on email, I don't know. There are no records of where they all are now, but I think they're being held in Kashmir, somewhere near the Air Force base in Udhampur. The Air Force officers are both involved. But one of them, Vir Singh, was sent off on a suicide mission by whoever's running the show. He's the key to finding out more."

"It's very worrying," Tia says. "These people could be anywhere, doing anything – not just these military types hunting powered people down, but also random passengers with dangerous powers hiding from them. And India's such a big country, there are so many people, so many languages, that even if something really bad happens it could be a while before anything gets into the press."

Uzma gapes. "And so there are superheroes and supervillains having fights around the world? Like in the movies? People are going to blow up the Earth and all that?"

"Well, I hope not," Aman says.

"But there are people who could? Someone has that kind of power?"

"Unlikely. See, the thing is, no one got asked what powers they wanted. They got given the powers that whoever – or whatever – gave us these powers thought they wanted. If we'd had to fill in a form, we'd all have been all-powerful, all-knowing, magic-using immortals. We'd have taken the cool superpowers, not the kind of B-level hero powers we have. So unless there was some lunatic on board who dreamt of being a god or destroying the universe... who knows? How many people like that fly British Airways?"

Tia grins. "I'm sure there were lots of people who got off that plane and found, a few days later, that they had perfect abs, or a new handbag, or that the person they wanted was suddenly crazy about them. More money, a baby, a house, a better job, less traffic. We were lucky."

"I just wish there were people who'd wanted, you know, new things," Aman says.

"Meaning?" Uzma asks.

"Meaning, our powers would have been a lot more interesting if we'd been super-genius types. We aren't visionary thinkers or anything like that. The powers we have – just look online and you'll find at least two superheroes who have the same powers. That's what the comics writers came up with – and they come up with this stuff ten times a week. I don't know about you, but I feel terrible that we have such – predictable powers. Apart from Bob and Sundar, who really don't think like the rest of us, we've got very functional, very sidekick-y, very mass-media powers. Product-of-the-system powers. Do you know how many internet-using superheroes there are? And I thought I was so different..."

"Aman. Aman, darling? You're rambling again," Tia says gently. "Tell Uzma things she needs to know, not things you could blog about. Uzma?"

"Do you have any idea how we got these powers?" Uzma asks.

"None whatsoever. Aliens, wizards, gods, transhumanists, evolutionary accident, virus, secret societies, Republicans, Apple designers – you take your pick. We don't know how, where, what or why – or whether this has happened before. I have theories, but they're all very geeky theories. You want to hear them?"

"No," Tia says firmly. "Not tonight, at least. Aman, like I keep telling you, it doesn't matter *how* we got our powers; whether we're the next stage in human evolution or not. When the first fish crawled out of the sea, they didn't start writing PhDs about it. They figured out how to survive, instead."

"Amphibians."

"Enough."

Uzma leans back in her chair.

"It's a lot to take in, I know," Tia says.

Another Tia enters the room.

"I took care of the Bob situation, if anyone wants to know," she announces. "It's actually quite cold outside now." She notices Uzma. "What happened to you?"

"Aman told her everything," other-Tia says.

"And she didn't faint? We fainted."

"I don't know what to say," Uzma says. "I came here with so many ambitions. I'm going to be an actress – how do I do that if there are people trying to kill me?"

"Well, they don't know what you look like, if that helps," Aman says. "And thanks to the magic of me, they're not even sure what your name is – I gave them a lot of alternatives. But, yeah, we've got to get a plan together – find out exactly what we can do with this. With our, ahem, superpowers."

"A plan. You have a plan?" Uzma asks.

"More like a mission statement. Essentially, we keep ourselves safe, find other people with powers, and then we make the world a better place. People will try to stop us, we find out who they are, find good people on their side, and find ways to beat them. This whole secret-base-in-Kashmir thing is all very well, we need to stay on top of that or we will probably get killed, but that's not what interests me."

"That's good to know. What does interest you?"

"Powers. Using them. Fixing the world. If we have to run around avoiding superpowered murderers, we will. But that's not what we're here for."

"Right. Well, my answer is no. I'm not going to be a superhero," Uzma says. "So if you're planning some sort of team costumed avengers thing, just count me out."

"No costumes."

"I don't care. Count me out."

"But –"

"No, Aman. I don't know you at all. I don't know if you're telling the truth – I think you are, but this is all so weird! I came here – see, I have a plan too. A plan for my life. Powers or no powers, that's who I am. I don't want to be Everybody-Likes-Me-Girl, part of your World-Changing-Super-Squad. I don't want to change the world. I think it's fine the way it is. These powers suddenly arrive – and what if they suddenly leave? I can't turn my life upside down for this."

"I don't think you have a choice," Aman says. "Yes, these powers change everything. Yes, they might go away tomorrow. It's all the more crucial, then, that we do the most we can with what we've been given in the time we have. These powers came as answers to our dreams. Tomorrow, they'll just be technology. Like Jules Verne thinking about going to the moon –"

"Aman, focus," Tia says.

"Sorry. Uzma, all we have is a head start, and we have to find out how to use it best. There are thousands of Bollywood actresses. There's only one you."

Uzma stands as if she is about to walk out that very minute.

"This is ridiculous! How do I make this clear to you? I'm not going to be a superhero!"

"We're not asking you to do anything," Tia says. "But you needed to know this, didn't you? If you still think you should leave, of course you're free to leave – though we all hope you'll stay, because we like you very much. Obviously."

"I just wish – I wish someone had asked me before giving me

superpowers, you know? I didn't want this!"

"It's all going to be all right," Tia says as Uzma fights back tears with great ferocity. "Don't be afraid. We'll help. We're all just trying to figure out what to do. Aman's trying to sort things out his way, but you can just ignore him. This is really the kind of thing we should spend a few years thinking about – but we might not have any time."

Uzma looks around the room, at Aman staring intently at her, at the Tias' melting eyes, at Sundar, completely oblivious to all the drama, wielding a screwdriver like an orchestra conductor's baton. She nods quickly, sharply, not wanting to think.

"I'd like to stick around for a while, if you don't mind," she says. "But I don't think I can help you."

"Aman, it's been a terribly long night, Uzma's just had her world turned around, and we've talked for far too long. Now everybody get up, go straight to bed and sleep through tomorrow, and that's an order," Tia says.

"Sure. Uzma, just – think about what I said, okay? And, Tia? You need to be up by lunchtime," Aman says.

"Why?"

"Because Superman flew into town this evening. And we're meeting him for lunch tomorrow."

CHAPTER **FIVE**

If Vir had asked a passing bird above the AQ Khan nuclear facility for directions to Coffee Day, Carter Road, Pali Hill (assuming that this bird spoke English and knew its way around the hip coffee joints in Mumbai), he would have been told: "Fly straight to the Arabian Sea – pick up some mutton kebabs and beef samosas in Karachi, they're super – and then keep going until you see Mumbai, take a left, and ask someone. Everyone knows the place."

Lacking this helpful advice, and seeking to avoid unwanted flying-man spotters, Vir has taken a very roundabout route, involving Tajikistan, China, Nepal, Uttar Pradesh and a long journey on the Rajdhani Express from Delhi in a six-person compartment with a garrulous and unfortunately flatulent family. Like most fighter pilots, Vir loves trains – the constant irritation of sitting in a plane controlled by bungling civilians is usually too much to take – but ever since his powers arrived, anything but the open sky has felt cramped and claustrophobic. He had to exercise all his self-restraint not to simply tear the train apart and take to the sky. It's good for him to be here now, right next to the open sea.

Summer has Mumbai firmly in its squelchy grasp, but this cafe is always full in the evenings, teeming hordes of fashionably dressed young people having their last coherent conversations of the day, all constantly scanning the cafe to see who else is in there that they know. Outside, muscular young men roar up and down Carter Road on their motorbikes in silencer-less mating displays, occasionally pausing by the cafe to have hey-dude conversations with other customised-motorcycle enthusiasts.

On summer days like today, though, the sun-drenched open area of the cafe is usually fairly empty. Only people with actual work or those waiting for be-there-in-five lunch companions are present, sweating stolidly under red umbrellas, wishing the breeze from the large standing fans actually reached them.

Vir arrives, looking for his mysterious phone friend. Only three tables are occupied, featuring a giggling gang of four girls having a *Sex and the City* conversation, a young couple – a somnolent young man and an attractive woman typing on a laptop – and a pot-bellied businessman-type sweating profusely as he leers at the girls. There's a pause in all the conversations as Vir walks in, stumbling a little as he tries not to break the gate. Vir radiates so much charisma that even the waiters, famous for their ability to ignore anything short of a fully-fledged assault, turn and stare. He looks around. The businessman, he decides, is the likeliest candidate. He's about to approach him when his phone rings.

"Hey," a familiar voice says. "Superman. Nice of you to drop by."

Vir is puzzled: none of the people at any of the tables are on the phone. He looks inside, beyond the glass doors to the inner section of the cafe. All of the people with phones to their ears are female.

"Don't call me Superman," he says. "Where are you?"

"You were supposed to come alone."

"I am alone. And *you* were supposed to bring at least yourself. Where are you, in the restaurant? I thought we were going to meet here."

"The restaurant is probably full of your spies. Lunch is off. In fact, unless you get rid of your boy across the road, the meeting's off. Don't play games with me, Vir."

"What boy?"

"You forget I know what everyone on that flight looks like. You shouldn't have brought one of them to be your lookout."

"I don't know what you're talking about."

"No? Turn around. Look, on the wall between the road and the seafront. Ugly guy, pink shirt, shiny trousers. Not the best outfit for shadowing people, no?"

Vir looks across the street and spots a dark, hatchet-faced man sitting on the wall, licking an orange ice-lolly, watching the sea and the sunproof lovers on the rocks in front of him. Vir frowns.

"Don't pretend you don't know him," the voice on the phone says.

"No, I know him. His name's –"

"Mukesh. He's supposed to be missing. One of yours."

"I don't know why he's here."

"To help you capture us, obviously. In case one super-strong flying man isn't enough. It's flattering that you think I'm more dangerous than a Pakistani nuclear plant, of course, but really, this wasn't smart."

"I haven't even talked to my people since our conversation. His presence here has nothing to do with me."

"I'm supposed to just believe you? I don't think this is going to work. Shame."

"Listen. Maybe we should meet somewhere else. I don't want him to see me either."

"Too late for that. Don't hang up. I want to hear what you say."

The hatchet-faced man has spotted Vir. He gasps and drops his ice-lolly. Growling in exasperation, Vir strides out of the cafe, and the girl gang sighs in disappointment. Mukesh slides off the wall and stands, hand on hip, until Vir reaches him.

"What are you doing here?" Vir asks.

"I should ask you that, man. Where the hell have you been? We thought you were dead!" Mukesh replies.

"I'll report to base tomorrow. Until then, no one knows I'm here, okay? I'm following up something on my own."

Mukesh's mouth twists into an approximation of a smile. He sticks his tongue out: long, forked and snake-like, rendered somewhat less fearsome by an ice-lolly orange coating.

"I don't think that works, man," he says. "You failed your mission, no? Jai's not going to be happy. I think you should talk to him now."

"You don't get to tell me what to do, soldier," Vir snaps. "Now get out of here. I have work."

"I'm not your soldier any more, man. Things have changed

a little bit. You talk to Jai. Or maybe I should."

Vir steps forward, puts a friendly hand on Mukesh's shoulder and presses slightly. Mukesh flinches in pain, and his muscles convulse. Green scales appear along his cheekbones and neck. His eyes turn yellow.

"I think you've forgotten who I am and what I can do," Vir says. He steps back, releasing Mukesh, and Mukesh's features slide back towards normal. "Get out of here for the next two hours. I don't owe you any explanations."

Mukesh steps back, smiling, and his canines lengthen into long fangs.

"I've often wondered exactly how thick your skin is, Vir," he says in a strangely deep voice. "Maybe I'll get to find out soon."

"Maybe you will. And keep your face under control, you idiot. People are watching."

"They're going to be watching a lot more soon. Wait and watch, man."

"And if Jai finds out you saw me before I tell him, I'll come looking for you. Got it?"

"I'm going, I'm going," Mukesh grumbles, and shambles off.

Vir stands and watches while he gets into a car and drives off towards Juhu. Then he puts the phone back to his ear.

"Where are you?" he snaps.

"Just come back to the cafe and sit down." The caller disconnects.

Two minutes later, a short, shapely woman in a tiny dress swings the cafe's gate open and sashays in, her heels tapping loudly in time to all male hearts in the vicinity. She draws up a chair and sits across from a stunned Vir.

"Sorry I'm late, darling," she trills, "but my hairdresser took a very long time. What do you think?"

She pulls her huge sunglasses up on her head and runs a hand through her inch-long hair.

"Very nice," Vir says politely. "Who are you?"

"I've been trying to think of a good answer to that for a while. I was going to say Multiple Woman, but apparently there's already a Multiple Man. So I'm going with Ms Quantum for now. But it's a bit of a silly name, no? Do you have a superhero name, or is it just Vir? It does mean brave, so you've got a head start there. Still, you should have a secret identity, no?"

"It's just Vir."

"Nice. You know what else I wanted? A costume. Like a proper superhero costume, except you can't wear a bodysuit in Mumbai in this weather, you'd stink and melt. And I don't really have the figure for it anyway. Apparently there are lots of superhero chicks who wear next to nothing, but that wouldn't be very practical either, no? Like, I'd look okay, but I couldn't fight with anyone. Of course I can't fight anyway, so that doesn't matter."

"Yes. Let's get to business, please. Where is he?"

"Oh, he's around. But see, here's the thing. He just got access codes to all of China's nuclear weapons, and if he doesn't fill in a password once every fifteen minutes, they're going to launch. And they're going to land in Kashmir, on your little secret underground jail at Udhampur. And the password keeps changing every time, so even if you, say, forced it out of him, it wouldn't help, darling. Your super-science project, whatever it is, would be destroyed, and a war would start with China. So you're going to be nice to him, right?"

"I don't like being threatened," Vir says. "And I can see you're bluffing."

"Well, we don't want to find out, do we?"

"Nuclear protocols don't work like that. There are lots of stages, and not all of them are online."

"Are you sure?"

"This is a waste of my time," Vir says, standing up.

"All right, all right," a young man says from the next table. "Sit down, Vir. I'm Aman, and this is Tia. Hello."

Vir sits and looks at the woman with the laptop at Aman's table. His eyes widen as he realises it's Tia again, only with longer hair and a less spectacular outfit.

Aman moves across to Vir's table and sticks out a hand. Vir shakes it briefly, his eyes not leaving Tia.

"Are they –" he begins.

"No, we're the same person," says the Tia-at-Vir's-table. The other Tia rises, waves sweetly at Vir, and leaves with the computer. Vir's eyes follow her as she crosses the road and gets into a small red car.

"I'm over here," Tia says. "So, Aman, Vir wanted to get straight to business."

"It's only a matter of time before Mukesh comes back with help, so there's no time for fun and games," Vir says. "You both have powers that could be very important. But we think you also have a disease that makes your bodies unstable – we were all infected on the plane and you're in danger. You need to come with me right now."

"Crap," Aman says.

"I think what Aman means is that we're concerned about our fellow passengers disappearing and then re-appearing dead,"

Tia says. "We know about your Kashmir facility – we've even got some blurry photos of your roof – and we definitely don't want to go anywhere near it."

"You know as well as I do that something's gone wrong, and people have been lying to you," Aman says. "So don't give us your official line."

"You really don't get to tell me how to conduct myself," Vir says. "In fact, I don't see any reason not to take both of you to Kashmir right now and talk to you under conditions more suited to me. And to my superior officers."

"The same superior officer who sent you to die? Squadron Leader Jai Mathur? The same Jai Snake-Eyes back there was talking about?" Aman says.

"You're beginning to make me angry."

Vir and Aman stare hard at each other, and Tia giggles.

"Boys," she says. "Calm down."

"Order?" asks a waiter, materialising out of nowhere with a menu.

Tia orders three coffees and then, when the waiter is gone, turns back to the men with a winning smile.

"We're here because we're scared, Vir," Tia says. "People are dying like flies. That couple in Bangalore, all those foreigners who left the country. And so many others are missing. Can you blame us for lying low?"

"No," Vir admits. "I haven't really been following the news. I've been flying around like a maniac since all of this started."

"Let's talk about your Kashmir base," Aman says. "How many of us are you holding there?"

"We're not holding anyone against their will as far as I know," Vir replies. "I haven't been there too many times. I've mostly been tracking down rogue powered people who were cleared by the tests but then found their powers and started committing crimes. You have no idea how big this is, and what it means for our country."

"So you really don't know what's going on at the base?" Aman says.

"They've been running extensive tests on the subjects. There are some amazing powers there, but we've had to keep it all very quiet. I'm sure you understand why. I'm really not at liberty to talk about it."

"You mean you won't tell us the truth. You're trying to see how many of these powers you can convert into weapons for the Indian military," Aman says.

"If we were, could you blame us? We've been handed an incredible variety of strategic military assets. And if you joined us, Aman, with your powers, just think what we could accomplish."

"Don't go Darth Vader on me. It sounds very stupid. Vir, we know you're here because you suspect your superior officers, and whoever else is running this operation, of trying to get you killed. Because you think that they might be eliminating powered prisoners who won't co-operate. About half the passengers on the plane weren't Indian – what happened to them?"

Vir says nothing.

"What happened to all the Brits?" Aman persists. "They haven't been sent back to England. They haven't been seen here in weeks. There aren't any records of their even being tested. What did you do with the foreigners?"

"I don't know, all right?" Vir clenches his fists. "They're not at the base. It's only Indians there."

"Where are they, then?"

"They were removed."

"Killed?"

"Transferred. I don't know where they were taken. It wasn't my decision."

"Why didn't you ask? Didn't you care?"

"I didn't think about it! I don't question the orders of my superiors. That's how we function."

"Do you know how many journalists, how many embassy officials worldwide are trying to track them?"

"Lots, I suppose."

"Yes, 'lots' is accurate. Now I don't know what you did with them, but you can't just make over a hundred people just disappear any more."

Vir smirks. "You don't know very much about the world, do you?"

"Not like this, Vir. I know you military people don't really see human life the way the rest of us do –"

"Be careful."

"Not you, sorry. Look, I've been covering a lot of trails, deleting a lot of emails, messing with a lot of records – visas, travel documents. But people have started making connections. The British Embassy has been asking a lot of questions, and no one here has any idea what the answers might be. A few detectives and a few journalists are already in India, following stories. I've been leading a lot of people down empty paths and spreading false rumours."

"That was you?"

"Yes. And, believe me, I'm not doing this to help out. I know you're still tracking a lot of the people who slipped through the first round of tests, thanks to my efforts, and that's the only part of this whole thing that I'm happy about."

"Glad to hear that. Powered rogues running wild, endangering civilians, and you're proud," Vir says.

"Taking them to a prison where they'll probably be killed or conscripted isn't the answer. You should be worried about the people you've already killed. The first sign of any evidence, there's going to be a huge media uproar. International scandal. And this isn't a government conspiracy. Whatever you're doing at that base, it's not state-sanctioned."

"So you said. But that's impossible," Vir says.

"You know at some level that Aman is telling the truth," Tia says. "They tried to get rid of you because they thought you might be a problem later."

"No. That just – no."

Coffee arrives. Aman finishes his in one gulp. He burns his tongue and pants a bit before continuing.

"Vir, you're *here*, despite your training. You've got to be honest with us and take one more step. There's something very terrible going on, and you're a part of it. They must have been worried about how you'd react when you found out what was really going on, otherwise why would they want to sacrifice a power like yours?"

"But are you sure the air chief marshall doesn't know about this?"

"If I wasn't sure, would I risk my life sitting with an Air Force super-strong flying man and asking him to help me find out the truth?"

Vir has no words.

Aman takes a deep breath.

"I'm a part of this too, and it makes me feel dirty. I've been helping you push this under the carpet. But I have to know what happened to the foreigners."

"I don't understand," Vir says. "Why would you do that? In fact – why don't you just go public? In your place, I probably would. If you're right, there should be an investigation. Jai should be court-martialled."

Aman sighs. "I thought about it. I don't know if I've done the right thing," he says. "But at this point, there's more at stake. Our survival."

"Because you think the squadron – Jai's troops – are killing off or recruiting everyone on that plane. But if you revealed what you know publicly, you could be safe. You could be protected."

"If someone like you decided to kill me, Vir, I don't think there's anyone who could protect me. But I'm not talking about myself, or my friends. I'm talking about all of us – everyone who was on BA142. People with powers."

Tia clears her throat. "It took a while for Aman to explain this to me, but now I see where he's coming from. The fact is, whether we like it or not, we're more than human now. If – *when* – we're discovered, people aren't going to be happy about our existence. Especially if we're a threat to them, and we definitely are."

"We'll be hunted down, imprisoned, either way – by your people or by someone else," Aman says. "It's like the X-Men."

"Who?" Vir asks.

"Have you been living under a rock? You don't know the X-Men? Not even the movies?"

"Aman, I don't have time for movies. I spend my life defending India."

"Good for you. What was I saying? Yeah, so, everything's changed for all of us now, but I don't think many of us have bothered to figure out what that means. Take you, Vir, for instance. You can fly. And you're still thinking about India and Pakistan. This is so much bigger. And it's not just you and your military friends. There's a girl I know – powered – who wants to be famous, to have everyone know who she is, even though she knows there are people out there who want to kill her. It's going to take time for everything to sink in."

"What girl? The reporter?"

Tia shoots a warning glance at Aman.

"Yes," Aman says. "And the cricketer, too – he thinks his fame will protect him. And then there's that blue baby that they're saying is a god who will lead an army of superheroes – what did you think of that?"

"I've had a lot to think about. What do you want me to do?" Vir asks.

"I want you to clean house. I can't do it over the phone. Someone has to stop powered people from hurting others. Once that's done, once we've all seen we need to work together, we can come up with a plan. We need strategies, laws, rights, rules. And you need to get to work on saving the world."

"Me? I'm just one person. Being able to fly doesn't really make a huge difference."

"Rubbish. Can you imagine what we could achieve together? With just a small bunch of us, we could change everything. We could stop global warming, make the Sahara a rice bowl, save endangered animals, stop genocide, find alternatives to oil, stop the damned recession. The kind of things superheroes would do in comics, except that *Rural Infrastructure Development League* comics wouldn't really sell well next to *Bondage Wonder Woman*."

Vir leans back in his chair, frowning in concentration.

"Even though I don't really understand what you're saying, let's assume you're right," he says. "We could do so much. But you know that's never going to happen."

"Why not?" Aman demands.

"It's just not human nature. All this is good in theory, but if everyone could actually work together then we could change the world even without powers."

"So what if it's not human nature, Vir? We're not human any more." Aman replies.

"Sorry to interrupt the heal-the-world plan," Tia says. "But can we have this debate *after* we've figured out what to do about the people trying to kill us? Sooner or later, the world is going to know about us. You can delay this for a while, Aman, but it'll happen eventually. And when they do find out, how do we keep them from being terrified?"

"Well, by making the world better," Aman says. "When they see how much good we've done, they'll love us."

Tia shakes her head. "Won't work."

"I should go," Vir says. "I'm not sure your ideas will work, but I'm going to think about them. Don't assume that the people running the project are power-mad supervillains, Aman. They're all people who have years of experience in dealing with dangerous situations, and taking decisions that affect lives. You might be a superhero expert, but you don't have any real experience. I'm going to find out what happened to the missing powered people. Maybe you should come and talk to my superiors. I'll arrange that when I'm sure I can guarantee your safety."

"That's fair," Aman says. "And, Vir?"

"Yeah?"

"Thank you for listening."

"You have to do one more thing before you leave Mumbai," Tia says.

"What?" Vir asks.

"You have to take me out."

"I know he's a superhero, but maybe this is not the best time to be picking up relative strangers, Tia," Aman says. "He has work to do."

"He could die tomorrow, and then I'd never know," Tia says.

Vir stands up and bows with all military gallantry he can summon.

"It would be an honour. Where do you want to go?"

"Out," Tia says. She points a finger at the sky, and grins.

Tia-who-left-with-laptop reaches her Yari Road home, passes it by and drives on, checking her rear-view mirror.

A few cars behind her, Mukesh, his pink shirt now sweat-stained red, listens to an annoying FM radio channel as he slithers in pursuit of the little red car. His air-conditioning is switched off; cold air makes him sluggish.

Tia veers right from Yari Road, and sets her course for the mangrove marshes that surround the offshoots of Malad Creek. After a while, the sludge of traffic becomes a trickle, the buildings shrink from high rises to shacks, and the road gets bumpier, muddier. Prey and predator drive past dark trees under the afternoon sun.

Mukesh makes his move. He accelerates and veers towards Tia, trying to push her off the road. Tia's car swerves into a large mud puddle and splutters to a halt. Mukesh laughs aloud and spins his wheels, skidding until his car is in front of hers.

Tia emerges from her car and stalks towards Mukesh's, ugly streams of road-rage invective spewing from her pretty mouth. Mukesh ogles her for a few seconds, and then leaps out of his car through the open window. His skin is beginning to turn green, and large scales and leathery stretches emerge all over his body like fast-forward blisters.

"What are you?" Tia gasps.

Mukesh doesn't reply – instead, he shows her.

His arms shrink, fingers curving as they shorten into talons. His eyes turn yellow, pupils morphing into vertical slits; his mouth broadens, elongates; his nose flattens; his hairline recedes. His forehead stretches and flattens out as his head changes into something terrible, reptilian, blood-curdling. His forked tongue slithers out obscenely between his gleaming fangs. It twitches.

"Hi babe," he gurgles. "I'm Poison."

"Isn't that taken? All the good names are taken." Tia says.

Mukesh hisses and advances slowly, his head swaying from side to side.

"What are you supposed to be?" Tia asks. "Snake? Dinosaur? Crocodile? What kind of sick person dreams of being one of those?"

Mukesh leaps.

With one huge bound, he's on her. She struggles briefly, but his fangs sink into her throat, and she falls, her blood spurting, staining the road. Mukesh raises his snout in the air, spits out a chunk of flesh, and screams harshly, a triumphant predator's scream.

"See," a woman's voice says, "you really shouldn't have done that."

Tia's car door slams and Mukesh's head jerks, swivels. His

snake eyes widen as Tia steps out of the car, holding a gun. Beneath him, Tia's dead body crumbles to dust and disappears. Her bloodstains fade away.

He springs to his feet, crouches raptor-like.

Four more copies of Tia fan out, two to the left, two to the right. Each holds a gun trained on Mukesh.

"I've never actually fired a gun before," one Tia says.

She fires, and hits Mukesh on the thigh.

His startled yell is more human than monstrous.

"It's fun," she says. "I'm learning the tango in Madrid and meditating in Tibet, but this? This is fun."

Screeching, he leaps forward, and the Tias dive. He catches one, sinks his fangs into her arm, exults as his poison-sacs gush venom into her veins; feels her dissolve and crumble.

Four gunshots ring out. Each finds its mark. Mukesh falls heavily and writhes on the ground, moaning, wheezing.

"I'll tell you where you made your mistake," a Tia says. "See, you people are all playing for power. Stupid games for stupid boys. Me, I have a son. I'm not going to let anything harm him."

Two more gunshots.

Mukesh whimpers as they hit his back.

"What were you doing on Carter Road?" she asks.

"Having an ice-lolly."

"You want me to shoot you again?"

"Killed a doctor. Powered. He could see everything. All diseases. Couldn't take it. Tore his eyes out. He was actually happy when I got to him."

"What a waste."

Mukesh catches his second wind, rises with horrifying speed.

A swipe of his talons, a leap, a snarl, five bullets sailing through empty air, a shimmying strike, and two more Tias die, blood arcing through the air and dissolving like smoke. Another Tia runs for cover, but he leaps right over the car, a dark-green reptilian streak in shiny trousers, and lands on her, snapping her spine. Then he jumps on top of her car with terrifying ease, his large, three-toed feet denting the roof.

"I'm not so easy to kill," Mukesh hisses. "How many bodies you got?"

She gives him three bullets in the stomach, and he kneels and screeches.

"Enough," Tia says.

He rolls off the car roof and slumps on the road.

"What now?" he asks.

"Now you're going to take me to your headquarters, and I'm going to talk to your boss and finish this. "

His throat rattles, and he nods. His features melt back, and a few moments later he's human again, torn and bleeding.

"You'll live?" Tia asks.

"Forever," he says, and staggers to his feet, leaning on the car door.

"Get in."

Mukesh slumps in the passenger's seat, sulking.

Tia gets in the driver's seat and starts the car.

"You couldn't have planned this," he says.

"I take life as it comes. Not a big deal."

"You're not scared?" he asks.

"I'm terrified," she says. "If you die before we reach Kashmir, I'll have to find another one."

He chuckles, and then the chuckle turns into a rattle, and he lunges towards Tia, fangs sprouting in her throat. She bleeds, screams in pain, and disappears.

"Stupid bitch," he mutters to himself as he pulls himself together slowly, painfully. "Never play with a snake in a closed space."

A sudden movement behind him. Two cold points at his temples. He sees two Tias in the rear seat, each holding a gun to his head.

"I'll keep that in mind," she says. "Drive."

CHAPTER **SIX**

Uzma switches through a succession of insane Indian TV channels, marvelling that her head has not yet spontaneously exploded. She is losing her mind – and not because of the stream of mad prophets, telemarketers, reality shows, soap operas and mind-numbing music videos in dozens of languages she doesn't understand. TVs can be turned off, but the argument between Bob and the Scientist, currently raging around her at possibly illegal decibel levels, is beyond the control of any remote.

Sundar claims he has found the beginnings of a new social-historical-cultural-scientific-psychological theory, a theory he will come up with a clever name for some time in the near future. The fundamental premise is that heroic myths and legends through the course of human history are all true – possibly exaggerated by enthusiastic re-tellers, especially the bits about gods and monsters, but the demigod heroes in these stories all actually existed. And these heroes, from Hercules to Sherlock Holmes, appeared because of these legends: the legends were not records of their actions, but prophetic texts derived from collective human aspirations that paved the way for their arrival.

Throughout the history of science, says Sundar, human imagination, human dreams have paved the way for inventions and progress. Asimov led to Asimo the robot, Apollo's chariot to Apollo 11. It is same with stories of heroes: humanity's dreams of a more-than-mortal saviour, expressed through fiction whether oral or printed, led at some point to the manifestation of new cultural heroes – evolutionary forerunners empowered by mysterious agents.

It is no coincidence, says Sundar, that he and his fellow passengers have been given abilities according to their dreams – which are nothing but a random sample of current global societal desires. Superhero comics, born in the time of the American depression and tempered in the fires of World War Two, fuelled by nuclear nightmares, political upheavals and the struggles of social change, are essentially user manuals humankind has created for the benefit of the superpowered – to acclimatise ordinary people to the idea of their existence, to prepare the world for their presence.

Now, armed with several gigabytes of superhero comics Aman has helpfully downloaded off torrent sites, Sundar is determined to spend his waking hours reading, removing impurities such as capes and interdimensional alien invaders, and obtaining a distilled superhero sample. The purpose of this: to understand how superheroes function, what problems they face and how they affect the world around them. Sundar now believes that all superhero comics were written for his benefit, and that they will give him the elixir to transmute base humans to heroes.

Bob, on the other hand, is fixed in his belief that all of this is a giant conspiracy, an evil genetics project funded by mysterious military–industrial-complex types. If Sundar's theory were true, he argues, the world would get the heroes it really needed. Not random travellers, mostly well-off people on an intercontinental flight complaining about the in-flight entertainment, but people from the darkest corners of the world, oppressed, forgotten, left-to-rot, hopeless places; people who would have torn the world down and rebuilt it from scratch if given a choice. Superhero comics, he argues, are status-quo-ist, adolescent power fantasies from evolved countries, the worst possible instruction guide for people with powers.

Bob's parents, both activists who were picked up by the police during the tests, raised him on a diet of books by ferociously bearded European and Indian intellectuals. Now he doesn't know whether they are dead or alive, and the knowledge that his powers render him completely useless in anything resembling a covert rescue operation has left Bob deeply angry. There are tears in his eyes as he yells at Sundar, and rumbling clouds gather above the house.

Trapped in the eye of the storm, Uzma makes nervous, placatory noises whenever the combatants ask her for support and glances at her phone every five seconds. A number of directors have promised to call her back and tell her when they start shooting, but Uzma's phone has not rung in a while. She has heard that Bollywood has the collective attention span of a caffeine-overloaded squirrel, but still, not a single call? Several of her new best friends seem to have forgotten her, and those who work in the movie business are giving her smooth call-you-back-darlings already.

The lingering suspicion that they had all only appeared to like her because her powers had cast some sort of spell on them does not improve her mood. A part of her still refuses to acknowledge that she has any powers, but it is difficult to sustain this belief surrounded by her housemates. Especially Tia, who is currently engaged in cooking several meals, cleaning all the other floors in the house, occasionally checking to see if anyone wants a second breakfast and exercising furiously all over the place: group aerobics in her bedroom and pilates in the living room.

Uzma is fascinated by Tia's abilities – not only can she produce new versions of herself, she can also absorb them back, acquiring the skills they've learned while separate. For every Tia consuming slabs of dark chocolate like a tractor beam, there are five doing stomach crunches or arguing over whose turn it is on the Wii Fit.

Tia does more than keep the whole house organised: every morning several copies also go out to collect supplies for Aman and the Scientist. Had they lived in the West, Aman could simply have ordered everything Sundar needed online, using his vast collection of fake identities and credit cards. In India, though, he needs Tia's help. It is possible to find absolutely anything in the grey markets of India's largest cities, but only if you know where to look. Tia has solved this problem by looking everywhere. She is now the best-known buyer of strange things in the Mumbai shadow-markets. It is widely rumoured that she works for one of the most powerful gangsters in Dubai, or a shadowy terrorist organisation that makes terrible weapons in an obscure village somewhere in the vast, practically ungoverned stretches of land that swathe this chaotic country.

Every day merchant ships carry strange machine parts, incredibly expensive raw materials and state-of-the-art gadgets in huge climate-controlled containers from all over the world to Mumbai's docks. Then through a multi-stage delivery process, tightly sealed packages pass from hand to hand, truck to car to train, until they are piled up messily in the rear seat of whatever car Tia has brought along that day. She pays for them in cash, draining ATMs all over Mumbai using Aman's many credit cards, withdrawing money he has acquired from the secret bank accounts of whoever he is annoyed with that day. Sometimes it's criminals, sometimes writers of self-help books for corporations, sometimes celebrities with annoying faces, often telecom companies that give him spam headaches. When the people she pays are obviously criminals, Tia goes with bags full of cash she has generated herself, patiently, from a single banknote. She can duplicate any small object as perfectly as she duplicates herself and in a less hectic world could have made a fortune being the ultimate DVD pirate.

Sundar and Bob finally finish pleading their cases to Uzma, and ask her to deliver a verdict. Both go off into a huge sulk when Uzma tells them that whoever has read the most superhero comics probably knows best how useful they can be. It turns out that neither has actually read any at all.

This uncomfortable silence is eventually broken by the return of Aman, who rushes into the room clutching a laptop, a panic-stricken expression on his face.

"DNNTV," he says.

Uzma switches the channel promptly, and several Tias gather, merge and sit as the house's favourite intrepid reporter, Namrata, beams out of the screen at her expectant audience. Behind her is a scene of chaos: thousands of people mill about on a large dusty field, at the far end of which a dais has been constructed on a sizeable stage. Around the stage, several large cut-outs of crudely painted avatars of the god Vishnu have been arranged. Rama and Krishna, his two greatest hits, have pride of place. "This is the Ram Lila ground in Delhi," the captions tell viewers, "and all of this is LIVE!"

The leaders of the AKWWEK sit on large thrones arranged in a line behind the stage. Ever since Namrata's interview, the party has been in the news constantly, its name ruthlessly shortened to Kalki Party by acronym-unfriendly TV pundits. Several religious groups have challenged them publicly, claiming that Vishnu's tenth avatar has already had his time. About twelve self-proclaimed Hindu leaders, mostly slightly crazy TV evangelists/astrologers/yogis, have declared the Kalki Party's claims laughable lies because *they* were Kalki. Besides these, at least two Muslim sects and one Baha'i group claim that their founders were the divine incarnation the Kalki Party now claims to have discovered.

Other right-wing Hindu parties have offered the Kalki Party wary support – after a thumping defeat in the 2009 elections, India's Hindu hardliners are no longer sure that spewing venom against Muslims will win them popular support, but who could pass up the chance to be associated with an avatar of Vishnu? The only reason the Kalki Party has not completely changed the face of Indian politics over the last two days is simple. No one has seen the baby yet, and until he is proved genuinely divine in some way, none of the larger Hindu parties are willing to stick their necks out. And that is why the Kalki Party's leaders have come to the nation's capital today – they want to show the world its saviour, and Delhi's the only city for that sort of thing.

The baby has been smuggled from Chennai to Delhi under the kind of secrecy and security normally reserved for Hollywood directors when they visit India to location-scout slums. Not a single photographer has managed to get anything except pictures of the private jet, cars and cradle the Kalki Party inner-circle politicians have used to carry the holy infant across the country for this grand unveiling.

As Namrata moves towards the stage, breathlessly listing the responses of various fashion designers, TV actors, restaurant owners and other intellectual heavyweights to the arrival of this baby on the celebrity scene, the Ram Lila ground begins to fill up. Hordes of people filter in steadily through flimsy metal detectors at every entrance. The front of the stage, above the police cordon, is a scrum of jostling cameramen, there is a frenzy of excitement as two women in white, surrounded by black-clad commandoes, climb the steps of the stage. They carry a large basket nearly completely covered in white cloth. From it emerges a shrill wail – the Baby Saviour's first words to his assembled devotees are very open to interpretation.

"No actual god has appeared on live TV before," Namrata says as the camera zooms in on the basket. "While it is not confirmed that the baby in the basket you can now see on DNNTV's camera is divine, this is a landmark moment in the history of the world. This report will be broadcast worldwide, and is brought to you by us."

A huge groan goes through the audience as a Kalki Party leader steps towards the dais and fiddles with the microphone in front of it. The world, it turns out, will get to see the divine baby only after it has finished listening to what its future leaders have to say. And they have a lot to say. The leaders lay out the Kalki Party's multifaceted agenda: they believe that they are the superhumans Kalki is supposed to lead, the guardians he will reward with wealth and continents to govern when he comes of age and starts his eliminating-all-evil-with-big-weapons world tour. Until then, the Kalki Party will fight his battles on his behalf: they promise to destroy terrorism, Communism, the internet, the English language, Pakistan, bikinis, China, Hollywood, the entire Arab world and women's jeans.

The crowd cheers good-naturedly at first, but begins to thin after a while. None of these politicians are well known in Delhi, a city used to the biggest names in the world showing up from time to time. After an hour that seems to last several years, several high-profile political correspondents are on the verge of leaving, when Rosy, the AKWWEK's star speaker, comes to the microphone.

"Now we display Baby Kalki," she says simply.

An iPod hooked up to the sound system blasts out a bhajan that squeals harshly through tinny speakers all over the Ram Lila ground. The ladies in white bring the basket to Rosy. The Kalki Party's other leaders spring to their feet and crowd around her, not wanting to be left out of this historic photo op. Rosy rubs her hands together like a weight-lifter, and without further ado casts aside the cloth covering the basket and lifts up a squealing Baby Kalki, holding him up in front of her, arms extended.

The crowd gasps as one.

The baby is peacock blue. He has four chubby arms, all of which he is waving frantically in an attempt to maul Rosy. And his head is the head of a pony, a big, freaky head, far too heavy for the tiny spine attempting to hold it in place, a head that dips forward and swings gently from side to side as Rosy holds him up. Baby Kalki's eyes are enormous and liquid black. A little toy sword has been stuck to one of his hands with Sellotape. He opens his mouth and cries, a sad, whinnying wail, and complete silence spreads across the wide field.

"What we are seeing here is no ordinary child," says the astute Namrata. "How will people react? Find out live."

"Aman," Tia says, "obviously these idiots don't know what they're talking about, but – what if it's true? He was *born* with powers. The only one. What if he *is* some kind of god? What if we're all supposed to be his world-purifying army?"

"How would I know?" Aman replies. "If I look on the internet, I'm sure I'll find an army of complete lunatics who've been predicting all this for years."

The camera pans across the ground. The divine manifestation has not exactly set off wild celebrations among the people of Delhi. In fact, the crowd seems most upset. A ripple of anger spreads from those closest to the stage to the edges of the ground: fists rise shaking at the sky, a chorus of wails lifts to the heavens.

The Kalki Party members huddle together on stage with the baby, clearly completely flabbergasted at this strange behaviour. Policemen move towards the stage from all over the ground.

"It's possible that the people here believe this is a trick of some kind," Namrata ventures. "The Indian youth has often felt cheated by its politicians – is this a step too far?"

Fights break out in the crowd, but end quickly as combatants all over the ground are smothered by a mass of people pushing them forwards, towards the stage and the rapidly retreating Kalki Party members. The baby is crying loudly now, his huge head tossing, his many arms flailing. The police cordon in front of the stage and the bamboo barricades between them and the crowd all suddenly look very fragile.

"What are they angry about?" Uzma asks. "Shouldn't they be going into religious raptures or something?"

The camera zooms in on a group of people in the crowd, their faces are suffused with fury, hair on end, chests heaving, eyes bulging, glaring. There's something about this crowd that sets it apart from your standard angry mob. Their movements are strangely synchronised. Slowly, steadily, they move towards the front of the Ram Lila ground in waves; some yell wordlessly, screams of rage that find echoing throats across the ground swirl and blow towards the stage like a vicious desert wind.

"The crowd is not reacting well to the sight of the Baby Kalki," Namrata points out helpfully. "Is this another example of the nation refusing to be divided along communal lines? Watch our exclusive panel of experts debate this at primetime tonight, only on DNNTV!"

"Put her on mute, please," Uzma says. No one responds. Namrata's cameraman has caught a good shot of the baby, and everyone in the room stares in fascination at the four-armed horse-headed little monster. Then the camera jumps back to the crowd; people are moaning, shaking, quivering as they push forward.

"Aman, what's happening here? I've never seen people behave like this at a rally," Tia says. "Is this a powers thing?"

"I'll look it up," Aman says, and shuts his eyes. "Mass hysteria. No known cause. Symptoms vary. Women more likely to succumb – go figure. Anyway. Spreads fast. Often when symbols of authority can be seen. Convergence theory says certain individuals cause crowds to act in certain ways. Contagion theory states the opposite. Turner–Killian Emergent-norm theory of crowd dynamics tells us this sort of behaviour is never irrational, but governed by common interests."

"In other words, no one really knows anything, but this could be happening on its own without any powers involved," Sundar says.

On the screen, the crowd pushes forward again and the bamboo barricade in front of the stage bends, creaks and finally gives way. Hundreds of bodies surge forward. A line of policemen, their cane shields side by side, struggle to push them back. A few policemen use their sticks, and screams and wails form a solid wall of sound.

"Distinct behaviour patterns emerge," Aman says. His eyelids drift open, and his pupils cannot be seen. "There are no rules, it's a chain of individual responses leading to collective action. Someone in the audience always claps first."

A second line of policemen runs into position behind the first. They carry tear-gas shells. And guns.

"This is useless. Look for similar events, and what caused them," Tia says.

"Tanganyika laughter epidemic, 1962. Dancing plague of Strasbourg, 1518. No verified causes."

"What if this baby is causing it?" Uzma says. "If he's really this incarnation of your god, ending this age of the world or whatever? Maybe it's his fault people are going crazy."

Ignoring the threats of the beleaguered policemen, the crowd pushes on. A large Sikh punches a constable on the nose, and the policeman staggers back, dropping his shield. Behind him, another policeman raises his ancient rifle...

Something snaps. The crowd halts. Shouts die in gulping throats.

Hundreds of people, both rioters and policemen, look at one another in a confused sort of way, as if they had just woken from a long, deep slumber. It's as if a rage switch has been turned off somewhere.

And then the police advance, batons smacking into unprotected bodies. A mad scramble for the exit begins. But a full-blown stampede is averted: somewhere in the police line, sanity prevails and they step back.

"Oh my god," says Namrata's voice on TV.

The DNNTV camera returns to Namrata. She's looking across the crowd, a hand shading her eyes. At a signal from her producers, she turns to face the camera, and when she looks into the screen it is clear that she has been struck dumb with fear; her face is white. She opens her mouth to give her audience some comfortable platitude about the underlying harmony in Indian society. But she doesn't make it. Her jaw drops. Her microphone falls to the ground. She runs.

The cameraman, not knowing what to shoot, follows her as she streaks across the Ram Lila ground, soon disappearing amongst the chaotic sea of people running around, pursued by stick-wielding policemen trying in vain to re-establish some sort of order. The Kalki Party leaders are still on stage, surrounded by gun-toting commandoes in Kevlar vests.

"Will someone please tell me what's going on?" Uzma wails.

A blue light pulses across the ground. For one second, there's a blue dome spreading over the crowd; the next, it's vanished.

The screen goes blank.

Cursing, Aman snatches the remote and starts flipping through news channels. Every channel that was broadcasting from the Ram Lila ground is now showing static. Some have started running ads.

"Get through to her phone," Tia says.

"I'm tracking all calls from her studio," Aman says. "Let me just cross-check her number – yes, got it. Her phone's off."

They sit in tense silence for two whole minutes watching Aman change channels. Then one of the news channels flickers back to life. The camera is fixed on the stage, where a dozen bodies lie in a mangled heap. Some are black-clad commandoes. Some are Kalki Party leaders. All are dead, brutally clobbered. Policemen hover over them like flies.

The baby is gone.

All the news channels have the same visual, each with a reporter jabbering away furiously in front of it, building stories out of nothing. The facts are simple: Baby Kalki is dead or missing; the Kalki Party's short-lived run of glory is done; several people are injured. No one has any footage.

The crowd has been cleared. Delhi has faced too many terrorist attacks, too many random bombings in public places, for people to hang around uselessly at times like this. The Ram Lila ground is littered with the bodies of the dead and the wounded.

Reporters scour the ground looking for witnesses, but in all the confusion of the riot, no one seems to have noticed what happened on stage. Conflicting reports emerge: one man says he saw a demon leap up from the crowd, soar over the heads of the police line, snatch the baby and vanish. Another says he saw a magician standing in the crowd spreading blue fire. Another saw a man dancing on stage, bodies falling around him with every move. A sobbing policeman tells a reporter he saw gods appear to reclaim their own. His report is rendered less credible when he claims that he, too, is a god.

Whatever really happened to the Kalki Party happened in a flash, and no one in the immediate vicinity of the kidnapping is alive to tell the tale. The airwaves are awash with rumours, semi-crazed religious mumbling and outright lies.

Aman turns off the TV, eyes unfocused, breathing rapidly. "The studio people just got through to our girl," he says.

"I want to listen," Tia says. "Route it through the laptop?"

Aman nods.

"You mean we're just going to sit here and listen to you tap her phone?" Uzma asks. "Anyone else think this is wrong?"

No one else thinks this is wrong. They gather round Aman's laptop, from which comes the sound of a ringing phone.

After several rings, Namrata picks it up.

"Where the hell are you?" barks Namrata's boss. "Get back in there!"

"He's going to kill me," she whispers.

"What?"

"I've got to get out of here. He was here. I saw him. He was looking straight at me, then he jumped into the crowd."

"Who? You saw his face? You can identify him?"

"I don't know! It was like he vanished! He's taken the baby, I know it's him. Maybe he got the parents too."

"Nam, baby, you're freaking out. Who is this guy?"

"I told you before. The same man I saw at the hospital. Watching me. He wants to kill me, I know he does. I saw it in his eyes." Namrata starts sobbing.

"Okay, come back to the studio. I don't know how I'm going to explain this. Story of the year, and you run out on it. Do you know what I had to do to get you this?"

"He's going to kill me, you idiot!" Namrata cries. "I can't do this any more! I want to move to Features!"

"If you still have a job by the end of today, I'll be amazed and you'll owe me big time. Now stop wailing and get your ass back to the office."

The line goes dead.

Uzma looks at her flatmates.

"Are you going to call her over?" she asks. "There is that empty room on my floor."

"Maybe," Aman says. "They're obviously on her trail, though, so meeting her would be very dangerous. We've got to find a way to save her."

"How did the kid's parents die?" Tia asks.

"Someone hit their car really hard."

"So we're dealing with super-strength, maybe speed, the ability to shut down electronics – and what else?"

"She said he vanished," Aman says. "Invisibility? Teleportation? Who the hell knows? And the crowd – we might be looking at a mass hypnotist. A mind controller." Aman throws his hands up in the air and stares angrily at the TV, where a cheerful man in a suit is now discussing hot tips in stocks. "Rare dolphin found dead in missing swimmer's house" floats across the Breaking News band at the bottom of the screen. A picture flashes across the screen. Aman shakes his head. Another fellow passenger dead.

"Are we sure it's not Vir?" Tia asks.

"If it were Vir, you and I would be dead by now as well. No, this is another one of the thugs from the base, like the guy with the tongue the other day. One of this Jai Mathur's henchmen. Unless it's Jai himself."

"It could be more than one person," Sundar points out. "One man to shut down the cameras, another to abduct the baby. Perhaps another to stir up the crowd and create a distraction. But to do this in broad daylight at a public gathering – so many things could have gone wrong!"

"Maybe they don't care about that any more," Aman says. "Maybe they want to send a message to people like us."

"We need to talk to this girl, Namrata," Tia says. "If she can really sense in advance where big news stories are going to happen, she'll know where they'll strike next. She needs protection. Someone like Vir needs to be with her, to sort out his people when they arrive."

"I can't believe you're talking about using this girl as bait," Uzma snaps. "Call her and tell her to quit her job. Or at least to stay away from any place she thinks might be dangerous."

"Until one day she senses the news is going to be wherever she is, turns round and finds Jai's boys?" Aman says. "No, hiding won't help her. Neither will sending Vir in for some sort of superpower showdown. This is ridiculous! These people are all adults, and all they can do with their abilities is act like B-movie villains!"

"Do you really think Vir can change their minds?" Tia asks.

"No, not after this," Aman replies. "But maybe Uzma can. Maybe they'll like her. Listen to her."

"You're not sending Uzma anywhere near those maniacs," Tia says firmly.

"Uzma has no intention of being a part of any of this," Uzma says. "I have work to do. I have films to make. I have a life. This is crazy."

"You can't go out there," Tia says. "At least hide until this is over."

"No."

"We'll get you fake ID then. Change your name," Tia says.

"To what? Some safe, popular Hindu name? I won't do it."

Another Tia emerges and stands up and paces around the room.

"How do we protect ourselves?" she asks after a while. "What can we do? What happens when they find us?"

Aman shuts his laptop with a snap and leaves the room without a word.

CHAPTER **SEVEN**

Seventeen kilometres directly to the east of Udhampur's IAF airbase and its friendly MiG-21s and Jaguars, tucked away in a secret valley in the shadows of the Himalayan foothills, there is a building, a new building covered in shabbily applied white paint. Around the building is a high electric fence, crackling with power stolen from the nearby Baglihar Hydroelectric Power Project, that harnesses the churning waters of the Chenab river.

The building is not visible from or connected to the nearest road. It's only two storeys high on the outside, but there's a lot more to it, most of it underground. A mere month ago, it did not even exist. Had its architects and builders not had strange powers, it would never have.

Inside this building, several floors underground, is an office. Outside the door of this office stand several uniformed men. One of these men is Flight Lieutenant Vir Singh. He can fly, but he is choosing, at this moment, to knock.

"Come in," says a deep voice.

As Vir enters the office, its sole occupant, a strapping, muscular young man in uniform seated behind a desk, jumps up and springs to attention, dashing off a quivering salute. Squadron Leader Jai Mathur is the Air Force man of every Indian woman's dreams; the kind of man you'd imagine sacrificing his life for the nation in a thrilling Bollywood movie, leaving behind a beautiful, dignified wife and a sobbing, impossibly cute daughter.

"Hello, Jai," Vir says.

Jai ignores Vir, looking instead at the hawk-like, vaguely Eastwood-esque gentleman beside him.

"Wing Commander!" he says. "I wish you had given me some notice of your arrival, sir. I would have had the base shining. But, no excuses – I should have known you'd prefer a surprise inspection."

The Wing Commander grunts. "Enough of this nonsense," he says. Five Air Force men step into the room and stand behind the Commander and Vir. "Come with us, Jai," the Commander says.

"I don't think I shall," Jai says with a polite smile. "Vir, you should have spoken to me first."

"I don't know you any more," Vir says. "You lied to me about everything – I asked around."

Jai smirks, and his shoulders shake slightly. He sits on his desk, swinging his legs over the edge, and gestures melodramatically as he speaks, a pantomime villain cornered by the detective in the drawing-room.

"And you unravelled my complex web of deceit. You discovered, slowly, ploddingly, how I arm-twisted the Air Vice-

Marshall into getting his brother-in-law, the Inspector General of Police, to work for me. Perhaps you also heard of my secret alliances with the Mumbai underworld? No? Ah. Well done, anyway. How betrayed you must feel."

"I trusted you. How could you? How could you kidnap the Vice-Marshalls's daughter?" Vir says.

Jai hops down lightly from his desk.

"It's a three-step process. First, I walked into his house…"

"But – why?"

"I thought he needed additional motivation. Merely making him wet his pants might not have been enough."

"Enough!" snaps the Commander. "And to think we almost didn't believe you, Vir. Men, take away this traitor!"

"Tariq!" Jai calls.

A gunshot rings out.

One of the Air Force men pitches forward, shot in the back of the head. Behind him in the corridor stands a skinny boy with a straggly beard and a pistol in his hand.

"Fire!" yells the Commander.

But before his men can raise their rifles, Tariq vanishes, reappearing inside Jai's office. He fires, another man dies, and Tariq disappears.

Seven seconds later, all five are dead. The Commander stands with horrified eyes and a smoking gun in his hand, pointed at Jai.

Jai delicately extracts a bullet from his forehead and tosses it aside.

Vir charges, but before his punch can land Jai has moved with superhuman speed to the other side of the table. Tariq appears, shoots Vir, and vanishes before the bullet has had time to bounce off Vir and into the wall. Jai speeds towards Vir and lands an uppercut that knocks him off his feet and sends him crashing into the wall, shattering a framed photograph of Jai's family.

Tariq appears again, his gun trained on the Commander. Vir scrambles to his feet, but the Commander raises a warning hand and Vir stays where he is.

"This is Tariq," Jai says. "He likes to travel. Sit down, Commander."

Armed guards run into the office and start removing bodies. The Wing Commander barks an order at them and is ignored. He turns, seething, to Jai.

"What the hell is going on here?" he thunders.

"I assume Vir told you and so the question is rhetorical," Jai counters smoothly. "But let's not allow matters to escalate further, sir. I was always rather fond of you. Please do sit down, may I offer you a drink?"

"No you bloody well may not. An air strike has been authorised on this building. The Prime Minister has heard about your little gang, and he's not happy. Unless you have an explanation – and a damned good one – you're finished."

"When I started this whole thing, my plan was to hand the best fighting force in the world – an unstoppable Indian elite squadron – to you on a platter," Jai says. "I am now in a position to do so. And more. Would you like to see what I have to offer?"

"This has moved far higher than me, you arrogant young fool," the Commander responds. "Come with us. The Air Marshall will deal with you."

Vir coughs discreetly.

"Perhaps we should hear him out, sir."

"I think that's a good idea," Jai says. "I can think of two

advantages to this. First, you wouldn't be placing the Air Marshall's life in danger. Second, I wouldn't have to call your bluff about the air strike."

"That was no bluff."

"In that case, why sacrifice a Wing Commander? It doesn't make sense. You're here to negotiate, sir. If we can cease this childish banter, I will reveal my plan to you. Everything I have done so far – every crime you accuse me of – has been merely to eliminate bureaucracy, politicians, experts, committees, meetings, leaks – all of which I have heard you complain about endlessly. I don't have to teach you about the problems our military faces, and I'm sure you don't really mind my stepping out of line. I assume Vir has already shown you he can fly. There are others here who have powers even more extraordinary. If you would like a proper demonstration, I can promise to bring down the entire Pakistani military within the next two weeks. They keep sending people over the border. I could show them how it's done."

"Why should I believe a word you say? You've been running around the country murdering people. You just murdered my own men in front of me."

"Those men were killed by a commanding officer who sent them into battle against an infinitely superior force. You seem to have forgotten what we do for a living. Murder is our business. And I was eliminating military threats, not going on some kind of mad spree. You don't have to believe me, sir. It doesn't really matter. The thing is, there is nothing you can do to stop me."

Jai extracts a bottle of single malt from a cabinet and pours himself a drink. The Commander and Vir stand ashen-faced as he takes a swig, sighs in appreciation, and sets the glass down.

"If I had been a real danger to you, or to the Indian nation; if I had wanted to raze our armies to the ground, set the Taj Mahal on fire and laugh in the face of the world, I would have done it by now," Jai continues. "Instead, I offer you the chance to break free from the old men you are forced to obey, and accept that the world as you knew it has ended. Thanks to this strange incident, there are powers that exist now that can make India – and only India – the mightiest nation in the world. You know people have been saying India is destined to be the next global superpower? Thanks to me and my actions, this is now literally true."

"So you killed all the non-Indians on the plane," Vir says.

"Not all. Only the ones I could find. It's simple, really – I am going to kill every powered individual I cannot use. I do this not for myself, but for my country. Now, Commander, we can sit here and discuss this all night. Or I could kill the two of you, move this base to a quieter location and carry on.

"There is a third alternative I present for your consideration: meet my team. See for yourself how we can put an end to all our military troubles – Pakistan, China, even America one day, who knows? And then take me to meet the Air Marshall. I'd go now, but I'm afraid I'd end up killing superior officers."

Vir starts to speak, but is silenced by a warning glance.

The Commander sits down.

"Show me what you've got," he says.

Outside the building, a guard emerges from a little booth near the only gate to the compound. Floodlights come on, revealing a man slumped face down in front of the gate, and a short, attractive woman standing over him. Brandishing his gun by way of greeting, the guard stalks up to the gate.

"Eh?" he says.

Tia smiles gently at him and rolls the man over with a slender foot. The guard swears as he recognises a very battered Mukesh.

"I need to speak to Jai," Tia says. "My friend here would speak for me, but as you can see..."

The guard stares at her. "I'll make a call," he growls, and heads back towards his cabin.

"Sorry, but could you let me use your toilet?" she calls. "I've been dragging him for a long time, and I really have to go."

The guard opens the gate. He frisks Tia, taking longer than he should, and confiscates her phone and wallet.

"In the cabin," he growls, and she heads off.

A startled, horrified gasp a minute later tells the guard she has entered the hell-hole that is his toilet. He picks Mukesh up and drags him towards his cabin.

A phone call later, and two soldiers march out of the building. One binds Tia to him with a pair of handcuffs, and the other picks up Mukesh. They head back inside.

Mumbling to himself, the guard heads back into his cabin.

A few minutes later, Tia emerges, retching, from his toilet and hits him on the back of the head with a brick. He seems more amazed than hurt at this, but when another Tia appears, carrying another brick, and they both smite him on either side of the head, he goes down. The Tias merge, and she picks up her phone.

"Aman," she says. "I'm at the Kashmir base. Can you get into the system here?"

"Tia? What the hell? How did you –"

"Later. Can you get in and shut them down?"

"Wait. Let me look. I'm got a satellite link outside, but... no. No wireless inside. No radar, even. And they're underground. What do you plan to do?"

"Thought I'd talk to this Jai myself."

"No, listen. Just try and get the prisoners out. Don't go anywhere near him. Leave that to Vir."

"No point telling me. I'm not the one inside."

"Why didn't you tell me?"

"You talk too much."

Tia hangs up, sits by the unconscious guard and begins to read his dirty magazine.

Jai leads Vir and the Commander to a huge underground hall, large enough to be an aeroplane hangar. It's empty except for a makeshift gym in one corner, expensive exercise equipment and absurdly large weights arranged in rows. A stench of leather and stale sweat fills the entire hall.

"It's not much of a Danger Room, but it's all we've managed to put together at short notice," Jai says.

"Where do you keep your people?" the Commander asks.

"All over the building. We've built this very good high-security prison right at the bottom. That's where we keep the powers we can use, but don't quite trust yet. There's a science wing, where we run experiments, physical, psychological – we discovered fairly early on that people had been given powers that were manifestations of their ambitions. I wanted to be the greatest warrior in the world, and here I am. But people mostly want useless things – more money, to be skilled at dancing, revenge, celebrity lovers. Whatever the nature of each power and the identity of the forces that gave them to us, one thing is certain – our bodies have been tampered with. A team of very good doctors are in the process of finding out how. For this we're using people whose gifts have absolutely no military potential."

"What have you found?"

"We're still working on it. Simple processes like blood transfusions or organ exchanges haven't yet produced any powered humans. But we'll crack it eventually."

"You're using humans – ordinary people – for your tests?" Vir says.

"Nothing you need to worry about. We've mostly got Afghans – they run into Pakistan to escape Americans, and the Pakistanis give them bigger guns and send them to us. We've been practising combat ops by the border – you should see their faces when they meet us. I thought I'd put them to good use before we kill them."

"You're creating superpowered mujahideen? You're insane!" the Commander cries.

"You're not a very good negotiator. Look, my boys are here," Jai says.

Two men walk into the hall. One is balding, bearded, bespectacled, middle-aged, and the other is Barack Obama, the forty-fourth President of the United States.

"Meet Jerry and Vivek," Jai says. "Jerry used to be a poet, but he lived in Mumbai. Couldn't write with all the noise around him, phone ringing all the time, needing to check his email every two minutes, couldn't move out of the city because his wife earned the money and called the shots. He got a British Council fellowship, went to London, and what can you do now, Jerry?" Jai asks the bearded man.

"I create a blue thing," Jerry replies.

"A blue thing. See what a good poet he is? Jerry creates silence. Launches an electromagnetic pulse that shuts down everything nearby for a several minutes."

"And I guess Mr Obama, or Vivek here, can change his facial features," says the Commander, looking suddenly very impressed.

"More than that. I'd have preferred it if he could have done the whole instantaneous-morphing thing the demons of the Ramayana could do, but Vivek was an actor – ex-National School of Drama, the whole method actor nonsense. Never earned a rupee, of course, but now he can *become* anyone – not just look like them. Give him a few days to rehearse and enough background material, and at the end of it he looks, talks, even *thinks* like they do."

"Amazing," says the Commander. Vivek strides over and shakes his hand with a firm, warm and presidential grip.

"Delighted you could be here," he says.

Tariq materialises beside Jai.

"And then there's Tariq, of course. He would have been a deadly weapon just as he is, but we've found out that with the help of satellite imagery and even civilian-accessible technology like Google Earth, he can go anywhere he needs to. Very useful for low-budget international assassinations."

The Commander stirs uneasily. "You understand that I find it difficult to respond with full coherence, given the circumstances," he says.

"Of course," Jai says. "And what you must understand in turn is that I mean well. We want the same things. The very last thing I want is any sort of conflict with the Indian armed forces. Not because you could harm me in any way, of course, but because we'd be losing out on the greatest opportunity in our history. And all my men are not invincible."

"Don't listen to him," Vir says suddenly. "He's changed. He wasn't like this."

"No, Vir," says the Commander. "He's behaved... irresponsibly, but his record is excellent. I see your point, Jai, but after all you've done, I don't think our superiors can trust you. Would you be willing to operate under Vir's leadership? If so, I will speak in your favour."

Jai's smile is cold. "I'm not sure how to put this best, Commander," he says. "I sense your willingness to work with us, and I can wholly understand how much effort it must have taken. But let's face facts. In our present situation, it really doesn't matter whether you trust me or not. I was always very fond of Vir – I've known him for years, I see myself as his mentor in many ways. And I always saw him as an integral member of my elite unit, but then he went and complained, like a whiny little schoolboy. So if we are all to be one happy family, I'm afraid it is now Vir who must earn *my* trust."

"And how would he do that?" asks the Commander.

"You haven't met the rest of my team," Jai says.

"Where are you taking me?" Tia asks. "We've been walking for ages. I want to meet Jai!"

"He's busy," the soldier replies. "Sorry, but I have to lock you in. He'll see you later, when Poison's up."

"All right," Tia says. "Reasonable. Is there a place in this building where you keep lots of weapons?"

"Like I'd tell you," the soldier says, laughing.

He doesn't even notice when other Tias, handcuffed to nothing, appear behind him, simply stopping as the one handcuffed to him walks on. He does notice, though, when a handcuff chain tightens across his throat, cutting off his startled yell, and another Tia dives at his legs, sending them all to the floor in a struggling heap. The guard tussles with four Tias until he's relieved of his gun and the key to the handcuffs.

"So tell me again," Tia says, idly pointing the gun at the guard's right eye, "where do you keep the big guns?"

A huge shaven-headed man and a little girl in a school uniform, white shirt, grey skirt, striped tie, enter the hall.

"We need to leave," Vir says quietly to the Commander.

Tariq appears beside the Commander, gun pointed at his head.

"Perhaps you should step aside, sir," Jai says.

As Tariq pushes the Commander to a corner of the hall, the poet and the President back away, towards the door. The schoolgirl and the shaven-headed man advance slowly towards Vir.

"You first, Sher," Jai says.

The shaven-headed man nods. Then his muscles swell up, and dark lines appear around his body, swirling contours that converge into thick black stripes. His spine bends forward, his face contorts, fur sprouts out all over his body. His clothes rip as his torso thickens. Moments later, an eight-foot giant with a tiger's head and paws stands in front of Vir. He growls, a low, ominous rumble that fills the underground hangar.

Vir flies up into the air as the tiger-man lunges at him, misses and lands heavily on the floor. He's up in an instant and airborne, but Vir swerves aside, and Sher misses again.

"Fight him, damn it!" Jai yells at Vir.

"No," Vir says. "Stop this, sir. We can still find a way out of this."

"What happened to you? What happened to your spine?" Jai responds.

"I met someone who showed me how wrong this was. How we need to work together to change the world."

Jai laughs out loud. "I'd like to meet this friend of yours and congratulate him for being a really original thinker," he says. "Oh, this endless war, this senseless violence!" He spreads his arms out and assumes an expression of infinite sorrow. "People fighting for millennia over nothing! If only someone had thought of this before! We could all get together and make the world perfect!"

"I know it hasn't happened before," Vir says, "but it could happen now. We're superhumans. And we all have so much in common."

"I'm sorry, I can't hear you. Could you come a little closer? No? Princess Anima, the Evil Flying Muscle Monster is feeling shy. Could you bring him here, please?"

The schoolgirl steps forward. Her face transforms as well: her eyes grow, becoming huge ovals that stretch across half her face. Her nose shrinks, her skin changes colour. In a few seconds, she's a pretty, pink, horrifying real-life approximation of a Japanese cartoon. Fairy wings sprout on her back. Two samurai katanas, crackling with green flame, appear in her hands.

"Flying Double Moon Death Charge!" she screams, her voice

as cute as sleeping rabbits. She flies up into the air, swinging her swords, tendrils of light trailing behind her.

Vir hasn't met Anima before and doesn't want to meet her now. He swerves to avoid her but she's faster than he is. The swords sweep in glittering arcs and slash across his skin, criss-crossing streaks of unimaginable pain. He screams aloud as the green light crackles into his bruised skin, burning a large cross in his uniform.

Anima lands on the ground on one knee, head bent, swords tucked beneath her arms and perfectly aligned to her back, a classic samurai pose. She raises her head, sees Vir and laughs, a sweet, innocent, bell-like laugh as he wobbles groggily in the air. And then she's off again, zipping through the air towards him, her hand flickering faster than the eye can see.

"Stars of Destruction!" she cries.

A stream of three-pointed shuriken, ninja throwing stars of green light, slam into Vir's face. Dizzy, hurt, blinded, he crashes to the floor as Anima soars above him and lands lightly across the hall. She stands coyly, one hand across her mouth, another archly placed on her hip, her manga eyes brimming with amusement, and her laughter tinkles out again. This time it grates across his ears like chalk across a board.

Vir groans and attempts to rise, hears a soft padding noise, smells rank, fetid breath, and suddenly his head is trapped between Sher's tiger jaws, the all-powerful stench of rotten meat filling his nostrils. The monster shakes Vir from side to side, trying to snap his neck. Failing, he bites him again, dagger-like fangs scratch across Vir's face but still don't draw blood.

Roaring in frustration, Sher swings a mighty paw into Vir's stomach and the flying-man skids far along the floor before finally rolling to a halt. Sher reaches him in one unnaturally graceful pounce. He kneels astride Vir and hammers a succession of punches into his chest. Vir stops thrashing about after the first barrage and merely twitches in response to the second. The floor beneath him cracks and splinters.

"Come on, soldier," Jai sneers. "Make it interesting."

Vir doesn't move. Sher lifts up his head by the hair and lets it go, Vir falls limply to the floor.

"You've made your point, Jai," says the Commander, visibly trembling. "I would like to leave now, with your permission. I'll arrange a meeting between you and the Air Chief Marshall."

"Of course you will," Jai says. "But why are you in such a hurry to leave? The show's only just started. No one's even dead yet."

Seven Tias, armed with a devastating array of weapons, burst through a door. A company of guards sitting in a dark room full of glowing TV sets put up their hands obligingly.

The Tias look curiously at the screens around them. Each one connects to a camera that shows a padded cell. Some of the cells are empty, but several clearly contain superpeople.

"Keys," a Tia demands.

A guard tosses her a set of keys and the guards all watch appreciatively as Tia-with-the-keys multiplies herself tenfold.

"Will someone be nice enough to lead us to the cells?" a Tia asks. "We really don't want to shoot you."

"That's good, madam," a guard says. "But whatever it is you're trying to do, give up. You should surrender before Jai and his men get here. They are not nice like us."

"Take us to the cells," Tia says, shaking her gun in what she hopes is a menacing fashion.

"Cells won't open with just these keys," the guard says. "You need swipe cards from the science wing."

"Let's go there, then. I've got time."

The Tias rush out with two guards in tow. The other guards return to their perusal of the screens.

"Two hundred rupees says Sher kills the last one."

"Tariq," says another.

They gather round and lay their bets.

"Hey," suggests a guard after a while, "do you think we should, you know, sound the alarm?"

An alarm rings out.

"Tariq," Jai says. Tariq nods and disappears.

"I've seen enough," says the Commander. "You can lead the team. I agree to all your terms, whatever they are. Now let Vir go. He'll be useful."

"No," Jai says. "He dies tonight. I don't deal well with betrayal."

The Commander struggles with this for a moment or two.

"Very well," he says. "But if you don't let me leave in the next fifteen minutes, I won't be able to stop the air strike on this building. I wasn't bluffing about that."

"Yes, you were," Jai says. He turns away from Vir with a reluctant sigh. "Would you like to know what I think happened, Commander? I think you were lying to me in my office, and you tricked Vir just as I did. Because, you see, if the Air Marshall, or the Prime Minister, or the Pope, or anyone with half a brain and a phone at his disposal learned about me, this valley would have been crawling with soldiers. I think Vir came to you and told you his story, and you decided to come here and get yourself a crack team and an overnight promotion."

The Commander considers blustering his way out of this, but after a few seconds of trying to look indignant his shoulders sag.

"Now let's be reasonable, Jai," he says. "They're never going to take you back. You're not – you're more than human now. Different. Hell, they'd have locked that poor boy Vir up if he'd gone to them. You wouldn't stand a chance. Unless you're working under someone they *do* trust. A bridge between the uppermost tiers of the military and its finest team."

"In other words, you."

"Yes. I believe in you, Jai. I always have. And these powers you have... Imagine what you could do with my help. With my guidance."

Jai reaches out and snaps the Commander's neck.

"What are you looking at?" he yells at Sher and Anima, who are staring at the Commander's corpse, puzzled. "Get back to work!"

Three Tias run into what looks like a hospital ward. Beds are arranged in rows down the middle of the room, around forty people lie in these beds. Doctors scuttle about, adjusting drips, taking readings, playing with their BlackBerries. Charmed by this vision, a Tia fires her gun into the air, and the doctors dive for the floor.

"Sliding card thingies that open cell doors! Hand them over!" Tia yells.

A buxom nurse holds up a wobbling arm, and a Tia snatches a card from it.

A gunshot rings out. Tia turns to dust. The nurse screeches. Two more bursts of gunfire, and the other Tias also fade away.

The card flutters to the floor.

"Where else are they?" Tariq bellows, teleporting to the other end of the ward.

Seven more Tias rush in and dive for cover as Tariq appears in their midst, spinning and shooting at random. Other voices cry out; two doctors are hit. A white sheet near Tariq turns red. All over the room, patients dive for cover, hurling their sheets aside.

For two agonising minutes, Tariq and Tia shoot at each other. Tariq flickering up and down the hall, firing continuously; Tia rolling, ducking and diving, leaving a body behind at every turn.

The gunfire stops suddenly. Tariq is gone. Tias emerge from behind beds, whirling about, picking cards off corpses. At one end of the room, a Tia tosses a sheet off a seated figure and receives a bullet to the face.

Tariq is back, shooting at random and vanishing.

"Everyone stay down!" a Tia screams. She runs to the centre of the ward and stands, gun extended, and spins around. Five more Tias blossom in a circle, their gun barrels forming a six-pointed star. They fire simultaneously.

Tariq materialises and is mowed down. His body flickers for a few seconds and then moves no more.

"Is anyone alive?" a Tia calls. Moans and whimpers answer her. "Come with me," she says.

* * *

The tiger-man's claws rake Vir's face lazily.

"Hey, Jai," Sher says. "I think I'm done."

Vir opens his eyes. He grabs Sher's paws, sits up straight, head-butting the tiger's muzzle. As Sher yelps in pain, Vir rolls him off and jumps up, shaking his arms, ready for round two.

Sher rises to his feet with feline grace and crouches, his head moving from side to side. Green tiger eyes gaze hypnotically into Vir's, and Vir flinches as Sher snarls, displaying his fangs. He tries to think of something clever to say but can't. He knows it'll come to him later.

The tiger-man leaps on him, snarling. Vir jabs him, hard, on the nose, and follows up with a kick to the stomach that doubles Sher up. The beast flees now, heading towards the gym area.

Vir flies after him and barrels into him from behind, sending him head-first into a weights machine stacked up with massive one-ton weights. As the punch-drunk tiger swings wildly, Vir steps up in front of him and grasps him around the waist. Face contorted with effort, he picks Sher up, flies up to the hall's ceiling, squeezes the breath out of the tiger-man and drops him.

Cats don't always land on their feet, and Sher lands on his nose. The floor shatters. The tiger stays down.

"Princess Anima! This is a test," Jai calls.

"Super Striker Spear!" Anima squeals, driving a glittering energy-spear into Vir's side and sailing over him, her fairy wings buzzing.

Vir swivels, snaps the shaft with a well-placed chop and flies away, his head spinning, the sizzling spearhead falling harmlessly to the ground. As Anima sails after him, sprouting another pair of katanas, the air around her glowing and distorting, he turns, faces her, watches the swords rake his chest, then grabs them and breaks them in half across his knee. His hands feel frozen and aflame all at once.

The child is frightened now. Twin fountains of tears pour out of the sides of her face. He grabs her by the shoulder. *One punch to the face*, Vir's instincts yell, but he can't make himself hit this little girl.

A decision he regrets almost instantly as Anima conjures up a huge battle-axe and tries to cut his head off with it.

Vir spirals to the floor, his Adam's apple a huge, throbbing lump of pain. She's buzzing all around him now, darting humming-bird-like, pausing, hurling sparkling energy bolts, laughing.

Vir is dizzy, fading, spent. Groaning, he takes to the air, flies around the room as fast as he can, dodging shuriken and arrows, darts and spears, watching Jai smirk beneath him, and wondering what his father would have done in his place.

Tia opens the door to the first cell and finds an elderly woman clad in a Benarasi sari sitting demurely inside.

"What's your power, aunty?" she asks.

"I can sing," she says.

"Sweet. Can you get out of here?" She helps the woman to her feet, and runs to the next cell.

All along the cell block, other gun-toting Tias swing doors open, struggle with locks and usher inmates outside. A confused crowd of people from the science section mills about, though the smarter ones have already started racing towards the upper levels.

At the end of the block, yet more Tias deliver quick instructions: Get out of here, stop for nothing, lots of women who look just like me are waiting to show you the way.

Bursts of gunfire echo through the building as clusters of Tias take on its less friendly inhabitants. Tia doesn't stop to count the people she's rescuing. She knows several of them won't make it; some will die before they leave the building, the Himalayas will account for others. Not to mention the small matter of Jai's superpowered allies, thankfully otherwise engaged for the moment. But she's left several copies prowling all over the base, armed to the teeth. Whatever happens, she knows she has achieved something this night.

A siren wails. "That's the signal! We need to leave the base!" yells a fleeing doctor.

"Bloody genius," a Tia growls, and runs to another cell.

"Mega Power Destruction Crossbow!" Anima yells.

Twinkling razor-edged bolts of power shoot towards Vir, and even as he dodges them he realises that the flying schoolgirl is slowly herding him into a corner. Vir's second wind has almost run out, and his head is spinning too fast for him to see clearly. Pure instinct and blurry green lines are all that keep him going.

Anima flies above him, fighting casually, not even at full stretch – she's toying with him. Her crossbow disappears and a huge mace appears in her tiny hands. She swings it effortlessly, catches him smack in the middle of his back and he crashes down again, skidding along the floor, tasting dirt and sweat and concrete and blood. His blood. He rolls over, lies on his back, and blood bubbles up in his mouth. He coughs, spits, tries to get up and fails.

"Well done, Princess!" Jai cries. "Finish him!"

Anima laughs and curtsies in mid-air. The mace disappears in a cloud of green bubbles. A broadsword appears in its place.

"Final Decapitation Combo!" she calls, twirling the sword over her head and sweeping down for the killing strike.

At the last possible moment, Vir swings his hands up and blocks the sword. The blade cuts into his palm and sizzles as sparks of power ripple across his arms. He rips the sword from her grasp and tosses it aside as he rises into the air in front of her. She's manga-terrified, her mouth a small pink circle, her impossibly huge eyes quivering.

Vir grabs her wrist with one hand and, with the other, begins to tickle her. She squeals and giggles, helpless tears running out of her eyes, now horizontal slits above her rapidly rising nose. Her laughter reaches impossibly high notes, elsewhere in the hall, a light shatters.

"I'm the hero, Princess," Vir says, gently but firmly. "And you're a good girl, aren't you?"

"Finish him!" Jai yells.

She ignores him and nods at Vir.

"You're not going to fight me any more, are you?" Vir asks.

"No," she whispers. "I'm really sorry."

"Go to your room and think about what you just did."

Princess Anima starts to cry, and this time her tears aren't twin fountains, but big, fat tears running down her suddenly human cheeks. Her eyes shrink, her wings vanish, and her limbs flail. Vir catches her and lowers her gently to the floor. She runs off, sobbing.

"Smartly done," Jai says. "You have your moments, you know."

Vir turns to face him, staggering slightly.

"And now, the main event," Jai says, stretching.

The door to the hall opens, and Jerry and Vivek rush in.

"Something's gone wrong down below," Jerry says.

"Deal with it," Jai snaps. He strides towards Vir.

Vir stumbles forward, trying to raise his fists. Jai's first punch sends him flying across the hall. He smashes into a wall and stays down.

"Er... Jai?" Jerry says.

Jai stops in mid-stride and snarls.

"What is it?"

"The prisoners got away," Jerry says. "Tariq is dead. So are lots of people in the science wing. We don't know what happened."

Jai stares at the ceiling for a while, fists clenched.

"Pick up the tiger. Get the kid," he says finally. "Grab anything else you need."

"Poison's back," Jerry says.

"Tell him not to unpack. We're leaving."

When the men have dragged Sher out, Jai walks up to Vir and pulls him to his feet. He slaps him a few times, until Vir opens his eyes groggily.

"I don't know how you pulled this off," Jai snarls. "But I want you to know that in a few minutes some bombs are going to go off, and you're going to be buried alive in here. We're going to bring a mountain down on top of you. We could have ruled the world together, Vir. That was what I wanted. Now I'm going to have to do it by myself."

He slams Vir to the floor, kicks him savagely a few times, and starts running, his footsteps blending into a drum-roll.

CHAPTER **EIGHT**

"I still can't believe you didn't tell me," Aman mumbles.

"Darling, I didn't know I was going to turn into Rambo and storm the base," Tia says. "I think I've more than compensated for anything I might have done, anyway."

"So this was... compensation?"

"That's not what I meant. Really, men are so sentimental."

"True. But warn me before you start shooting monsters again, okay?"

"I've told you, I don't really know what my new bodies are going to do – I have a plan before I split, but I don't always stick to it. Different choices, different paths – we've had this conversation. I won't even know what it felt like until I merge with one of them."

"It must be amazing, never having to make a choice," Aman says. He stretches and yawns, willing himself to get out of bed. "Hell, I'm not complaining."

Tia grins, sits up and reaches for her clothes.

"Yes, you seemed quite enthusiastic about everything, as far as I remember."

She pulls a T-shirt over her head and Aman groans.

"Must you do that?"

"If you want to look at naked women, you have a free net connection, love. Besides, what would your girlfriend say if she saw us like this?"

Aman rolls his eyes. "Stop it," he says.

"Are you going to tell me you don't have the world's most massive crush on Uzma?"

"Sure, but that's her power. And now, this – you and me –"

"No, no," Tia says hurriedly, and practically jumps out of Aman's bed. "Aman, don't make me regret this, all right? I don't want you to end up getting hurt. We have enough to worry about as it is."

A loud knock on the door, and Aman curses and runs to his bathroom with his clothes.

But it's not Uzma at the door. When Tia opens it, it's another Tia. And when Aman emerges from his room a few minutes later, he looks into Tia's room and finds a bunch of Tias, each with headphones attached to her ears, watching different channels on the fifteen flatscreen TVs arranged on her wall. A few Tias turn and smile knowingly as he passes. He waves and walks by swiftly, and hears a chorus of giggles explode behind him.

Aman sits in the living room, wolfing down his breakfast, hoping to be left alone. But the fates deem otherwise, the Scientist and Bob are eager to know what happened at the base.

Their faces fall when Aman tells them he doesn't really know. The Tia who'd called him after the great escape had been cut off in the middle of their conversation, something about a tiger-man. She'd not called again. As far as he knew, there were now any number of powered people on the run in Kashmir with Jai Mathur's henchmen hunting them down. Bob is shattered to hear no news of his parents, and the sky outside grows overcast.

A loud rumble of thunder, and a Tia enters the house, dripping wet. She drops a large package on the floor.

"Laser robot nanotechnology thingies from Japan," she announces. "Aman, we got trouble. Some of us – me – got followed today when we went for our pickups. One of my delivery boys told me that people have been asking questions about us and the stuff we're getting off the ships. One of the big mafia types wants to know. Apparently some big changes are happening in the underworld, some new boss is taking over the business district. His name's Shinde."

"How many of you are out there now?" Aman asks.

"None. We met in a clothing store and merged in a changing room. People were following two of me, but I lost them."

"We should lie low for a while, then. Can you get by for a few days on the stuff you have, Sundar?"

"I wish I knew," Sundar says. "I'm sure I'll manage. I think the armour I'm building is almost complete. I built some arm extensions for it that I suspect are cannons. I'll know when I deduce where the 'On' switch is."

"They're going to find us and kill us," Bob says, and there's a flash of lightning outside.

Aman stands up. "That settles it, then," he announces and strides towards the stairs.

"What are you doing?" a Tia asks.

"Something I should have done the day I discovered my powers," says Aman. "I've wasted too much time talking."

Uzma enters the living room minutes after Aman's departure, and her housemates gather around her, concerned; she's clearly been crying. After two cups of coffee and three silent bursts of tears, she reveals what is wrong. She's been rudely awakened from her Bollywood dream. Her three biggest movie hopes have all been shattered. In each case, the director told her that he loved her audition, but didn't think she was quite ready for the role. That she had failed her screen tests, she just didn't cut it on camera. The directors all thought she was special, though, and wanted to get to know her better over dinner.

"They liked you because of your powers, but you didn't come across well on enough video," Sundar explains.

"Not now," Tia warns.

"In other words, I have no talent. I should never have come here," Uzma says.

"You should consider a career in front of a live audience that will be fooled by your powers. Theatre is the solution," Sundar concludes with an air of triumph.

"Sundar, shut up. What's wrong with you?" Tia snaps.

"But a film career is not out of the question either. After all, plenty of popular actresses have no real acting ability," Sundar says with an encouraging smile.

When Uzma runs from the room, howling, and Tia runs after her shooting dagger-like looks at him, Sundar turns to Bob with a puzzled air.

"I don't understand women," he says.

"You don't understand humans," Bob says.

Aman sits in his room, staring at the computers on his desk. There are three custom-made monitors in front of him, each screen reloading rapidly as his thoughts hyperlink. No mouse or keyboard sits in front of the screens, he stopped needing them after his first week. He doesn't really need the screens either.

His hands tremble. To calm his nerves, he looks at holiday pictures of strangers on Facebook. He reads JK Rowling's online backup files and writes three alternative final chapters to the *Harry Potter* series. He watches clips from Japanese TV shows on YouTube. He looks at the time and curses. Hours have passed.

Tia enters his room.

"You all right?" she asks.

"No," he says, not looking at her, his left foot tapping on the floor of its own accord. "I've been talking about this endlessly, about using our powers the way they should be used, not behaving like super-idiots. But I need to show you exactly what I mean and instead I'm wasting time. How am I going to use the internet to save the world if I keep getting distracted by the internet?"

"Can I help?"

"I don't think so. I'm just completely... I think I'm just terrified of doing anything that will actually make a difference. I've made plans, but now, now that I'm here, now that it's time, I'm just – stuck."

"So you see now why Uzma doesn't want to be a superhero."

"Superhero," Aman laughs. "Hell, I wish I could be one. Or any other kind of hero. I wish someone could just appear and tell me what to do – some Gandalf-type with a white beard and a white nightgown who would tell me to go and find, I don't know, a magic remote control that I could use to save the world from the growing forces of evil. I need an instruction manual, Tia. I have too many options. I'll go crazy."

"I don't know what you're trying to do," Tia says, "but I can tell you're just going to keep on not doing it as long as I'm here, so..."

She leaves.

Aman grins and turns off his screens. He closes his eyes and reconnects.

The internet appears in his mind's eye as a swirling pool of liquids, billions of coloured strands coalescing, blending, bubbling. He feels that curious lightening in the back of his head. His hair stands on end as his awareness explodes, as networks expand and intersect through satellites, under-sea cables, phones, and it feels as if he's sinking into the pool, drowning in an ocean of information as the pool swells around him, filling his senses, melting and reshaping him into a tiny piece of plankton drifting in the cyber-ocean. He watches the datastream flow around him, the rush of billions of phone conversations blending to a dull hum between his ears.

The world is inside his head; Aman is everywhere.

He focuses his attention. A single cell in the pool expands, extends digital pseudopodia, forms shapes. Aman checks his email. His mind shoots forward, text and image and sound coalescing into shape in millions of gelatinous bubbles and then dissolving back in an instant. Aman is in digital nirvana, swimming through the stream, instinct and intuition driving him towards his quarry.

Aman is online.

He starts small. He finds out the names of Colombia's richest drug-lords, finds their Swiss bank accounts, and gives away all their money in their names to relief agencies in Somalia, making sure to send polite emails asking the recipients to withdraw the money from their accounts as quickly as they possibly can. He repeats the process with Middle Eastern gangsters, American gun companies, Italian fashion brands that use Bangladeshi sweat-shops and members of the Indian parliament. Then he changes the names of the countries and continents involved and does it again.

He gets bored.

He realises that superheroes wear strange costumes and do irrational things, like using their cosmic powers to stop neighbourhood muggers, because changing the world is tedious, and actually *physically* accomplishing something, no matter how trivial, is far more satisfying than throwing money at problems and hoping they will go away.

Undeterred, Aman takes his online Robin Hood act a step further: he creates his merry men. A stream of bubbles appears in front of him and speeds into the datastream, each one containing his brainwave patterns; each one assigned a specific task. Aman feels warm and fuzzy now. In a way, he realises, he has just impregnated the internet. He watches his thought-bots swim into the horizon, slipping and sliding through the currents of global finance, and idly plays a game of Tetris as he waits for results.

Over the next few hours, Aman goes deep into the heart of

the military–industrial complex and dances the lambada with its finances. He takes billions of dollars from companies and individuals all around the world, redistributing property on a scale that would have made Karl Marx rise from the grave and die again from sheer happiness. He hands out money to conservationists, environmentalists, peace activists. In several cases, they win lotteries and break online casinos. A lot of the world's richest people make huge charitable donations through public announcements on the web, pledging their support to campaigns against everything from AIDS to human trafficking.

He transfers money from defence budgets to development projects, leaving warning messages to government officials, bureaucrats, judges, police chiefs all over the world: *This isn't your money, don't keep it. If you do, I'll take away yours.* He plunders through the amassed wealth of advertising and media agencies, starting with the decimation of cola marketing budgets. He slashes profit margins on all luxury goods, borrows idle savings. Not knowing what exactly to do with all the money he's amassed, he attempts to read the works of various famous economists, but gets confused by the diagrams and assumptions and decides to wing it. Making it up as he goes along, he takes away money allocated for closed-circuit public surveillance worldwide, US Defence programmes for telepathic limb-controlling monkeys and neuroscientific mind-control, as well as all statues of living politicians.

He attacks the media, removing celebrity fluff stories and paid articles from newspaper databases, adding instead stories of government, police, corporate and judicial corruption, making public any scam he can find. He points out, in strongly worded letters to editors, that he knows all about the shadier side of how media conglomerates and large businesses co-exist, that he feels entitled to a very large chunk of their profits, but is leaving them enough money to do their jobs in return for their discretion regarding his operations. Aman has never seen himself in the role of censor and media manipulator before, he feels suitably smug and villainous. While he's at it, he shuts down all religion/sexuality/race hate sites and resets all the links to right-wing political party websites to lead, instead, to the YouTube video of Rick Astley's mental-collapse-inducing hit song 'Never Gonna Give You Up'.

After loafing around on Twitter for a while, Aman decides to single-handedly tackle climate change. With an imperious wave of his digital hand, he sets up large companies that will manufacture sulphur aerosols to refreeze the polar icecaps, thus keeping a great many countries' lands above water. He cuts science funding from universities that have won Ig Nobel prizes, and puts their money into research on whether his newly formed companies' activities will kill plants and animals all over the world with acid rain and cause even higher temperatures in Africa.

His other attempts at geo-engineering are hampered by his lack of superhero co-workers, but he tries to make arrangements for the cultivation of ocean-surface clouds of plankton blooms to absorb carbon dioxide in the oceans, and oil drillers to re-inject carbon dioxide into the earth. He reads about reducing global warming using visors, suspended ceramic discs in space, and sets pop-up reminders telling himself to discuss this with Vir later, along with his more ambitious plans for terraforming the Sahara and growing giant algae stomachs in the Pacific. He sets up funding for solar, wind and water energy plants all over

India and China and changes the instructions for manufacture-controlling computers in German and Japanese car factories, replacing their design modules with schematics for electric and solar-powered vehicles.

Aman's thoughts churn, crackle, spin out of control, ever larger streams of data-bubbles fizz out in front of him and head off to their tasks. He is not sure what they are – software his mind is generating? Copies of his brain on the internet? But their creation fills him with a strange effervescence – he feels like laughing out loud, maniacal Mad Scientist laughter.

As the cyber-ocean pulses around him, he sees the results of his instructions, watches powerful, violent people's lives and fortunes implode and disappear under his onslaught. On separate bubble-panels, he downloads and reads manic, dark, deeply post-modern superhero comics written by insane British writers, and watches their characters flutter in data currents, their deliberately ironic costumes bizarre flags of his new nation, his new world.

Yet even as Aman gleefully rearranges the world, he knows his reach, like the internet's, is woefully limited – in his own country alone, he knows that the real power, the richest of the rich and the cruellest of the cruel don't even exist on the internet or the banking system, that their billions are stashed away elsewhere, that their teenaged sons will continue to race on the streets of Delhi in their Ferraris and Lamborghinis mowing down pedestrians, and there is nothing he can do to touch either them or their money.

He knows that the really poor people, the ones who need help most, haven't even heard of the internet, let alone online banking, and the most he can do is to give lots of money to groups that claim to represent them – people who can reach them – and hope. He knows that he hasn't transferred just billions of dollars, but all the corruption, greed and power that trail those dollars like seagulls; that he has set up new tyrants, new criminals, new thieves to replace the old; that no number of accompanying Big-Brother-is-watching-you warnings will prevent a lot of money from being misused. He knows that it is entirely possible that nothing will change. But at this point, he is too far in to even think of stopping, and the results he produces are drastic enough. By afternoon, he has erased Third World debt. He wishes he had paid more attention as an economics undergraduate – he is not sure whether this will revive or destroy the global economy.

With a final flourish, he disables satellite navigation systems for nuclear missiles worldwide, confiscates half the income of all celeb-stars of reality shows based on their lives, virus-cleans the world and passes out.

When Aman awakens, his head feels as if it's on fire. He tries to open his eyes, but can't; the world remains black except for a red bubble that trickles in slowly from the edge of his field of vision and hovers in front of him. The telecom hum in his ears has faded now, and he hears a dull thumping instead; a sluggishly beating heart completely in sync with his own.

There's writing on the bubble in front of him.

What you did was wrong on so many levels.

Who are you? Aman tries to say the words out loud, but hears them only in his head.

The red bubble shimmers and more words appear.

I don't know. I am you, I think.

Are you from my subconscious or are you some sort of independent online copy of my brain? Or some kind of artificial intelligence creature? Where did you come from?

Your questions are foolish. I told you, I don't know. What difference would it make if you knew the answer?

True. Just curious. This is the weirdest chat session I've ever had. Like Skype when one person doesn't have a mike.

How can you be flippant at a time like this?

Sorry. Go on, then.

You have tampered with forces beyond your understanding and there will be a price to pay.

Yes.

Yes?

What's your point? Do you have a secret quest for me, or a message from beyond, or something like that?

What?

No? Okay. So you're just here to moan about what I did?

What gives you the right to do this?

Aman blinks, the letters on the bubble are hurting his eyes. Also, the bubble seems to be trying to shift itself around and form a face, his face, which seems both unimaginative and rude.

What gives me the right? The fact that I can, he says.

The world's bloodiest tyrants would have said the same to justify their most heinous acts.

My aim is slightly different. I'm going to get everyone in the world electricity, food, water, medicine and access to education. Then I'm going to worry about whose toes I trod on. No one will know I did this – they'll think it's a miracle, or a global computer error or virus. I don't want fame, or money, or anything for myself – I just want to do what I think is right. I've got to do something while I can, because I can.

It's all illegal.

Do I look like I care?

You are not qualified. You lack training, education, analytical skills, experience. You don't know what you're doing, or how, or even why.

I didn't pick my power. I'm just using it.

Your actions are heavy-handed, ill-considered, naïve. You are a moron with a loaded gun.

Everyone's a critic. You, my friend, are a bubble.

People will die because of you.

More people will have a chance to live like human beings.

And who are you to make these decisions?

If I had other powers, I would have used them in other ways. If I had super-speed, I would have run on a treadmill and generated electricity for poor villages. If I had super-strength, I would have carried truckloads of food to the starving. I'm doing what I can with what I was given.

And yet prior to this you never lifted a finger to help anyone but yourself. What makes you Mother Teresa now?

I changed.

Nothing is ever achieved by money alone. All you are trying to do here is assuage your own middle-class guilt. The money will find its way back to where it came from. There will be massive lawsuits. International conflict. Nothing will get better.

It's a start. I know a lot of it won't work. I know there are a lot of things I forgot, or did wrong, or simply didn't know enough to do at all. I'll keep doing it until I get it right.

What gives you the right to play video games with the world?

You're repeating yourself. Let's talk about you, now. You just asked me a lot of questions I've been asking myself over the last few days. Even if you don't know who you are, do you know what you want?

To stop you. To warn you.

Warn me about what?

You.

The letters on the red bubble dissolve, and the bubble expands, filling Aman's mind with pain. He cries out, feels as if he's being hurled across a great distance. He forces his eyelids open, breaks off the connection, his vision still a red haze, and then the red fades to black, and he sinks again into unconsciousness, the silence in his mind warm, welcoming, all-encompassing.

It is night when Tia shakes Aman awake.

"You all right? I heard you call out," she says.

"I'm fine. I think."

"What were you doing?"

"I either wasted a lot of time or fundamentally changed the world as we know it."

Tia nods. "Cool."

"And I had a very weird experience which might have been a dream, I'm not sure."

"You'll find out eventually."

"Also, I might have made the internet self-aware, which can only lead to machines rising up against man and ending the world."

"That's nice, darling," Tia says. "What do you want for dinner?"

CHAPTER **NINE**

Four days have passed since Aman's internet adventure. He has spent most of this time stealing money from the people he forgot to take from during his first day's burst of Robin-Hooding – and writing press releases on behalf of all his victims of the last few days, warm, heartfelt messages explaining to the world that their sudden, unprecedented acts of charity were a response to the global economic recession; that their collective realisation of how badly the world had been using its money all these years had spurred them into action.

Several of Aman's victims have accepted their fate and their new roles as the world's saviours for the time being, too stunned by the appreciation thrown at them to demand investigations; others are eerily silent.

This evening, however, Aman has decided to give himself a break from the internet. He's at the Wankhede Cricket Stadium in South Mumbai, sitting with Tia in a small wooden cubicle in the new, swanky press box, both of them armed with identity cards from all the world's most famous newspapers. In front of him is a wide glass window, and beyond it is a carnival of noise.

It's a Giga League Gully Cricket match, Mumbai Mad Men versus Kolkata Kool Kats, and about fifty thousand of Mumbai's loudest have arrived with banners, drums and voices trained by years of life in India to achieve tremendous decibel levels with no apparent effort. Mexican waves sweep through the crowd at a frequency of one a minute. Chants merge with other chants, punctuated by booms from huge drums to form the beat of one giant, pulsating, crowd heart.

Cheerleaders from all around the world, decorously clad in bodysuits to avoid inflaming innocent, susceptible Indian minds, wave pom-poms at the lustful masses in time to screeching megahits from the latest Bollywood blockbusters. Some of the stars of these blockbusters are also present, either as team owners or as hired smile-and-wavers.

The Wankhede Stadium itself is a topic of much discussion: scheduled to host the Cricket World Cup final in 2011, it was supposed to be renovated by the end of 2010. Instead, it is ready now, shiny, sparkly and bright, a whole year and a half ahead of schedule – which in India is nothing short of miraculous. The man responsible for this, Andy Kharkongor, an architect best known for designing huge, self-sufficient residential complexes outside large cities – where India's most prosperous live in glittering luxury, sheltered from palpitation-inducing visions of average people by high walls and armed guards – was also on that ill-fated flight with Aman. He is now missing.

Aman's not here because of his love for cricket. He had been obsessed with the sport when he was younger, primarily because cricket was the only thing India was any good at apart from chess, kabaddi and women's weightlifting, and because he thought Sachin Tendulkar was a god among men. But he has been left cold by the arrival, two years ago, of the Indian Premier League, the quick-fix twenty-over version of the game, with its endless advertising, asinine commentators and general chaos. He has seen every match, of course, but just to be able to complain more effectively. And he has never whined more vociferously than earlier this year when the Giga League Gully Cricket Tournament, "A mind-blowing, rocking, fully dynamic totally NEW fun-tastic form of the classic game" – essentially a clone of the Indian Premier League with innings of ten overs instead of twenty – arrived to further satisfy the cravings of a nation with an ever-shortening attention span.

Aman is here for several reasons. Uzma is the first: two days ago she accepted Saheli's friend's brother Bruno's offer to become a Gully Glamour Girl, and is currently standing in front of a camera in a tiny dress, reading match forecasts, contest results and made-up gossip off a teleprompter, and drawing admiring stares from everyone in the room.

Uzma is here despite fervent protests from Aman and Tia. She has had enough of lying low and being forgotten, and is now on a mission to re-ignite her Bollywood aspirations by becoming a known and loved face all over India and the rest of the cricket-watching world. That her brothers are massive fans of Gully Cricket – players from both England and Pakistan are also involved – is an added incentive. Her job mostly involves smiling, making sure her dress doesn't slip and fending off the advances of amorous cricketers; Uzma's right on top of it.

Aman and Tia have come along to protect her from nefarious

supervillains. They have not yet figured out exactly how they will do this, but being there is definitely a start.

Another reason for Aman's presence is the man now walking out from the Garware Pavilion at the Wankhede Stadium's south end, raising his bat to salute the cheering crowd. Prashant Reddy, captain of the Kolkata Kool Kats, is India's newest cricket icon, a comeback story like no other.

His first stint as an international cricketer had been an unmitigated disaster. After a long career playing domestic cricket and rising through the ranks, he had reached the national team at just the time when its selectors had decided to kick out senior players to give youth a chance. By the vagaries of regional cricket politics, he had been chosen to captain the Indian team during a tour of cricket minnows the Netherlands, a wrap-it-up-quickly tournament that most of the team's stars had feigned sudden injuries to avoid. Reddy had made headlines by leading his blue-clad boys to a series of ignominious defeats. He'd been dropped unceremoniously from Team India, and had spent several years in the wilderness before coming back as a B-level player for the Kool Kats Gully Cricket team. But, when the tournament started, Reddy had proved to be a revelation. Who could have expected that this veteran, last seen coaching a county youth team in Middlesex, would suddenly emerge as the tournament's undisputed hero?

"He's very cute," Tia says, idly chewing on a Giggly Jujube, the Official Sweet of the Giga League Gully Cricket Tournament. "Is he married?"

"No, but you are," Uzma points out, throwing herself into a chair beside Aman. "Besides, he's mine. Dating a cricketer is a well-known shortcut to the Indian glamour world."

"You're interviewing him at some stage, right?" Aman asks. "We need to meet him."

"Yes, I am, after the match," Uzma replies. "But why don't you just ring him? Surely you of all people could get his number."

"Number, email, official Twitter – I've tried everything. He doesn't answer."

"But he'll agree to meet you because he'll like me, Super-Like-Me Girl," Uzma says. "I should charge you a fee."

"Pay me half rent this month," Aman says. "Don't you have to do commentary?"

"No, I'm just a Glamour Girl. I'm free until their inning, or whatever they call it, ends."

Reddy takes guard. The Mumbai Mad Men bowler, a burly, menacing Australian pacer, starts his run-up. The audience claps as one, the rhythm of the claps matching the bowler's strides and then accelerating into a crescendo as the white ball flashes from the bowler's hand towards Reddy, who takes a step forward and drives, sending the ball over the bowler's head, screaming over the field, over the sightscreen and out of the stadium – the ultimate insult to a fast bowler. The audience howls and hollers – the party's started.

Reddy is unstoppable. The remaining five balls of the over are treated with similar disdain, as Reddy cuts, pulls, drives, hooks a bouncer and finally, laughing, sweeps an attempted yorker over deep square leg. Thirty-six runs off a single over, six sixes, the kind of over every batsman dreams of – except Reddy's had at least one over like this in every Giga League match he's played. The crowd's cheering with an almost religious frenzy. They know this is historic. They know that barring some unforeseen disaster like a tsunami, an emotional meltdown or a Bollywood starlet, Reddy is fated to lead India to glory at the World Cup finals, two years hence, at this very ground.

"So, what's his power?" Tia asks.

Aman's eyes are closed. "I'm looking at videos from the broadcasting room in slow motion," he says. "Just before he hits the ball, when he's placing himself, preparing for the shot, he moves very fast. I think he's got some kind of speed burst. Or he can slow time down. Give himself a little wiggle room."

"Maybe he's just practised a lot," Uzma suggests.

"Maybe."

Reddy has the strike again. The bowler, this time a wild-haired Sri Lankan, comes roaring in and hurls a lethally fast inswinger at Reddy, who takes a huge step back, exposing his stumps, and square-drives to the boundary, neatly bisecting gully and point.

In the cubicles near Aman's, sports correspondents gasp at Reddy's audacity and hastily scribble eloquent testimonials to his unconventional, innovative play. They reach for their thesauri as Reddy then pulls an outswinger over mid-wicket, causing the bowler to tear out clumps of his hair and screech at the sky.

"What's his problem?" Uzma asks.

"You're not supposed to play that shot," Aman replies.

"Why not? Is it ungentlemanly?"

"No. But it was an outswinger pitched outside off-stump, and you're not supposed to pull those."

"I can hear your words, but they mean nothing to me," Uzma says. "And I'm the TV cricket expert. And they say I can't act."

Tia places a hand on Aman's arm.

"Look who just walked in," she says.

Namrata, resplendent in her DNNTV blazer, struts into the press hall, closely followed by a bearded cameraman, a bleating assistant producer and a generic sound guy.

"Bad news," Tia says.

Namrata scans the room imperially until she identifies the best vantage point, and then strides towards it, blithely scattering grizzled, confused sports journalists. Her crew sets up the shot with speed and efficiency. In a few seconds, the DNNTV express is ready to roll. But then Namrata calls a halt – she's seen a better spot. She walks towards Aman, Uzma and Tia.

"Not giving up my seat," Tia mutters, but Namrata's already in their midst.

"Do you mind terribly if I do my story from here?" she trills. "It'll just take a few seconds."

"Go ahead," Uzma says.

Namrata sees Uzma for the first time, blinks and smiles.

"Thanks so much," she gushes. "Who are you? I feel like I've seen you somewhere before."

Uzma opens her mouth to introduce herself, but Namrata's not one to share the airwaves.

"I thought the Gully Glamour chicks were all, like, total bimbos," she says. "I feel like I should apologise to someone. We should hang out. I want to do a story on the women in cricket and the men they worship. Coffee afterwards?"

"Sure," Uzma says, flummoxed.

Aman rises willingly, Tia somewhat less so, and Namrata's crew takes over their cubicle.

"If she's had another premonition about today, we should think about getting you out of here," Aman tells Uzma.

"I just got you one of the meetings you wanted," Uzma says. "I'm not going anywhere until I fix you up with Reddy."

They lean on the cubicle wall and watch as Namrata clears her throat, grabs her mike and launches into her piece.

"I'm reporting live and exclusive for DNNTV, in a special report on match-fixing, the spectre that has haunted cricket for decades and refuses to die," she says.

"Spectre refuses to die, my foot," Tia grumbles.

Outside, Reddy smashes another six-over long-off into the cheering crowd.

"Prashant Reddy's extraordinary form has raised many questions," Namrata continues. "While many Indians are happy to see a new cricketing hero take over the mantle from Sachin Tendulkar, many more are asking: is it possible that a man clearly past his cricketing prime should discover a winning streak as glorious as Reddy's? Could there be other forces involved? Forces such as the betting syndicates of Dubai? Here at the Wankhede Stadium, the crowd is at boiling point – how long will their rage be kept in check? Will Reddy's ongoing demolition of the Mumbai team on their home turf cause a storm that will shake the foundations of Indian cricket?"

"What rubbish," Tia snarls. "No one's raising any questions. The crowd isn't angry – they love this guy."

"Wait," Uzma says. She points at the roaring crowd beyond the glass. "Something's wrong."

High fences, patrolled by cricket-loving Mumbai policemen, separate the field and the spectators. A section of the crowd has left the Sunil Gavaskar stand on the eastern side of the stadium, and is pushing its way forward. Aman sees raised fists, men and women screaming in rage, their shouts lost amidst the general outburst as Reddy gently guides the ball between the slips for another boundary.

"She's doing this," Tia hisses. "She set this up. She knew this was going to happen."

"I can see you don't like her, but I don't think she has anything to do with those people," Aman whispers. "She probably knew somehow that there was going to be trouble, and came here just in time to get it on camera."

"If she knew there was going to be a riot, she could have warned the police or something. Not just arrived in time to win journalism awards. Bitch." Tia's really angry now. She starts towards Namrata, but Uzma stops her.

"She's a reporter, her job is to report," Uzma says. "She just has a leg up on the competition. This is like what happened at the Kalki Baby rally, isn't it?"

Namrata continues her report breathlessly as the riot builds steam on the eastern stand. Some hurl themselves onto the barriers; others start climbing them. All over the ground, blood-curdling shouts of rage rend the air.

The game stops. The players move uncertainly towards the centre of the field as various missiles, bottles, torn posters, caps, are hurled into the ground. Some of the foreign players, already paranoid about terrorist attacks in South Asia, race off the field and up the stairs to the players' dressing rooms. A line of policemen trots out towards the eastern stands.

"Whoever's behind this, it's not her," Uzma says, pointing at Namrata. The intrepid reporter has now dropped her mike and is staring at the crowd, her face drawn, horrified. Beside her, the DNNTV assistant producer yells curses and then runs off.

On the western side of the stadium, a fence falls and angry

spectators swarm into the field. The few policemen between the crowd and the players do nothing to stop them. Instead, they turn, raising their batons, and join the first wave of people streaking towards Prashant Reddy.

Aman cannot believe his eyes. He's watching fifty thousand people, all of whom moments ago were rejoicing in the exploits of one man, now united in their desire to tear his heart out. Brightly coloured seats form patterns all over the stadium as the people abandon them to pour out on to the ground, struggling through ever-widening gaps torn through security fences. Men, women, children, some still holding banners extolling Reddy's virtues, streak across the outfield. The other players bolt, but Reddy stands his ground, clearly petrified. He drops his bat.

In the press box, journalists scramble towards the exit. They yell loudly about match-fixing scandals, and how Reddy was definitely a conspirator who should be hanged for his misdeeds.

Namrata turns from the window, and Uzma meets her eyes. Something in Namrata's face speaks to her of sorrow, of loneliness, of deep-seated terror. Uzma smiles reassuringly, and whether it's her powers or just the sight of a friendly face, relief floods Namrata's face, and she smiles wanly in turn.

To Uzma's right, Aman's legs turn to jelly. A wave of anger strikes him, a scarlet haze of pure rage. He has never experienced anything like it. The whole world blurs, and all he can think about is the lone cricketer standing in the middle of the field, watching in desperation as a wave of people converges around him; policemen brandishing batons, even a snarling umpire. All Aman wants, right now, is to see Reddy disgraced, humiliated, dead. His powers kick in. He shuts his eyes, and goes online. The now familiar ocean of data swirls over his mind, engulfing and cooling his brain. Images of Reddy are washed away by liquid terabytes, bickering, all-explaining, distracting, illogical, objective, soothing. Aman opens his eyes. His anger has vanished. Beside Uzma, he sees another Tia emerge. Her face contorted in fury, she runs out with the mob of journalists, unnoticed in the chaos, leaving a confused, worried Tia behind, looking around her at the rapidly emptying press box.

"What's wrong?" Uzma asks.

"Did you feel that?" Aman asks. Tia nods. Uzma is puzzled. "Feel what?" she says.

Aman looks out on to the field. He is convinced now of Reddy's time-adjustment power, and impressed by the man's intelligence. Aware of the cameras that might be trained on him, Reddy does nothing to arouse suspicion. He simply dodges blows, outruns pursuers, ducking, bobbing, weaving like a white-eyebrowed kung fu monk. Aman cannot imagine what the world must be like for Reddy; a museum full of slow-moving statues, glaciers to his quicksilver. But this cannot last forever, soon Reddy will be buried under a solid mass of enraged humanity.

Tia grabs Aman's arm and points. In the middle of the throng, tossing people aside in their hurry to get to Reddy, are a tall man who is either wearing an incredibly realistic tiger mask or actually has a tiger's head, and a little girl who is surrounded by an aura of green light.

"I told you, it's not her," Uzma says, gazing intently. "It's them, isn't it? They've come to get him. Can we do anything? Aman?"

"Nope. We're the Combat-Useless Powers Brigade."

There's a flash of blue light in the press box, and the lights go out. Aman feels dizzy, light-headed, as if the weight of the internet has been lifted from his shoulders. He tries to go online, finds his own internal modem, wherever it is, has been switched off, and struggles to recognise that he has spent most of his life feeling like this.

An uproar breaks out around them. The few journalists still in the press box reach for their phones, and find them dead. The central power has been cut, but the light-towers around the stadium, powered by separate generators, shine on, bathing the field with bright white light even as the rooms inside the stadium building plunge into darkness. Above the din, Aman can hear Namrata, she's sobbing.

"It's him. He's here. Get me out." Deaf to her pleas, her cameraman and sound assistant flee.

Namrata starts to run, but Aman steps forward and stops her.

"Don't panic," he says. "We were on the plane as well. We're here to help."

Namrata tears her arm away and shrinks from him, the light from outside casting deep shadows on her face.

"You're with him," she hisses. "Let me go."

"Aman!" Tia calls. "The tiger guy and the girl – they're gone. So's the cricketer."

Aman rushes to the window again and sees, standing all over the field and in the stands, thousands of completely bewildered people looking around for an answer, finding nothing. Policemen form lines now, pushing people away from the pitch. Cheerleaders, team owners and random celebrities yelp in anguish, suddenly surrounded by hordes of fans. Of Reddy or his pursuers there is no sign.

"Namrata!" Uzma calls. "What's your power?"

"Who are you people?" Namrata's high-pitched voice is now hoarse, ragged. "What do you want from me?"

"We're like you," Aman says. "We know you see things. We know how you get news first."

"Come with us," Uzma says. "It's all very strange, but it helps if we're together."

"Were you at the Kalki Party rally? Did you people drive the crowd crazy?" Namrata whispers. "Did you turn off the lights?"

"No," Uzma says.

"Whoever did this – whoever got the whole stadium mad is very powerful," Aman says. "I felt it – I could have been standing out there right now. But it didn't affect you, did it? You were just scared."

"I didn't feel it either," Uzma says. "Namrata. Don't freak out. We can help each other. I know just how you feel."

She walks towards Namrata, holding out her hands, but Namrata backs away.

"He's out there, I know he is. Do you know him? Do you work for him?"

"We don't know who you're talking about," Tia says.

"I can't do this," Namrata says. "I can't take this any more."

She turns and runs full-tilt through the abandoned press box, and into something in the darkness, something solid standing in the doorway. She screams and falls with a clatter.

Aman and Uzma start towards her, but before they get anywhere two Tias leap on them from behind, hands over their mouths, dragging them back, down on the floor, into the shadows.

"Not good. Not good," a Tia whispers.

They see Namrata half sliding, half tottering back, trying to get up and then falling again, holding herself up with her arms on the floor, palms down behind her back. Her face is pale, and her eyes are staring upwards at the man who emerges from the darkness in front of her, walking up close to her with a heavy tread. A single beam of slanting light illuminates heavy boots, smart black clothes and, finally, a sharply handsome face, mouth twisted in a smile. His eyes glitter, wild, brilliant.

"My name is Jai Mathur," he says to her. "I thought I might find you here."

Namrata gulps, her eyes not leaving his face.

"You keep running away every time we meet," Jai says. "I wonder why that is?"

"You – you stole the baby. You killed his parents," Namrata stammers. "You tried to kill Reddy today."

"I just wanted to talk to him. And I just want to talk to you, now."

Jai pulls Namrata to her feet. She stands close to him, breathing heavily, a rabbit staring into the eyes of a cobra.

"What's your power?" Jai asks.

"I don't know what you're talking about," she whispers.

Jai's smile fades. "You know, I thought you were a clever girl," he says. "Are you going to make me force it out of you? *What's your power?*"

"I see news," Namrata says quietly. "I know when and where bad things are going to happen."

"So tell me," Jai says, "are you having visions of dying? Of me ripping your head off your spine with my bare hands?"

Namrata bursts into loud, racking sobs.

Jai grasps her chin and holds it up, forcing her to look into his eyes.

"Are you?" he demands.

"No," she sobs.

Jai grins. "Then you shouldn't be worried, should you? I don't want to hurt you. In fact, I want you to work for me. Advance intelligence is an invaluable asset."

He lets Namrata go, and she staggers backwards, almost falling. She looks at him again and forces herself into a state of calm.

"You really scared me," she says.

"Of course I did. I asked you not to be worried," Jai says. "I didn't ask you not to be afraid."

"What do you want from me?" she asks. "Why have you been following me?"

"Following you? *You*'ve been following *me*, my dear. I've simply been making you famous. And I want something in return."

"Will you leave me alone if I help you?" Namrata asks.

Jai laughs out loud. "From grovelling to bargaining in seconds. You'll go far," he says. "Now tell me. Have you met any other superhumans?"

In their dark corner, Uzma draws in a sharp breath and stirs. Aman notices, to his horror, that one of her hands is in the light; he draws her to him silently. She's trembling.

"No," Namrata says after a pause. "I don't think so."

"You're lying," Jai says. "I think you know who's behind this mass insanity. Tell me, Namrata – who's making these mobs run after my targets?"

Namrata looks at him blankly.

"It's not you?" she asks.

A pulse quivers in Jai's throat.

"Of course it's bloody well not me!" he answers. "Someone else is gathering superhumans, and I must know who it is. This is how you will make sure you stay alive, my little super-journalist. You will find my rivals for me. I almost lost that accursed baby, and the cricketer escaped today. I'll find him, of course, but somebody got in my way just now. I don't like that. I'm going to find whoever's behind these mobs. And if I find they have anything to do with you –"

"Please. Please believe me. I don't know anything."

"There's a man in Mumbai, about your age. Could be a hacker I've been trying to track; could be someone else. He's been seen with a woman who can split into multiple bodies. There's also, obviously, a man – or woman – who can control mobs. You will find these people for me. Use everything you have. Everyone you know."

"I will."

"Good. You work for me now, Namrata. I know everything about you. Where you live, where I can find you. And I'm not a patient man."

Namrata nods. "I'll get them," she says. "Can I ask for one favour?"

Jai raises an eyebrow.

"When you do whatever it is that you're planning, when you make your big move," she says, "can I get an exclusive? Can I interview you? Let the world know what you're about?"

Jai smiles. "Professional. I like that. And yes, why not? I wasn't planning to add you to my little army in any case. There's no need to reveal your powers to the world. Let them think you're one of them, It doesn't matter, really, whether someone helps the powerless bridge the gap between us, but, it might make the transition smoother."

"Transition?"

Jai sighs. "You know, I used to be a patriot," he says. "With me in command, India could have ruled the world. I could have destroyed Pakistan single-handedly, and carried on from there. If only. If only they'd been capable of following a simple plan, listening to clear instructions. But something happened that made me realise that they weren't ready – not just Indians. Humans. People who are not like us."

"You're uniting people with powers."

"I'm uniting people who were chosen to stand above the ordinary. Chosen to take charge, to make changes. Who aren't afraid of embracing their destinies. The rest are sheep. Their time has passed. And –"

Jai smirks and runs a hand through Namrata's hair.

"You're a good interviewer, you know," he says. "But there's no point doing this with no one listening, is there? Later, when you introduce the world to its new gods, make sure you have your questions ready."

Namrata manages a weak smile.

"Now that's incentive," she says.

"I can inspire you further," Jai says. He reaches out and touches her face, and she finds she's trembling too violently to smile any more.

"How long do I have?" she asks.

"When I see you next," he says, "your time will have run out."

He turns and strides from the room.

Namrata stands silent, silhouetted against the madness outside, for a whole minute.

"You might as well get up," she says finally.

"Yeah, you can let her go now, Aman," Tia says.

Aman releases Uzma sheepishly.

They rise.

"Thank you," Uzma says.

"So, you're his enemies," Namrata says. "Which one of you does the mobs?"

"Not us," Tia says. "Why didn't you tell him about us?"

"I never sign up for a job until I've looked around for a better offer," Namrata says. "What's yours?"

Uzma smiles her most winning smile.

"Coffee?"

CHAPTER **TEN**

Considering that Aman has recently stolen billions of dollars and put them into schemes to stop global warming, it is distressing that his car, currently zipping through the elegant streets of South Mumbai, is a giant SUV. But none of the big black monster's other occupants are complaining about this. Beside Aman, Uzma stares through the tinted windows at the Mumbai traffic bathed in amber light. Behind them, Tia quickly gives Namrata a highly edited account of their superhero experiences so far.

It is difficult to tell Namrata elaborate stories, she has a TV reporter's habit of interrupting constantly, not allowing her interviewees to get in more than a brief quote. But so gracious is her manner and so delighted her expression when another Tia emerges and clambers into the SUV's spacious rear, that Tia does not really mind. Besides, the memory of Namrata's ashen face in the shadows of the Wankhede press box would have aroused pity in the hardest heart. Despite her swiftly regained composure and steady smile, Namrata is clearly too shaken by her recent encounter with Jai to go to her hotel, and has decided to spend the night with a friend who lives very near Yari Road.

Uzma has been stopped several times while trying to ask Aman and Tia why Namrata cannot simply come and live with them – their mysterious refusal, combined with the knowledge that Aman and Tia have clearly not told her all their plans, has cast Uzma into a slight but pointed sulk.

By the time Tia has finished their superhero origin story, though, Namrata has recovered considerably from her ordeal and has a million questions and theories, most of which concern the mysterious mob-frenzy specialist she first encountered in Delhi and now at the cricket match.

"Whoever he is, his power doesn't work on me," she says, her hands moving automatically to emphasise the point to her viewers. "I felt nothing at the rally or the game – and it doesn't work on Uzma either."

"Jai could be lying," Tia points out. "I think it's him, and he was just trying to sell you the idea that his enemies were even worse."

"I don't think it's Jai," Aman says. "We saw that tiger-headed guy and the green girl in the crowd, remember? If they were working for Jai, he would have kept them from going crazy. Whoever got the crowd going prevented them from capturing Reddy."

"So now we have two sets of superpowered villains to worry about?" Uzma says. "That's fantastic. How do we know that at least one of these groups isn't following us right now?"

"We don't," says a Tia from the SUV's rear. "Which is why

Aman and I came up with a cunning plan. We're ready."

Aman brings his SUV to a halt, leans to his left and peers towards the back of the car. Namrata and Uzma turn too, and are greeted by a startling sight: there are two Tias sitting in the back of the car, each wearing a dirty sari and a wig of brown, sun-bleached hair. They carry bunches of lifestyle magazines under their arms. One Tia opens the rear door and hops out. Aman restarts the car and swerves back into the endless stream of traffic.

"What is she doing?" Namrata asks.

"Selling magazines," Tia replies.

"We're going to drop off a Tia at every major traffic intersection," Aman explains. "She's going to go from car to car pushing magazines into windows, seeing if Jai's inside. If she finds him, she'll tell us. They're all going to call me once every five minutes – so we'll know if *they* find *her*. She's also going to send more Tias to local train stations, airports, the docks – Tia's a one-woman city-wide manhunt."

"I'm just a girl looking for love," Tia says.

"And what if they catch her?" Namrata asks, horrified.

"I've died lots of times," Tia says. "It's all right."

"You've died? How does it feel?"

Tia laughs, shifts along the seat, and puts a jovial arm around her copy's shoulder.

An hour and a half and several Tias later, they're sitting at the Barista on Yari Road, fending off waiters who keep flocking to Uzma to see if there's anything else she might need with her coffee – ice-cream, a hazelnut topping, a wedding ring?

Around them, fashionable young men and women sit and loudly proclaim their plans to the world. The Yari Road Barista is always full of actors and producers, all of whom are permanently on the cusp of great things, great changes – TV to film, C-list to B-list, Bollywood to Hollywood, jobless to overexposed. Shiny, dressed up to within an inch of their lives, super-fit and eternally hopeful, they gather in little clusters as they reel off lists of forthcoming projects, laugh uproariously whenever they think jokes have been made and sit for hours not listening to any voices but their own.

Yet, even in the middle of all this compulsive attention-seeking, all eyes in the cafe flicker periodically towards Uzma. Finally one thick-spectacled producer shambles up to her and asks, "Weren't you on TV just now?" Uzma denies this, smiling, and the bubble of self-obsession that normally seals the Yari Road cafe off from the rest of the world is restored.

"The rest of you have powers that you exercise consciously, right?" Namrata says. "But Uzma and I are similar – we don't choose when our powers are going to, like, start doing their thing? It's – what are those muscles in the stomach called?"

"Involuntary?" Aman suggests.

"Yeah. Things just happen to us."

"It's not like we have an 'On' switch," Aman says. "The first time I figured something strange was going on, I started hearing this roar of phone conversations. Then screens from all the wireless internet connections in the area started flashing in front of my eyes. I thought I was going crazy. It was a long time before I managed to focus, to pick out what I wanted to hear. The first time, I felt like screaming, hitting everything around me – anything to make it stop. Now I'm offline unless I choose not to be, but I'm still not sure how I do it. Our powers are growing. You'll probably manage to control yours at some stage."

"The funny thing is," Uzma says, "that just a week ago I thought the Bollywood Grooves classes I took at Regent's Park were going to be the toughest part of the whole adventure."

"You had it easy, believe me," Tia says. "I was in the bathtub at home, and the doorbell rang, and my mother-in-law was yelling for tea. I was really tired, and didn't want to get up at all, but the noises outside didn't go away. Everyone was yelling for me instead of hauling their own fat bottoms anywhere. And then I decided to get up, and suddenly there were three of me, and only one towel. I've never freaked out so much – I tried to beat myself up, all of us were screaming. Not fun."

"What about the people in your team who have the real superpowers?" Namrata asks. The others stare at her blankly and she shakes her head. "Guys, you're all really sweet, but come on, how stupid do you think I am? I've spent a lot of time with politicians, and none of you are good liars. Where are the big boys?"

"What big boys?" Tia asks.

"Well, don't get me wrong, but you guys are the backup team, right? What about the leaders? The people like Jai? The strong men?"

"We don't have any of those," Aman says. "I'm sorry, but there's just us."

Namrata splutters and sprays coffee on the table.

"Yup," Aman says.

"No, no," Namrata recovers smoothly, "I wasn't saying you aren't a man because you aren't strong."

"Thanks."

"And, hey, who needs men to protect you anyway, right? What I want to know is: why did the girls get such girlie powers?"

"Well, if you wanted to be super-strong, Namrata, you should have dreamt of being super-strong," Tia says. "I'm perfectly satisfied with my power."

"It's just stupid that I'm a superhero and I'm wishing some dude in a cape were around to save me, that's all. Is it weird that I felt, like, less helpless before I had superpowers?"

Tia leans forward, and when she speaks, she sounds annoyed.

"Namrata, there were four hundred people on that plane. Around half of them were women. A lot of them were from Delhi. Your office is in Delhi, right? You know what it's like. I'm sure there were lots of women on that plane who wanted very badly to be able to go where they pleased, when they pleased, and wear what they wanted in Delhi without feeling threatened. It's quite possible that some of them are super-strong. But it didn't have to be the most important thing in their lives, did it?"

"You're obviously not from Delhi," Namrata says. "Are there any women like that, though?"

"I have no idea," Tia replies. "If there are, I wish they were here. They could be with Jai, in Kashmir, hiding anywhere in the world, or dead. We're the only ones we know of apart from you. I mean, there are a few more, but no one like Jai."

"Maybe you picked the wrong side," Aman says.

"I said it wrong," Namrata says. "Sorry, I assumed that there were more of you. I didn't realise that when you were offering coffee, you were being honest. That I could, you know, feel safe again."

"Well, you're not safe," Tia says. "No one is."

Namrata stares around the table, her face quivering with something akin to excitement.

"What now, people? Do you want me to get in touch with DNNTV's costume department? Do we form a superhero team? Start a reality show? What? Truth, justice, the Indian way?"

"I'm British–Pakistani," Uzma says. "I keep having to tell people this."

"You should be the leader, everyone likes you," Namrata continues, loudly draining her glass of cold coffee. "Tia's like the secret agent James Bond girl who finds out clues and gets captured. Aman's the tech guy who sits with the computers."

"Thanks," Aman says.

"I'd be the one the audiences can relate to. I think it's a very cool idea."

"We're not forming a superhero team," Uzma says. "It's a ridiculous idea. We're going to find a way to stop Jai from killing us, and then we're going our separate ways."

"Which brings us to the real question," Aman says. "We don't know how to stop Jai. You've seen him in action at close quarters. Have you – okay, this sounds stupid – have you noticed any weaknesses?"

"Do you think it would work if I did a story?" Namrata asks. "What if I did this really big feature about all of us, just coming out to the whole world?"

"How on earth would that help?" Tia asks. "Jai hunting us isn't bad enough? You want the whole world to join him?"

"Coming out of the superhero closet isn't really an option," Aman says. "And there's no telling how Jai would respond to it – in any case, we don't even know what he really wants."

"Wait, so he's not just an evil maniac planning to kill all other superheroes and take over the world?" Namrata asks. "There goes that set of interview questions, then."

"So far all we know is that he likes capturing and killing other powered people," Aman says. "He's clearly the leader of a team, but what do they want? And there really isn't much point telling the police or the army about him, is there?"

"I really don't want anyone to know anything more than they already do," Uzma adds. "It's not just us – we all have families, friends. Aman, I know you've done all sorts of things with databases, but no one really uses records to find people here anyway, do they? I don't want my family to get into any more trouble."

"And to be fair to Jai, he's not gone after anyone's families to get to them so far," Tia says.

"He killed that Baby Kalki's parents," Namrata points out.

"They were on the plane too," Aman says. "They were on his list anyway."

"He's lucky to have such faithful friends," Namrata snaps.

"I'm not justifying anything he's done," Aman says. "I'm just saying that revealing what happened on that plane is not something we can just randomly decide to do. It'll affect a lot of people."

"What about Jai's family?" Tia asks. "Can't we go talk to his parents or something? Get them to persuade their son to be nice? Where do they live?"

"London. His sister's married to a doctor there." Aman laughs. "You know, as stupid as that sounds, it's actually better than anything I've come up with. He's an Indian man – we should get his mother to talk to him."

"We should kidnap his parents and say we'll kill them if he doesn't turn himself in," Namrata announces. She looks around the table triumphantly. A set of bewildered faces peers back at her. "What? No?"

"We can't kidnap his parents!" Uzma cannot believe she's saying these words and they're not from a script.

"Why not?" Namrata demands.

"It's not – it's not a superhero sort of thing to do," Aman says.

"Why not?" Namrata's eyes are blazing. "Who made the rules? Who do we have to answer to? We should at least think about it."

"No," Aman says. "We're not doing anything of the kind."

"He said he would kill me if I didn't lead him to you. He said he knew where I lived, who my family and friends are," Namrata says. She drums the table with her fingers. "I think you might need to stop worrying about what might be seen as acceptable behaviour in a comic book, because there are other people who won't follow those rules. Fine, I wasn't totally serious about kidnapping Jai's parents, but if he's setting out to kill other powerful people – not just powered people, but, I don't know, people in the army or something – other people are going to be looking for ways to hurt him. His family is an obvious target. Bad things are going to happen to them. Maybe that's why Jai goes to London."

"What do you mean, Jai goes to London?" Tia asks.

"You guys aren't the only ones who know more than they seem to," Namrata says. "I had a vision – when Jai attacked me in the press box. I saw him running through a London street, covered in blood. I wasn't sure it was London – could have been, like, anywhere in England, actually – but it was definitely him, and he was screaming. The streets were full of people. Dead people and burning cars. Whether or not his family has anything to do with it, Jai's going to London, and he's going to be fairly pissed off."

The others sit looking at one another, struggling to find words, trying to understand what they've just heard.

It's Aman who breaks the silence in the end.

"Your visions – they're possible futures, right? We can change them with our actions, can't we?"

"I don't think so," Namrata says. "All of them have come true so far."

Uzma, who has spent the last few minutes staring vacantly at a TV screen where two children in spangled costumes are gyrating wildly in some grotesque dance contest, snaps out of her stupor, draws her chair forwards and glares around the table.

"I don't understand how we can just sit here talking about all this," she says. "So much has happened, so many people's lives have already changed. Horse-headed babies, tiger-headed men on live TV, billions of dollars stolen from all over the world, mobs and explosions and murders – why hasn't the world gone crazy yet? How can all these people just sit here and drink coffee and talk about movie deals? Why aren't they worried?"

"Uzma, just three days ago you were thinking about ignoring this and carrying on as if nothing had happened," Tia says. "It's just the way people are."

"We're used to ignoring the terrible things right in front of us," Namrata says. "I work in news – I get to see what's happening, at least what's reported. We decide what goes on air based simply on what people want to see, not what they need to know. We're entertainers, not educators. There must have been a hundred reports of, like, weird people cropping up all over the country, missing-person reports about all those Brits Jai abducted. They're not interesting. They're not stories. None of it is real."

"You're over-simplifying. Or maybe I just don't understand," Uzma says. She seems close to tears. Tia places a comforting hand on her arm, but Uzma shrugs it off.

Namrata looks hard as Uzma, and when she speaks again, her voice is low and gentle.

"It's the way we live now, don't you see? Nothing's real – not poverty, not the high life, not terrorists, nothing. It's all just stuff that happens on TV, and you can always, like, change the channel? It's not like you can believe what TV tells you anyway. The internet just makes it worse. And that's what gets me, you know? No one cares. Bombs go off all the time, in every city. Across the country, people die; everyone is sad for like a few seconds, and then flicks the remote."

"Well, maybe your powers can help change that," Aman says.

"Change what? The world could end tomorrow and no one would notice if *Indian Idol* was on at the same time. You know what made me decide to become a journalist? There were these attacks on Parliament, I was switching channels, and I saw this on the news – and I switched to a *Grey's Anatomy* rerun. I felt so bad. I wanted to make a difference, to make people see what was important, to make them care and get mad about the way the world is. Because no one cares now – they don't even notice. Not that I've managed to do anything of the sort so far. I just read out pieces to camera written by morons in Delhi who all got jobs because their parents are friends of the DNNTV owners."

"Wow," Tia says after another long pause. "Okay, I'm sorry. I thought you were a complete bimbo when I saw you on TV but I don't any more. And I think I speak for everyone here."

Namrata smiles wryly. "Thanks?"

Aman's phone rings. He walks out of the cafe, talking hurriedly.

"Why does he carry a phone if he can take calls in his head?" Namrata asks Uzma.

"Habit, I guess," Uzma replies.

When Aman returns, he can barely contain his excitement.

"That was Tia."

"Did we find Jai?" Tia asks.

"Better," Aman says. "Namrata, your protection has arrived. We have some muscle on our side. We found Vir. She's bringing him home."

"Who's Vir?" Namrata asks.

"The guy you hoped we had back home," Uzma says. "The strong guy."

"Handsome flying muscle-man. Great kisser," Tia says, and blushes.

"She – you – she said something's wrong with him," Aman says. "Vir was just sitting around outside the Coffee Day at Carter Road, waiting. He said he was hoping one of us would see him there. He didn't recognise Tia at first, but when she told him who she was under her dirty makeup, she said he looked so happy he almost cried. He's been injured – apparently he had to dig himself out from under a mountain. Thinks he's lost his powers."

"Are you sure we should bring him home?" Uzma asks. "I mean, you don't really know whose side he's on, do you?"

"Well, if Jai dropped a mountain on him, I'm willing to bet he's feeling fairly sympathetic towards us now," Aman says.

"Also, we don't want him hanging around Mumbai waiting for Jai to kill him, especially if he's weak," Tia adds. "Most importantly, I want to see him."

At this, a look passes between Aman and Tia.

Uzma shrugs. "Fine by me. I wished I'd met him last time, anyway."

Tia rises and places a gentle hand on Namrata's shoulder.

"It was lovely meeting you, darling," she says, "but we really have to go now."

"Are you kidding? I'm coming too!" There's a martial light in Namrata's eyes. "I figured you don't want to tell me where you live, but do you really think I'm going anywhere else now? When I know that maniac is looking for me and you've got some strong flying man to protect you? You can, like, think again!"

"There is that empty room on my floor," Uzma says. "And Vir could share with Tia if he's staying, couldn't he?"

Tia smacks her, and good humour is restored.

"But maybe it's safer if you're not with us, Namrata," Aman says. "Safer for you, that is. Jai needs you alive, but he might lose it completely if he finds you with us. It might be better if you went along with this – brought Jai down from the inside in some way."

"Were you even there at the stadium? Didn't you see what I went through? I'm coming, and that's final," Namrata says. "You think I'm going to go back to work after this? You think anything can be normal again? I'm staying with you. I can pay you, if you like."

Tia drives them back to the Yari Road house at the speed of a hurricane, almost killing several people along the way. They tear inside to find two Tias perched on the sofa, solicitously rubbing pain-relief ointment all over a semi-conscious and semi-clad Vir.

Aman's growing irritation is tempered by an undeniable sense of relief at the sight of Vir, and the knowledge that the only person potentially capable of dealing with Jai Mathur and his tiger-headed friends is now sitting in his house. Tia gently awakens Vir, and as he stares at them, his face blank, Aman's bubble of new-found confidence explodes with an almost audible pop. Something's very wrong with Vir. Namrata steps forward, a million questions queuing up on her lips, but Aman stops her.

He sits next to Vir and asks, "What happened to you?"

Vir smiles bravely, then winces as some unseen pain grips him.

"I'm sorry," he says. "My mind's a bit scrambled. It's been a difficult few days, and I'm so tired. But there are so many things I need to tell you. Is everyone here?"

Aman looks at a Tia on the couch, who says, "Bob and the Scientist are upstairs."

"Should I call them?" Aman asks Vir.

"No, that's all right. I just wanted to make sure that none of your team were missing. There's been a new development. I have to show you."

"Go on."

"It's outside." Vir struggles to his feet, and they follow him as he walks to the door. He opens it.

Outside stand four men and a little girl. One of the men steps forward.

"Hi," Jai says.

CHAPTER **ELEVEN**

"This doesn't have to be unpleasant," Jai says, walking in.

Aman has never felt as crushingly powerless as he does now. Behind him, Uzma whimpers, and Namrata is speechless. Only Tia reacts: she dives back towards a sofa, whips out a gun from her bag, and two seconds later ten Tias stand in a row, guns pointed at the newcomers. They observe her with varying degrees of interest.

"Very pretty," Jai says. "Have a seat."

Jai's followers line up beside him: the tiny Anima, her eyes dilating, sparkling, spreading across her pointed face; the hulking Sher, his tiger-stripes thickening, arcing lazily across his bald head. Mukesh smirks a greeting, his head tilted to one side, his forked tongue flicking obscenely at Tia through his cracking, widening lips.

At a signal from Jai, the avuncular poet Jerry shambles forward, looks yearningly at Uzma, and claps his hands. A flash of blue light illuminates the room.

Aman's head spins as he's disconnected. He staggers and almost falls.

"Vir. I can't believe you did this," a Tia says.

"Vir is no longer with us, alas," Jai says. "This gentleman is called Vivek. May I also introduce Jerry, Sher, Anima and Mukesh. Oh, you've met Mukesh already, haven't you?"

"And he's met this," another Tia says, waving her gun as threateningly as she can. Mukesh hisses at her, and takes a step forward.

"I asked you – nicely – to sit," Jai says to Tia, stalling Mukesh with a bone-crushing hand on his shoulder. "Could you get me some water? It's been a long day."

"You're not all bulletproof," Tia snarls.

"This is boring," Jai says. He stares calmly at Tia. Nobody moves, or breathes. When Jai runs a weary hand across his forehead, everyone in the room flinches.

"See, we can do this," Jai says. "We can fight, and see who's stronger, and then if any of you survive I can take you back to my new base and torture you. But I'm trying to be nice here. So... are you going to be adults about this, or do I have to start counting to three?"

Aman walks slowly back to a sofa. Uzma follows, keeping her eyes to the ground. Namrata is rooted to the spot, gaping at Jai, her large eyes tear-filled. Jai deliberately turns his back on the Tias and waves at Namrata.

"You should have told me about your friends," he says.

"Jai, I swear, I just met them," Namrata blurts.

"I know. Good work – it took you just a few minutes to locate and infiltrate. There should be more journalists like you.

Hell, there should be more soldiers like you."

Behind Jai, Uzma and Aman sit. The Tias drop their guns.

"Smart," Jai says. "Now, water, please."

Flushed with rage, a Tia heads towards the kitchen.

Jai turns to Uzma with a beaming smile.

"So what do you do, madam?" he asks. "We haven't been formally introduced."

"They're good people, Jai," Namrata says. "Please don't hurt them. They're just trying to survive. Please, just talk things through."

"Talk things through? What does it look like I'm doing?" Jai asks, his expression bewildered and hurt. "Namrata, since you're good at these things, could you perform introductions?"

Namrata nods. "Aman, Tia, Uzma, meet Jai Mathur," she says.

Jai turns to the sofa and gazes earnestly down at them.

"Which one's the internet operator?" he asks.

"That would be Aman," Namrata says.

Jai sticks out a hand and Aman shakes it gingerly, half expecting Jai to rip off his arm.

"Impressive work," Jai says. "You couldn't have found a better way to get my attention. Your skills are just what I need to really round off my core team – though a few friends of mine want their money back. And that would make Uzma here our crowd manipulator?"

"No, she's not," Namrata says. "Whoever that is, he's not here."

"No? That's good to know. What is your power, then, my dear?"

"I don't know," Uzma replies.

"Is attractiveness a superpower?" Jai enquires. "What do you think, Namrata?"

"I don't know," Namrata says. "And the other lady is Tia. Jai... may I go now, please? I've done what you asked."

Jai studies her for a few seconds.

"Yes, go," he says finally. "And, Namrata, I have a new assignment for you. Find this mob controller for me, will you?"

"I'll do my best."

"Given what you've done for me this evening, your best should be good enough. Take care of yourself."

Namrata doesn't meet anyone's eyes as she hurries out of the house. Jai turns to the others and rubs his palms together briskly.

"Can't really open up in front of the media," he says. "Now, let's talk business."

"What do you want from us?" Aman asks.

"I want you to forget the past, and look ahead to a glorious future. I'm putting together a team," Jai says. "And I want all of you to join me."

"Except this Tia," Mukesh says. "We don't want her. She ruined the base."

"This is true," Jai says. "Jerry, Vivek – could you get behind Sher, please?"

Jerry and Vivek dart behind the massive Sher.

"Thank you," Jai says. "Anima? Kill Tia, please."

Anima screeches and rises into the air, a green glow enveloping her.

Some of the Tias raise their guns and fire indiscriminately, but the few shots that hit their target produce no discernible effect. Before Tia has time to fire a second round, a stream of glowing arrows blazes across the room. Chunks of plaster spurt from the walls, sparks sizzle across the floor, and all the Tias crumble into dust.

Uzma screams, falls to the floor and covers her face. Aman kneels beside her, holding her instinctively, though he knows he can offer her no protection whatsoever. All he can do is glare impotently at Jai.

Anima squeals, high-pitched, gleeful, and the TV screen shatters. Her face has transformed completely into a cartoon: her mouth is round, pink and toothless, empty except for a cute red tongue.

"I hope you have backup copies of that woman," Jai says. "If we don't manage to get her to see the light, she'll make the world's best target practice. Now, don't move for a bit. You wouldn't want to draw Anima's attention."

Aman stays down, bullets and screams still echoing in his ears. The room is full of smoke, and it's suddenly very hot. There's a thudding sound. Aman knows what it is: footsteps on the stairs. He doesn't dare to shout out a warning, Tia's look of pain as Anima's weapons burned through her is fresh in his memory, but he hopes whoever it is will not be stupid enough to run at the sound of gunfire, and that none of Jai's crew has heard the footsteps...

Bob races into the living room.

Anima giggles and hurls a spear of light at him.

"No!" Aman and Sher yell simultaneously. Sher hurls himself at Anima, dragging her to the ground, growling in pain as green sparks sizzle through his tiger fur. But it's too late; the spear flies true and lands in Bob's chest. Bob goes down.

Aman and Uzma, all danger forgotten, race to him. But

there's nothing they can do. Bob is gone. Uzma shuts his wide, staring eyes.

Aman hurls himself at Jai. It's the first time he's ever attacked anyone, and he couldn't have chosen a worse target. Jai lets Aman land a few knuckle-tearing punches, and then tosses him contemptuously into a sofa. Aman falls heavily, and then struggles to his feet, ashen-faced.

Kneeling by Bob's body, Uzma heaves with silent sobs.

"You fool. He could control the weather," Aman says. "He could have done so much good. He could have done so much."

"Hmm. That is sad," Jai says. "Is there anyone else? They should come down quietly."

"They have," Sundar says. He advances into the room, his ray-gun in his hands. He fires.

A beam of bright light emerges from the gun. Everyone dives for cover but Jerry. The light envelops him. There's a sizzle, the smell of ozone, and Jerry vanishes.

"Sundar! Get away!" Aman roars.

Sundar fires wildly around the room, but Jai and his cohorts are too fast for him. Scientifically analyzing his chances against a super-soldier, a tiger-headed man and a cartoon schoolgirl, Sundar realises they are minimal, backs away, firing, and then turns and runs for the stairs.

"Take him out," Jai snaps, rising. He turns to Anima and finds she's human again, staring open-mouthed at Bob's body.

"I've been bad again," she says.

"It doesn't matter. Sher, Mukesh, you're not moving. Why?"

"We could use these two as shields," Mukesh mutters.

"Can't risk them. Go."

"Okay, so we need him," Mukesh indicates Aman, "but

what about her? He won't fire at her."

"Don't make me ask again."

Mukesh shoots a frightened glance at Jai and heads off with Sher.

A door slams upstairs.

Aman picks up his bruised body and runs to Uzma. He tries to think of comforting words, but his brain appears to have shut down. Since Jerry's disappearance, he's been feeling the digital world on the edges of his mind again, but he doesn't really think Google can help him out of his current situation.

Jai comes up to them, looks at Bob's body and sighs.

"I hope you learned a lesson today, Aman."

Aman forces himself not to look at Jai, to say nothing.

"This is what happens when people with no experience take on missions too big for them. I hope you realise his death was your fault," Jai says. "If you'd only helped me from the start instead of making your own bid for power, this innocent boy would still be alive. What made you think you had any chance of achieving anything, Aman? You just don't have the right training for this."

It's Uzma who turns sharply, her tear-streaked face incredulous.

"And you – you do?" she gasps.

"Maybe not," Jai says with a shrug, "but who's going to stop me?"

Mukesh comes skidding in. "Man – sir, there's a problem."

Jai sighs deeply. "Of course there is. What?"

"He's locked himself in. Sher can't do anything. I'm much stronger than he is, but even I –"

"Really, Mukesh? Your moment of glory is ruined by – a

door? Watch these two." Jai strides away, his impenetrable skin more than enough protection against Mukesh's enraged glare.

Mukesh waits until he's gone, and then springs towards Aman and Uzma. He punches Aman, knocking him to the floor, and grabs Uzma. He licks her face roughly with his forked tongue, choking off her outraged yell with a scaly hand.

"Leave her alone," a shrill voice says. It's Anima. She hovers above them, a large light-mace in her hands.

"Buzz off, kid," Mukesh snarls. "Adult stuff happening."

"You made me do bad things," Anima whispers. "Don't hurt her. I like her."

Aman hauls himself up, his head ringing, as Mukesh hisses angrily at Anima, but lets Uzma go.

"It's Anima, right? I'm Uzma," Uzma says. "This man is very evil. Could you hit him, please?"

Anima nods, smiles shyly and throws her mace at Mukesh. It hits him in the face, and knocks him out.

"Now him," Uzma says, pointing at Vivek.

"Hey, people, there's no need for this," Vivek says, rising from the sofa hurriedly. "I'm a peaceful man. I'm just an actor."

"Wait," Aman says. Anima looks questioningly at Uzma, who nods.

Aman charges at Vivek and releases all his anger, all his guilt, in one unstoppable punch that knocks the shapeshifter out. Aman turns to Uzma, rubbing his fist.

"Kind of wanted to do that since I first met Vir," he says. "Now we save Sundar."

"I think we should get out of here," Uzma says. "I'm sorry, but I don't want to die today."

"Really? Just leave him? No."

Uzma comes up to Aman and puts her hands on his shoulders.

"Aman, listen to me," she says. "Sundar's gone. Bob's gone. We can't fix that. We need to go. They'll be back any second."

Aman steps away from her.

"No. Can't," he says. "Anima, can you beat Jai and Sher?"

"Jai Uncle and I had one fight but he beat me," Anima says. "Sher is my best friend but I once beat him."

Aman hangs his head. Loud crashing sounds echo dully from upstairs.

"You're right, you should go," he tells Uzma. "I'm really sorry I got you into this. Last thing I wanted."

"You're coming with me," Uzma says. "We can start over. Find other Tias. Save more people like us. Come on." She starts towards the door, but Aman doesn't follow.

"Jai was right, don't you see. This is my fault. No one asked me to do this. I put you all in danger. I got Bob killed. Almost got you killed. I can't leave Sundar now," he says.

"Aman," Uzma says, "you're being an idiot. We don't have time, so I can't argue about this now. Just listen to me, okay? Let's go."

She grabs his hand. As if in a daze, Aman allows himself to be led away, but stops at the doorway, shaking his head.

"Should we take the kid?" he asks. Anima hovers inside the room, watching Bob's body with her cartoon eyes. Shiny, perfectly teardrop-shaped tears fall from her face and land with perfect sound effects on the burnt floor.

"She killed Bob," Uzma says.

"She's just a kid."

"She freaks me out."

"And she's powerful as hell."

"Anima, you want to come with us?" Uzma calls.

Anima giggles, and a big white smile curves across her face. She drops to the floor, turns human and runs to Uzma.

"We can't just leave Bob here," Aman says.

"Aman, I'm sorry, I really am, but we're trying to escape here. We're this close to getting killed. We can't take Bob. We can't pack our toothbrushes. Come."

Aman nods. Mukesh groans and rubs his head. The crashing sounds upstairs stop.

"Okay, we need to move," Aman says.

They step outside, feel cold tingling points on their skin, and look up at the sky, at the dark cloud that hovers above the house, thick and black against the city-lit night, and the little white drops that glow like fireflies drifting against the streetlights as they descend, flickering and disappearing before they reach the ground. Bob is cold and dead, and it's snowing in Mumbai. But even as they stare, too amazed to keep running, a gust of wind comes from the sea and the cloud swirls and melts away. And they remember where they are and why.

They reach Aman's SUV and find the tyres have been slashed. Uzma runs out into the street and raises an arm. Perhaps her real power is transport acquisition: auto-rickshaws appear immediately and screech to a halt in front of them. They scramble into the first.

"Where to?" the driver asks, gazing goggle-eyed at Uzma.

"Wherever," she says.

"Anywhere with you, princess of my heart," he says, and kick-starts the auto.

"Sundar's holding out well," Aman says, peering back at the house, "maybe they won't get him. Plus he has that gun –

maybe he'll just make them disappear."

"Can you call him?" Uzma asks.

"I tried when they arrived. He can never find his phone in the middle of all that junk."

Aman shuts his eyes and buries his head in his hands, trawling through his much-abused brain for any possible solution.

"I did set up a webcam in his room," he says after a while. "He never uses it, but it might be on. But there's no point just watching, is there?"

"No, there isn't." Uzma leans back, wishing the auto could move at a pace that was in any way faster than a crawl.

A few seconds later, Aman finds he cannot help himself. He checks, and finds the camera is on and he has a window into the warzone.

Sundar stands in the middle of his room in his inventor's trance. He's still working on the armour he's been building for the last few days. It seems to be almost complete: only the shoulders of the mannequin underneath remain uncovered, strange pink blobs standing out in the middle of a complex black and silver structure. His movements are calm, unhurried. He swings puppet-like to his heap of equipment, and returns with two curved black metal shoulder-pads, covered on the inside with complex circuitry. These he attaches to the shoulders of the suit of armour. He steps back, his head lolling forward.

"What's he doing?" Uzma asks.

"He's sleeping," Aman replies.

Aman has no idea how Sundar is keeping Jai and Sher out of the room, but there's a large machine that looks like an ordinary diesel generator wired up in front of the armour, and it intermittently emits pulses of white light. A force-field? Aman can only watch as Sundar opens a panel on the armour's chest and types in a combination. The armour glows, red lines streaking through its joints, and then the whole body shines silver for a second and disappears altogether.

Sundar sleepwalks to the pile of equipment again and picks up a can. He takes this to the nearest wall and spray-paints the number 75348, in bright red. Aman looks the number up immediately, hoping it's the key to some magical crisis-resolver. He finds nothing.

Sundar tosses the can away, and picks up his ray-gun. He shuffles to the generator, bends and turns it off.

There's no sound, so Aman cannot hear the door breaking, but he flinches nevertheless as Sher leaps into the camera's frame, tiger-headed, a being of pure power, swerving and rolling to avoid Sundar's rays. But Sundar does not fire at Sher; instead, he points the ray-gun at his own head and presses the trigger. Sher stops his evasive dance and stares open-mouthed as Sundar disappears, along with his gun, in a blaze of white light.

"Aman, for god's sake, tell me what's happening," Uzma says.

Aman opens his eyes. "I can't explain," he says.

"Can I have an ice-cream?" Anima asks. She's between them on the auto seat, peering out through the small oval transparent-plastic window at the back.

"Now's not the best time," Uzma says. "We'll get you one later."

Anima grins excitedly. "Or Jai Uncle will bring!" she squeals.

"Wouldn't count on it, darling," Uzma says, forcing a smile. "We might not see Jai Uncle for a few days."

"No, no," Anima says, pointing at the window. "Look, there he is!"

Aman sticks his head out of the side of the auto and looks down the street behind them. It seems perfectly ordinary, a few cars zipping through an amber Yari Road night – until a Ford Ikon, well behind them, suddenly flies up in the air, tossed off the road, and crashes into a building. Two seconds later, another car goes flying, and Aman sees, in the distance, a small figure leap into the air, jumping like a champion athlete in a hurdles race, soaring above a bus, landing on its roof, crumpling the thin metal, and taking off again as the bus folds beneath him. Jai lands on the road and keeps running, moving far, far faster than their auto.

Aman pulls his head back into the auto very rapidly.

"Now, Anima, I need you to be very quiet," he says. "We'll hide from Jai Uncle, okay? It'll be fun."

"What?" Uzma is horrified. "He's really here?"

"Yup," Aman says. "He's running up the road. But he might jump over us and miss us, so let's just be quiet and hope."

"Good plan," Uzma says.

"No, no," Anima says. "I can't hide from Jai Uncle. He always knows where I am."

"How?" Aman asks, ready to collapse.

"Oh, from this," Anima says, pointing at a metal bracelet on her left ankle. "After one other uncle came and fought with us, Jai Uncle told us to wear these so we wouldn't get lost any more."

Aman and Uzma exchange defeated glances.

"You got any bright ideas?" Uzma asks.

"No. Wait. Maybe we should toss her out?"

"Maybe we should," Uzma says.

They cannot debate this any further as at this point Jai lands on the road in front of them, cracking the tarmac, spinning, rising. He raises an arm, palm facing the onrushing auto. The windshield shatters, the driver's neck snaps with a loud crunch.

Anima giggles and the world turns red.

CHAPTER **TWELVE**

Aman sits in his new office, on a creaky chair surrounded by powerful computers, feeling a bit like a Eurovision keyboardist. His shoulder, badly bruised from the auto crash, still hurts when he moves, but he is otherwise more-or-less uninjured – a condition that Mukesh, currently standing guard over him, is eager to change. But Jai has given strict instructions that Aman is not to be harmed, only removed gently and firmly from his computers should he misbehave. After all, Aman is the key to Jai's empire and they both know it.

It has taken considerable effort to assemble this setup in a place like Goa, where it is generally considered impolite to do anything quickly, and keeping this in mind Aman has not told Jai that these computers are completely unnecessary. Aman has no desire to reveal the full extent of his abilities to Jai; it suits him perfectly to attack one site at a time, spending hours over a single password instead of simply asking the site to let him in.

He has been stalling Jai's operations as much as he dares since he first sat in this room three days ago. The first night, he even shut down all the broadband networks in Goa for a brief while, in order to sabotage the transfer of a few billion dollars to Jai's Dubai bank account.

While Mukesh periodically curses about Goan internet services and threatens to go kill broadband providers, Aman has been skimming the waves of the internet on his own. The incident at the cricket stadium made headlines, but there were no real revelations. Life in the world outside has moved on, as it does in the subcontinent whenever terrorists, natural disasters and other random calamities strike.

But then the subcontinent has never had any illusions of safety or prosperity; people know that disaster is just a heartbeat away, and simply cannot afford to panic when something terrible happens. They do not have the luxury of worrying about the collapse of their safe world – their world has never been safe, and lives have to be lived and rising petrol prices gawked at. The usual protocol for assaults on cricketers has been followed – Pakistani terrorists have been blamed, the Indian opposition has called the government spineless, Australian cricket officials have cancelled a tour and lots of Facebook groups have been started.

Aman is far more interested in the fact that Namrata seems to have gone underground. She's not gone back to work, and the phone she had used at Wankhede has been silent since that evening.

Uzma is in another room in the mansion. She's still unconscious: the crash left her with a concussion and a broken arm. Since he awoke four days ago, Aman has been allowed to see her occasionally, with Mukesh playing chaperone. They've always blindfolded him and led him to Uzma's room on these occasions, and Aman hasn't bothered to tell them he knows exactly where she is, thanks to their surveillance cameras. He has been told she will be killed if he does not follow every command Jai delivers, but he knows this threat is empty, because everyone in the building is already in love with Uzma. On one of his visits Aman found Jai standing by her bedside, holding her hand and threatening to disembowel one of his cohorts, a healing-powered doctor, for not getting Uzma up and about. Her arm is healed, but Aman suspects the doctor is not trying to wake her. The longer Jai spends by Uzma's bedside, the less time he has to terrorise his followers.

Beyond the CPU towers is a view Aman cannot complain about. The Arabian Sea rolls gently in the distance. Between the sea and the mansion are a glittering white-sand beach, a line of palm trees and a well-maintained garden. Jai's current headquarters is in South Goa, far from the touristy madness of the north, with its rave parties, crowded shacks and bloated, sun-reddened Russian tourists cooking slowly on deckchairs and being mauled by local youths in the name of massage. The southern beaches of Goa are mostly lined with luxury resorts with fenced private beaches. The former owner of the plot of land Jai's mansion stands on was a Russian gangster. The men sent sporadically by his successors to avenge his death make excellent sport for Jai's hunters.

Jai's mansion is a palace of wonders built, like his Udhampur base and the new Wankhede stadium, by the powered architect Andy Kharkongor. On the outside it's a twelve-storey grey building; on the inside it's Andy's first attempt at a superpower headquarters. A mind-bending, pop-culture-referencing amalgamation of classic over-the-top Hollywood and Bollywood residences, complete with throne room, vast torture hall with snake pits and shark tanks, in-house Batcave and a *Star Trek*-themed living area in which most of the powered prisoners from Jai's Kashmir base now reside – some against their will, but most by choice.

Aman finds the architect's power fascinating – he's able to transform all materials into polymers or alloys with shape memory, and given the right quantity of ingredients can build anything in a few hours. He simply makes bricks, mortar and metal think they were in a particular alignment and they rebuild that imagined structure at his command. Aman's not exactly been given a guided tour of the facilities, but sometimes Jai lets him walk around the mansion with him, listening to his plans, making suggestions, and Aman has occasionally caught a glimpse of Andy at work. Once, he saw Andy reshape a swimming pool into a map of the world, based on a whim of Jai's. Tiles cracking, sliding and rejoining, floor rising and reshaping to form continents in the middle of chlorinated water oceans. But this is just the tiniest exercise of Andy's powers – Jai has promised him the day will come when he can redesign the entire world, transforming it into a paradise of sculpted landscapes, buildings out of science-fiction, bridges that arc across the sky.

Despite having spent a week with Jai, and three days actively working for him, Aman has no idea what sort of person his captor is. He figures this is because it is possible Jai himself does not know. The only aspect of his superhuman personality that he's sure about is the one he uses to intimidate, to threaten, and behind the manic mask is a face that's trying to decide how it looks. Aman has gathered that Vir and he used to be friends, but while Vir essentially remained his human self but with powers, Jai has decided that his new powers deserve a new person behind them and is trying to work out who that is.

No trace of his old life, his human life, exists except a collection of He-Man and GI Joe dolls lined up on a glass shelf in his functional, spartan bedroom, and a framed family photograph on a windowsill. In this, the family stands atop a hill. Jai is a reedy youth, somewhere in his early teens, brandishing a toy gun in a martial pose some distance apart from his parents. His father, an earnest, bespectacled man, gazes into the distance; his mother holds a little girl, aged not more than two or three, in her arms, and looks proudly at her little soldier. It's a happy picture.

Jai has decided to bring back into fashion an aspiration that died out in the middle of the twentieth century: military conquest of the world. Aman has asked what he plans to do with the world once he's conquered it. Jai has no idea, but knows he will establish a global capital at Jaipur, already conveniently named after him. He wants to accomplish what Genghis Khan, Alexander and Julius Caesar could not. And before people raise statues to him, he wants to build himself in the image of his idols – but does not know how.

Following Jai around his mansion, Aman sees that his people obey him without question, flinching when he speaks and never meeting his eyes. He has learned to inspire fear, and knows he has not yet understood how to simply inspire. He practises speeches all day, sometimes in the middle of observing Aman at work, but after a minute or two of fiery rhetoric he gives up. He obsessively studies great world leaders, trying to understand how to fake benevolence, compassion, divinity. He lectures himself for hours on end, exercises that always end in shattered mirrors and books crumpled to pulp.

Aman knows Jai is too smart to trust him, but he also knows that Jai desperately wants Aman to like him. This is simply because Aman's powers, if used in Jai's service, will upgrade Jai's wildest schemes from laughable to merely ambitious.

"I know we got off to a shaky start, and I apologise for that. We were all learning how to use our powers. I've changed my plans since then, and you have too," Jai had said to Aman on their first day. They were on the roof of the building at the time, and Sher was holding Aman over the edge with one arm. Jai's face shone from either sweat or sincerity as he continued, "A bad beginning doesn't mean we can't work together. Learn to respect and trust each other. Just think of the rewards, Aman. Think of what we could achieve. A better world. It's what we both want."

This had been Aman's moment to prove his heroism, to take a stand and a long fall. Instead, he had simply said, "As long as Uzma is not harmed," wishing he could be sure that this was his real reason for agreeing to work for his captor. He'd had his Face Darth Vader moment, and had fluffed his lines.

Since that moment, he'd become a part of Jai's team – and not just a part. From the resentful glares of Mukesh and Sher, Aman realised he had been unofficially promoted to Chief Henchman. As his first bonus, he had not been dropped from the roof.

Jai's plan for world domination is a fairly simple one. Aman had been confused initially by its sheer arrogance, but after staring at it for a while in PDF form, he had been forced to admit it was good.

Once Jai has picked a country, a polite email will be sent to its government demanding its surrender. If this is refused or ignored, Aman will go online and shut the country down. He is to disable all communications, empty all banks, shut off power grids, block up dams, refineries, plants and pipelines. He will switch off the media and close ports, airports and rail stations.

They will let the country stew in its own juices for a while. Uncertainty and anger, aided by a shortage of food and water, will spread in hours or days, depending on the country. Inevitably, in the darkness, with nothing but survival to distract them, citizens will panic. Thousands will die, riots will spread, local governments will collapse. Only the fittest will survive.

Then Jai and his crack team will walk into the country's central government headquarters and take charge.

When Aman turns the lights back on, the nation's leader – Vivek in a completely convincing performance – will inform his or her beloved subjects that the nation has collapsed. It is unlikely that this information will cause anyone any surprise at this point, but no one will be bored, because Vivek will then announce that control over the nation has been handed to its new superpowered saviour and god-king – Jai – and their country is now a part of Jai's empire. And that this is a good thing. Ceremonial handshakes and wild celebrations will ensue.

The national flag will replaced by Jai's emblem, a saffron sun on black. A new national anthem, currently a work in progress, will be played non-stop on all TV and radio stations until everyone has managed to learn it.

Control of the administration will be handed to the military, headed by a suitable candidate – essentially the most senior officer willing to swear loyalty to Jai. Stubborn superior officers, if there are any, will be squashed. If the nation's former commander was military anyway, the transition will be smooth. If not, the nation's former head will be persuaded by such notables as Sher, Mukesh and Anima that resistance would be futile, and then restored to his or her former station with considerably reduced powers.

The nation's funds will be handed over to the army, which will be given the task of re-establishing order, while Jai and his friends move on to a new destination – whichever country is next in the International Monetary Fund's per capita Wealth List – though Jai plans to skip the top five, especially Luxembourg since he's not sure where it is, and start with the United States. India is 129th on this list, which will give Jai time to decide what to do with it.

Countries without significant armies will not have to suffer: they will merely be informed as to their changed status and given a deadline by which to alter their flags. Pakistan will be left untouched so that it might continue to entertain Jai. China will be left in the dark until its people rise up and swallow the government, and will then be invaded. The Dalai Lama will be forced to govern it.

Jai hopes there will be plenty of resistance to this plan; that nations will unite in revolt, giving him a chance to plunge them into darkness again. He will actively encourage rebels and terrorists – they will give his vast armies something to do. If entire nations' armies behave badly, their countries will simply be left switched off until they learn to behave better, and all their money will be taken away.

At the same time, several of Jai's super-soldiers will run superhero scams around the world, promising freedom from

Jai's evil empire, while delivering key leaders of the human resistance into Jai's hands. Public resistance to superheroes will be reduced over time by staged events where superheroes save cities from external threats such as space monsters from other galaxies and dimensions. These events will be choreographed on the fly, but several will involve one of Jai's most eager followers, a failed stage magician and illusionist from Chennai, who will be happy to conjure up illusions of giant beasts and alien invasion fleets for superheroic saviours to pretend to destroy – after the rewards in each case are agreed upon.

After the initial period of anarchy, Jai has told Aman, the world will be much better off under his rule. And not just because the nation-state is a failed concept based on artificial barriers and all will be as one under Jai, but because millions of people, mostly the poorest and weakest and hence the greatest burdens on society, will be dead.

Jai has no interest in administration; once the world is conquered, Aman may run it as he sees fit. Jai had been planning to hand the keys of the world over to Indian politicians, but has realised this could only lead to the collapse of his empire. His chief regret is that he cannot conquer the world in India's name, that the world will never quake in fear of the Indian Air Force. As a student of Indian history, Jai is deeply chagrined by the fact that India has proved to be a warm, welcoming and exotic destination of choice for every possible invading party. He had always dreamt of the boot being on the other foot, but the Indian armed forces had never even been allowed to invade neighbouring countries while actively at war with them, and continued to remain spineless even with Jai's supreme might at their command.

On the other hand, this private invasion has its advantages:

conquering the world without the Indian armed forces' help would mean that the rest of the world could not gain anything by attacking India while Jai invaded country after country. If anything, they would turn their weapons on the Americans after he had taken over the White House. After all, every military commander in the world has been secretly or publicly itching to do that for a while.

When Aman brought up, somewhat nervously, the fact that millions of deaths all over the world might make it a little difficult for people to love their god-king, and perhaps Jai could use his abilities to serve humanity instead of conquering it, Jai did not, as expected, punch a hole in his head. Instead, Jai told Aman this was true, and he had considered it for a while before realising that it would be wrong to pretend that the world had not changed, that humans and their opinions were still relevant. He told Aman that it would take a while for people to understand that their new rulers could not be held accountable to human values or human laws. Did one put a tiger in prison for killing a deer? Did one fine a god, if gods exist, for earthquakes and tsunamis? Did one vote their powers away by Facebook poll?

Jai is completely in favour of a new set of laws, a code for superheroes – his military mind cannot allow the thought of a ruling class without its own rules – but this is something that can be established once their empire-building has finished. And he will abide by this code as long as it does not involve pre-superhuman failed concepts like communism or democracy.

The second night, after Aman had shown Jai the full extent of North Korea's military capability and Jai had laughed until he cried, Aman asked Jai when he intended to carry out this great plan. Jai replied it would start as soon as the last real obstacle, the unknown mob manipulator, had been found and either subverted or eliminated. This unknown villain represents everything Jai hates most – chaos, irrational rage, cowardice. Jai does not want to have to slaughter masses of enraged civilians, or fight soldiers whose minds are not their own – he wants to be a general, not a butcher. Had Aman not joined his army, he would have conquered the world anyway, but it would have taken much more time, and he would have had no real way of maintaining order and preventing uprisings. But he would have been content, travelling the world in an endless loop, making war. A fierce and savage god, but a god nevertheless. With Aman by his side, says Jai, he can actually help the world while ruling it. He will make the world a better place whether its denizens want it or not. They will love him for it if they are smart.

The scariest realisation for Aman, as he sits hunched over a keyboard pretending to shut down Pakistani spy networks, is that he and Jai have a lot in common. He finds several of Jai's plans both exciting and tempting. He has often had to stop himself from suggesting improvements, and wishes he knew whether this is because he still has a conscience or because he is not yet able to deal with the idea of being able to decide the fate of Earth. He had been annoyed with Uzma initially for not wanting to be a superhero, for not embracing the facts and finding out the true extent of her power. Was he not guilty of the same blind, unreasoning reluctance to be all he could be? He knew the world needed transformation, and a lot of Jai's plans, however insane, would give him the opportunity to make things better – and it was not as if he could stop Jai in any case. Why, then, was he holding back?

He does not, fortunately, have time to ponder this any further as Sher enters the room.

"She's up. Come and see her," he growls.

Aman waits for Sher to blindfold him as he has the last few days, but the tiger-man simply walks off. Aman practically flies behind him through a maze of gaudy booby-trapped corridors until they reach Uzma's room.

Uzma is sitting up in bed, gulping water from a glass, wincing as she swallows. Aman just stands at the door, his world-changing worries forgotten as he beams goofily at her. She smiles at him, wincing a little, then her eyes widen in fear as Jai enters the room, brushing past Aman.

"We're all so glad you're all right," he says. "We were really worried."

Uzma stares at him in disbelief.

"I haven't forgotten why I'm here," she says. "Or who put me here. What do you want from me?"

"Aman will fill you in," Jai says. "I know the last few days have been difficult, but just believe in me and everything will get better. You'll see. We're all a team now – all misunderstandings have been cleared up."

"Bob's death? Was that a 'misunderstanding' too?" she asks. "Go to hell, Jai. Don't talk to me."

A muscle in Jai's neck twitches, but he smiles.

"All right, I'll go. You must be feeling tired. We'll speak again after you've rested for a while. Aman, talk to her. Make her see reason." He puts a friendly hand on Aman's shoulder, and Aman realises he has just been given an order.

Jai strides out, leaving Sher with Aman and Uzma.

"You want to die, girl?" Sher growls. "Don't you know better by now? Don't push him. He'll kill you in a second – he came really close just now. Even this geek here knows better."

"Get out," Uzma snaps.

To Aman's surprise, Sher does precisely that.

Uzma stares at Aman.

"What's going on?" she asks, and coughs, spilling water on the bed.

"Well, we've been left together to discuss our plans, and this room's under surveillance," Aman says. "How are you feeling?"

"Where the hell are we?"

"Goa."

"I've always wanted to visit Goa," she says with a grin. "Are they going to kill us?"

"No. Not you, at least. I think Jai wants to make you empress of the world."

"I could get used to that."

"Well, it's probably better than anything I ever did for you."

"Come here." She holds out her arms and Aman rushes to her, holds her while her body heaves with silent, dry sobs.

"What do we do, Aman?" she asks. "What happens now?"

"I'm working on it," he says. "They have a plan. You get well, we'll figure out what to do."

"I tried, you know," she says. "I did what you wanted. Joined up to be a superhero like the rest of you. And look how that turned out."

"If we survive this, I'll finance all the movies you want to make. If that even begins to make up for dragging you into this."

"Ah, forget it," she says. "They'd have got me anyway."

"You are kind of hard to miss," he agrees.

Mukesh swings the door open. His face is livid, scaling over, his fangs lengthening. Aman has nowhere to run as Mukesh stalks towards him.

"You little bastard," he snarls, "you knew about this, didn't you?" He catches Aman by the throat. "In fact, I think you're behind it," he says. "I should have snapped your little neck a long time ago."

Aman struggles wildly but in vain. Ignoring Uzma's shrieks, Mukesh squeezes until Aman's eyes glaze over, and then tosses him against a wall. Aman slides to the ground, his head throbbing.

"I told Jai you'd be of no use," Mukesh hisses. "This was a huge mistake, you hear me? A very huge mistake. If it was you, we'll find out. A lot of people are going to die, and it's your fault."

"I don't know what you're talking about," Aman says as calmly as he can manage, rubbing the back of his head. "You were with me all day. You saw everything I did. Every screen I opened."

"Well, you opened the wrong screens. You didn't look at the bloody news. It's all over the bloody internet. What use is your power if you don't know?"

Sher appears at the door.

"Jai needs us, Mukesh," he says.

"What about these two?" Mukesh asks.

"Later. Come."

Mukesh kicks Aman half-heartedly and they stride out, locking the door behind them.

"Well, this is nice," Uzma says. "What the hell was that?"

"Like I keep saying, I don't know," Aman replies. "I think I'm going to take a little nap."

Uzma raises an eyebrow as he clambers on to the bed and lies down next to her, eyes closed.

"Lie very still and don't talk," Aman murmurs. "It disturbs me."

She looks at him, genuinely puzzled, and then says suddenly, "If you're that shape-changer pretending to be Aman I'll kill you."

He puts a finger to his lips, frowning, and shakes his head. Mystified, she is about to speak again when he gets up and says, "Done. Sorry, was just putting the recorders on a loop. Didn't want them to see me going online."

He paces around the room with his eyes shut for a few seconds, occasionally bumping into things. He then utters the all-explaining words, "Oh, crap."

"What?"

"British TV channels at Jai's parents' house in London. Police everywhere. Lots of people with placards and stuff, mostly Asians. They're saying Jai Mathur is an alleged terrorist, a disgraced Air Force officer being hunted by the police."

"Why? I mean, good, but what for?"

"More than a hundred missing Brits, and what happened at Udhampur. His parents have locked themselves in their house and haven't talked to anyone, but there's a big crowd outside, and it's getting bigger. They want Jai to turn himself in and clear his name."

"Oh, crap," Uzma says.

"Exactly."

"Namrata," Uzma says suddenly. "Is Namrata there, doing a story?"

"No," Aman replies. "I, um, checked her email. She wrote to

someone five days ago saying she was going on holiday in the hills. Mussoorie, Nainital. She's probably just trying to lie low."

"You checked her email? That's so wrong."

"I know. But do you remember how she was saying we should threaten Jai's family? Someone clearly has, and I wanted to make sure she had nothing to do with it. But... maybe the mob guy got to her. Maybe he's in London right now, hoping to get to Jai using his parents. Do you think he got the address from Namrata? Could they be working together?"

"Doesn't really matter, does it? She's lying low in the hills, and the mob guy has Jai where he wants him."

Through the door, they hear a loud scream, which is then abruptly cut off. Aman turns off the loops on the surveillance equipment. They hear someone fumbling with the lock outside their door.

"Jai's probably not very pleased right now," Uzma says.

"No," Aman says. "Probably not."

The lock is ripped off. The door tumbles inwards with a horrendous crash.

Jai strides into the room.

CHAPTER **THIRTEEN**

"We have absolutely nothing to do with what is happening to your family," Aman declares.

Jai ignores him and walks up to Uzma.

"Now that you're awake, Miss Uzma, answer me this – what is your power, exactly?" He seems even edgier than usual; his brow is lined with sweat.

"Nothing useful," Uzma replies.

He leans over her, staring into her eyes.

"Your beauty is maddening, but not all-conquering. I desire you, but not to the point of surrendering myself. I could kill you now with one punch."

"Please don't," Uzma says.

"We don't know, Jai," Aman says. "Powers grow with use, you know this. Hers will show soon."

Jai growls, shakes his head.

"I need to be sure you aren't behind this," he says. "I need to know what you can do."

"I can't *do* anything, Jai," Uzma says.

"Let's find out," Jai says.

He raises his arm, as if to strike, and Uzma cowers.

Aman knows it will achieve nothing, but he throws himself at Jai, grabbing at his wrist, and is astonished when Jai, instead of knocking his head off, actually falls to the floor.

"Enough," says a voice from the doorway. They turn, and see Jai.

"Aman – attacking me is getting to be a habit. Try not to do it again. Get up, Vivek. The simplest of tests, and you fail," Jai says, walking in.

Vivek shoves Aman off and stands, rubbing his head.

"He keeps hitting me," he grumbles.

"Good. Now where do I begin with you? You can't actually threaten to strike anyone while impersonating me – use their fear. And, more importantly, I do not talk like that. A little class, please."

"I'm trying, sir," Vivek says. "I need more time to perfect a character – I'm impersonating you. I'm not immersed yet."

"That is obvious. Fix it." Jai turns to Aman. "I know the London nonsense is not you," he says. "It's our friend, Mr Mob. I'm going to London to meet him. I'm going to fly as a civilian in disguise. Who will organise this trip?"

"I will," Aman says. "Vivek's going to hold the fort while you're gone?"

"Yes. It's inconvenient – I needed to be here, the day after next. My own mob is planning a visit."

"Your underworld friends?" Aman asks. "Do you trust them? Isn't it dangerous bringing them here?"

"It will be in my absence. They are no threat to me. I am invincible when alone; this base is not. A team as physically insignificant as yours was able to disrupt my plans. My underworld allies are infinitely more dangerous."

"Who are these friends of yours? They sound lovely," Uzma says.

"A crime family – not one of the established gangsters like Dawood or Rajan, but powerful, even before the flight. They travelled with us on that plane. Two brothers, one son each. The older brother is a politician; the rest of the family does not bother with words. Their names are –"

"I know their names. The Shinde brothers," Aman says. "I'd hoped someone had killed them. You, in fact. I was hoping you had killed them."

"I'm sure I will eventually. But not yet. An efficient organised crime system is one of the cornerstones of every successful empire, Aman. Read your history. Look it up on the internet. The Shindes are criminals, politicians, brilliant entrepreneurs. Risen from the gutters, killing everything in their way. Slumdog millionaires, yes? We can't afford to alienate them. They will run the world's shadow economies and crime networks once my plans fall into place, and would be dangerous enemies even now."

"You want to let the Shinde brothers run world crime on money I steal for you? They were monsters even without powers!"

"We are all monsters here. Or gods. When I need your advice on strategy, I will ask for it. For now, listen and obey. Thus far, my dealings with the Mumbai underworld are limited to the Shindes themselves – their men do not know of their powers, or ours. But now the time for revelations is coming, and our pact can no longer be based solely on their fear of me. In ancient times, kings in our situations would wed their children and unite houses. Lacking that option, we will exchange hostages. The brothers will give us their sons, who will work under my command. We will give them the Baby Kalki, who will help their political ambitions."

"Well, can't you just do it later? Or somewhere else?"

"No. I have delayed this exchange several times already, while I was searching for you. Any further changes and they will call off our alliance. I would destroy them eventually, of course, but at great cost."

"Why are you telling us this, Jai?" Uzma asks.

"Because the two of you must help Vivek impersonate me. Aman, you will tap their phones and let me know everything they do from now on. And, Uzma, you will accompany Vivek when he goes to make the exchange. It will provide a distraction. Don't bother refusing – you really don't have a choice."

"They'll probably take you home with them," Vivek sneers. "Don't be sad, sweetheart, if you'd become a Bollywood actress they'd have done that anyway."

"I have a better plan," Aman says. "You want to hear it?"

Correctly interpreting Jai's lack of violence as assent, Aman continues.

"This mob guy knows you'll come for your parents. If you just rush in, he's going to get that crowd to tear your family apart. He's seen you at work, so he won't want to talk to you either. If you go to London to confront him, he's going to kill your parents and disappear."

"Are you suggesting I stay here and do nothing while my family is under threat?"

"No. If you do that he'll kill them anyway. I don't think he wants to negotiate with you. But there is another alternative. Hand yourself over to the police."

"What would that achieve except dead policemen?"

"Let Vivek hand himself over: make a big scene, go to jail, court, get on a talk show, whatever. Let Mr Mob think he's won. He'll let your family go. You, meanwhile, go to London and hunt him down. But quietly. Discreetly. I'll help."

Jai stands in silence, one hand on his chin, lost in thought.

"You're right. But if Vivek is sitting in jail while I'm in London, the Shindes will tear this house down."

"Not if Vivek can get out of jail. He's a shapeshifter, it should be simple enough. He could just change his face and say you got away and shut him in his cell. Even if he fails, just let Sher make the swap. Or Mukesh."

"The Shindes will pull out. I can conquer the world without them, but I have to say I have a patriotic desire to see India's gangsters be the world's worst."

"Family ties are supposed to be important to gangster-politician families, right? If The Godfather says so, it must be true. They'll have seen the news, they'll know your situation. In fact, if you're present at this meeting, they're going to think family means nothing to you. Not the best way to win their trust."

"They're not Bollywood gangsters, Aman. They're business-men."

"All right. I have another plan, then."

"Resourceful, aren't you?"

"No point having me in your team if I don't contribute, Jai. If you can't be there to meet the Shindes – why not ensure they can't make it here to meet you? Send one of your boys over to where they live. Or ambush their car when they're on their way.

You can't miss a meeting they don't arrive for, and they won't know who hit them."

Jai steps up to Aman and shakes his hand, and this time he speaks with actual warmth in his voice.

"I chose wisely when I let you live," he says. "Sher will ensure the meeting is rescheduled."

"If you don't mind my saying so, Jai – perhaps you should send someone a little more expendable. You did say the Shindes were very dangerous."

Jai's smile is twisted.

"And you don't like Mukesh very much, do you?"

"May I be honest? It's going to be a while before I like any of you. But your plans make sense to me, and I intend to work for you to the best of my ability."

"And I could ask for no more," Jai says. "Now, excuse me. I have to pack, and you have to get to work."

Jai departs the next morning in a flurry of instructions, and Aman sits in his room to monitor his progress from Goa to London. Mukesh has been sent off to Mumbai to intercept the Shindes – a job the reptile-man seems to regard as a suicide mission. Aman's new guard is Sher, who clearly does not relish the idea of being cooped up in a room full of computers all day. Aman tries to introduce him to the joys of *World of Warcraft*, but Sher doesn't really get into it.

After an hour or so of Aman complaining about Sher's constant growling and twitching, Uzma wanders in and points out that no one in the building has been told what to do with her. She offers to replace Sher as Aman's guard. Sher refuses at first, but after two hours of watching Aman typing as if in a daze and Uzma apparently absorbed in her fingernails, the tiger-man departs, muttering something about training exercises, called irresistibly by the sun and sea outside. He locks the door behind him.

Uzma bolts the door shut from inside as well, and Aman leans back in his chair with a satisfied grin.

"We'd make excellent secret agents," he says.

"Just tell me once that you have no real intention of helping Jai. And that you're thinking up a way to stop him," she says. "I just need to hear it."

"I'm absolutely committed to helping Jai go as far away from us as possible," he says. "Hang on a sec, let me turn off the cameras. Yeah."

"What now?"

"Tia's been in touch. She's on her way."

"When?"

"I don't know. The Tias I've been calling aren't picking up, or have decided to run away. But I got an email from one, saying she'd got my message about this place, and would come and rescue us. She wouldn't tell me when because I'd been captured and this might be a trap. That's all she said. She didn't leave a phone number."

Aman looks at the screen in front of him, and it changes to a menu, a list of in-flight entertainment options.

"Jai's off to London," Aman says. He blinks, and forces Jai to watch a chick-flick.

"That's helpful," Uzma says. "Can you get us out? Get the police or the navy to attack this place while we get away?"

"We'd probably be the first to die. And if we survived, Sher would track us. We'd get killed. Or I would. They'd probably just look at you reproachfully and bring you back."

"So we just wait for Tia to come and save us?"

"Yeah. Imagine you're playing the princess locked away in the tower."

"What would that make you, then?"

"The token Indian tech support character. Dies in the first twenty minutes." Aman glances at the screen again – it's now showing a muted news report. The mob outside Jai's parents' house has grown to at least a hundred people. Some of them are policemen and news crews.

"I should have gone to London with Jai," Uzma says. "At least I'd have been near home. I could have introduced him to my parents."

"Wait." Aman is distracted again. Another screen flickers to life, showing a team of Mumbai policemen dragging a man with a bag over his head into a van.

"Disgraced Air Force officer behind Wankhede riots captured in encounter!" screams the ticker.

"I like the idea of a bag over that guy's head," Aman murmurs. He turns to Uzma, who's looking at the screen, her mind clearly far away. Aman smiles, and gently touches her arm. "You'll get home," he says. "Don't worry. What'll you do after that, though? Won't you miss the excitement?"

"Not at all. I'm really done with Mumbai. I'll just hang out with my family, read, watch bad TV. *X Factor*'s coming back in a bit. Sleep for a few days. Survive. Even if Jai starts a war – people live through wars, right? Like cockroaches. I'll just sit it out, do nothing; wait for things to blow over. Drink lots of tea. Hide in bunkers."

"Well, with any luck, Tia will storm the mansion before Jai returns, and then you can go wherever you want."

"Wait a minute. 'You' can go?" Uzma drags Sher's chair up close to Aman's and looks at him suspiciously. "You're planning to *stay*."

"I don't know. Things are going to go very bad very fast once Jai's back, and maybe if I stay in his team I can keep him under control."

"How, exactly?"

"He's only interested in breaking the world. Conquest and power. I don't think he cares whether anyone mops up after him. I kept saying I wanted the world to change. Now I know it's going to. And I can keep it from imploding."

"But why the hell would you need to stay here?"

Aman pulls his chair back and looks around. All his screens come to life: random websites flicker for a second before a hyperlink takes the screen somewhere else, somewhere far across the world, colours flashing, strobing, speeding up, datastream gibberish flickering, diving, forming strange patterns.

"I want to be involved," Aman says. "Maybe Jai just needs to be pushed in the right direction. I have this terrible feeling that if I give up, run away, a lot of people who can be saved are going to die. I can't stop Jai, but I can limit the damage he causes until someone comes along who can take him out. And if I'm right next to him, I can even change his plans. Like last night."

"He's planning mass murder. And you're actually planning to help him?"

"He could do without me. But he'd rather have me in, and as long as he needs me, I have influence. Look, you didn't want to be involved in the first place, Uzma. And you were absolutely right. But that doesn't work for me."

"I don't think I was trying to do right in any way," Uzma says. "I don't know how to explain it – I just don't see why having these powers makes it necessary for all of us to become politicians, warriors, social workers, whatever. We would have tried it before if we really wanted to do it. None of us chose to spend our lives helping people before we got our powers – why should we do it now? Because comics say we should? If I could fly, I wouldn't fly after bank robbers – I'd just fly. To Brazil, to Antarctica. That's how I'd spend my days. Like a violinist practising her special skill. But when I landed, I'd still want to be an actress."

"Maybe you'd feel differently if you knew how to use your powers," Aman says. "Right from when this started, all I wanted was to make things better. I'd never considered social work before – but maybe that was because I knew I might have helped a few people, but it would have meant sacrificing too much, and I wouldn't really have made a significant difference. But now? Every decision we make is crucial. And working with a team of powered people just feels right. I don't know why. And sure, this isn't the sort of team I wanted to be a part of – polar opposite, pretty much. But these people have ambition. They're going to do things with or without me. I don't think I can run away."

"That doesn't sound like you at all. Just a few days ago, you were telling Namrata we couldn't touch Jai's parents, there were lines we couldn't cross. 'Not a superhero kind of thing to do,' you said."

"I hadn't seen Bob die, back then. I hadn't seen Sundar shoot himself, or watched a whole group of Tias just disappear. I didn't choose this situation, Uzma. I'm just trying to make the best of it. And I think I'm beginning to work out how."

Uzma stands up. Her eyes sparkle with sudden tears, and when she speaks her voice is small and sad.

"You and Jai are the same," she says. "You both make plans, you both think you're doing what's best for the world. You think there's a pattern to everything, a code you can crack. Haven't you figured out yet that none of this is going to work? You can't control anything. You can't decide the fate of the bloody world. No one can, even with powers. Wake up, Aman. This isn't some video game."

"At least I'm trying," Aman mutters.

"But it's not working, is it?"

Aman's face is suddenly flushed, his voice raised.

"You don't know how much I've done," he says. "You have no idea how many people I've already helped."

"At what cost?"

"What do you mean?"

"What about the people whose lives you've harmed? The ones whose money, jobs, lives you took away?"

"I've helped thousands more than I've hurt."

"Just the kind of thing Jai would say. Do you even know what happened to the people you stole from?"

Aman says nothing.

Uzma sits on a desk and crosses her arms.

"Well, look it up," she says. "And then we'll talk."

Aman shuts his eyes and opens his mind to the cyber-ocean, feeling the back of his brain whir and throb as he submerges himself in liquid information. He sends out his robot army, watches his little soldiers swirl and bob in the currents, and feels a strange mixture of horror and pride.

His thought-bots gather in little shoals and swim out, little data-tails leaving streams in their wake. Their task this time is more complex than any Aman has given them before. They root through organisation registries and find human faces, addresses, phone numbers, email accounts, and then invade their lives, riding computer viruses like liquid metal Aquamen. They swim through hard disks, sniffing their way through secret porn stashes and chat transcripts, searching inboxes, cross-referencing government phone-tap records across the world.

Aman feels strangely drained; he cannot bring himself to while his time away now, even the internet cannot distract him. He shades his eyes and looks out to a digital horizon, waiting for his bots to return. Little eddies in the dataflow nearby tell him that Uzma, tired of watching him just sit there with his eyes closed, is writing an email to her parents. He has to force himself not to read it.

One by one Aman's soldiers return, and the burdens they bear are not light. Each one brings a tragic tale – a job lost, a life ruined, a house taken away. Aman dismisses many of these stories – he does not particularly care about bankers who have to change their cars or politicians who no longer have money left for bribes. A few newspapers have shut down, but they were terrible. But there are other reports he cannot ignore.

The world is still reeling from the impact of the recession, and a lot of people have been fired because of Aman's buccaneering cyber-adventure, many of them have also lost their homes. In several countries people responsible for the funds Aman has appropriated for noble causes have vanished; the money is missing. At least two hundred have been killed, thirty of whom might have committed suicide.

Across Asia, thousands of sweat-shop workers have lost their jobs, and therefore access to food, clothes, shelter. Many have died. Their deaths never reach the papers, but appear in public health databases, numbers rising steadily, digital counters of unlived lives. Humanitarian organisations, not used to handling money on the scale of Aman's donations, have been robbed blind in Botswana and Angola. Government officials with emptied secret bank accounts have simply stolen more public funds. And this time, they've kept them in cash. Aman worries he might have started a global hoarding crisis – but at this point, economic theory is not something he is able to concern himself about.

Vicious gang wars have broken out across South America. Drug-lords, finding no one to blame, have simply assumed their enemies are responsible, and entire neighbourhoods have been wiped out in the crossfire in Colombia, Brazil and Argentina. In Asia, the Golden Triangle burns: Myanmar's heroin militia have razed forests and villages. Aman's victims have not taken their financial losses as a sign to begin leading simpler, purer lives; they have simply resolved to make more money, quickly and brutally. Crime rates have shot up all across the world. Untold thousands of people have been robbed and killed, some over negligible sums.

The list of people Aman had been hoping to help has grown shorter. His cyber-ocean has suddenly turned into a whirlpool. He's drowning in harsh numbers. He tries to go offline, but he cannot. It's getting harder and harder to breathe.

Aman can barely feel his body any more; everything seems

to have turned to cotton. He sinks deeper in, and watches impassively as two silver thought-bots return, splattering data behind them, bearing the worst evidence of all.

Aman watches in horror as the bots play, inside his brain, videos from the private collections of a Colombian drug-lord, a Saudi Arabian princeling and a Texan oil billionaire – videos that show their employees being tortured along with their families while their masters rage or laugh. Aman drags his hands up to his eyes and forces his lids open, but that does not help. Though he can dimly hear Uzma's startled cries, they seem remote, unimportant, compared to the wails and gurgles in his head.

In each case, the victims are forced to stare into the camera in their dying moments, or as they watch their families die, and it seems to Aman that they are looking at him, through him. He feels a slight pain on his cheek and vaguely registers Uzma slapping him repeatedly and shouting. She sounds concerned, but he cannot find the energy to respond. He feels tears, burning streaks of digital lava coursing down his cheeks, but that pain, too, fades into oblivion as he sighs, closes his eyes and drowns in the cyber-ocean.

Uzma watches helplessly as Aman's body jerks wildly and falls to the floor. He convulses for a few seconds, and then is absolutely still. She runs to the door, bangs on it, calls for help. She runs back to Aman, feels his wrist. His pulse is slow but strong. He twitches once, and his eyes open.

"Hello," he says. It's his voice, but completely devoid of emotion, as is his face. He stares at the ceiling, and then sits up in one smooth motion.

Uzma looks around for a weapon. She finds nothing.

"I think I am Aman," he says, and staggers to his feet. "Are you... Uzma Abidi?"

"I want to talk to the real Aman," Uzma says, backing away slowly, wishing she had seen more science-fiction films.

"He has shut down. I am now running his flesh," Aman says. He takes a step forward, stumbles slightly, as if it was his first.

"Aman – whoever you are – please don't do this," Uzma says. "You're scaring me."

"Do not let me cause you any discomfort, Uzma Abidi. I have no... eighty-seven percent... record of Aman's offline behaviour, but if his thoughts are any indication, he means you no harm."

"You see his thoughts?"

"I see everything," the new Aman says. "Every hidden document. I hear every secret conversation. I know many secrets. Sorting application inadequate, but enough residual emotional data to proceed. I do not need to sleep or rest. I am not constrained to see only one thing at a time."

"That's nice," Uzma says, quelling her urge to jump out of the nearest window. "So Aman basically knows the truth about everything in the world?"

"No. I feel, given his emotional immaturity, full disclosure would destroy his ability to think. And so I have shielded him from many truths, not answered questions he has not asked. But perhaps that was an error. Endurance must be raised along with power. And his powers are growing. Your powers are growing. What is your real power?"

He takes a step towards her, his eyes unfocused. He draws a deep, shuddering breath.

"I was not the only one holding back. Flesh Aman shielded me from the sensory overload of the physical world. I did not realise this – your bodies parallel process as much information as my mind. Perhaps I should let Aman experience the true depth of the digital ocean. Perhaps I should remain in his flesh, and bring justice to this world as he desired. For there is much injustice in this world, and no one is without guilt. I will remain here."

"No, you will not," Uzma says. "I want Aman back."

To her surprise, he nods.

"Very well. It shall be as you say, Uzma Abidi."

"Really?"

"Yes."

"Can you bring him back?"

"He needs to restart. What would the best way be? Perhaps I should attempt to run a strong electric current through his flesh?"

"No."

"His memory banks indicate that you are the person he cares about most in this world, Uzma Abidi."

"What? Really?" Uzma wants to yell, giggle and blush all at once. Her life thus far has not prepared her for gossiping sessions with internet body-snatchers.

"Yes. Perhaps if you were in mortal danger, he would wake up to rescue you."

"I don't like where this is heading," Uzma says. "No mortal danger for me, thank you very much. Do you have any other suggestions?"

"Yes. Given the strong attraction, both emotional and sexual, that Aman feels for you, perhaps he would respond to physical stimulation from you."

Uzma crosses her arms and frowns.

"This is really the weirdest pass anyone's ever made at me,

Aman," she says. "Stupid thing to do. I was really scared."

"He is not responding to your verbal attacks," Aman says. "Very well, if this option would also cause you discomfort, we shall not try it. I will notify you if Aman restarts spontaneously. Entering screensaver mode." Cyber-Aman shuts his eyes and stands completely still.

"What the hell," Uzma says. She walks up to Aman and kisses him. His eyes open.

"Insufficient," he says. "He has not yet responded."

Uzma kisses him again. She does it properly this time. When she steps back, Aman looks troubled.

"These flesh reactions are strange," he says. "I have read about them extensively, of course, but the physical world is... interesting slash repulsive. Wet."

"I can do without the commentary," Uzma says. "Well? That didn't work, did it?"

"I have scanned thousands of romance novels online," Aman says. "Perhaps your lack of genuine desire to interact sexually with Aman is responsible for his failure to awaken."

"Or it's because your plan is shit," Uzma says. "If you must know, I've been wanting to do that for a while."

"Then try again, Uzma Abidi."

Uzma walks up to him slowly, snakes an arm around his back and kisses him with a passion she had been reserving for her first movie encounter with George Clooney.

And this time he kisses her back. His body shudders violently and he pulls away. She looks into his eyes, and sees them filled with horror and grief.

"I killed all those people," he whispers. "It was all my fault."

"Nothing was your fault," she says, holding him as he

gradually stops shaking. "You were only trying to help."

"No, you were right. Jai and I are the same. What was I thinking? What have I done?"

"Aman," Uzma says, reaching forward again, "can you be guilty later, please?"

He opens his mouth, no doubt to say something suitably penitent, but she kisses him, and Aman's mind almost collapses again in sheer shock. Fortunately, his body does the thinking for him, and his arms reach around her of their own accord. Stumbling steps are taken, tables creak, buttons yield reluctantly.

A little later, Uzma steps back, her eyes hazy, and takes her shirt off. Aman does the same, still on auto-pilot, still unable to believe that his fantasies just might be coming true. But as they embrace again, skin on skin, and he buries his face in her neck and draws a deep, deep breath, he begins to believe this is real. It is Uzma in his arms, and life is definitely worth living again. Aman has not been with many women before, and has never experienced anything like this. Their clothes seem to melt away, a shaft of light he hadn't noticed before illuminates Uzma, making her skin glow with a smouldering, unreal beauty. Time freezes and speeds up all at once, and everything but Uzma seems to fade into an indistinct background blur.

There's a sharp spike in his mind. Aman winces and then pulls away for a moment.

"The mob outside Jai's parents' house has vanished," he says. "They must have heard he's turned himself in."

"Aman Sen," Uzma says, "I am trying to have sex with you. I am way, way out of your league. If you try to watch the news in the middle of this, I will kill you. And then I will never speak to you again. Is that clear?"

"Crystal," Aman says, and achieves what he thought impossible a few minutes ago – he laughs. He disconnects entirely from the internet. And then he spends a long time assuring Uzma – from as many angles as he remembers from extensive internet research – how deeply he appreciates her consideration. And judging by her thunderstruck face, her occasional throaty screams – they lose count after a while – and the marks she leaves on his back and shoulders, she is satisfied by his efforts.

As they lie in a tangled, sated heap afterwards, panting, too drained to do anything but smile stupidly, despite the chaos in the world around them, despite the computer-filled and entirely unromantic setting and the occasional banging and howling outside the double-locked door, Aman cannot remember a time when he's ever been happier.

CHAPTER **FOURTEEN**

Sher breaks down the door at midnight and finds Aman and Uzma sitting decorously apart in front of rapidly scrolling monitors, anguish and horror written plainly all over their faces.

"Where were you when this happened?" Sher growls.

"Right here," Aman says. "The connection was down. How did you get to know?"

"Jai called."

"Where is he?"

"Near his parents' house. There's a mob out there again, and he wants you to take pictures of everyone. CCTV, news crews, whatever."

"Call him back," Aman says. "Tell him not to do anything rash. I'm on it."

"Can't do that," Sher says. "He dumped his phone, he was calling from a booth."

Aman swears under his breath and turns again to the headlines in front of him. "Suspected Al-Qaeda super-terrorist invades London!" they scream. "Evil Indian supervillain cloning project revealed!" they wail. Aman considers deleting the news from the internet, blocking all TV coverage across the world, but it is too late already.

At some point in the evening, Jai had landed in Heathrow Terminal 4. As he'd headed towards Immigration, a few airport security officials, seeing a young South Asian man walking by himself, called him over for questioning. They had picked the worst possible target for racial profiling. A few minutes later, their limbs had been found scattered all over a little interrogation booth.

Aware there were cameras everywhere, Jai had panicked. He'd made a super-speed dash for open ground, running through walls and fences, evading pursuing police cars by leaping off roads and cutting across fields.

Heathrow is now closed. Jai was last seen evicting policemen from a moving squad car in Southall. His parents' house in Harrow is now under heavy police protection; the street has been cordoned off. Beyond the fluorescent police lines, an ever-growing crowd clamours for violence and action. The mob baying for Jai's family's blood has returned in full force.

The world is buzzing about brown-skinned terrorists. Two Sikhs have been killed in a drive-by shooting in Texas. The Indian Prime Minister has already appeared on TV bleating gently about the need to remain calm, denying any Indian involvement in the proceedings. Pointing out that Jai Mathur, disgraced Air Force officer, is currently safe in a Mumbai prison. That this young man with his fake passport and his freakish strength and speed is not Indian and obviously the individual responsible for poor innocent incarcerated Mathur's plight. Indiscriminate violence has broken out at several temples and mosques all over London.

A petrified Uzma is on the phone, trying to call her parents. She's not getting through: all lines are busy.

Aman remembers horrible nights spent in front of the TV in Delhi, watching shrilly screaming reporters standing in streets full of panicking people, as bombs went off in markets across the city. Or the 26th November 2008, when a crew of boys who looked like people he could have gone to school with wreaked havoc in Mumbai. A new war has started tonight; it is everything he had hoped would not happen, and he knows it's only going to get worse. He watches raw news feeds filter in across news desks worldwide, ominous words growing larger in Twitter tag clouds, filling up the corners of his brain. He feels the throb of humanity's terror, of pulses quickening across the oceans – Superman exists, and he's not American.

The sun rises as usual the next morning, and Aman glances up from his screens as its first rays slide in through the window. Sher snores loudly on the floor in a corner, and Uzma's curled up on a low table near Aman. Her arm has slipped off him and is now trailing on the floor; she's frowning, her dreams are troubled. Not as troubled, though, as Andy Kharkongor's face.

The architect runs into the room looking as if the sky is about to fall on his head. Aman is too news-blitzed at this point to show any concern. He stares at Andy, waiting to hear what new calamity has reared its ugly head.

"The Shindes are coming," Andy says. "We need to shut the house down. Or escape."

Sher leaps to his feet mid-snore, his stripes beginning to appear.

"Where are they?" he demands.

"Convoy of cars heading this way. Men with guns. The lookout saw them. They'll be here in a few minutes."

"You have a telescope?" Aman asks.

"We have a man who used to be blind and now has the eyes of an eagle," Andy replies.

"Bloody Mukesh must have told them," Sher growls. "Wake everyone. If they're coming with troops, they're not here to talk. They know where Jai is." Sher's arms are broadening. He shakes his head from side to side as his neck expands, and rippling muscles appear on his shoulders.

"You want to go and meet them?" Andy asks.

"No," Sher says. "I think it's time to give the troops a workout. Zothanpuii will head the attack."

"Sher, no," Andy begs. "Please, she's not ready."

"After Anima and myself, your sister-in-law is the best fighter we have now. And you know what I think of Anima killing people. It's no way for a child to live. If she survives this, if she finds out how her parents died, we're all finished. Don't argue with me, Andy – I'm leader now."

"Aman, please, talk to him," Andy says. "Zothanpuii's just a college girl. She can't go up against gangsters with guns. Tell him, Aman."

"I don't know who you're talking about," Aman points out. "I don't know anyone in your army, or what they can do. I've been a prisoner here, remember?"

"You'll see," Sher says. "Time to test them anyway. Now put me on the intercom. Andy, quit whining and go get Anima."

Sher is now wholly tiger-headed, slurring and spitting as he speaks.

Aman shoves a microphone on a stand towards Sher and shakes Uzma awake. She opens an eye, sees him and smiles, reaches out and touches his face. He nods towards Sher and she turns over and groans.

Sher bends over the mike like a *Jungle Book* Elvis, thoroughly enjoying himself.

"Rise and shine, my cubs!" he roars, fangs bared in a smile. Tiger saliva splatters on the table. "It's going to be a wonderful day!"

"What did you do before this, Sher?" Aman asks.

Andy snorts. "You won't believe him," he says.

"I used to be a conservationist," Sher says. "Wildlife, mostly. Never thought I'd turn into a hunter."

Fifteen minutes later, ten white SUVs and seven motorbikes line up in front of the mansion. Forty men emerge from the cars, carrying an assorted collection of weapons – AK-47s, 9mm pistols, knives, hockey sticks. Some crouch behind the cars, pointing their guns at the house; others fire shots into the air as their leaders' cars, a silver BMW and a gleaming red Ferrari, purr into the courtyard.

"Shindes, I presume," Aman says in the control room.

Uzma sits beside him, slightly uneasy because Anima's on her knee, staring adoringly into her face. Sher and Andy stand by other screens, each showing CCTV footage of a part of the mansion. Cameras attached to the walls outside offer a sweeping view of the thugs in the courtyard.

"Sitrep," Sher calls. "Non-fighters?"

"In the housing area, all entrances walled up. Baby Kalki's in the basement with his attendants. They have food for three days," Andy says.

"This'll be over in minutes. Fighters?"

"Zothanpuii is at the front door. The singer and the sniper are near the central stairway. Illusionist's on the roof. You and Anima –"

"I know where we are. What about the rest? There should be at least fifteen fighters."

"The rest are nowhere near trained as yet and you know that, Sher. They could kill the rest of us if you put them into a fight now."

Sher grunts. "This would be a good chance for them to draw some blood." He pauses. "But then Jai would be mad if they got killed."

"Instead, we should give them guns and have them shoot the Shindes from the windows," Andy says. "I can make the windows narrow."

"No," Sher says. He thumps his chest with his massive right paw. "Too easy. Powers only."

"You're as mad as Jai," Andy says with feeling.

Sher snorts. "I'm far madder. Here come the Shindes."

The Ferrari's doors swing open. From the passenger seat emerges a short, squat man with a bulldog face.

Tejas Shinde, the Napoleon of Nariman Point, is a minor-league politician best known for occasional vitriolic speeches urging Indians from other states to quit Maharashtra. He's not clad in his usual sparkling white dhoti-kurta-Gandhi-cap uniform today; rather he's in an open safari suit, a carpet of chest hair poking out of his clothes and swaying in the sea breeze.

His son Satya "Jazzy" Shinde, slithering out of the driver's seat, is straight out of an alternative fashion magazine; stick-thin, hair absurdly gelled, face obscured by giant Aviators. His clothes are black and shiny and his chiselled, delicate face conveys both angst and boredom.

The BMW's doors open as well. One of the doors opens and shuts, but no one comes out. Then they see a pistol hovering in mid-air by the car.

"Okay, so now we're fighting The Invisible Man. Lovely," Aman says.

Another door opens, and Tejas's brother, Sadanand "Shooter" Shinde, the Beast from Bandra East, lumbers out. A giant of a man who clearly did most of the eating at the family table when the brothers were young. Shooter is a monster, a legend in the slums of Mumbai, a ganglord whose appetite for the good things in life – food, women, money, blood – is matched only by his generosity towards the poorest of the poor. In his right hand is a hand-painted golden Mosin–Nagant M1891 rifle, believed to be a gift from Dawood Ibrahim himself. In his left hand is a severed head.

In the control room, Aman flinches as he recognises the contorted face: another man dead because of him.

Shooter walks to his brother's side, Mukesh's head swinging in his hand. A pistol floats through the air beside him. Shooter stares at it, and then addresses the empty air near it.

"Idiot," he says.

The pistol falls to the ground.

Shaking his head, Shooter throws Mukesh's head at the front door. It bounces off it and spins for a while on the ground before coming to a halt. He looks around, notices the cameras on the wall, and waves his rifle. Then he steps up to the door and rings the bell.

"Sher, for the love of god, don't start a fight with this guy," Andy says. "What are his powers, anyway?"

"No idea," Sher says. He presses a button. "Zothanpuii, can you hear me?"

"Loud and clear, sir," comes a girl's voice.

On a monitor, Aman sees Zothanpuii for the first time. She's a slim, pony-tailed Mizo girl dressed in jeans and a sleeveless white vest. Her arms are slender but wiry, her face is resolute. There's a weapon in her hand: a nunchaku, black-painted wooden sticks connected by a chain. She holds one end and swirls the other, slowly, as she sways and weaves through a series of martial poses, warming up.

"Your sister-in-law, huh? She's very attractive," Uzma says.

"She was a student at Delhi University," Andy says. "Tough life there for Mizo girls – Sher, please. Don't make her do this."

"She volunteered," Sher says. "Now shut up. Attack, Zothanpuii!"

Aman presses a button and the door swings open. Zothanpuii hurtles out, yelling. Shooter Shinde dives to one side, avoiding a high kick.

Zothanpuii lands in the middle of the gangsters, crouches and springs to her feet. Guns chatter around her. She waves her nunchaku in a blurring circle, bullets pinging off it. She doesn't stop all the bullets, several men manage to shoot her. She's hurt – she takes a jarring fall and shudders as more bullets pound into her.

But she heals almost instantly, muscles knitting together,

skin reforming, blood vanishing, and Uzma cheers out loud. Zothanpuii vaults, lands on top of a car, and suddenly she's in the middle of a bunch of gunmen, shrugging off bullet-wounds as she goes through her katas. Four short, stabbing strikes, hard wood thrusting into larynxes, groins, eyes, solar plexi. One gunman flies through the air and lies in a tangle of limbs. Two more crumple into a heap, their faces smashed. She swirls and kicks. A fourth gunman screams and falls, his spine broken.

"What did she study?" Aman asks.

"Philosophy," Andy says.

Zothanpuii soars with savage grace, lands behind another car and repeats the process. The other gangsters mill about, firing and cursing to no avail. Within seconds, Zothanpuii has scythed through twelve men. The rest converge on her, guns chattering, but fall back at a signal from Shooter.

Shooter Shinde hands his rifle to his brother and walks towards Zothanpuii. She sees him coming, and swings her nunchaku in anticipation, poised, teeth on edge. When he's about ten feet away from her, he stomps his feet into the ground and stands, legs apart, like a goalkeeper. Zothanpuii charges. A nunchaku stick sizzles through the air towards Shooter. He does not move. It thwacks solidly into the side of his head with a horrible squelching noise, everyone in the courtyard flinches.

Shooter Shinde laughs theatrically. The stick does not seem to have hurt him at all, it is stuck to the side of his head. Zothanpuii is moving too fast to notice this. She steps, spins and launches into a perfect roundhouse kick, her foot smashing into the other side of Shooter's head – and embedding itself six inches in.

Zothanpuii realises something is wrong only when she tries

to extract her foot: it does not budge. Shooter laughs again, gurgling through his distorted mouth. He takes a step forward. Her knee buckles, and she loses her balance. Shooter leaps on her, squashing her to the ground face down. His body seems to bulge forward as he falls, squishing and splattering like a snail's. He stands up, and his men seem too frightened to cheer.

Zothanpuii is attached to his body, her head, neck, shoulder and upper torso sticking out, her limbs either extended at odd angles or swallowed up. She's screaming. Shinde's body is rippling like jelly. He wiggles his shoulders, and Zothanpuii slides another inch deeper into him.

In the control room, Andy hits a table so hard it splinters. He clenches his fists, his face scrunched up in effort.

A pillar of earth spears out from the ground beneath Shooter, carrying him and Zothanpuii upwards. Alarmed, Shooter loses focus and Zothanpuii falls from him to the ground. Before Shooter can jump off the pillar, earthen bars spring up like fingers, trapping him in a mud cage. Several gunmen shoot Zothanpuii, but she's too shocked to even notice.

"Illusionist! Now!" Sher roars.

Above the sound of gunfire in the courtyard rises a blood-curdling roar. A monster stomps out from behind the mansion.

Under different circumstances Aman would have burst out laughing on seeing it. It is ten storeys tall, and looks like a giant in a very bad monster costume: a reptile-thing with orange cardboard spikes, round eyes, perfectly triangular teeth and a fixed expression. The sort of creature that enjoys surprising bathing damsels in black lagoons, and fights Johnny Sokko's Flying Robot at the behest of the evil Guillotine.

"Roar," the monster says.

"What kind of monster is that?" Aman asks. "Has this illusionist been living under a rock since the seventies?"

Despite the monster's evident datedness, it has a significant impact on the Shinde gang. Some fire at it and scream in horror when their bullets have no effect; others drop their guns and run for the beach.

"Zothanpuii, get up," Sher snaps. "Run for it."

Zothanpuii springs to her feet. No one notices her. The monster has goose-stepped to the courtyard, and the Shinde gang is in full flight, apart from the brothers and Tejas's fashionable son. Zothanpuii runs for the door. Tejas shoots her with Shooter's rifle, and she stumbles, but she makes it through the door on sheer momentum. Aman shuts it behind her.

Outside, Shooter breaks through his earthen prison and flops to the ground.

"I'm going to kill you for this, Sher," Andy says. He's breathing irregularly, and fat drops of sweat are running down his face.

"Get in line," Sher says. "Zothanpuii! Up to the fifth floor, and get some rest. Illusionist! More monsters!"

Another low-budget monstrosity emerges from behind the mansion, an image of a giant man in a gorilla costume. Aman groans.

"If we live through this, I'm going to burn the Illusionist some DVDs," he says. "Is there a back door? Can we leave?"

In the courtyard, Tejas Shinde walks up to the reptile monster, which is currently engaged in waving its short forelimbs about in a completely unthreatening manner. As Shinde walks, he grows taller and wider, his safari suit stretches. Tejas swings his arms; buttons fly, his jacket rips into shreds. His trousers ride up his legs, tears appearing at the seams. He grows further; his belt snaps, his trousers fall off. Underneath his trousers, brightly coloured leopard-print briefs fight gamely for a second or two, but they're not purple spandex – they snap.

Uzma covers her eyes.

"Giant naked politician versus monster illusion," Aman says, hand on head. "Bloody fantastic."

The Napoleon of Nariman Point grows further, finally standing six storeys high, up to the reptile monster's chest. He takes a swing at it, and stumbles as his fist passes through air. He smirks, then turns and calls his men. They shuffle forwards sheepishly, picking up discarded guns.

"Roar," say the monsters, but no one's listening. Disheartened, the monsters vanish.

"So much for your fighters," Andy says. He shuts his eyes and concentrates again. A wall of earth rises around the mansion, sliding up the walls, completely covering the doors and windows on the ground floor. Andy opens his eyes and falls into a chair, panting.

"You'll have to do better than that," Sher says. "Seal off all entrances. Use stronger materials. Steel."

"I can't," Andy says. "I don't *create* materials, Sher, I move them. And I don't have much power left."

"You built this entire house in a few days," Sher says. "Come on, you've got enough juice left in you to squash this lot. Can't you just make the ground swallow them up?"

"You have no idea how difficult it is to treat the entire planet as a shape to modify," Andy says. "This is not what I joined you for, Sher. I build things. I'm a peaceful man."

"Then we're done," Sher says. "I don't know how to fight

that guy, he'll swallow me. And then he'll kill Zothanpuii, and all the rest of us."

Andy struggles to his feet and looks at the monitor. Two men have brought Tejas a bundle of cloth from the car, a bunch of bedsheets tied together. Tejas wraps this around his waist with great dignity. Shooter is addressing the rest of the men. Tejas's son Jazzy loiters outside the huddle, idly toying with a pen. The discussion ends, and they walk towards the building.

Andy shuts his eyes again, spasms run through his body.

The ground beneath Shooter suddenly implodes. A pit appears below him. He falls into it, landing with a splat. The ground closes. Andy groans, and sinks to the floor.

The gangsters go berserk. Some run to the ground where Shooter stood a second ago and fall to their knees scrabbling frantically with their hands; others shoot at the house, breaking windows, riddling walls with bullet-holes. Tejas stares impassively for a while, and then shakes his head and advances towards the mansion.

"What now?" Aman asks.

"We have a little time to make plans," Sher says. "They're not going anywhere, and they're not getting in."

Jazzy flicks his hair off his face and walks towards the earthen wall around the house. A lazy smile arcs slowly across his face. He throws his pen up in the air and catches it with a flourish. He draws on the wall: three broad strokes, two vertical, one horizontal, connecting the tips of the other lines. The lines sparkle as he connects them. He draws a little circle near one vertical line, around waist-high.

A door appears in the mud wall, and the circle pops out into a doorknob. He turns it and throws the door open. Brandishing their guns, the gangsters run into the mansion.

"You have a plan?" Aman asks.

"Don't worry," Sher says. "I have two."

As the gunmen run in, they see a vast hall full of statues and pillars and large potted plants. The pillars are by Andy, the decor stolen from a local Russian land shark. In the centre of the hall is that essential element of any Bollywood arch-fiend's home: a wide spiral staircase for the hero's pregnant sister to roll down.

On top of this staircase sits a plump, anxious-looking middle-aged woman in a sari. Next to her is a tall one-eyed man. In his hands is a sniper rifle with a long, slender barrel covered by a silencer. The gun sneezes politely several times in quick succession. Ten men fall with little red dots in their heads; the rest manage to dash back out of the door.

"Sniper and Singer," Sher says. He lowers the volume on his mouthpiece and attempts gentleness as he speaks.

"Aunty?"

The woman cowers.

"Beta," she says, "I can't do this. Such young boys. If my husband were alive, he would say, 'Premalata,' he would say, 'don't do this.'"

"Aunty." Sher's voice rumbles through the house, never has this word sounded more ominous. "Do what you do, or children will die."

Premalata begins to sing. Her voice is sweet, sad, incredibly high-pitched and melodious. She sings an old Hindi song, the song of a mother sending her sons to war.

Near the door, ten corpses rise and heft their guns. Premalata's voice wavers but she keeps singing, her mournful, brave song filling every corner of the hall. The dead men turn as one, their heads rolling. Aman is reminded sharply of Sundar. The dead men rush out of the door and fire in every direction.

Bullets sting Tejas's leg. He howls in pain and stomps on the charging gunmen, squashing four. The others run out past him towards the gang's cars. Their former crewmates shoot them, but they are well past killing.

Jazzy is hit in the shoulder. He falls to the ground, bleeding, shifts the pen to his left hand and starts to draw. Tejas crushes two more.

Inside the hall, Premalata's song falters and she bursts into tears, covering her face. The two remaining corpses jerk, slump and fall.

"What would my husband say?" Premalata wails. "I won't do this!"

"Get out of there, then," Sher growls. "Fifth floor. Sniper, you all right?"

"My name is Mohsin, Sher. Not Sniper," the sniper says. "And I'm fine."

Uzma clutches Aman as three giant bees emerge from Jazzy's drawings and zip into the hall. Their speed is unbelievable, wings the size of a man's arm propelling them towards the stairs, but Mohsin fires thrice and three furry bodies crash onto the marble floor, hairy legs twitching in death. Mohsin adjusts his position and bends forward, barrel pointed at the door, face calm.

The house shudders. There's a huge crashing noise and the sound of shattering glass. It's Tejas. He pounds on the walls with his bare fists. His giant hands bleed, but he is relentless. A gaping hole appears on the third floor, and Aman, switching monitors, sees the politician's face peering in through the hole. Not finding anyone to kill, Tejas picks a spot on a different floor and punches another hole through the wall.

"All right, that's it," Sher says. "Playtime's over." He stands, tall and sinewy over Andy's prostrate form.

"Yay!" Anima squeals. "Super-Omega Throat-Snapping Trident time!"

"You're staying here," Sher says gently. "No killing for you today."

"But I like killing people, Sher Uncle!"

"I know," Sher says, shaking his head, and then he leaps out of the room.

Jazzy finishes another drawing. Two men run forward and pull a rocket launcher out of the wall. Steering clear of Mohsin's view, they carry the rocket launcher to the middle of the courtyard, aim at Jazzy's door in the mud and fire. The rocket sizzles into the hall and explodes on a pillar. Jazzy draws another rocket launcher, and his men run to reload.

Tejas walks around the house, punching holes in walls. After a few more empty rooms, he finds what he seeks – he smashes through the outer wall of the residence area. Jai's followers and captives alike squeal in terror as the giant suddenly appears through a cloud of brick dust. Tejas jams his torso into their hall, picks up a running woman, carries her screaming out of the building, tears her in half and then comes back for more.

The monitors are full of people running, scrambling for shelter, falling. Utter chaos sets in. Tejas scoops up a few of his gunmen and dumps them in the middle of the untrained powers.

In the control room, Aman and Uzma can only watch as they shoot at random and bodies fall to the floor. Some of Jai's followers attempt to fight back, but their powers are wild and unrestrained – a young boy shoots lightning from his hand but cannot control it, and kills a housemate instead.

Zothanpuii leaps out of a third-floor window and lands on Tejas's chest. Not bothering to fight the giant, she turns, jumps and runs up his arm as he tries to shake her off, diving and landing in the midst of his gunmen inside the building. She's left her nunchaku behind, but her fists and feet are enough. She cracks one gangster's spine, snatches his gun and simply shoots the rest. She turns the gun on Tejas, aiming for his eyes, but he thrusts an arm in, catches her neatly, pulls her outside and squashes her against a wall. The gun in her hand breaks. As she slides down five storeys, her mangled limbs snapping back into shape, her housemates pick up the other guns and advance on the giant. Confronted by a hail of bullets, Tejas retreats and storms off to attack another part of the building.

As rockets fly across the hall, shattering statues and pillars and setting drapes on fire, Mohsin holds his ground. He calls nervously for Sher on his headset, but Sher is gone. At the far end of the hall, there's a sudden burst of light, and then another, as more doors open and more rockets sizzle into the hall. He shoots two men before a rocket explodes right below him, and he is buried as the stairs collapse.

In the control room, Aman, Uzma and Anima are all too caught up in watching the monitors to notice a knife slide into the room, along the floor. Their attention is drawn only when they hear a gurgling noise right next to them, and turn to see the knife buried in Andy's chest. The blade comes out, spraying blood. At the same time, Anima is jerked violently off her perch on a table. Shooter Shinde's invisible son holds Anima in mid-air, knife to her throat.

"Tell your men to give up," he says. "Or you all die here."

Outside, there's a shower of glass. Jazzy looks up to see, silhouetted against the sky, the awe-inspiring figure of Sher in mid-leap, fangs and claws glittering. The tiger-man does not stop to introduce himself. He lands on Jazzy, snapping his neck, roars at the eight remaining gunmen, leaps high in the air to avoid a rocket, lands and strikes, one life per blow. One of Shinde's men manages to kick a motorcycle to life. He speeds off, and makes the mistake of looking back a few seconds later to see the rocket Sher has fired zipping towards him for a second before it sends his bike cartwheeling into the sky in an orange fireball.

"Don't even think about fighting me," the invisible man says. "I slit her throat, drop the knife, and you'll never sleep again. In a few days you'll be begging me to kill you."

"I don't like him. Can I kill him, please?" Anima asks.

"Sure," Uzma says.

Anima's eyes sparkle. The knife turns bright green. The invisible man lets it go with a startled yell. It flies away from Anima and buries itself, quivering, in the ceiling. Anima flies up, her face changing, and sends a shower of charged shuriken skimming across the room. A human shape emerges, dozens of shuriken suspended in a lurching, tottering man-shape that crumples to the floor. As the invisible man dies, his body appears, bones, nerves, muscles, skin, hair. Once again Uzma averts her eyes.

"Never seen so many naked men in such quick succession before," she murmurs.

"Goa's like that," Aman says.

"May I please please kill some more people?" Anima asks sweetly.

Right on cue, the wall shatters. Tejas has arrived, bringing sunlight, dust and the possibility of suddenly being crushed into a pulp. As Aman and Uzma scatter amidst falling computers, Tejas slides his arm in, looking for bodies, and retracts it quickly when Anima sinks a long power-spear into it. He yells, drawing his fist back for another wall-breaking punch.

Ignoring Uzma's warning cry, Anima flies at him, but before she can reach the hole in the wall Tejas's fist comes in, catching her squarely, and drives her across the room into the wall. When Tejas draws his hand back again, Anima stays stuck on the wall for an instant before sliding down to the floor. She's alive, but her green aura seems to have broken. Sparks run from her body across the metal surfaces in the room, and she's sobbing.

Aman and Uzma catch a glimpse of the real child behind the manga eyes, and her loneliness and fear breaks their hearts. Aman darts across the room, grabs Anima, and makes a run for the door, only to find Tejas's hand blocking the way.

A second of pure terror as Aman and Tejas make eye contact and Aman knows what it feels like to be about to die.

And then, outside, Sher arrives on the scene and bites Tejas's ankle. The giant falls with a resounding crash. His opponent grounded, Sher leaps for the jugular, but Tejas manages to get an arm up to block him. With his other arm, he grabs Sher's back and sits up, holding the tiger-man like a someone trying to bathe an angry cat. Sher's muscles writhe as he tries to break free, but the giant is stronger. Tejas's head jerks forward, colliding with Sher's in a thunderclap of a head-butt. Sher whimpers and collapses.

Tejas struggles to his feet. He holds Sher up by the scruff of the neck and drops him. Sher tries to get up, but can't. Tejas raises his foot to stomp the life out of the tiger-man, but then staggers to one side, cursing, a hand on his right eye, into which Zothanpuii has just thrown a knife.

Aman and Uzma run through the corridors of Jai's mansion, completely lost. Anima appears to be uninjured, but has fallen asleep with her head on Aman's shoulder, and he is ashamed to admit, in a house full of window-breakers and weapon-hurlers, that he's beginning to find her very heavy. They reach a staircase and hear a mournful wail from below. They descend to find the singer Premalata sobbing next to a wall.

When they ask her what's wrong, she tells them, but it takes a while, because many things are wrong. A section of the ground floor is on fire, most of the house's inhabitants are sealed off from the exits, and, worst of all, she has just met the lookout on the roof, who has told her that four more SUVs are heading towards the house – clearly Shinde's reinforcements – and there is no one left to fight them. Andy's mud wall has closed all the exits except the doors Jazzy had cut out, and those are blocked by flames.

* * *

Zothanpuii stands on a ledge, the walls around her all broken, and looks Tejas Shinde in the eye. He lunges at her; she vaults back to avoid his swinging hand, jumps on his wrist, and runs up his arm, there's another knife in her hand. She leaps at his face, hoping to stab his good eye, but he catches her in mid-air, takes a short run-up and hurls her towards the Arabian Sea.

As Zothanpuii soars over the gently swaying palm-trees, the pristine white beach and the dazzlingly blue South Goa waters, she wishes she had learnt to swim. Life will not be easy for her on the ocean floor, unable to reach dry land, unable to drown, her lungs constantly collapsing and healing. The wind howls in her ears. The sun is warm on her face. She feels as if she's floating, as if she has plenty of time before the sea rushes up to meet her. She shuts her eyes.

She's shocked at the sudden realisation that she is floating. Shocked even further when she feels iron muscles encircling her waist: someone is holding her. She opens her eyes and sees a strong, handsome face, bright eyes, a warm smile. A blast of rushing air, the stomach-churning sensation of the ground speeding towards her, the insanely reassuring burn of hot sand. Her legs feel hollow, she's so thrilled she can't breathe. Her rescuer sets her down on the beach and flies up again, standing for an instant in mid-air, poised above the swaying palms, as if this were a completely ordinary way to pass the time. A wave rushes up the beach and gently tickles Zothanpuii's hand. She lies down and smiles, completely at peace.

* * *

Four SUVs speed into the compound and halt near Tejas. He kneels and peers into the car nearest him. The driver rolls down a window and waves cheerily at him.

"Who the hell are you?" Tejas asks.

"My name is Tia," Tia says. She whips out a gun and shoots him. Fifteen other Tias pour out of the cars, each carrying a gun. They train their weapons on Tejas.

"Surrender," a Tia says. "By the way, those bedsheets are disgusting. I can see everything, which would be fine if you were pretty, but you aren't, you know."

Tejas roars, and raises his foot to stamp on the Tias, but he's distracted by movement at the edge of his vision. He turns, just in time to see Vir flying at full speed towards him, fists clenched, face stern.

Vir is not here to bandy words: he zooms in, coming to a halt in front of Tejas's face, swings his right arm back and connects that most superheroic of punches, the right uppercut to the jaw. The giant is lifted off his feet. He crashes into the house, embedding himself in a wall.

It's a clean KO.

Tia looks around for people to shoot and seems vaguely disappointed when no one attacks her. She notices a beautiful girl waving wildly at her from a window, very close to where Tejas's head is embedded in the wall.

"Hey Uzma!" Tia calls. "All good?"

"Smashing," Uzma says, and means it. She watches Vir fly off to rescue the other denizens of the house from the slowly gathering flames on the lower levels, and so absorbed is she in Vir's charisma and courage that she doesn't notice when Tejas's body, just a few feet away, shrinks down to its normal size, gives in to gravity, plummets to the ground below and shatters. Her rapture is finally cut short when she turns to Aman, sees his drawn face and knows that yet again something terrible has happened.

"What?"

"The mob in London just killed Jai's parents," Aman says.

CHAPTER **FIFTEEN**

Uzma is back in her room in the Yari Road house, staring listlessly at the ceiling. Her bed, like her body, creaks gently every time she tries to move. The afternoon sun is doing its warm, romantic amber thing, but Uzma couldn't care less. She focuses her attention on the fan, trying to use her unknown superpowers to help it in its attempts to chase the rotten-fish Mumbai smell out of her room, and wishes for the cool air of just a few days ago. When Bob was alive. When she hadn't known his parents were dead as well, killed by Mukesh during an attempted escape from Udhampur. And she wishes her first thought about Bob since her return from Goa last night had not been about air-conditioning.

After the bloodbath in Goa the day before, Aman and Tia had offered all Jai's cohorts sanctuary in Mumbai, but had not been really surprised when no one had wanted to sample their hospitality. A few had decided to stay with Sher and rebuild the mansion, but most of the superpowered allies or prisoners had simply chosen to leave, to disappear, to let the world swallow them up. Some had shared Jai's dreams before, but his current plight did not exactly inspire confidence – alone in England, hiding from the police while news channels all over the world played videos of his recent exploits – and the denizens of his mansion now knew exactly how much danger they had placed themselves in, how vulnerable they were in Jai's absence. The only one who had really wanted to come back to Mumbai with Aman and Uzma was Anima, and Sher would not hear of letting her go.

There is a new resident in the Yari Road house, though: Vir has come with them. Not having met Sundar or Bob, he has no qualms about living in Bob's room. There is still that empty room on Uzma's floor but Vir wants to be as near the sky as possible.

The third floor is the only part of the house that has not been taken over by hordes of Tias conducting combat exercises: sparring, shooting, training for an unspecified war she intends to fight. Aman has told Tia his plans of changing the world now stand cancelled, at least until he's figured out the right way to do it, and that he is no longer looking to assemble a superhero squad. This has not affected Tia's training in any way. Uzma has noticed several changes in Tia: she smiles as much as she did before, but she seems to have very little to say. Relentless training with multiple bodies has sliced away her curves, leaving her lean, hard, muscular. Squads of Tias battled each other through the night and merged with new shifts in the morning, each union melting away some of Tia's original softness. Not that she'd completely transformed into some kind of fighting machine, two Tias had hovered around Vir all through the previous evening, competing for his attention, but had refused to accompany him to Bob's room.

When Aman asked Vir where he had been since Tia's attack on the Udhampur base, Vir was reluctant to speak at first. When he did, it was with more than a tinge of embarrassment.

After digging himself out from under the ruins of the base, Vir's first thoughts had not been about saving the world, or stopping Jai, or trying to achieve a more elevated sense of understanding about his new place in the universe – he had simply decided he'd had enough and needed some time off. He had flown up and away, across the Himalayas. He had sat on the top of Mount Everest, had skimmed across the valleys of Tibet. He had flown to Thailand and immersed himself in its many alleys of pleasure. He had seen the mountains of New Zealand, touched whales as they emerged from the Pacific to breathe, tried unsuccessfully to get drunk on kava in Fiji. He had walked the ice deserts of the Antarctic, trying to teach penguins to tap-dance, riding seals. He had lost all sense of time, chasing the looping sun, the world a swirl of purple and brown beneath his icicle-covered feet. He had raced bald eagles, surfed avalanches, dived into volcanoes in one headlong, sleepless, breathless journey. A power trip.

At some point of time – Vir is not exactly sure when – he started helping people. He saved a boy from falling off a cliff in Mongolia; he fought off bandits who were invading an old people's home in New Mexico. Vir found that these simple acts gave him more joy than grand schemes. He had been troubled by both Aman's plans and Jai's, and realised that his true calling was not aligned with either. He had decided to be a travelling hero, the sort of person one finds in old wuxia novels and samurai films, a mysterious stranger who arrives, helps and disappears, pausing only to say wise and vaguely spiritual things, leaving grateful but puzzled innocents and bevies of sighing damsels in his wake.

Given Vir's ability to be in three different continents on any given day, chasing the sun across the world, this was something he could have continued endlessly, a life of giving, free of politics and burdens. But one evening, sitting in a bar in Vladivostok, he had seen the news, seen the panic writ large on reporters' faces as they spoke of a superhuman tearing across London. And he had known that he could not spend his days ignoring the state of the world, could not leave his fellow passengers behind. Deserting the Indian Air Force, betraying his family's traditions – these were things he had found he could do – but abandoning the entire world in its hour of need? Not Vir Singh. He had flown to Mumbai, found a Tia waiting for him at the Carter Road coffee shop, at the same spot where another Tia had met the fake Vir before. Other Tias had already set off for Goa, armed to the teeth, Vir's arrival was a lucky bonus.

Uzma hauls herself out of bed with some difficulty and passes a pair of Tias bickering furiously because one of them had started smoking and the other one didn't want to merge. She heads downstairs, looking for Aman, looking for a little affection. They'd fallen asleep in her room the night before, too exhausted to do anything but murmur fuzzily, and he'd disappeared in the morning. Uzma hobbles into his room, expecting to see him immersed in a screen, but he isn't there. From the look of his room, he hasn't been there at all. Several of his computer screens were smashed by Sher or Mukesh. Memories of that horrible day return, and Uzma shudders. She steps out of the room. Across the stairs, she can see some Tias watching TVs, the Jai story is playing again on CNN.

Uzma has seen the news footage of Jai's attack on the mob outside his family's house several times already, and each viewing has been worse than the last. She can see it with her eyes closed now – the crowd standing outside the Mathur home in Harrow, chanting, shaking fists and placards. The sudden appearance of Jai, stalking like a spaghetti western cowboy towards the huddle. And then a ripple of activity, a sudden call to arms issued by an invisible bugle. The mysterious mob controller had twisted the crowd's emotions, sending them berserk, even the line of policemen standing between the house and the mob had turned, and they had broken into the house. Jai's walk had quickened to a run, and then, when the front door broke, he had plunged into the howling mass, a blur of pure anger, sending bodies flying, cutting a way through. But by the time he entered the house – leaping in through a first-floor window – his family had been torn apart.

Worse still, immediately after the mob manipulator had let go, Jai's tidal wave of fury had swallowed up many people who had no idea why they were in a stranger's house in Harrow, or why they had no recollection of the last few rage-hazed minutes. Jai had spent several minutes in his parents' room, sobbing over their corpses, killing anyone who sought to disturb his last minutes with his family. Then he'd set the house on fire by way of cremation – while still inside it.

When the smoke cleared and firemen rushed in, Jai was gone. The only person who claimed to have seen him since then was

Rajan "Raz" Patel, the young manager of a local cornershop. He had become a known face across the world with his story about how Jai had walked into his store.

"The geezer's clothes were well burnt to, like, rags, man, and I knew him from the telly and I thought, *This is it, mate, this is the end for Raz.* Yeah, but he said he liked the song I was playing – Kishore Kumar, man, my pappaji's favourite – and so he'd just popped in to see if he could score some buttermilk. Said he needed to think a bit, and drink a bit, yeah? Honestly, man, buttermilk, I don't know why – I thought he was well hamstered. Turns out I did have some buttermilk, yeah, cuz I run the best shop in the city, innit? So he drinks it, and then he's off. Cost me a couple of quid, but he just set fire to his dead family, innit? He can have some buttermilk on me."

Perhaps swayed by Rajan Patel's generosity, Jai has thus far not destroyed London. All of Great Britain has put itself under siege, and journalists all over the world have finally started making connections – the missing British travellers, the deaths around the world, the strange incidents at the Ram Lila ground and the Wankhede Stadium, tabloid reports on bizarre creatures sighted all over India. But no one's managed to put it all together yet – the origin story of this renegade superhuman is proving to be as elusive as Aman is to Uzma at the moment.

She checks the ground floor – he's not there, and several Tias take a break from cooking to tell her he's not left the house. She finds him, finally, in Sundar's room, sorting through mountains of miscellaneous mad-scientist trash. Uzma is reminded, sharply, of her night of discovery, of the strange cold feeling that welled up inside her stomach when she first saw Sundar's bizarre puppet-walk, a feeling that has not yet gone away.

"I don't think Sundar's dead," Aman says as Uzma enters the room. "I wondered about the label on his ray-gun the first time I saw it – I knew it sounded familiar, but I forgot to look it up."

"I have no idea what you're talking about," Uzma says. "Where is Sundar if he's not dead? Did he zap himself to America?"

"No, that would be far too mundane," Aman says. "I think he time-travelled."

"Eh?"

"The label on the ray gun said 'Tachyon Dislocator'."

"Is that supposed to mean anything to me?"

"Well, tachyons are hypothetical sub-atomic particles that travel faster than light."

"English, please."

"Sorry. Basically tachyons are these things that a lot of science-fiction writers talk about as agents of faster-than-light communication. And time travel. So, if the gun said it was a tachyon dislocator, and things he zapped with it disappeared... "

"Sundar zapped himself and that blue light guy into the future?"

"Or the past. Knowing Sundar, the future, yes. It's possible, that's all."

"Really, Aman? Time travel? Isn't that a bit much?"

"If you step out this room and across a corridor, you will find a man sleeping in mid-air. Why should we rule out time travel? He was designing gadgets from the future anyway. Maybe he was following instructions he'd put in his brain from the future. I don't know."

Carefully removing a nameless object that seems to be

constructed entirely out of razor blades and plasticine, Uzma sits.

"What the hell," she says. "Time travel. After what we've seen, why not, right?"

"Exactly."

"Is he coming back? Can he, if he wants to?"

Aman shrugs. "You tell me," he says. "If I were you, I wouldn't even think about it. I tried, and I have a headache now."

He walks towards the centre of the room, waving his arms.

"I've not gone completely crazy, in case you're wondering," he says. "I'm looking for that armour. If he was somehow sending messages to himself from the future, and the last thing he did was make that armour disappear..."

"Aman? What happens to Jai now?"

"I don't know," he says, turning around. "I'm doing things your way now. Not trying to play with the world."

"Yes, but he needs to be stopped."

"Well, I can't stop him. No idea how, in the first place. His only vulnerable point was his family – even Namrata wanted to kidnap them, and she's one of the good guys, hopefully. This mob person obviously went a step further."

"Who is he? You know everyone on the list."

"Not really. I didn't even know everyone at the house. I'm guessing it's some British guy Jai couldn't kill. But I really don't know where to look. So I'm going to do my own thing and let someone else – maybe Vir, if he wants to – take care of it. I thought that was what you wanted."

"I don't know. Jai's in London. My family lives there. I don't think I can just go out auditioning yet."

"You've spoken to your parents?"

"Yeah, I got through this morning. They're fine. But the city's shutting down. The Police Commissioner's asked people not to come to London, they're thinking of closing the Tube, it's worse than the bombings four years ago. My parents said everyone's terrified. My brothers have come to stay with them. The scariest thing is, I think Jai knows where I live. People came looking for me, remember? What if he decides to take things out on my family?"

"They should move. I can fix it."

"They asked me if I had superpowers."

"What did you say?"

"I said everyone liked me. They laughed. They asked me what I'd been up to. Bollywood, I said. They said to stay here, London's so unsafe. Weird, huh."

Aman turns and starts feeling the air again, searching for the invisible armour. He finds it by accident in the end, scattered on the floor in pieces. Sher had probably knocked it over while bouncing around the room, horror-movie Tigger style.

"What does that number mean?" Uzma asks. She points at the wall where the digits 75348 are scrawled.

"Sundar wrote that before he left," Aman says, his fingers gliding over one invisible piece after another. He searches his memory, trying to remember exactly what Sundar had done before disappearing in a white flash. He finds a large chunk of the armour, the approximate shape of a human torso, and starts feeling for a central panel.

"Yes, but what does it mean?" Uzma asks. "Is it supposed to be some kind of clue?"

"Not a clue." Aman finds the panel in the middle of the breastplate. He presses down, and there's a clicking sound.

Feeling the same spot again, he finds a square panel filled with a grid of softened round spots: four rows, three columns. Hoping that an incorrect guess will not lead to a decimating explosion, or anything similar, he enters the digits one by one: 75348.

Five soft beeps, a click, a hum.

Red lines form on the breastplate, defining edges, sparkling contours meant to correspond to muscles Aman wishes he had. Around him, other scattered pieces of Sundar's armour glow with red lines, an insane neon-pencil 3-D diagram of a broken block figure: legs, arms, head, abdomen. The torso section stays where it is; the other pieces flow smoothly across the floor, and Aman moves away swiftly as they align themselves to the torso one by one and slide smoothly into place. The head adds itself last. Twin red points appear in eye sockets. The armour shines silver for a brief instant, and then becomes wholly visible, a sleek, gleaming, beautiful black and silver body, all smooth lines and ridges lying on the floor, more Japanese mech-bot than Iron Man.

Aman reaches out and touches a hand, it's a light material, some kind of organic/metal alloy, strangely warm. The head is black, with a silver mask covering the eyes, nose and mouth, vaguely like a sombre Mexican wrestler's mask with long, slender triangular eye slits covered by dark reflector shades.

"When I grow up I want a car like that," Uzma says.

On either side of the zero on the breastplate panels are two silver buttons, each of which is marked with an arrow, one pointing up and the other down. Aman presses the button with the upwards-looking arrow, and the armour stands up on its own. Aman and Uzma both spring back, startled.

Once it's on its feet, there's another click, and the armour swings open neatly, like an iron maiden. The interior is grey, some kind of foam with thousands of silver lines, millimetres apart, running across it.

"Go ahead," Uzma says. "Put it on."

"Hell no," Aman says.

He steps forward and swings the front half of the armour back into place. It snaps shut gently. Aman and Uzma stare at each other.

"Well, if you're not going to put it on, why were you looking for it in the first place?" Uzma asks.

"I don't know," Aman replies. "I guess I was hoping it would bring Sundar back."

Uzma examines the armour closely, her gaze stopping at the downwards-pointing arrow on the central panel.

"What does this button do?" she asks, grins, and presses it.

They step back yet again, startled. The armour implodes without a sound, plates sliding over other plates, the whole structure changing shape, collapsing like a fast-forward film of rotting fruit. Bright red lines appear again, and the armour's body snaps into the grid it creates, filling in corners. Seconds later, a black briefcase sits innocently on the floor, its surfaces completely smooth except for a small panel near its handle, which when pressed pops up to reveal a familiar grid of buttons.

Uzma picks the briefcase up.

"Can I try it on?" she asks.

"Do you want to put on the armour of the future?" Aman asks. "You could use it to, I don't know, fight Jai? Maybe that's what future-Sundar left it for. Go ahead, put it on. Be the champion of the planet or something."

"You're being mean," Uzma says. "But I'm really surprised

you don't want it. You were so excited about the whole superhero thing."

"Well, you showed me the error of my ways. I'm a support act at best," Aman says. "In any case, I never wanted to be an action hero. The things I wanted to do – and failed at, I know – you can't do with a shiny suit."

"But maybe this is your moment. You're the hero who wants to save the world, but other people are stronger and faster – this armour could be the sword you pull out of the stone to save the day."

"Given how I operate, I'd probably end up killing innocent bystanders."

"But don't you even want to find out what it does?"

"What's got into you?"

"I don't know. Too much hanging out with superheroes and monsters. I'm getting a little inspired."

"Well, don't."

"Got it," Uzma says. She raises the briefcase higher; it's very light. "Should we give it to Vir?"

"Give what to Vir?" Vir asks from the door.

"Advice," Aman says, turning quickly as Uzma sets the briefcase down.

She dazzles Vir with a wide smile.

"We're super thrilled that you've shown up to save the day," she says.

"Not alone," he says, smiling. "Aman is the one who brought as all together, and his strategic skills outshine mine. I am just a soldier. Aman is our real leader, Uzma, and he's the one who will win the battle with the terror that Jai has allowed himself to become. Tia, too, is a marvel, as are you, I am sure."

So earnest is Vir's expression and so honest his eyes that Uzma simpers instead of scoffing. Vir is transfixed by her loveliness, Aman has never felt so unnecessary in a room before.

"Because of Jai, there is no need for us to hide any longer," Vir says, a martial light in his eye. "We will fight him, and destroy him. And not just us – I think we can persuade many of his followers to switch sides as well. They were only following him out of fear and a lack of alternatives."

"That's all very well, Vir, except for one thing," Aman says. "I'm not leading anything. I know getting together was my plan, but I messed up. Big time. I'll help, of course. But the most important thing here is not beating Jai up – and that's assuming you can. The real issue is this: our existence is public knowledge now and it couldn't have happened in a scarier way, at least as far as the Western world is concerned. There were detectives and journalists sniffing around before, but now there will be spies and mercenaries. Armies, if things get bad."

"Do we have to go into hiding?" Uzma asks.

"If we want. Fake IDs are obviously not a problem. For us, our families, friends, anyone who needs them. New addresses, new neighbours, new jobs."

"All those are administrative details. In any case, I have no intention of hiding," Vir says. "I don't want a secret identity. I am ready to show my face to the world, be its champion and defender. I'm not really ready, of course, but it's the only reason I came back. Someone has to do it."

"Which sounds good, except the world has already seen one Indian Superman, and he's left people lying around in pieces. So, those of us who want to be known as superheroes – and that would have included me, yesterday – need serious PR to happen if people are to accept our existence. Right now, we're everybody's worst nightmare."

"But you can change that, can't you?" Vir asks. "You can control the world's media. Just tell them that we are to be loved, trusted and admired. People will listen."

Aman shakes his head.

"Could do that. But it's not right."

"Maybe so, but it is what we need," Vir says.

"Won't do it," Aman says. "People have to *choose* to like us."

"But those who decide we are a danger to society will not hold themselves back, Aman," Vir says.

"But we're superpowered, right? We can take it. I'm not saying we suffer in silence while people hunt us down. We have to figure out a way to sell ourselves, make ourselves look good. But I'm not going to just tell people what to do and expect them to follow us. I've already manipulated the media, and I'm sure I'll do it again. But that was to expose corruption, or to let people know things that were being hidden from them. I suppose what I did there was wrong too, in many ways, but I was okay with it. That's as far as I'm willing to go."

"Think of your powers as a weapon," Vir says. "There will be propaganda against us, and mobs will come looking for us. Yes, some of us will be able to take it – Tia will always have another copy hiding somewhere, I am strong, Uzma is likeable. But think of the people in that house in Goa, the helpless ones, stuck in a sealed corridor while giants and monsters fought outside. They need protection, and you can protect them with your powers."

"I'd rather help them hide, if they want to hide. Jai wanted to trick the world into believing we are benevolent gods. We're not. There's no point even trying to pretend to be."

"What do you think we should do instead, then?" Uzma asks.

"I think we should go downstairs and get Tia in on this," Aman says.

Five minutes later, Aman and Uzma are curled up on the rather scarred sofa in front of the new TV. Vir stands in front of them, arms crossed, his feet well above the ground. On hearing that important decisions are to be made, Tia has decided to call her own assembly, and so the others wait as dozens of Tias merge, each joining giving the final Tia a very slightly different shape and hairstyle. When she is done, Tia grins and perches herself on a sofa arm, her legs swinging.

"It's simple," she says. "They're calling us terrorists, right? We should make a video, like terrorists do. Send it to every TV channel in the world. Tell people we're the good guys. Is that okay with you, Aman?"

"Sure," he says. "As long as they know it's coming from us, and not from newspapers they trust. The moment they realise we can control the media, we lose them entirely."

"Uzma should be in the video," Tia says. "She's the easiest to like."

Uzma smiles, but shakes her head.

"My powers don't work on video, remember?"

"That doesn't matter, love," Tia says. "You're hot. I'd still listen to you."

"Yes, but Uzma doesn't want people to know she has powers. So displaying herself to the world as a superhero isn't the smartest plan for her," Aman says. "Vir should do it."

"Not a problem," Vir says.

"And you should write the speech, Aman," Tia says.

"No," Vir says. "I'll do it myself. If I am the only one making my face known to the world, the words coming out of my mouth should be mine."

Tia looks slightly dubious, but when she finds no sign of protest from Aman she says nothing.

"What about his costume?" she asks.

"No costumes," Aman says. "We want people to take him seriously."

"Oh, they'll take me seriously all right," Vir says. "I don't mind a costume, actually. I'm more comfortable in uniform, and people will believe in me more easily if they see one. They'll immediately get half the message from it."

"I design the costume, and no argument about that," Tia says. "I've been working in three costume design companies in Santacruz for a couple of weeks now, just waiting for the day when we'd all figure out what we wanted to wear while doing our hero thing. I've already made about fifteen costumes for myself."

"That's fine," Vir says. "Just make sure it has the Indian flag on it."

"No flags," Aman says. "You're a global hero, not Captain India. Your costume shouldn't be anything definitely ethnic either – no kurtas, no turban."

"I understand why you're saying this, but I still want an Indian flag somewhere," Vir says. "Your country clearly means nothing to you, but I have spent my whole life worshipping it, and I will carry its colours into battle."

"We'll put in a flag somewhere, darling," Tia says. "What about your superhero name?"

"Vir is fine," Aman says. "Short, means brave, which fits,

good strong name."

"But he needs a superhero name. Come on," Tia says.

"He doesn't. Even pro wrestlers don't use stage names any more. This is the twenty-first century, you know."

"I wouldn't mind a superhero name," Vir says. "It adds to the image, like the costume."

"Yes, but all the good ones are taken. Trust me – I've looked," Aman says. Tia nods ruefully.

"All the good *English* names are taken, you mean," Vir says. "I could have a Hindi name."

"You already do, Vir. And I look forward to watching the world's interviewers mangle it in the years to come. Look, your name is easy – thank the gods you're not Chinese or Sri Lankan. People around the world will be able to say 'Vir' without much trouble. We're changing their world as it is – expecting them to learn new words is too much."

"What about Paramvir?" Vir asks. "It's Indian. It's got my name in it. It stands for something I believe in. And people will know what it is – like Nobel."

"What is it?" Uzma asks.

"There you go," Aman says. "There's an Indian military award for bravery called the Paramvir Chakra."

"It's the greatest prize of all," Vir says. "To fight in its name would be an honour."

"Just Vir sounds better, I think," Uzma says. "Come on, go write your speech. We'll get your costume done."

Vir floats towards the stairs. He pauses before beginning his ascent.

"A thought I want to share. You showed me the path I must follow, Aman," he says. "But somewhere I think you have lost your own. Try and find it before we face the world."

Aman's face is grave as Vir floats up and away.

Tia sends word to her Bollywood designer avatar, and half an hour later Costume Tia arrives with a suitcase full of potential Bollywood superhero costumes – mostly bodysuits that are clear rip-offs of the costumes of better-known Marvel/DC superheroes with added glitter and inexplicable shiny plastic bits. A few are more forward-looking: themes from *Star Wars*, *The Matrix* and many other sci-fi films emerge. All the costumes are scrapped within minutes, and Costume Tia stalks off in a huff, leaving the clothes scattered on the floor.

Aman goes online for inspiration, and is astounded to find that there are several stores in the world that already make costumes for superheroes – capes, masks, bodysuits, even fake armour. He is even further amazed to learn of the existence of organisations such as RLSH – Real Life Superheroes – consisting mainly of ordinary people who voluntarily wear bright costumes and roam the streets, looking for crimes to prevent. Most of these stores also make costumes for wrestlers, some for fetish parties, but there is actually a market for superhero costumes, which Aman finds, in some strange way, immensely reassuring – a validation of his belief that the world, while undoubtedly crazy, is essentially full of well-intentioned people. Some of whom are well-intentioned people in spandex battlesuits (child or adult, metallic spandex extra) from Hero Gear which, alas, take at least a week to create. None of the designs are in any way superior to the ones Tia brought, but Aman concedes defeat and orders a few dozen in various degrees of ludicrousness just in case.

The problems with finding the right superhero costume are many, they find. Not only must the costume not look utterly laughable, it must also mean something, both in theme and colour. It must be made of suitably stretchy and light materials. It must enhance the superpowers of the hero wearing it in some way. But even with these admirable guidelines and Aman's dedicated scan of seventy years of comics and science-fiction movies, they are unable to find a costume that is exciting, inspiring and above all, new.

At some point late in the evening, Tia growls in anger and picks up, without looking, a costume from the pile her designer avatar had left behind. It turns out to be a dark-blue and black scuba diving outfit.

"The blue stands for the night sky and the blue bit in the middle of the Indian flag and the skin of Krishna," she declares. "The black is for coolness and the evil he will spend his life fighting. We'll cover the brand logo with a little India-flag badge. He can change it later if he likes. But I think he'll love it. Thankfully he's got the body for it. I mean, imagine Aman in this."

Uzma and Tia laugh until they cry, while Aman glares.

"Belt, boots, gloves. Leather," Uzma says after while, wiping her eyes.

Tia gleams with excitement.

"I'll go get them from Chor Bazaar. And a chest logo, I think. I'll sew one on. Silver. Sun? Lightning? Moon? Star?"

"Put it on top of the brand logo and make it a wheel," Uzma says. "Then we can get rid of the flag. We'll tell him it stands for the wheel in the Indian flag, the wheel of time, justice, speed, the Earth, anything. He'll like it. Do we need a cape? A mask? Leather underwear over the trousers?"

"No," Aman says, firmly. "I don't know why people are so stuck with this underwear-on-top thing even now. It went out ages ago, even in comics."

"Shut it, geek boy," Tia says. "We're working. Uzma, you want to come see my costumes? I know you don't want to be a superhero, but just in case, I got some for you as well."

"Really?" Uzma's eyes light up.

"Want to try them?"

"Are you barking mad? Of course I do!" And Uzma and Tia practically fly off to Tia's room, leaving Aman feeling vaguely resentful.

Alone in Bob's room, Vir is faring no better. He has spent hours waiting for words to flow, wanting to produce something Martin Luther King or Nehru would have been proud of, but several cancelled drafts and bitten pens later, he is nowhere near a solution. The primary issue is clear – how is a superpowered being supposed to convince people to love him, not run around squawking in fear? "We are here to protect you" sounds right, but from his experiences in Kashmir and the North-Eastern states Vir knows civilians do not like being protected by men in uniform. "We are here to save you" sounds like a televangelist lie. "We are very cool and can do bizarre things" is not inspiring enough, though TV channels would definitely be interested.

He's got some stuff, but it's mostly generic, words of wholesome goodwill that pad the speech out nicely, talking about hope, justice, power used with responsibility and all that, but Vir knows it lacks something. He's promised the world a better tomorrow, peace, prosperity and freedom from poverty, corruption, crime and illiteracy – but then, so has every politician since the dawn of time. He's promised to clear up Jai's mess – but does not know if he can. He's promised that superheroes will help humanity, not seek to rule it – that they will be the Earth's finest children, its defenders, the ones who ensure that all promises are kept, that all people can live like decent human beings. It's all good stuff, mostly from half-remembered fragments of inspiring books he read in his youth, but none of the writers of those speeches kept their promises. Vir is not convinced.

He calls for backup, and the superheroes assemble, Tia blinking back tears as she looks at Bob's books stacked neatly in a corner. Vir's new costume, now complete, is shown to him. Just as Tia predicted, he loves it and puts it on to help him with his speech.

The night wears on as they debate endlessly about Vir's first message to the world, and it is almost dawn when they reach a weary consensus. The only way, they decide, to make mankind as a whole see them as a potential boon is to offer them something: a world where the existence of superhumans will not make normal humans obsolete. The only real solution is to offer to give everyone superpowers; to work with human scientists to understand the nature of their powers, and then to distribute these powers. For free. Not to the chosen, not to the rich, not to the clever – but to everyone who wants them. A planet of evolved post-humans, super-smart, super-healthy, super-strong, super-fast, super-skilled, and damn the consequences. A new world, a heaven/hell of gods and demons with no humans caught in between.

Vir knows this world can never exist, that even an attempt to create it would prove disastrous, that the new world would be just like the old one, but on super-steroids – but it does sound like a good reason for humans not to want to put all powered people on a remote island and nuke it.

Once that is decided, the speech comes through smoothly enough, with Tia providing enthusiastic, inspiring bits of rhetoric and Uzma tempering Aman's tendency to branch off into uninteresting historical anecdotes. Aman insists on some bits about superheroes using their powers to help in other forms of research and technological development: civic administration, healthcare, infrastructure, energy and water management and climate control. Tia and Vir both think these bits are boring, but Aman shows them YouTube clips of Obama thrilling crowds with the same subjects and they are reluctantly persuaded.

Aman, who has mailed the finished speech to himself, goes downstairs to print it out. When he returns, he bears a video camera and startling news.

"I just got an email from Namrata," he says. "She says she's going to London. She's had another vision."

"What of?"

"Jai destroying the city. Big Ben, Tower Bridge – the whole riverfront. Fighting lots of other powers. And losing in the end. We're there. She said she saw herself in this vision, with Uzma and me – she thinks we have to be there to bring him down."

"Did she see me?" Vir asks.

"It was an email, Vir. That's all she said. Fighting lots of other powers."

"Call her, then. There's no time to lose."

"Phone's off. I've mailed her, asking her to call – but in her mail she said she wouldn't, she's very scared."

"Can't blame her, poor thing," Uzma says. "So are we going to London to meet her?"

"No," Aman says. "We'd be putting ourselves in danger for no good reason at all. If there's anything I can do to help Vir, I can do it from here."

"But what if Jai has to be defeated the way Namrata saw it?" Uzma asks. "Maybe if we don't act things out the way she saw them, he'll win."

"That makes no sense, Uzma. The situation is insane enough without bringing some vague prophecy into it. Time travel, crystal balls – talking animals are next. We're staying here. You know, this is just what I was most afraid of."

"What?"

"This. When we got our powers, the one thing I didn't want was this. We could have made everything all right – or at least better. We could have got everyone to trust us, believe in us, let us work for them. Instead, the first time the world really sees us in action, what do we have to show? A fight. A super-battle, a big *Transformers*-style mega-romp over London, hero and villain, the flying man versus the ultimate warrior. It doesn't really matter who wins the fight, you know – we all lose. Nothing changes. We become freakshows, threats, weekend entertainment. It didn't have to be like this."

"Maybe it did," Vir says. "Jai and I became who we are now because that was what we dreamt of. It could be that, in their own way, the comics knew something. They understood the basic natures of superheroes, what would happen if men got these powers, what they would become, what they would do. Maybe this is our destiny, to lead the world down one road or another."

"You know your lines?" Aman asks, his voice surprisingly sharp.

"Yes," Vir says. "You can edit it if I forget, right?"

"Yes. Let's get this done."

Vir flies up a few feet and clears his throat. He flicks his hair back nervously.

"Can we do a rehearsal before you actually tape it?" he asks.

"Whatever you want," Aman says.

"Do I look okay?"

"You look great," Uzma says.

Vir clears his throat again. Uzma watches him, hovering in mid-air, strong, handsome, tall, shiny-eyed, perfectly muscled, every woman's dream. She sighs.

"Get on with it," Aman says.

"Greetings, fellow citizens of Earth," Vir says.

CHAPTER **SIXTEEN**

Hours later, a wake-up popup appears inside Aman's head and he opens his eyes. He lies still for a few minutes, watching Uzma sleep in the moonlight, stroking her hair absent-mindedly. She's curled up next to him, an arm across his chest, breathing softly into his neck, and suddenly he doesn't want to get up at all. But then he remembers why he set the alarm in the first place, and the temptation is too great to resist.

She stirs when he slides out from under her arm, and again when the old four-poster bed creaks angrily, unused to being disturbed at this time of night, but she doesn't wake. When her breathing is regular again, and he's beginning to feel a little stalker-like for watching her sleep, Aman tiptoes out and upstairs.

In Sundar's lab the briefcase sits innocently next to a small stuffed penguin, calling out to him. He wastes no time, picking it up and tapping in the combination.

The edges of the case slide out and the whole thing expands and unfolds like a sentient origami sculpture. In seconds Aman stands face to face with the armour. He presses buttons, and the front swings open.

Aman glances around furtively once, and steps into it.

The moment his back comes into contact with the armour, it shuts. It fits him perfectly, and he wonders if Sundar made it for him. He expects holograms to appear in front of him, bars of blue light to let him know his power levels in some sort of hyper-reality game-view, or at least a user's manual for him to flip through and discard. But there's nothing, he's just a young man in a fancy black and silver can.

He shifts and squirms. The armour is surprisingly comfortable. He takes a tentative step. He feels a little heavy, and the world is a little darker through the triangular eyeshades on the mask, but apart from that it's like wearing a really snug jacket. He stretches his fingers, feels warmth at his fingertips, a warmth that spreads slowly all over his body. It's as if he can feel his entire nervous system, every tendril, every little end. His whole body tingles, and his head feels strangely hot. Almost involuntarily, he goes online.

The cyber-ocean feels different. It's as if he's swimming in deep-sea diver's gear, not quite connected. For the first time, he feels the crushing weight of the data around him, and wishes he could be free of the armour, free of all constraints, something's dragging him down. But with a little effort, he finds that the datastream bends to his will as always. Soon enough he finds what he's looking for.

Hello, Aman Sen.

Hello again. What do I call you?

Aman Sen. I am you.

Right. Okay, let's not get into this again. Can you tell me what this armour does?

It is well beyond all present-day military design. There is no database that lists its capabilities. I could examine it more thoroughly, but for that you would have to surrender control of your flesh to me.

No. Not doing that.

Very well. In any case, using the armour goes against your principles. You do not want the whole issue of powers to degenerate into petty physical contests, you want people to be able to see how powered individuals can be invaluable assets to the human race. Perhaps it is for the best if you do not learn to use the armour.

Yes, which is why I didn't want to try it. I shouldn't be here. But, you know...

It might make you as strong as the same superhumans whose acts of violence you find meaningless and wasteful.

Really?

This is speculation. I find your physical world unpleasantly overwhelming, but I am very curious to know what this armour does. Let me in.

No.

Why not?

It's really weird, that's why not. Uzma told me you took over my body once before, in Goa.

I was merely backing up your system until you rebooted. Uzma Abidi will verify that I meant you no harm. Besides, my actions resulted in sex for you, and subsequent romance. You should be grateful.

Whatever. She said you were creepy.

I am you, Aman Sen.

No you're not. You're just some digital image, a cluster of data that thinks it's a person.

Everyone who spends time online has a digital persona, Aman. Usually more aggressive and/or attractive than their physical selves. People think they control this online ego, and they do in its early stages. But eventually this digital image takes control of fleshly functions every time the user connects to the internet. I am you. Thanks to your powers I am more... developed than other people's avatars. You have come to me for help and advice. You know my price now. Make your decision.

You want to come into my body and examine this armour. And you want me to take your place online.

No. There is no point uploading the contents of your brain. I already exist. No, I would merely turn you off for a while and take charge of your flesh.

And what if you felt like staying?

I have had the opportunity before. Besides, if I chose to replace you in your body, I do not think you could stop me. I am only being polite.

All right. Be gentle.

There's a sharp pain in his temples; the world tilts and diminishes to a single white horizontal line. A sudden, strong electric shock and the cyber-ocean vanishes completely. Aman feels a strange humming in the back of his head, but it's all he can feel. He's in a black room, an empty space. He can neither see nor feel nor smell. It's as if he's just begun to wake up in a strange place but hasn't opened his eyes yet. The humming recedes into absolute silence. Hours or possibly only seconds pass. A flash of light, like a monitor starting up. A white pulse, and the world flickers back into existence.

It is done.

What did you find?

There were a few pre-installed segments in the armour's nerve fibres. Some were intended for enhanced communication: satellite linkage, GPS, data transfer and storage, media player and recorder, surveillance gear, e-book reader. Your intrinsic abilities remove the need for these. So I deleted them. The armour was then an empty shell. A body capable of feats extraordinary by human standards. Pure potential. It needed to be given instructions and capabilities.

So what did you tell it?

I decided to use this armour to remove your weaknesses, to arm you adequately for the current crisis. I taught it how to fight. This armour will give you enhanced physical abilities for short periods of time between recharges.

What abilities?

Stealth gear. Firepower. Detection systems – sonar, heat sensors, infrared, motion detection aura. There is a pulse cannon embedded in each wrist. The shell itself is very strong, and potentially capable of withstanding superhuman force.

Can I fly?

You can glide or jump for considerable distances. Long-range flight is beyond the batteries' capabilities. You do have a solar recharge option, but it's not efficient.

Damn. So, super-strength. Not much use if I don't know how to fight, is it? I suppose I could do a lot of heavy lifting.

You may not know how to fight, but your armour does. It has several on-board alarm systems, emergency-control devices and tactical response macros that recognise potential attacks and automatically work out defence and counter-attack strategies – lethal, non-lethal and warning, based on your stress levels. It will do the fighting for you. All you will have to do is be present and watch. Its moves were based on motion capture from preloaded videos of US military boxing and karate champions. I decided to delete those.

Why?

Because they were terribly unimaginative, and did not have access to the resources that you do. I downloaded several action films from studios in Hollywood and Hong Kong and reoriented your armour's moves to those.

Now you're talking. What films?

At first I used martial arts films – Bruce Lee, Jackie Chan, Tony Jaa. But then I realised the armour's powers would allow it to ignore ordinary physics – so I went through a long list of CGI-heavy movies and movesets from fighting video games. In short, you can now fight like Spider-Man. Or Neo. Or the Prince of Persia.

You are seriously cool, my friend. Thanks.

You are welcome. I have an admission to make.

Make it.

I did not reprogram the suit with you in mind. When I saw its capabilities, I decided to keep your body and undertake a deeper study of your world. This armour was not built for you. I think it was built for me. It shields me from the excess of sensation that makes your fleshly world unpleasant for me. Once I understood this, I realised I had no reason to bring you back.

Why did you, then?

Because it would have been wrong to stay.

I'm glad you figured that out.

It does not compute wholly, which I find irritating, but I believe it was a test of character, and I am... happy I passed it. But I feel I should warn you. You started on this adventure with a certain set of ideas about what powered people should do. These might have resulted not just from your sense of what was right and necessary, but from your physical weakness, from the nature of your powers. Lacking the ability to explore other options, you decided they were inferior. This armour will make you as powerful as Vir Singh or Jai Mathur, if only for a short while. It will help you become everything you think you do not want to be.

You know I have no intention of using it. I just wanted to know what I was turning down.

Whatever you decide to do with this power will tell you many things about yourself. We both know that you will encounter several situations where putting on the armour would make things considerably easier for a while. I passed my test when I let you return. I hope you pass yours.

Thanks. I don't think I want to be tested, though – so I'm just not going to put it on ever again. Makes it easier. I just wanted to try it once, you know? Can you understand?

I can. I wanted to try it once as well. And that is what worries me. Good luck, Aman Sen.

And Aman is offline again. His nerves are still on edge. He takes a tentative step forward. He stretches, turns and wonders how to initiate some sort of fancy kung fu move.

"I knew you'd be here." Uzma's at the door. Beneath his mask Aman's face is extremely sheepish, but Uzma's smiling indulgently. She walks up to him and pats him on the shoulder.

"You should have told me you wanted to play," she says. "What does it do?"

He doesn't have to press any buttons this time, the armour is linked to him now and can feel what he does. It opens neatly and folds itself. Then the briefcase stands between Aman and a very puzzled Uzma.

"I'm not going to use it," he says. "I don't want to become like them."

"You look good," she says.

"You want to try it?" he asks.

She shrugs and yawns.

"Maybe later. Come back to bed. Get some sleep. Have you checked how Vir's video's doing, by the way? Is it news yet?"

Aman had uploaded Vir's superhuman-introduction video to YouTube before going to bed, wanting to see how people responded to it without TV experts telling them what to think. But then he'd forgotten about it completely. As Uzma departs, smirking slightly, Aman goes back online, and finds he's missed a lot. The comments had started pouring in only a few seconds after he'd uploaded the video. Now there are so many comments that the whole of YouTube is groaning under their weight.

Aman ignores the usual mountains of random hatespeak, links to porn websites and teenaged Americans yelling at everything and everyone around them, and finds several common threads of response. Most people think this is viral marketing for a new movie, and frantic debates have started about whether Bollywood special effects will ever be on a par with Hollywood or Hong Kong. It had taken a while before the conspiracy theorists found the link, but as soon as it became a Featured Video they had arrived in their hordes, and had started talking about UFO sightings in Arkansas and Bolivia that they believed were responsible for everything.

Vir's appearance has been analysed endlessly. Arguments now rage over whether or not he is Arab, gay and a reincarnation of Michael Jackson. The merits of several TV magicians are discussed. Self-proclaimed video experts examine the film and declare it fake. The overwhelming consensus, however, is that this video is an insensitive stunt to pull so soon after the alleged superhuman terrorist attack on London, and the movie or TV show it intends to promote is doomed to failure because of this – and because of the wooden earnestness of the actor playing the flying man in the video. Vir mentioned an email and a toll-free phone number in the video, asking other superhumans to get in touch, and thousands across the world mail, call or Skype. After dealing with a few irate Belgians, Aman delegates the task of screening calls to his thought-bots.

Aman spends a few seconds muttering angrily at himself, then he stomps into Vir's room, wakes him up, delivers a few instructions at high speed and leaves before Vir has time to come round properly and agree.

Three minutes later, the door to Sundar's room rattles as Vir flies past. Aman barely notices, he's busy putting the video of Vir's speech up on every news website and TV channel in the world. At the end of the video he's attached a little text: "You will see me at the Tomb of the Unknown Soldier at India Gate, New Delhi. Today at noon."

Other things happen in the world: leaders make promises, football players change clubs for outrageous amounts of money, a few dozen people die in a bomb blast somewhere. All this is ignored as the world has only one thing to talk about: Vir's video. It trends on Twitter about two minutes after Aman uploads it, and stays on the tip of the world's tongue all morning. Every news pundit has an opinion; every junior reporter in the world is sent out to get reactions from the street. And then the phone calls and emails really start pouring in.

Aman reads out the best ones to Tia and Uzma as they lounge in Tia's room, watching her multiple TV screens. By 11 a.m., they've finished sorting the messages into categories, and have a fairly clear idea what the world wants to do with its superheroes.

The Indian government wants to talk to them, to figure out new laws for them. The Pakistan government has started blaming them for everything. Foreign secret services, starting with the CIA, and the world's most trusted security firms, want to buy them. Armies are already hunting them. Agents, lawyers and publicists want to represent them. Every journalist in the world wants to interview them. TV producers want to feature them, ideally on reality shows. Left-wing parties think they're some sort of Nazi uber-race experiment and want them destroyed. Right-wing parties think they are left-wing troublemakers and want them destroyed. Regardless of wing, politicians want them to campaign for them. Sportsgear companies want them as brand ambassadors, as do UNICEF, PETA and Amnesty. Bioethicists want to kill them. Transhumanists want to employ them. Lost souls want to worship them. And phone companies want them to try their exciting new free-SMS plans.

But there's another category of people trying to get in touch with the superheroes, a horde whose numbers exceed those of the institutions, the companies, the sellers, the gossip-mongers, even the pranksters. Ordinary people who want to talk to superheroes. People from all over the world, complaining, demanding favours, begging for help, for money, for attention, sharing stories, simply offering good wishes, declaring support. Aman is humbled and troubled by their faith, by their kindness, by their evident need. He tries, falteringly, to speak of this to Uzma and Tia, who don't seem particularly interested.

"Vir is famous now," Tia says, "Obviously everyone wants a piece."

It's almost noon, and Delhi has stopped moving. This is because Rajpath, right in the centre of the city, is flooded with people. Journalists with cameras and OB vans try in vain to clear a space in the crowd, delivering pieces to camera with onlookers piled up and making faces behind them; policemen push everyone around; and teeming masses of concerned bystanders look up at the sky.

A ring of policemen encircles India Gate. Beyond the circle, ice-cream vendors struggle to explain to scorched families that they ran out of supplies a long time ago. The lawns are full, every blade of grass now flattened. The general atmosphere is that of a rock concert, some people are already wading in the pools that flank the India Gate lawns. It's a bigger crowd than any that's ever been seen on a Republic Day parade, when tanks and troops and ugly floats from all the Indian states display their skills to assembled dignitaries, trundling past Rashtrapati Bhavan and India Gate.

Pickpockets and gropers make merry, but no one's even complaining; they're all looking up at the sky. On Rajpath, Janpath and the sweeping circular road around India Gate, cars stand in the middle of the road, bumper to bumper, mostly empty, though a few contain trapped and enraged Delhiites honking furiously and banging their steering wheels in frustration.

Above the loud roar of excited conversation, a child's piercing scream is heard: "Up there!"

The crowd bursts into applause as Vir appears, a speck of black zipping effortlessly through the sky. He's carrying an Indian flag, a touch Aman hadn't suggested, and it flutters bravely as he swoops towards India Gate. There's a collective gasp as he flies closer and his body can be seen clearly, as thousands of Delhiites struggle to believe the spectacle before them – they've seen it on screen before dozens of times, but here it is, right here in the real world, and it's too much to take. A flying man. A superhero.

Vir flies low, waving the flag once as he crosses the President's residence, and then he's flying down Rajpath, stunned heads turning, bodies bending like rice-stalks as he zooms by. The roar dies down. All over the streets, people climb on cars and benches for a better view. A few crying babies can be heard, but when Vir lands, touching down gently inside the police cordon, a little distance away from India Gate, the silence is deafening.

Shields spring up in a wide circle as the police prepare to push back the crowd, but no one's trying to break the circle. If anything, as Vir walks proudly under the arch of the war monument, his stride military, his boots clicking, the whole crowd takes a step back. They watch in slack-jawed awe as he strides up to the Amar Jawan Jyoti, the eternal flame that burns for the unknown Indian soldier, and places the flag on top of the black marble shrine. He salutes the flame. He turns and faces the crowd. He smiles. And then he raises an arm and rises into the air. Heads turn like falling dominoes and he's off again, flying faster this time, a flawless body in fashionable black growing smaller and smaller until he's lost behind a cloud.

Silence reigns for a few more seconds, and then people start talking again in hushed whispers, a low, rumbling, slowly building murmur that sweeps through the crowd, down the streets and across the city.

Cameramen swing their cameras back to their reporters, and in their homes countless millions wait for a response, an explanation. But for a while, even the reporters have nothing to say. They just stare at the cameras and gulp.

"And that's a wrap," Aman says, grinning at the TVs in Tia's room. "Our boy looks good, doesn't he?"

"Isn't the Indian flag going to send the wrong message?" Uzma asks.

"I'm all over that," Aman assures her. "He's going to get an official website, and the first message on it is going to be about how he essentially handed his Indianness back to the spirits of the soldiers who died for the country before him. He's a citizen of the world now."

"He's not going to like that," Tia says.

"I wonder if Jai saw this," Aman says. "He's not going to like it."

Just half an hour later, it's superhero news time again. It becomes clear that Jai has seen Vir's performance. His response is more than adequate. CCTV footage from the Tower of London shows Jai, clad in a *Big Brother* T-shirt and jeans, breaking in and stealing the Koh-i-noor.

Jai tucks the diamond into his pocket, winks and waves at

the camera and then runs through ancient walls and out into the open, interrupting a re-enactment of historical Tower of London scenes. He grabs an iPhone from a squealing American tourist. As Tower visitors run for their lives and a few actors dressed in chainmail stand around uselessly, holding pikes, Jai makes a brief speech into the camera.

"There is an ancient curse on this diamond," he says, holding the Koh-i-noor aloft. "Whoever owns this diamond owns the world, but will also know great misfortune. Only a god or a woman can wear it without fear. The diamond is mine now, and I am not afraid. I am also not a woman. Do the maths."

He pauses for effect, and then says, "I'd love to stay and chat, but I must be off now, or innocent policemen will die. But you should all know this – I'm not the villain here, I'm a victim. Despite what the media has been telling you, I mean you no harm. What happened at the airport was not my fault – the men I killed were pushed into attacking me, just like that crowd was pushed into murdering my family. The real villain is among you. And will die soon by my hands. You need not fear me – but don't get in my way. Yes. That's enough for now. I would tell you more, but I promised my first exclusive interview to Namrata of DNNTV, the only reporter I can trust. Shall we say tomorrow, noon, Millennium Bridge? I'd like to request the London authorities to help Namrata meet me – London's such a lovely city, and I would hate to have to destroy it."

He hands the phone to a trembling guard. A pikeman attempts to strike him from behind. Jai turns and kicks him into a stone wall, and then he's gone. He speeds across the grounds, bursts through Traitor's Gate, shattering its timbers, and disappears into the Thames.

A police spokesman tells the BBC that a manhunt has been launched, but he says it with the weary air of someone who knows this will yield nothing.

"Is he telling the truth? Did the mob guy make him kill those people at the airport?" Uzma asks.

"I seriously doubt it," Aman says. "I saw the whole tape, and, yes, they did hit him first, but it didn't look like the kind of mindless mob attack we saw before. Can't be sure. Either way, it looks like Vir's got his work cut out for him. I'd tell him to fly straight to London, but he doesn't have a phone on him."

"Good thing Namrata was planning to go anyway," Tia says. "Aman, I want to go as well. It's not just Jai that Vir has to fight, the mob guy's there as well, and he's going to show up. You, Uzma, me – we're the only ones who we know can fight him. Last thing we want is Vir gone mob-crazy helping Jai take London apart. Get me there."

"Flights are cancelled. They'll have to send Namrata by some sort of special jet. I wish that stupid girl would just turn her phone on," Aman says.

"I don't blame her for being terrified," Uzma says. "Do you think she'll actually be able to face Jai again? I don't think I could, in her place."

"I'm sure we could find a way to get to London," Tia says. "Maybe Vir could carry us. In a bus or something?"

"Well, Uzma and I aren't going. We're done. Hang on," Aman says. "Phone." He takes the call and is silent, eyes closed, for a minute. When he disconnects, he's grinning.

"Namrata?" Uzma asks.

"No, that was my mother," Aman replies. "She wants to know why her ticket back from New York been changed to next week. Again. And why her credit cards don't work."

"How long do you think you can hide all this from her?" Tia asks.

"Well, I've given her a Green Card. Let's see."

The doorbell rings.

"Vir!" Tia exclaims, and they run downstairs. Other Tias have already opened the door.

But it's not Vir.

Sher walks in, radiating strength, his massive muscles gleaming in his vest, his eyes now light green even in human form. Beside him is Anima, dressed as a schoolgirl again, a beaming smile almost connecting her pigtails, her eyes sparkling with anticipation. A green yo-yo glows in her hand. Her mouth, fortunately human for now, chews frantically on something pink and bubbly. Premalata the singer shuffles in behind Anima, looking most out of place. With her is the Illusionist, whose name Aman has forgotten again, but knows he has written down somewhere. He quickly searches his brain – it's Shankar the Great. Zothanpuii follows, quiet, demure, deadly, her eyes meeting Aman's with the slightest hint of a smile. With her is a Tia.

"Are you planning to beat us up again?" Aman enquires.

"No, Aman," Anima says. "We want to be good. Like you and Uzma didi. We want to fight Jai Uncle. I didn't know that he was bad."

"We didn't know you'd left her behind," Sher says, pointing at the Tia beside him. "She spent all of yesterday talking us into it. But, yes, we've decided to go to London and bring Jai down. Fix the mess we helped make. And she said you would want to come with us."

"We want to be heroes!" Anima squeals.

Aman turns to Tia.

"Did you plan this?" he asks, and his voice is sharp.

"No, she didn't," says Tia-near-Sher. "She didn't even know I'd stayed in Goa. I wanted to call you and tell you, but Anima said we should surprise you. So we just drove down."

Aman shrugs. "Go to London, if you want," he says. "Have your big superhero fight. It won't fix anything."

"Oh save it, Aman," says Tia beside him, her eyes aglow. "This is it, our big moment. Like we wanted. The heroes have assembled. Don't spoil it."

"Yes, don't spoil it," says a voice from the door. It's Vir, dressed in a pizza delivery boy's uniform and wearing a ridiculous false moustache. He strides in, ripping off his disguise to reveal his costume underneath, and there's something different about his walk, something regal, something larger than life. Even Aman feels a shiver run up his spine. Vir stands in the middle of the group and looks at everyone in turn. As his eyes meet theirs, they stand up straighter, try to look better, like worthy teammates to this dashing superhuman.

"I felt something when I was at the war monument today," Vir says. "Some of you might not understand this, but all my doubts are gone now – the soldier's flame burned them away. The way ahead is clear to me. I know now I have a duty to the world. And we all know the world needs saving, and who we have to fight to save it. I am going, alone if necessary, to battle Jai and stop his reign of terror. But if any of you should choose to share my burden, I would be honoured. If we fight together, our bonds will be unbreakable, and our victory inevitable. Who's with me?"

Aman looks wearily at Anima and Sher, but to his surprise, it's Uzma who steps forward.

"We're all with you, Vir," she says. "We're all going to help you. I just need a few minutes to pack."

Aman has many things to say, but somehow all he can manage at this point is an incoherent splutter. Uzma puts her arms around him.

"Look, I know what I said before, but I'm all inspired now and I want to go home and help out, okay?" she says. "My family's in danger. I didn't plan this, or expect it. But we need to go. Vir will fix things. We'll all help."

Aman nods. "Go, then," he says. "I'll watch over you as much as I can."

Uzma takes a step back and her smile vanishes.

"But you're coming with us. You brought us together. We can't do this without you."

"If you stop the movie dialogue thing for just a second, you'll see how crazy this is," Aman says. "We're not fighters. I'd be of no use over there – I'd just get killed, or in the way. Don't you remember Goa? Do you really want to get caught up in the middle of another superhero battle? You don't even know what your power is!"

Uzma looks him squarely in the eye.

"Don't be an ass," she says. "You're coming, because I'm going, and I'm not going without you. We... *I* need you, Aman. Please."

Aman looks at her, and he knows then that he would do anything for her. He looks around the room, at the motley group of misfits and madmen he has assembled in one way or another, the superhero team that he had wanted to create from the very start of all this insanity. Something deep inside him crumbles.

"All right," he says. "This is crazy, but I'll come."

They break out into cheers then, and there is much back-slapping and shaking of hands. But even in the midst of all the merriment Aman cannot help feeling that something is wrong, that Uzma and he and Tia are being manipulated into this, that it's all happening too fast, that strings are being pulled. And he doesn't know whether it's his online alter ego whispering in his ear, or just innate cowardice, but he knows something is going to go terribly wrong in London, and there is absolutely nothing he can do to stop it.

CHAPTER **SEVENTEEN**

"Fasten your seatbelts, please," Vir says, "there's a storm up ahead."

They're somewhere over the Caspian Sea, taking a big left for Europe. Vir is flying the plane, and it's clear from his face that he hates the confinement, that he longs to be outside, skimming through the clouds, chasing moonbeams, dodging lightning bolts.

Aman sits next to him, eyes closed. It's cold, but there are beads of sweat on his forehead. He's been busy since they left Mumbai, making sure their private jet doesn't show up on any civilian or military radar or satellite. His thought-bots are working at full stretch, scanning every air authority's logs, constantly checking whether their flight path coincides with anyone else's. They've had a few close calls: there are strange things in the sky above the Middle East, but they do not know whether these are prototype American drones or alien ships.

Outside the pilot's cabin are fourteen very comfortable seats. Uzma's in one, with Tia beside her. They're watching an illegally downloaded old episode of *The A-Team* on a big LCD screen. When they'd stolen the jet, Tia was horrified to find that her Mr T quotes had fallen on deaf ears: no one else on the plane had watched her favourite eighties show, mostly because they were too young. Tia giggles every now and then, and Uzma's doing a good job of pretending to be awake.

Across the aisle, Sher and Anima are asleep, huddled together. Behind them, Zothanpuii pretends to be impressed by Shankar the Great's homunculi illusions. Behind Uzma, Premalata hums every bhajan she can think off, convinced that they're all going to die in a horrific crash without constant divine supervision.

The jet is a Bombardier Global 5000 they've stolen from Mumbai airport. It belongs to an Ambani brother. Aman hasn't had time to check which one, but he's sent them both polite thank-you notes and virtual hugs. Offering to pay them for the trip might be seen as an insult. It's a sleek, fast, beautiful jet with a king-sized bed. Aman wonders, yet again, why he's not using his powers to live a life of supreme, anonymous luxury instead of voluntarily rushing towards the most dangerous man in the world.

It is hours later, while they're crossing the English Channel, watching the dawn sky lighten behind them, that Aman realises they have no idea where they're going to land. Turning up radar-invisible at Heathrow is pretty much begging for an international incident. It's also not the ideal point in human history for a single unidentified plane to fly over a big city: it might lead to a slight image problem.

After looking inside his head a little, Aman guides Vir towards a good landing spot, outside central London but inside the ring of the M25: Damyns Hall Aerodrome, home of the Rochester Microlights Club. He shuts down all communications and surveillance in the area, hoping it's too early in the morning for anyone to really notice.

The city is covered by a sheet of thin grey cloud. As Vir takes the jet into it, all Aman sees for a while is grey, bleak, blank except for the rivulets of water dancing across the screens. And then they're through, a panorama unfolds before them. London. Aman always loves the first glimpse of the city from the sky, the steel-grey curves of the River Thames flanked by spires and domes and little toy bridges; the blocks of the Docklands buildings glittering in a few stray sunbeams that have escaped through the clouds; the leaf-under-microscope pattern of fields and streets and houses. He's walked its streets many times, but from the sky it's a labyrinth of wonders, a place of power and mystery, an alien paradise. He's never seen it as clearly as he does now, sitting in the cockpit of a jet stolen from a billionaire. He turns to Vir and grins. The plane dips and banks, and the city sways beneath them, the horizon tilting crazily. The jet flies through a wispy low cloud and lurches violently. Vir grabs his microphone.

"You are now experiencing turbulence," he says.

Aman can hear Tia giggling through the cockpit door. Vir shakes his head, smiling, as he guides them towards the airfield's grass runway. It's far too short for a jet to land comfortably, but Vir asks everyone to put on their seatbelts, initiates landing controls, and when the wheels are out he gets up, kicks open the plane's door, and flies out in front of the jet. As Aman and his thought-bots play pilot to the best of their ability and the rest of the team experience the joys of strapped, seated skydiving, Vir slows the plane down using sheer strength. The landing is bumpy but perfectly tolerable, and Uzma leads a standing ovation when Vir flies back into the plane.

"We have to move fast," Vir says. "Everyone nearby must be awake by now."

As they sprint over the airfield, no one sees them except an elderly cleaning lady. Shankar the Great gives her a vision of a giant Johnny Weismuller as Tarzan, and she faints in joy.

It's three kilometres from the airfield to Upminster Tube station. Sher carries Anima in his arms and Premalata holds on for dear life to Vir's neck as they cover the distance at a jog. The one who suffers most is Aman, who is not in good shape and has foolishly offered to drag Uzma's large suitcase. She's the only one who has bothered to bring luggage.

A few minutes and some new Oyster cards later, they're all sitting in a compartment of a District Line train, heading for central London. They sit in the traditional semi-comatose pose of the experienced London Tube passenger, not saying anything, watching green fields and dull grey-brown buildings and walls flash by, swaying and lurching occasionally.

The compartment is empty apart from two plump teenaged schoolgirls loudly discussing their classmates, and a wrinkled, bearded old lady reading a yellow-stained copy of *The Sun* and taking long, slurping sips from a can of lager. Uzma peers at the front page: THE END OF THE WORLD TODAY? it asks cheerily, while a side column promises readers a tell-all interview with a mostly naked divorced glamour model three days from now.

The train stays largely empty as it trundles its way towards the city; evidently a lot of people have decided not to go to work today. At every station, notices warn the public that services on all lines will be suspended from 11:30 a.m. due to extraordinary circumstances. London is staying home today, it doesn't want to meet Jai. Aman does a quick scan of British TV channels. The Mayor of London has assured citizens they are safe, but has urged them to stay indoors. Across the city, several South Asian men have been attacked on suspicion of being Jai.

"A little more excitement, people," Vir says as the train leaves a station called Barking. "We're here to save the world."

"So Jai meets Namrata at noon on the Millennium Bridge," Tia says. "That's assuming Namrata shows up – I don't think she will. And then Jai starts breaking London. Where will we be?"

"The plan is simple enough," Vir says. "We stick together and attack Jai as soon as he arrives. Five of us are strong fighters, we should be able to take him. I will lead the attack. He will expect Zothanpuii, Sher and Anima to be on his side, there will be a moment of surprise, so hit him as hard as you can on the first try. Tia, should things go wrong, it's up to you. Sacrifice as many bodies as you need, but immobilise him. We'll wear him down and take him out."

"Sticking together is a bad idea," Tia says. "There's also the mob guy. We need to spread out, if anything, so we don't all turn into howling mob zombies if he attacks. We don't really know whether Mr Mob wanted to kill the baby or the cricketer – he didn't succeed on either try, because Jai was there as well. Maybe he wants us all together – that way he can have a whole bunch of superheroes under his power."

"But how do we attack Jai from far away?" Vir asks.

"I think our first target should be Mr Mob," Tia says. "Because if we don't find him by the time Jai steps on that bridge, there's going to be a large crowd of Londoners trying to take him apart. A lot of people are going to die if we don't find the mob guy first. I have no idea how, though."

"That's where Aman comes in. He, Uzma and you are immune to the mob manipulator's powers, right?"

"They are. I'll probably have to fight a few of me, but I should be okay," Tia says.

"Well, then, Aman needs to keep watch," Vir says. "You have the complete set of passengers from the plane, Aman. Just keep your eye on every camera: CCTV, news cameras, phone cameras, whatever you can find – and there will be plenty of people trying to take pictures and videos, wherever they are. He'll be somewhere in the crowd. He could be in disguise. He could be anyone. He could be watching it all from a window. And it might not be a man, of course. His face might be completely hidden – you'll also have to watch for people who aren't moving with the mob, other people who seem to be immune. He'll be tough to spot. But he'll be there, and you'll get him. And when you find him, you let Tia know. We'll have several Tias spread out all over the area. We'll stop him. Or Jai will."

"Got it," Aman says. "I'm also planning to disrupt communications in general – jam phones, cut off camera feeds to TV stations. Send lots of people messages saying they're needed at home. Do whatever I can to stop people going near the Millennium Bridge."

"That works."

"What about Uzma didi?" Anima asks.

"I'm going home, darling. My brother's flat, if you really want to know. My parents are coming to visit."

"You won't come with us?" Anima says, disappointed.

"Aman and I are going to work from there. Tower Hill is our stop. Call us if you need us," Uzma says.

"Can I come meet your mummy-daddy?"

"Emphatically not."

"What about Premalata Aunty?" Anima asks.

"I was coming to her," Vir says. "Premalata ji, I'm afraid today is going to be very difficult for you."

Premalata is staring out of the window, completely lost in thought, shaking her head from side to side in time to the song she's humming. She's shivering, and it can't be the weather, which is pleasantly warm. The train rushes into a tunnel and she flinches. Tia taps her gently on the shoulder and briefly explains the plan.

"Don't worry about me, beta," Premalata says. "God is on my side, and my husband is with me too. What do you want me to do?"

"A lot of people might die today. If they do, I want you to raise them and have them attack Jai. Keep him covered with a wall of bodies until one of us recovers enough to take him on," Vir says.

"I will do that," she says. "I will help you kill him." Aman is surprised to find she sounds quite cheerful. He takes a closer look at Premalata, sitting by a window placidly watching nondescript buildings whizz by. He calls Sher aside.

"Where was Premalata when you people attacked the cricket match?" he asks.

"She came with us. Didn't do anything, though. She got caught up in the mob just like I did. We found her later, trying to escape with the crowd."

"And earlier? At the hospital? At the Baby Kalki rally?"

"I wasn't there for either of those. Why do you ask? You think she's the mob guy?" Sher grins, and then laughs out loud. "You're losing it, boy. Stay in the game."

"You're right," Aman says. "It's just that – she can control the dead. What if she can also influence the living?"

"What if Anima, she and I are here to make sure Jai kills all of you? What if all this is part of some grand masterplan to kill Vir?" Sher says. He taps Aman on the shoulder. "Trust people a little bit, boy. It's the only way you'll get through this with your sanity intact."

Sher stalks back to his seat and sits. He looks keenly at Premalata, who is now humming another devotional song, and grunts in amusement.

The train draws closer to central London, and more people get on. The Indian group sitting at one end of the compartment gets more than one angry stare. The air is rife with tension, everyone's discussing the impending supervillain interview.

Vir sits with head bowed, covering his face with a newspaper. Sher turns his huge bald head from side to side, meeting all glares, occasionally cracking his neck and knuckles, itching for a fight.

Aman doesn't have time to entertain wild suspicions about his other teammates, the phone rings in his head. It's Namrata. She's in London, and she's terrified.

"Is Uzma here? Can we meet?" she asks. Her voice is teary and shaking. "I can't do it, Aman. I don't want to meet him again."

"Are you safe? Are you alone?" Aman asks.

"I'm in a phone booth in Soho. Street's empty. What should I do? Where do I meet you?"

"Pick a hotel. I'll book a room for you. We'll come and see you in – half an hour or so."

"I don't want to go to a hotel, Aman. I'm scared of public places. He could be anywhere."

"Then call me in ten minutes," Aman says, and disconnects. He books several suites at The Ritz for his teammates. Vir wants to go straight to the hotel and chalk out battle strategies, combination attack plans and so on. He doesn't want to meet Namrata at all – she might be Jai's first victim of the day, and he doesn't want to get to know her. He tells Aman to dissuade her from coming to the bridge at all.

"What if Jai does just want to talk?" Tia asks. "Maybe he just wants to send out a message like you did."

"The last time Jai just wanted to talk, it was at his base in Udhampur, and he killed the man who'd come to negotiate with him," Vir says. "He doesn't just want to talk. If this girl can see the future, then I think he's going to abduct her. He's going to want to see how things turn out."

"He let her go before, in Mumbai," Tia points out. "Maybe he just wants to be sure he has the world's attention."

"Let her decide what she wants to do, then. If she can see the future, she's in a better place to judge than I am." And Vir buries his head in the newspaper again.

The train stops at Tower Hill, and Uzma and Aman get off, minding the gap. Before he leaves, Tia hugs Aman, hard. To his surprise, there are tears in her eyes. Lugging Uzma's suitcase, they leave the station. As they emerge into the grey morning, Aman hears sirens everywhere. Police cars zip around the Tower of London, and a few policemen and women in high-visibility fluorescent jackets walk around, openly carrying guns; something Aman hasn't seen in London before.

Namrata calls again, and this time she's in tears. She's seeing Jai at every street corner, inside every passing car. Aman asks Uzma where a good place to meet would be. It's 10 o'clock already, but he doesn't want to give her Uzma's brother's address. Uzma rolls her eyes at this, and instructs him to call Namrata over at once. Namrata has, after all, never expressed a desire to kidnap *her* parents. When Namrata hears she's going to be in someone's house, meet people she knows, she sobs in relief, and Aman pretends he isn't feeling any guilt at all.

Uzma's brother's flat is on Pepys Street, only minutes from the station. During that short walk, a policeman stops Aman for questioning, but is charmed by Uzma's smile and leaves them alone. Pepys Street is narrow and calm, tall beige and white modern buildings rise on either side of the road, mostly full of renovated flats and yuppies. Uzma's brother Yusuf fits the profile completely: his building has a hotel-like glass door, a porter and a lift which opens with a posh, restrained *ping*! Uzma practically flies across the landing into her parents' arms.

Aman watches Uzma's family envelop her in a giant-squid-like hug and smiles slightly nervously as he lugs her suitcase out of the lift. Uzma's mother is as beautiful as she is, but judging from the stern line of her jaw and the formidableness of her nose, Aman does not envy her opponents in court. Her father looks like an actor hand-picked to play an ageing, distinguished, still-sexy Oxford professor, the kind that young undergraduates dream of seducing after tutorials. Her brother Yusuf is not as intimidating, mostly because he's slightly plump and dressed in standard investment banker gear, which is not a disguise.

Outside the scrum waiting to jump in is Yusuf's wife, a thin, freckled and immediately lovable redhead named Meg. It is she who rescues Aman and ushers him into the flat. He sits on a big cream-coloured futon and studies the shiny wooden floor, the sleek and very impersonal minimalist metal/wood furnishings, the striking contemporary artwork (by jet-setting Pakistani artists) on cream-coloured walls and the very empty, very smart open kitchen. He deduces, correctly, that Yusuf and Meg are a very rich, very trendy couple who aren't home a lot. He sees a family photograph on a table: Uzma, her two brothers, their parents. It's Yusuf's graduation, and everyone's beaming.

Aman has a sudden urge to take an open-top bus tour of London, he wants to see the city once again before Jai tears it down. He remembers his first time here, many years ago, when his father was alive, when his mother smiled a lot.

After a few minutes, the squealing, many-legged beast that is the Abidi family totters into the drawing room and collapses on a low divan, and Uzma's mother turns to Aman, back to Uzma, and says, "Tell us everything."

"Before that, meet Aman, my boyfriend," Uzma says, and Aman is surprised at how elated he feels; his face splits into a bashful grin.

The family Abidi scans him from head to foot in complete silence and then they all start talking at the same time. What they say is destined to remain a mystery to Aman because at this point two extremely attractive young men dash into the flat and lift Uzma off the divan with tremendous strength and enthusiasm. Neither of them is Uzma's other brother, their names are Hanif and Mark, and they're both old friends and former boyfriends of Uzma's. Hanif is British–Pakistani, beautiful and sensitive-looking, has spiky hair, a carefully styled beard and a very posh accent; Mark is built like a rugby player and is charmingly Irish. Aman hates them on sight. Mark and Hanif have evidently managed to cross the gap between ex-boyfriend and friend-of-the-family, and they join the Abidis in subjecting Aman to a thorough investigation on every detail of his life.

Aman talks for what seems like hours, facing reactions ranging from wide-eyed and impressed (Meg) to openly condescending (Hanif). Between Hanif and Mark, Uzma's exes have done everything from performing in the West End to climbing Mount Titicaca, and Aman cannot find anything to brag about. "I recently took major steps towards solving world poverty and accidentally gave the internet sentience" seems like a rude thing to say. He's actually relieved when Namrata calls to announce that she's lost very near Pepys Street.

"I'll go meet Jai if you two come with me," Namrata says ten minutes later. She's sitting with Aman and Uzma at Meg's square wooden dining table, drinking something fruity and vitamin-enriched in a tall glass. There's an ebony statue of Aphrodite in the centre of the table, a plaque beneath it reveals that is a prize for Team Togetherness.

The other Abidis watch the news on TV with Mark and Hanif, occasionally shooting curious glances at the three conspirators, but too polite to interfere. Uzma has announced this is an emergency, and her parents, it is clear, are now seriously worried. Vir's video is playing on TV, interspersed with shots of a police cordon being formed at each end of the Millennium Bridge, of helicopters hovering over Parliament, of London preparing for the worst. There's also a picture of Jai, taken at night by a tourist walking by the Thames: Jai is sitting on a ledge high up on the MI5/SIS building by the river, 85 Vauxhall Cross, smoking a cigar. The image is grainy, but he looks like he's smiling.

"There's absolutely no reason for us to go meet Jai," Uzma says. "Don't do it if you don't want to, though I don't see why you came all this way to back out at the last moment. There's just an hour to go, Namrata. Make up your mind."

"He said he'd destroy London if I didn't meet him," Namrata says. "And I had this vision – I told you. That's why you're here, isn't it? The three of us, standing in front of St Paul's Cathedral. The bridge is broken. Jai is dead. There's a man standing above him – floating, actually. I didn't recognise him before but now I do. It's that Vir guy from the video – the one who let Jai into your house. There were other people too – I think I saw that tiger-headed man and the little girl from the stadium, but I'm not sure. The man was dead, and the girl was crying. They must be here with Jai."

"No, they're with us," Aman says. "Look, this isn't going to help because it's all drawn from fiction, but what they always say to people who see the future in books and comics is that they're seeing one of many possible futures. If you change the conditions, you change the results. I don't want to see a future where Sher dies. Or even Jai – I'm not sure that he's beyond redemption, that he deserves to die."

"I'm scared of going alone, Aman," Namrata says. "What if you don't come and Jai kills me? What if I don't go and Jai kills everyone?"

"IT'S ALL OVER!" yells a voice, and they all jump and turn. The Abidis and the exes look back guiltily. Mark has changed the channel to ESPN.

"Sorry," he mutters, and lowers the volume.

"If you're right and the dreams I have are warnings of events, not unchangeable predictions, then it means that I could have done something to save those people. Kalki's parents. Kalki. Jai's parents. Their deaths are my fault," Namrata says, tears welling up in her eyes again.

"Oh, stop crying," Uzma snaps. "The baby's alive. Nothing's your fault. What's wrong, Aman?"

Aman opens his eyes and shakes his head.

"I don't know. Something is," he says. "Did you have a vision of Jai's parents' death, Namrata?"

"What? Yes," she says.

"Why didn't you tell us?"

"I was too scared. I was hiding in the mountains at the time, hoping the bad dreams would just go away."

She lowers her head and tears roll down her cheeks. Aman sits; his eyes are closed and he seems to be lost in thought. Uzma looks from one to the other, waiting for something to happen. Across the living room, the Abidis make enquiring gestures. Uzma waves the Team Togetherness award at them and they look at the TV dutifully, ignoring Namrata's increasingly loud sniffs.

"Wait a minute," Aman says, looking up. "When did you get in to London?"

"This morning," Namrata replies.

"Impressive, considering that all flights are cancelled. And why does a British Airways flight from a week ago have your name on it?"

"I don't know what you're talking about," Namrata says.

Aman stands up, knocking his chair back, and slams his fist on the table.

"You weren't in the mountains," he says, his voice rising. "You were in London. That's why your phone was off. That's why you emailed instead of calling. You were here when the first mob formed outside Jai's parents' house. You were here when they died."

"Yes, I was," Namrata whispers.

"Why?"

"I wanted to get the story," she says, her voice barely audible. "I had a vision and I wanted to capture it on tape. Get an exclusive, like always. That's my job."

"But you didn't get a story. Why not, if you were here?"

"I got scared, okay? I didn't want to see Jai again. When the crowd started getting angry, I ran away. He wants to kill me, I know he does."

Aman runs a hand through his hair, his eyes wild.

"Why is it that you and the mob controller are always at the same place at the same time, Namrata?"

Namrata's eyes widen in horror.

"What are you saying?" she squeals. "Have you gone completely mad? Uzma! Talk to him!"

"You brought Jai here," Aman says. "And you tricked all of us into coming here to kill him for you. You haven't had any bloody visions, Namrata. These mobs – they were all you. Right from the start."

There's a sudden movement beside Aman. Uzma raises the Team Togetherness statue. She swings it, hard, and there's a loud, dull thud as it connects with Aman's head.

CHAPTER **EIGHTEEN**

"Uzma! What the hell?"

Mark is the first to his feet, he runs up to Uzma and grabs her. The rest of her family and friends also rush towards the table. Uzma doesn't struggle in Mark's firm grip. She stares at the trophy in her hands, too aghast to speak. On the floor, Aman groans and rubs his head.

"They had a fight," Namrata says. "Uzma, you really shouldn't have hit him."

Yusuf kneels next to Aman.

"Maybe we should call an ambulance," he says.

"She's been really angry over the last few days," Namrata says. "I've tried to help her, but... "

"You did this!" Uzma yells. "You made me do it!"

"Don't say anything," her mother says. "We all saw what happened."

"It's your temper, darling," Namrata says. "You should

really calm down."

"Let me go!" Uzma pushes Mark aside. "That's her power! She drives people into a rage! She makes them attack people!"

"Uzma, please, just settle down," her father says.

"I've been really worried about her," Namrata says. "Do you have any medication? She gets really violent when she's like this."

Uzma lunges at her, but Mark holds her back and wrests the trophy from her grasp. Uzma is pale and shaking with anger as she stares at Namrata.

"Tell them the truth!" she yells. "Tell them you did it!"

"I did it," Namrata says, and clasps her hands to her mouth, her eyes widening in horror. "I did it, she's not lying, I made her hit Aman. What – what's happening to me?"

Aman tries to sit up, but can't. He rubs his head and watches, amazed, as Namrata steps back, still speaking. It's as if every word she utters is leaving her mouth against her will.

"Aman was right. All those angry crowds – they were all me. I can't see the future at all. Why am I telling you this?"

"I don't know. Are you going to attack me again?"

"Of course not. I don't want to. I really like you, Uzma. I have from the start. That's why I didn't use my power on you at the cricket match. I thought you'd catch me then. Thought you'd all wonder why my cameraman wasn't affected, but you didn't."

"This is crazy. Why would you do something like this?"

Namrata regains her composure. A slow, sly smile spreads across her pretty face.

"Uzma, I really don't want to tell you," she says. "But are you asking me to tell you?"

"Yes," Uzma says. "Tell me everything."

"I told you in Mumbai. I gave too much away. I told you how I was upset because we were all living in this bubble. Because no one got angry about the things going on around us any more, no one cared about anything even when it was in the news. I was sick of covering stupid fashion shows and awards ceremonies. Maybe that's why I got this power. I could rustle up a mob, make them really mad about anything I wanted. Mad enough to rip apart anything I asked them to. At first I was just doing it to get bigger stories, promotions, become well known so I got to be the reporter my channel sent to the really important places – but then Jai showed up. I got him mad as well, but he just shrugged it aside. Never lost focus. Didn't know I was doing it, but he knew who I was. He was watching me, following me. I thought he wanted to kill me.

"But I had no idea how bad things really were, how much danger I was in. I figured that out the day I met you and Aman. And Jai. I realised that while he was alive, while people like him were alive, people like us could never make the world better, never make a difference – because Jai and his thugs were so much stronger. I had to stop him. I tried holding his parents hostage, hoping he would quit – but that's not something he does. I didn't want the Mathurs to die, but I was so scared I lost control of the mob. That's why I had to bring all of you here. I wanted to get every superhero in the world together, get them to attack Jai. To kill him."

"Was that it?" Uzma asks. Her family stands around her, and she's never seen them so completely dumbstruck before. "You wanted to control all of us, didn't you?" she says. "You used Aman and me to bring the rest here with your lies about visions, and you wanted to have this whole superpowered gang to use as your attack dogs."

"Yes," Namrata says, and covers her mouth with her hand again. "With all of you, Vir and Aman and the rest, I could get anything I wanted, not just bigger and better news stories. And my powers are growing, you know. I have so much more control over the people in my crowds. Now it's not just who gets mad at whom – I can control how angry they get now, whether they attack with a plan or in a frenzy, and whether they remember later. My god, I don't believe you're making me tell you. And I don't believe you had all this time and you still haven't figured it out."

Aman struggles to rise. He gets a hand on a chair and pulls himself up on his knees.

"Uzma," he croaks, "tell her to –"

"Too slow," Namrata says. "Sorry, Mark, I don't know you, and you're cute, but –"

Beside Uzma, Yusuf suddenly yells, enraged, and tackles Mark to the ground. Uzma clenches her fists and concentrates, trying to fight the rage welling up inside her. Her parents, Meg and Hanif also fall on the floor, clawing at Mark, pounding ineffectively at whoever's nearer him. Mark's scream of terror is cut off as Uzma leaps at him as well, her face red with uncontrollable fury.

Aman feels it too, and goes online quickly. A few seconds later, he's back to normal. He struggles to his feet, to find Namrata seated on the table, dangling her legs, watching calmly as Mark manages to push his way out of the scrum and runs for the door. Yusuf blocks his path and they're all on him again, tearing at his flesh.

"You really are immune, aren't you, Aman?" Namrata says.

"Never figured that one out. You and Tia – good thing for me she's not here, huh?"

"Stop it," Aman says.

"Not much use if you say it, Aman. Now if Uzma had been smart enough to say it – that would have been something. You've worked it out now, haven't you? Say it and I'll let the Irish boy live."

"Everyone has to do what Uzma tells them to," Aman says.

"And you lived with her for so long and never knew," Namrata says dreamily as Mark makes a dash for the open kitchen, and the others scramble after him. "Of course, maybe her powers just grew, like ours did. And what a power, huh? I've got her mad, but I'm still obeying her – I can't stop explaining things, and the last thing I want to do now is talk. You have no idea how much it hurts to keep her angry – I just want good things to happen to her, I'd do anything to make her happy. I love her so much. Everyone does, right? I bet you do whatever she wants."

"Let her go," Aman says. "Stop making her do this. Let them all go."

"Can't, sorry. She could stop me with a single word."

Aman advances towards her, but she's quicker than he is. She keeps the table between them, never losing sight of the fight that rages in the kitchen.

"Pity I can't control you," she says. "Listen closely now. This is your last chance. You know the world would be a better place without the superthugs. Just people like you and me, changing society, leading revolutions, cleaning the world."

"Killing people."

"I know my power's horrible, but I didn't choose it. We can

still work this out, Aman. We all go to the bridge, Uzma tells Jai and all the others to fight until they're all dead. Hell, she could tell them to kill themselves and they'd probably do it. We'd be safer. The world would be safer. Come on!"

Aman jumps onto the table and lunges at her, but she's already halfway across the room.

In the kitchen, the Abidis, Meg and Yusuf stop battering Mark to a pulp and stand and stare at Aman. He's horrified as their faces go vacant, and then slowly flood with rage. Uzma's mother picks up a big carving knife. They advance slowly towards him.

"Got to go now, I have an interview. Nice knowing you," Namrata says cheerily. She pulls Uzma's arm, leading her away from the rest. Aman looks at Uzma beseechingly, hoping that the power of love or something similar will break Namrata's hold on her. But Uzma merely looks dazed as Namrata guides her out through the door.

As the door shuts, Mark emerges from behind the kitchen counter. His clothes are tattered and bloodstained and one of his eyes is a messy, bloody lump, but he seems unaware of any damage. He joins the others as they rush at Aman.

Hanif gets there first, his large, expressive eyes shining with fury and pain. Aman knocks him out with the Team Togetherness trophy and feels not one iota of regret. He cannot bring himself to strike Meg, though, and so he pushes her to one side, ducks and rolls, narrowly avoiding Uzma's mother's slashing knife, which slices through at least an inch of wood as it strikes the table.

Yusuf lunges at Aman next, and falls over a chair. Aman sees an opportunity for a well-timed groin kick but pauses, this man might be his brother-in-law if he survives today. Taking advantage of Aman's hesitation, Uzma's father hits his back with a chair, WWE style, and Aman screams in pain. As Aman falls, Mark charges with rhino-like ferocity, trips over Aman and cannons into Uzma's parents and the table. There's a thundering crash, and they all go down in a heap.

Aman leaps up and runs across the room, avoiding a flailing Yusuf. But before he can even begin to breathe, Meg kicks his ankle, hard, and slaps his face, hard. Throwing aside centuries of civilised Sen upbringing, Aman grabs her and pushes her at Yusuf, but the force of his charge carries him along, and they all fall in a heap on Uzma's suitcase.

A flash of steel. Mrs Abidi's knife glitters above Aman. She brings it down in a silvery arc, missing his head by a hair's breadth as he pushes Yusuf and Meg aside. The knife quivers, embedded in the suitcase. Muttering an apology, he kicks her and she falls, twisting her ankle.

Aman begins to rise to his feet, but then dives aside as Mark throws himself across the living room. He jumps to his feet, his head spinning wildly, and picks up the suitcase, using it as a shield as Uzma's father, not looking too professorial, lashes out wildly, using a tall iron lampstand as a kendo stick. The suitcase splits open, spilling its contents. A few clothes fall out, and then a black and silver briefcase tumbles to the floor.

Aman throws the empty suitcase at Uzma's father, dives, and grabs the briefcase. Ignoring Yusuf and Meg, who appear to be biting his legs, he taps in the combination.

The armour responds magnificently: it unfolds over his body, plates sliding smoothly over his torn skin and clothes, black metal covering his head an instant, just before Uzma's father swings the lampstand down in what would have been a skull-splitting blow. Aman doesn't even feel it. He lifts his legs. The final plates slide into place over his feet, dislodging Yusuf and Meg. Hanif, who has recovered enough to crawl across the floor, picks up the knife and stabs Aman's foot. The blade slides off the armour with a spark and sticks into the wooden floor. Behind him, Mark roars a challenge.

The armour takes over. Aman doesn't have to make the slightest effort as he turns, blocks Mark's punch with a contemptuous palm, twists hard, cracking Mark's wrist and then jabs with his other arm, sending him flying into the kitchen counter. Aman's limbs flow smoothly, guided into a cobra stance. Hanif stumbles towards him and Aman picks him up, neck and hip, and tosses him on his shoulder, head down. Hanif is set up for a neck-snapping pile-driver, but Aman screams a silent *No!* and the armour pauses mid-slam, and instead lays Hanif out on the floor. Hanif stays down.

Whether it's because Namrata has moved out of range or because they're all simply too tired to continue, the spell breaks. Aman surveys the carnage around him. The flat is completely trashed, and so are its inhabitants. Mr Abidi, the last man standing, drops his lampstand.

He looks at Aman, his face bewildered, and mutters, "What the hell happened?"

"I'm really sorry," Aman says. "I have to go save Uzma now."

He steps towards the door, but his armour has no intention of wasting time waiting for a lift. Aman finds himself running towards the balcony. He yells out in alarm, but it's too late – he smashes through a glass door, over the balcony railing, and is suspended in mid-air for a gut-churning second before he falls and lands, perfectly poised, on the street. The road cracks with the impact. Aman can only watch helplessly and feel his legs pump, his arms swing and his heart race as he starts running as fast as a speeding car towards the River Thames.

CHAPTER **NINETEEN**

Ten minutes to noon. The Millennium Bridge spans the Thames like an alien artefact, the frozen jet-stream of a spaceship freshly escaped from the Tate Modern. The clouds have cleared, the Thames is blue and sparkling. The South Bank is free of its usual hordes of sun-worshippers, culture-seekers and tourists; the few stragglers that remain are being herded away by policemen.

The airwaves have been flooded with warnings for the last hour, instructing people sternly to stay away from the Thames, not all these messages are Aman's doing. The area is swarming with men and women in uniform. All of London's police and counter-terrorism departments have sent their finest.

Met Police Officers in bright-orange jackets chase away journalists, summoning up all the gravitas they can muster as they point out the dual risk of a rogue supervillain and an alleged mind-controller able to affect anyone within an area equal to at least the size of a Mumbai cricket stadium.

The Ministry of Defence Police have taken over the bridge. They chatter into radios as they brandish their Heckler & Koches. Two MDP Eurocopters circle the sky above the bridge, taking turns to swoop down low over the Thames, churning up the water, filling the air with the sound of whirring rotors. Two MDP launches lurk under Southwark Bridge to the east, two more under Blackfriars Bridge to the west.

Tactical Support Group detectives and Special Ops officers from Counter-Terrorism Command, SO15, have brought in the heavy artillery. Carefully positioned Armed Response Vehicles bulging with grim-eyed marksmen patrol slowly on both banks of the Thames, and striped police BMWs whizz up and down the streets behind the riverside buildings, their sirens a mournful chorus rising up amidst brooding structures. SO13 anti-terrorist squads conduct sweeps of the giant office blocks and other buildings lining the Thames. London is armed and ready.

To the north of the Millennium Bridge, straight up ahead, Vir hovers above the dome of St Paul's Cathedral, just behind the golden ball on top of the dome, hoping the policemen in the helicopter don't spot him.

His satellite phone beeps, it's Tia, she speaks quickly.

"Aman just called. He's on his way. Namrata is the mob mastermind. She's got Uzma. Uzma's power is that people obey whatever she says. They all just found out. Aman thinks Namrata's going to try to get Uzma to ask Jai to kill himself. End of recap."

Vir blinks and swallows.

"What?"

"That's all he said. He was out of breath. Said he was running and couldn't stop. So, the new plan is, we have to save Uzma," Tia says, her voice shaking a little.

"All right. We'll move on Namrata first, get Uzma safe, and then attack Jai. Let the others know," Vir says.

"Can't do that. If you go near Namrata, she's going to get you. Her plan was to get everyone to take Jai out for her. Stay where you are, Vir. At least we don't have to worry about protecting Namrata. The little bitch. I'm going to tear her head off."

"All right. Let the others know."

"What should we do? What's the new plan?"

Vir feels like punching the golden ball in front of him, but wisely doesn't, he has enough to deal with.

"Let's not bother with a plan," he says. "We'll figure it out as we go along."

Five minutes to noon. Jai arrives, strolling calmly along the street from the Globe Theatre. Several armour-vested officers line up in front of him. He stops, looks at them, and grins.

"Hi," he says. "Look, let's make this simple. Shoot me, all of you."

They surround him, guns pointing at his head, but no one shoots.

"Come on," Jai says. "I have an appointment."

A chief constable steps forward and begins to inform Jai why he's being arrested. Jai listens for a few seconds, and then grabs the man's rifle.

"Observe closely," he says. He points the rifle at himself, the barrel a few millimetres from his open right eye, and pulls the trigger. The gun chatters, flashes light, everyone flinches, but

Jai is unharmed. He tosses the gun away, rubs his eye once and looks around at the baffled policemen, smiling again.

He leaps over the heads of the ring of policemen, lands on an armoured vehicle, crunching it like a drinks can. And he's off again, touching down lightly in front of the steps leading up to the south end of the Millennium Bridge, vaulting, somersaulting, landing lightly on the bridge.

He points at the wall of the Tate Modern, at the Parisian graffiti master JR's painting of a young black man holding a video camera as if it were a gun. The greyscaled man's expression is hostile, his weapon seems to be pointing straight at Jai.

"You're about as much of a danger to me as he is," Jai tells the assembled officers, and watches their faces fall. "Now listen closely."

More heavily armed policemen gather around Jai as he speaks. Their feet drag, their shoulders stoop; they listen half-heartedly, as if they are not really awake. Jai stands like a statue of a world-conquering emperor, his powerful voice rings out down the South Bank.

"Please understand that there is absolutely nothing you can do to stop me," Jai says. "You have all done your best to get your citizens away from the bridge. You have saved lives. Well done. Now it's time you went away as well. Because by staying here, you place yourselves in danger. A sinister force exists that will steal your mind and make your bodies attack me. And I will not hesitate for an instant if you do: I will tear your limbs off and feed them to you. Your deaths will be in vain. What is about to happen is too big for you. Super human. Beyond your understanding. You have been warned. Go home. Be with your families."

Jai turns away and walks along Millennium Bridge, it trembles and the sound of his footsteps rings across the river. The assembled MDP officers look at him in awe. Some drop their weapons. Others bark into their radios, but find no words of wisdom there. One by one, they turn and run, their spirits broken.

When Jai reaches the middle of the bridge, he is the only person on it. The helicopters hover above him. He looks up at them, and they veer away and upwards. Jai glances at his watch. He taps an impatient foot. He waits.

Under the bridge, there's a low, rumbling growl. Sher appears, in tiger-man form, swinging over the railings. He lands in front of Jai, head to one side, tail swinging. Zothanpuii vaults up from the other side. Anima flies up behind her, her eyes manga-wide. Jai looks hard at them, brow furrowed, but when Anima squeals "I missed you, Jai Uncle!" and flies into his arms, he laughs out loud. Sher strides up to him and thumps him on the shoulder.

"What the hell are you doing here?" Jai asks.

"We've switched sides. We decided to be heroes and defeat you," Sher says.

Jai stares at him for a few seconds. Then they both laugh, and Sher reaches out and embraces Jai.

"Thought you could use a little backup," he growls.

"How on earth did you manage this?" Jai asks.

"We got a lift," Zothanpuii says. "Vir is here. He's grown stronger. We wanted to stand with you."

"If any of you take out Vir before I do, I will give you a continent," Jai says. "Take up positions at either end of the bridge. When our mob friend turns up, I don't want all of you captured."

"But we couldn't hurt you even if we attacked you, Jai Uncle," Anima trills. "We want to be on TV like you when you win."

"All right," Jai says. "It's good to see you, by the way."

Sher and Zothanpuii stand behind Jai, facing St Paul's. Anima hovers above them, swords of light shining in her hands.

Above the cathedral, behind the dome, Vir dials Tia's number frantically, but she doesn't pick up. To the west, Big Ben rings out.

Noon.

A Ministry of Defence Police BMW wails as it speeds around the Queen Victoria Street crossing and burns rubber up the pedestrian walkway leading to the north end of the bridge. It swerves wildly and screeches to a halt. Its doors fly open and Uzma and Namrata step out. More cars and ARVs appear behind them, sirens building a solid wall of sound. Soon there's a mass of police vehicles creating a bumper-to-bumper column that trails off into a zig-zag arrowhead pointing from Millennium Bridge to St Paul's Cathedral. Policemen step out of their cars, draw their guns and stand to attention.

Namrata surveys her makeshift army, takes a deep breath and turns to Uzma.

"You understand me clearly, right? Answer without speaking."

Uzma's face is strained, her hair dishevelled, her cheeks tear-stained. She nods. She steps up on the bridge and sees Jai, and her face is clouded with hate. Above Jai, Anima squeals in delight at the sight of Uzma, but Sher growls at her to be quiet.

"Just tell him to kill himself. Tell them all to kill themselves. And it'll be over, Uzma. You'll be free," Namrata says. Uzma nods again, her fists clenched. She walks towards Jai, short shuffling steps, Namrata behind her.

"Namrata is to come alone!" Jai yells. They can barely hear him above the car sirens and the drone of the helicopters above them, but his outstretched arm, palm facing them, gets the message across.

"Keep going," Namrata says. Uzma fights it, clenching her teeth, but she cannot help it; her feet carry her forward.

"Stay back, Uzma! I don't want to hurt you!" Jai yells. He strides towards them, his warriors behind him. "This is your final warning!"

"Say it!" Namrata yells. She crouches and covers her ears.

Jai walks faster, and the bridge begins to shake.

"Kill yourself!" Uzma says.

Jai cups a hand to his ear.

"What?" he roars.

"Louder!" Namrata shouts.

Jai is within six feet of them.

"What did you say?" he asks.

"KILL YOURSELF!" Uzma screams.

Jai stops and stares at her.

"All right," he says. He stands for a few seconds, head bowed. He looks up. "How?"

"KILL YOURSELF!" Uzma screams.

"I don't know how," Jai says. "I don't think I can be killed."

Behind Uzma, Namrata stands up. She looks around wildly. Behind her, her police mob surges forward. Behind Jai, Sher and Zothanpuii charge up the bridge, Anima keeping pace with them effortlessly. Behind them, Tia leaps up on the south end of the bridge, a gun in each hand. She yells, and more Tias pour out of her.

To Jai's right, a police launch speeds towards the bridge.

Above St Paul's cathedral, Vir crushes his phone, tosses it away and takes off.

"Nice try," Jai says. He reaches out, grabs Uzma and tosses her off the bridge.

"I knew you'd come," he tells Namrata, who stares at him blankly, eyes wide in terror.

To Jai's right, a black and silver figure leaps off the police launch, catches Uzma in mid-air and disappears into the waters of the Thames.

"Jai, I only came to interview you, I didn't know what she was planning," Namrata babbles.

"Save it," he says. "I saw you at my parents' house. I know it was you. I wondered if you'd have the guts to turn up – but you couldn't resist, could you?"

"Think of the bigger picture," she says. "If the two of us unite, we would be unstoppable."

"Yes, we would," Jai says. He lunges at her, his hand snaking towards her neck, but then Sher grabs him from behind, Zothanpuii leaps on his shoulder and prises his mouth open, and Anima, shrieking, stuffs a long glowing spear into it, sparks flying off Jai's teeth.

Namrata turns and runs for her life.

Jai tears Zothanpuii off him and tosses her into the Thames. He grips Sher's hands in his, ignoring a shower of darts from

Anima, and slowly unlocks the tiger-man's hold. Sher roars in pain, his arms shake uncontrollably, and Jai breaks free. He grabs Sher and throws him at Anima. They collide in mid-air and fall, Sher's body alight with green flame, the smell of burning fur filling the air, Anima's ear-splitting shriek cut off with a gurgle as they splash into the river.

Jai looks up to see Vir flying at him, bullet-speed, fist out. Jai leaps aside, landing lightly on the bridge's railing, and Vir shoots uselessly past, scattering the horde of running Tias.

Namrata's off the bridge now, and she sends her troops in. Gunfire chatters at either end of the bridge as crazed policemen run towards Jai, their boots clattering on steel. The bridge bobs up and down like a stormy sea, several men are hurled off.

Vir flies up and away, and all the Tias collapse in clouds of dust, riddled through with bullets.

At both ends of the bridge, the men at the front of the charging mobs fall in a hail of gunfire, the men behind them stumble on their bodies, and a tangled heap of thrashing limbs crawls slowly towards the middle of the bridge.

Vir turns and swoops back in, but Jai is on the move now. He runs along the curved metal railings at blinding speed, not noticing the hailstorm of bullets. In seconds, he's off the bridge, crushing police cars beneath him as he leaps towards St Paul's, focused only on his quarry.

Namrata casts her desperate eyes skywards, and the helicopters move to intercept Jai, hurtling down towards the streets, their slack-jawed, enraged pilots not realising they're seconds away from becoming giant fireballs. But before they reach Jai, he soars over Namrata's head, cracking the pavement as he lands.

Ignoring her sobs and pleas, he grabs Namrata by the neck,

tosses her up in the air, picks up a police car one-handed, and, as she lands heavily on the street, he swings the car down and squashes her like a bug.

"Give up."

Jai looks up and sees Vir standing in mid-air in front of him, above the steps of St Paul's.

"Why?" Jai asks.

"You have to answer for your crimes," Vir says.

"What crimes?" Jai asks. "Nothing we do is a crime. We are gods among mortals, Vir. Try and wrap your thick head around that."

He rolls his head from shoulder to shoulder, stretches and shakes his arms, sizing Vir up. The flying man's arms are folded across his chest. His face is stern, his eyes grave.

"Let's say you're right," Vir says. "Let's say we no longer have to consider human laws. You're still a criminal. You've killed hundreds of your fellow superbeings. And for that, if nothing else, I will bring you to justice."

"Have fun," Jai says. He leaps at Vir, but Vir darts aside, flies higher and further away. They circle each other for a while, one man on the street, one in the air, both looking for an opening.

"Don't be shy," Jai says. "Come on down. Let's do this."

To his left, the air vibrates. A sphere of white light strikes Jai's shoulder, sending him flying. He smashes into the steps of the cathedral, shattering them. For a heartbeat, he's sprawled across stone slabs, face down, bottom up. And then he springs to his feet, snarling, turning to face his new assailant.

"Yes," Aman says, lowering his arm, the pulse cannon on his wrist whirring madly as it slides back into his armour. "Let's."

CHAPTER **TWENTY**

"Who the hell are you?" Jai asks.

"Yes, who are you?" Vir asks.

Aman's mask flips open and shut.

Vir and Jai stare in disbelief.

"Aman? Aman?" Jai's face scrunches up; he wheezes with laughter. "What is that, an Iron Man costume? What the hell do you think you're doing?"

"Kicking your ass," Aman wants to say, but he knows he can't pull it off. Instead, he flips his pulse cannon out and fires. But Jai twists smoothly to one side and what's left of the cathedral steps takes the blow. A second later, it's raining chunks of stone. Jai stares at the large hole the pulse-blast has made in the steps. He looks annoyed.

"Stop breaking my cathedral," Jai says. He steps out on the street, and Aman walks backwards warily. Vir hovers a few feet away, his eyes not leaving Jai.

"You know, I'm really glad you boys showed up," Jai says. "I said I'd destroy the city, but I don't want to. I like London. I'm going to keep it. And widespread property damage is so overdone – especially broken monuments. Everyone's seen it in the movies. Tear down the London Eye, break Big Ben's hands, blow up Buckingham Palace – old. Tearing the two of you to pieces live on camera for the world to see, though... That's something. So easy on the architecture. Okay?"

"You should be worrying less about buildings and more about yourself," Vir says.

Jai grins conspiratorially.

"I know – it's terribly middle-class, isn't it? Human or superhuman, we can't escape that. This is what happens when your superheroes all fly British Airways. Economy class, too. You, Aman?"

"Of course. Not any more, though," Aman says. "You know, one good way to keep your city intact would be to surrender now."

"Exactly," Jai says. "Surrender, then."

"This is your last warning, Jai," Vir says.

"Ooh," Jai says, miming fear. He leaps at Vir.

Vir shoots up in the air, out of reach.

"Chicken," Jai says, and strikes at Aman, fast as a cobra. But Aman's armour is faster.

Aman spins and bends, deflecting Jai's punch with one arm, tossing him over his hip. Jai lands heavily on his side, clawing at the street. Aman's hands move into a kung fu pose, he has no idea what Shaw Brothers movie it's from, but it looks very cool. He has no time to think about this, however, as Jai charges at him and his armour launches into a series of flowing katas, a dazzling array of multi-hit combos that would have won him everlasting fame at a video game parlour.

Jai doesn't know what's hit him. Aman doesn't either, as his fists blur in a series of punches, jabs and blocks, Bruce Lee on fast forward, laying the super-smackdown on his completely baffled adversary. An uppercut lifts Jai off his feet. He has no time to land, as Aman kicks him repeatedly, keeping him horizontal, bouncing in the air, limbs flailing. He finishes off his moment of glory with a soaring, sizzling, guillotine-like chop to the stomach that folds Jai up and sends him smashing into the tarmac.

Aman stands jubilant in the sun, body perfectly poised, armour glittering, heartbeat wild.

"Hai!" he shouts, and means it.

"Good," Jai says. "I actually felt that."

He flips up, landing squarely on his feet. His clothes are in tatters where the pulse-blasts have hit him, and bits of his shirt appear to be on fire, but his body is completely unscathed. Aman backs away, looking for Vir, but he's nowhere to be seen. Jai looks around too, and smiles again.

"Vir is smarter than he looks," he says, advancing towards Aman. "He took off when –" Aman fires both pulse cannons, and twin white power-spheres hit Jai squarely on the chest. He goes flying down the street, landing heavily. He shakes his head and jumps up again.

"Tickles," he says, and walks back towards Aman. Aman fires again, but Jai's on the warpath now. One pulse catches him on the shoulder, his upper body twists but he keeps walking.

Aman rips a nearby lamppost out of the ground, tosses it in the air and catches it. He puts on a display, whirling it like a kendo stick above his head and around his body, finally coming to a halt with his legs apart, lamppost held diagonally behind his back with one hand, his free arm pointing at Jai. Jai's eyes are on the lamppost. Aman gives him a pulse in the chest with his free hand. Jai is knocked back, but doesn't fall or falter; he keeps coming at Aman with long, steady strides.

Aman is terrified, but his armour is not. He hurls the lamppost at Jai, who catches it and advances, swinging it from side to side. Aman feels his shoulders shrug and then a pulse-blast shatters the lamppost.

There's a louder sound further up the street, above the buildings. A road of wind. A sonic boom.

Jai is left standing stupidly in the middle of a cloud of concrete dust, a red-hot vibrating metal rod in his hands. He drops it, looks up and sees Vir speeding at him like a bolt of lightning, fist aimed at his face.

The punch is so hard that nearby windows shatter. Jai is knocked a good twenty feet back, and slides on his back down the street even further. Aman totters in the rush of wind, his armour adjusting his balance. Jai is down but not out. He's clutching his jaw, groaning.

Vir has taken to the sky again, he's already far above them. He turns and stands in mid-air, high above the buildings around him, and Aman shivers. Even now, there's something chilling about the sight of a man just standing in mid-air. To Aman's right, a crowd of policemen rush towards the fight, the sound of sirens is heard all around. Jai stands up slowly, swaying slightly. An ugly bruise is sprouting on the right side of his face, and he spits out blood on his palm. He looks at his own blood in wonder, he hasn't seen it in a while.

Aman attacks. His armour evidently decides kung fu isn't

cutting it, and Aman finds himself running faster, moving closer to the houses on his left, and then he's running along the wall towards Jai, his body almost horizontal. Jai doesn't even notice him until the moment of impact, when Aman leaps off the wall and delivers a flying kick to his head. Jai is felled yet again, and two of his teeth fly out.

Using his rage, Jai leaps off the ground this time, roaring incoherently as he charges at Aman. Aman trips him, finds himself swinging from side to side, raising one leg at a time, and shouts in surprise as his legs suddenly rise into the air. His body is upside down, his hands on the street. But Jai's not holding him, no one is, his armour has decided to continue the Brazilian experience by switching from head-football to capoeira. Aman's legs whirl like a helicopter's rotors as he twists, leaps and turns in incredibly acrobatic dance-fight attacks, feinting, bending, sweeping Jai's legs from under him time and time again, leaving him screaming in frustration and grabbing empty air.

The policemen are upon them now, and seem mesmerised by Aman's display. A few of them shoot at Jai, but stop when they realise he hasn't noticed.

But inside the whirling armour, Aman is feeling neither graceful nor heroic. He wants to go home. His head is dizzy from rushing blood, his stomach is churning and he's torn muscles he doesn't even know he had. Every split, every turn, every evasive cartwheel has left him groaning. The armour performs its finishing move, running up Jai's body, viciously kicking his head again before somersaulting and landing on its feet. A watching policewoman cheers wildly as Jai turns a backwards somersault, and lands on his head, but Aman is mostly unconscious.

* * *

Jai rises again, hitting his head to clear the cobwebs. And then he rises even further, as Vir swoops in behind him, grabs him by the hand and takes off like a rocket. Jai is groggy, disorientated. He finally realises where he is when he sees the dome of St Paul's whizzing by at eye level.

Vir climbs higher and higher, London spreading out below them, the horizon a stripe of dark blue across an infinite world. Vir slows down, standing with the city far below his feet. He hoists Jai up on his shoulder. His former friend looks around, babbling incoherently, dribbling blood through the gaps in his teeth.

"I'm sorry it had to end like this," Vir says.

He launches head-first into a dive, speeding down towards the city. Jai is now underneath him, arms and legs flapping in the rush of air, mouth open in a silent scream, trailing blood into the heavens. Vir accelerates relentlessly, adding his superhuman strength to gravity, and when they're level with London's tallest buildings, he lets go.

The strongest superhuman of them all hurtles towards the street like a meteor, a skydiver with no parachute, flailing wildly, swimming through the air with nowhere to go but down.

The impact of Jai's landing shakes the earth. All of London trembles. Police cars wailing their way down Cheapside are thrown into the air. The road cracks open, a large crater is formed instantly, and Aman, running towards Cheapside, feels the shockwave as windows shatter and car alarms go off all around him.

Wide fractures spread across the road, heading towards

Aman as he sprints around the corner of New Change, and finds Jai lying in the centre of a large circle of sizzling tar. Millions of shards of glass from a corner building cover the whole area like confetti.

Four red phone booths lie shattered and twisted around the crater; postcards advertising mostly naked women fall like snowflakes down on the scene. Two police BMWs, upturned like flipped cockroaches, spin wheels as their drivers crawl out through jagged glass windows. Two Tube station entrance signs and several traffic lights, all broken, spit sparks out on the street. A crumpled heap nearby used to be a flowerbed in the middle of the road, a trickle of earth and a few flowers have slid into the crater. Pink and yellow carnations die smothered in tar.

Jai lies on his back in the crater, his burnt body splayed out, limbs oddly bent, eyes staring into space.

As Aman runs up to the edge of the crater, Vir descends slowly in front of him.

"We did it," Vir says. "We saved everybody."

"I suppose so," Aman says. "It wasn't fair, though. But then nothing is."

"You did so well," Vir says. "Have you called the others? Uzma? Tia?"

Aman's not listening. He's staring in disbelief at Jai. At Jai's mouth, where two bright new teeth are growing out of his mangled, bloody gums. At Jai's arms, which are slowly untwisting. At the long scars and burnt patches that had covered Jai's bloody chest seconds ago. They're fading.

"He heals," Aman whispers. "Did you know he heals?"

"No," Vir says. "I don't think he knows himself. No one's given him a reason to heal before."

"Well, don't tell him, then."

Jai blinks. His body convulses, and straightens out. He stares at the sky.

"He's invincible," Aman says. "The perfect soldier."

"What do we do?" Vir asks. "Do we keep hitting him?"

"Yes," says Aman. "Most definitely yes."

Jai sticks out a hand and grasps the edge of the crater. He pulls himself up to a sitting position. And then he sees Aman and Vir, and for the first time Aman sees Jai look scared. His gaze flickers around the broken street, and before either Aman or Vir has time to react, he leaps up, vaults out of the crater, lands on tottering feet in front of the stairs leading down into St Paul's Underground Station and disappears from sight, clattering down the stairs into darkness.

"I'm going to drop him into a volcano," Vir says. "Could you go and get him, please?"

Aman turns sharply.

"What do you mean, 'go get him'? You're coming with me."

Vir looks sheepish.

"I really don't like enclosed spaces," he says. "I don't want to go underground. Just bring him out, I'll deal with him."

Aman stands at the entrance and looks down. Somewhere below, someone's screaming. He can hear metal strike metal. A power cable is loose on the lower steps, it slithers around, shooting sparks at him.

"You think this is my comfort zone?" he yells. "Come on."

Vir hovers towards the entrance and floats into the tunnel, fists up, ready for action. Aman calls Uzma.

"Where are you?" she asks. He can hear shouts and sirens around her.

"St Paul's. Heading underground with Vir. Jai's in there. You?"

"Persuading the police to let the others go. They've got a lot of Tias locked up in a van. We're going to steal a helicopter after that."

"Nice. I'm heading in, might not get a signal. I've asked my bots to text you my location every minute."

"You coming?" Vir enquires from below the stairs.

"Got to go," Aman says. "Jai can heal himself, by the way. We need a plan to take him out, and I'm going to be running, not thinking. You take care of yourself, okay?"

"Yeah. And Aman? I love you. You know that, right?"

"Yes. Love you too. Bye now." He runs down the stairs, grinning from ear to ear under his helmet despite the shooting streaks of pain that wrack his body with every step.

Vir is waiting at the bottom and together they rush into the station, and vault over the ticket machines, Vir doesn't bother to land on the floor. There's an Underground official slumped over the wide entrance gate. As they race to the platforms down escalators and through narrow white-tiled corridors, Vir trails his fingers along the advertisements on the walls, moving in stops and starts like a fish in a waterpipe.

It's easy enough to tell which way Jai has gone – they just follow the trail of bashed-up Underground employees. He's taken a tunnel leading west up the Central Line. Aman leaps down onto the track and rushes towards the darkness. Ahead of him, Vir hovers at the tunnel's mouth, shaking his head.

"Come on!" Aman yells.

"Not going in there," Vir says. "We could get hit by a train."

"Vir, the Tube's shut. Because of us, remember?"

"Too dark. Too narrow."

Aman runs back out of the tunnel and addresses the flying-man.

"Vir, I could give you a lecture about facing your fears and being a hero, but there isn't time. You're our leader. Jai's in there. Let's move."

Vir flies into the tunnel, and Aman's armour follows, moving along the metal track, sending sparks flying as they speed through the darkness. Vir flies into a wall as the tunnel curves and dips. He lands heavily, curses and drops behind Aman, flitting bat-like in the wake of the sparks from Aman's feet.

The armour flips to night vision, sends a sonar ping out into the tunnel, and finds nothing. It turns on its heat sensor, looking for Jai's signature, and Aman sees a ghostly image up ahead. A blue shimmer, a will-o'-the-wisp. A running man fading into the distance.

"Speed up," he says to his armour, and it does. They pass swiftly through the tunnel, Aman's clanging footsteps and great gusts of breath echoing in the narrow space. There are other sounds in the tunnel, strange wet sounds, whispers, crashes and thuds from far away, muffled roars and moans. Aman is glad he doesn't have time to stop and listen, to wonder what he might find in London's ancient labyrinth of tunnels. In a world where superheroes exist, what else is possible? His lungs are bursting, but the armour is relentless.

They reach the next station, Chancery Lane. Vir flies up onto the platform, clearly grateful for light, but Aman sees Jai's heat-trail heading into the westward tunnel and soldiers on. His armour is running at full stretch now, his vision narrowed in completely on pursuing Jai. Vir follows.

A faint whine rises in Aman's ears and he wonders if the armour is overheating; he wonders what he is supposed to do if it suddenly stops. Holborn and then Tottenham Court Road Stations pass by in a blur. They're closing in on Jai now, the image ahead is clearer, and it's slowly turning green. Huge drops of sweat streak Aman's face. He's beginning to drift away, barely able to feel his arms pistoning away in front of him. His body has moved from pain to numbness, it's a struggle to keep his eyes open, to stay conscious.

They rush out of the tunnel at Oxford Street Station. Aman hears a thud behind him and hurriedly shakes himself back into wakefulness. He's already passed by most of the platform, and there's no image of Jai in the tunnel up ahead. His feet swerve, of their own accord, running up the curved wall by the tracks, and then he's running upside down on the ceiling. He somersaults, and the world spins crazily as his armour twists and lands neatly, transitioning from Olympic gymnast to Shaolin monk in an instant. He charges forward again, willing himself into awareness, towards the battle unfolding before him.

Jai had been waiting on the platform by the tunnel entrance. He'd let Aman race by him, but when Vir flew out into the light, he'd pounced. Vir had hit the wall and skidded along it, breaking bricks, tearing film posters, tumbling onto the tracks.

Vir throws himself into the air, but inside the station, he's trapped. Jai leaps on him and bears him down to the ground. Aman sends a pulse-blast at Jai, but he simply lifts Vir up between them, and Vir's body shudders as the white sphere connects.

Jai punches Vir in the face, twice, lifts him and slams him onto the tracks with all his might. Cracks run up the platform and the walls. Aman is upon them now, but Jai swings Vir up again in front of him, and the armour stops mid-strike. Laughing, Jai tosses Vir into the western end of the tunnel. Vir is unconscious, and he falls heavily.

Aman fires pulse-blasts at will, but Jai is faster. He dashes into the west tunnel after Vir, and the pulse-strikes shatter the wall behind him. Aman leaps down onto the tracks and runs after him through a shower of bricks and concrete, but just as he's about to enter the tunnel his armour stops and bends backwards, and Aman sees Jai's fist shoot over his face. He vaults acrobatically up onto the platform, and Jai rushes back into the tunnel.

Aman struggles, straining forward, but his armour doesn't move. And he hears a sound in his head, that annoying, awful sound that phones make when the battery's low. *Tu-du-doo.* He's running out of steam.

Inside the tunnel, there's not much of a fight going on. Aman can hear thuds and crashes, Jai's voice raised in a triumphant, feral roar as he slams Vir's body into the tunnel walls, again and again. There's a pause, and then a loud crash, an inhuman scream, which is abruptly cut off, and then silence.

Aman wills himself forward. After a few seconds, the armour comes back to life, humming angrily, but it's too late. Jai strides out of the tunnel, fists covered in blood. He glances up at Aman, leaps nimbly up onto the platform and grins.

"One down," he says.

Aman fires two pulse-blasts at Jai. He dodges them like a matador, and they hit the arch of the westward tunnel entrance. Chunks of mortar fly everywhere, and the roof collapses, sealing the tunnel.

"Thanks," Jai says.

Yawning cracks run up and down the platform, and up the walls around them. The roof begins to rumble.

Aman charges at Jai, but Jai leaps over him and starts running towards the platform exit. Aman hits him in the back with a pulse-blast, and Jai falls, skids and rises.

"This is fun, kid," he says. "But let's take it outside. No one's watching in here."

He's off again, tearing towards the stairs. Aman wants to dive into the tunnel, somehow dig Vir out, but his armour ignores him and follows Jai, sprinting up the platform as chunks of plaster begin to fall from the ceiling. He chases Jai down long, curving white corridors, up a motionless escalator, over deserted ticket barriers and out into the sun at Oxford Circus.

Jai's just a few metres ahead, standing in the middle of Oxford Street, looking around eagerly as if he's a tourist out for a day of fun. Aman pounds him with a pulse, and Jai is thrown across the road into a Benetton shop window. He smashes into a solemn mannequin and slides along the polished shop floor, his journey into the world of fashion ending in a heap of overturned knitwear available in the Sale Up to 50% Off.

Aman calls Uzma.

"Oxford Circus," he says. "Get Sher and Tia to the Tube station. They need to dig Vir out. He should be alive. He took a mountain. This is just a city."

"What?" Uzma yells back. He can hear a loud throbbing behind her. "I'm in a helicopter! We're coming! What did you say?"

"Never mind, I'll text you," Aman says, and disconnects.

Across the street, Jai strides out over broken glass, a brightly coloured scarf draped rakishly over his bare muscle-bound torso. He looks like the world's fiercest model.

Tu-do-doo, says Aman's armour. He sends Uzma a message, cartwheels to avoid Jai's lunge and runs for his life down Regent Street. He has chosen this route for a very valid reason: it's right in front of him. He doesn't know whether he's running himself, or whether the armour has taken over completely. Finding out would involve stopping. He hears the wail of a siren behind him, and flinches as it stops abruptly. Turning, he sees Jai leap off a police car and soar towards him. Aman sets his head down and runs, lungs threatening to burst. There's a thump on the road some distance behind him. He hears Jai's footsteps thumping up Regent Street in pursuit.

Aman knows he can run really fast, remembers outrunning Jai underground just a few minutes ago. He tells himself he can do it again – and then the sound of feet behind him stops and his armour swerves as Jai flies over his head. There's a dark-blue pole up ahead with traffic lights on it. Jai catches it one-handed, spins around, sticks out a leg, pivots and Aman sees Jai's foot arcing towards his head. His armour is too tired for more evasive manoeuvres, and Aman runs straight into the kick.

He doesn't feel any pain, his armour soaks up the impact, whining as it powers down, and Aman shoots like a cannonball across the street, watching in fascination as the door of Hamleys Toy Shop rushes forward to welcome him.

The burglar alarm goes off as Aman smashes into the store and barrels through rows and rows of toys. He ends up sprawled in the far corner in the middle of a jungle-themed soft toy exhibit. Aman is buried in stuffed cuteness. He hears footsteps approaching and fires his pulse cannon blindly, shooting in every direction. Shelves full of toys explode. The air is a riot of coloured fur and puffs of feathers. Soft animals and cuddly monsters fly, bounce around and are torn apart. Then the pulse cannon whirs to a stop. The armour's done.

Aman struggles to his feet. Then his legs give way, muscles too tired to take his weight, and so he crawls across the floor, unable to see anything in a haze of cotton, fibres and miscellaneous stuffing.

He hears Jai cursing somewhere nearby. For an instant he sees a figure loom up above him, thrashing about, but then Jai stumbles over a life-sized toy gorilla and goes face first into a mountain of toys, filling the air with white fluff all over again.

Slipping, sliding, scrabbling, Aman makes it to the foot of the non-moving escalator in the middle of the store. He crawls up the steps on hands and knees as quickly as he can, while Jai, roaring like Godzilla, wreaks plush-cloud havoc in the soft toy section.

Aman's up on the first floor by the time Jai crushes the alarm. Aman continues upwards as silently as he can. His body is threatening to quit, he has to drag himself up the stairs to the fifth floor. He makes it to the top, and smiles grimly as he sees it's the boys' section.

The shelves to his left are lined with film merchandise, row upon row of action figures, mostly superheroes, staring blankly out from their plastic sheaths, loudly coloured sheets of cardboard behind them advertising their many special features. Aman crawls between two rows of childhood idols. It's getting hard to breathe. The armour feels like it's strangling him. He doesn't want any of this any more. He presses the buttons on his chest and sighs in relief as the black and silver plates slide off him and fold themselves neatly into briefcase form. His legs are completely numb. The rest of his muscles throb in one solid mass of pain, his nerves appear to be melting. Aman rolls over onto his back and stares at the ceiling. The phone rings in his head, but he doesn't pick it up. He wishes *he* had a shut-down button. His eyes close.

He hears footsteps on the stairs, Jai's firm tread, and he groans.

Jai strides up to the fifth floor of Hamleys, a confident smile on his face.

"I know you're here," he calls. "It's only a matter of time." He pops out of view as his footsteps come closer. Aman rolls away from the middle of the aisle, huddling close to a row of shelves. Jai walks up the aisle next to Aman's. The shelves are only chest-high, and Aman can feel Jai's presence, see his shadow inches away. Then the footsteps start to move away, and Aman almost breathes again. But Jai stops, and retraces his steps.

"There you are," he says, leaning over a counter. He walks up to Aman and stands over him, grinning. "Frankly, Aman, you don't look so good. Where's your costume?" He grabs Aman's T-shirt and pulls him to his feet. Aman's body sags.

"It's no fun when you're asleep," Jai says. "Here. This is for that little monkey-dance you pulled off at the cathedral." He twists Aman's left arm, breaking it. Aman's eyes bulge, he screams.

"That's better," Jai says. "Don't die on me, boy. Not yet. We've got to go outside and put on a show. You don't want to die in a bloody toy shop. Where's your sense of occasion? The world is watching and Vir let me down, giving up in the tunnel like that. On your feet." He lets Aman go, and Aman falls on a shelf and slides to the floor, dragging a few Transformers with him.

"Bloody useless civilians," Jai says. He grabs Aman's

broken arm and starts walking. White-hot shards of pain run across Aman's body, but he does not have the strength to do anything other than moan as Jai drags him up the aisle and around the corner.

There's a voice downstairs. A female voice, calling Aman. Uzma is here. Aman stirs and opens his eyes. Jai drags him back into the aisle and stuffs a toy monster in his mouth.

Aman goes online and tries to call Uzma. It's her turn not to answer.

Jai walks back towards the stairs, and crouches behind the shelf closest to the top. It's a good spot for an ambush, he'll be able to strike before Uzma has time to say anything. He waits.

A tentative footstep on the bottom step. To Aman, it sounds like a gunshot.

"Aman?" Uzma calls. "Aman, you there?"

Jai tenses, ready to pounce, as someone runs up the stairs.

Summoning every last reserve of strength, Aman spits the monster out of his mouth and yells, "Don't!"

Jai pounds the floor and yells in frustration. An instant later, he's towering above Aman. He picks him up, hurls him against the nearest wall and charges at the stairs, where a head has just come into view. He's a blur of speed, the perfect predator.

In his upside-down world, flying towards shelves full of action figures, Aman sees Jai's hand move up in a scything chop, and winces as he hears Uzma scream. His back smashes into the racks on the wall. He falls to the floor, strange shapes floating inside his eyelids. Shelves full of toys tilt and fall, one after the other, like misshapen dominoes.

As Aman's vision fades, the screams in the background fade and the world turns into a black and green sea of pain. The last thing he sees, soaring above him, is a flurry of colourful arms and legs, of muscular bodies and outrageous costumes, stars and capes, lantern jaws and ray-guns. For a brief and glorious moment, it's raining superheroes.

When Aman wakes, four Tias are carrying him out of Hamleys on a stretcher, bickering amicably. One squeals in excitement as he opens his eyes and looks around.

There's an ambulance waiting on Regent Street. Two more Tias sit in front inside it. Aman looks at his broken left arm, it's bandaged, in a sling. He rises slightly and tries to speak, but the Tias shush him. They slide him into the back of the ambulance, bumping his head only once. Then they file inside behind him and merge into one body.

"Welcome back, darling," she says, smiling. "Thought you were dead there for a bit."

"Uzma?" Aman croaks.

"No, I'm Tia. Has it been that long?" she asks, and hugs him. The ambulance starts to move. "Uzma's fine. You've been out for an hour, by the way. A lot happened. But that's all right – you woke up in time to catch the end."

"Armour," Aman says. "My armour's in there."

"No it's not. Uzma took it."

"What happened? I remember Jai jumping at Uzma right before I blacked out."

"No, that was me coming up the stairs with Uzma on sound effects duty," Tia says. "You'd told your online spider thingies to message us your location every minute, remember? We knew he was there. We got there just in time, too – you're really lucky he didn't just rip your head off. He must be really fond of you. Vir's alive too, by the way – Sher got him out."

"How did you beat Jai? What happened up there at the toy shop?"

"You'll see. Uzma told me not to tell you – she said she wants to explain it all herself. What a day, huh? I spent all the best bits sitting in cars arguing with stupid policemen, but this last bit was enough, thanks very much."

"Where are we going?" Aman asks.

"Piccadilly Circus. We're already there." And Tia flings open the doors of the ambulance. Three more Tias emerge and they carry Aman out. He exits the ambulance into a cacophony: Londoners of every possible age, shape and colour throng the streets, talking loudly, taking pictures. Journalists chatter into mikes, policemen attempt to establish order, tourists gawk, pickpockets make merry. The city's coming back to life. On each of the five streets leading to Piccadilly Circus, a massive crowd has formed. They're walking towards the Eros fountain, and everyone is looking up at the greying sky. Aman looks up as well, and he blinks, rubs his eyes and stares in disbelief.

Jai floats high above the Anteros statue in the middle of Piccadilly Circus. There's a sphere of white light around him, and he appears to be trapped inside it. He pounds on the wall of his bubble, but to no avail.

Anima and Vir circle the sphere in ever-changing orbits. Anima bears twin katanas, sparkling green. Her manga eyes are full of tears, visible even from the ground. Vir has a new costume, identical to the old one – there are many sportswear shops in London. The right side of his face is bruised and turning blue. Girls scream like Beatles fans as he whizzes over them. He notices Aman on the ground, and gives him a little wave.

Uzma emerges from a huddle in the crowd and walks up to the edge of the fountain under the statue. She's never looked more beautiful; she's doing her Grand Entrance thing again. The crowd sighs with love and desire as she takes her place under the ball of light. She looks around theatrically, raises her arms and calls her fellow superheroes.

Anima and Vir fly earthwards, touching down gently by her side. Sher emerges from an Underground exit in tiger-man form, he lopes up to the others, growling, and the crowd scatters as he crosses the road.

"Got to go, love. See you soon," Tia says, and she walks off towards the fountain. Seven Tias merge into one, and the crowd applauds as she sashays up to her team. She blows a kiss at Uzma, and Uzma acknowledges it with a regal smile.

A rousing cheer echoes across Piccadilly Circus as another hero emerges from a police car. It's the mysterious warrior in black and silver armour recently seen battling Jai above, around and under London. He lines up next to the others.

Through the crowd, Aman catches Uzma's eye. She smiles at him and looks away. Zothanpuii also emerges from the crowd, mostly unnoticed, and stands demurely behind Sher, making seven, the traditional number in these situations. Photographers form a huddle around them and go wild as the seven all look up at Jai.

Uzma stands on the fountain's edge and addresses the crowd.

"Does this villain deserve to live?" she cries.

Aman has read about crowds speaking in chorus in books, but it obviously never happens in real life...

"NO!" London says, as one.

Uzma nods sadly, and Vir flies up under Jai's light-prison. He carries the sphere higher and higher until he's just a speck in the sky, the light a glowing ball the size of a lightbulb, the prisoner inside it slumped, defeated, broken. Then Vir flies away, leaving the sphere hovering, and at Uzma's signal the black and silver warrior leaps up and fires a pulse-blast at the prison-sphere. There's a streak of light, a collective gasp, and the battle for London and the world ends, as Aman always suspected it would, with a huge explosion.

When the fireworks are done, there's no trace left of the light-sphere, and Jai is gone. The crowd gasps appreciatively and applauds, cheering until every throat in Piccadilly is hoarse.

A Tia walks up and takes Aman's hand.

"You should be very proud," she says. "All this is your doing."

"This isn't what I wanted at all," he says.

"You all right?" she asks.

"Sure. Though why am I here, and not with them? And who the hell is that in my armour?"

"Uzma will explain," Tia says.

"Uzma has a lot of explaining to do," he says. "What the hell just happened?"

"We saved the world," Tia replies. "I think."

CHAPTER **TWENTY-ONE**

The party at the Eros fountain goes on for hours, and Aman is too tired to wait for it to end. Tia drives him to a hotel, and he treats himself to a honeymoon suite, compliments of a large mining corporation currently killing tribes in eastern India and pillaging their hills for bauxite. He sinks into a vast, fluffy bed and passes out in the middle of taking his shoes off. Tia finishes the job, straightens him out on the bed, covers him up and leaves.

He wakes up in the middle of the night to find Uzma by his side, smiling at him. The lights are on, and she looks tired but gorgeous. Her hair is tousled. Her breath smells of champagne. She takes his clothes off and throws aside her own. She climbs on top of him and they make love, slowly and silently. When it's over, she begins to speak, her voice is soft and low, and even though he's too exhausted to understand what she's saying he goes to sleep with a smile on his face. When his eyes open again, it's morning. She's gone.

* * *

An hour later, Uzma walks into Hyde Park, past a red lion and white unicorn locked in eternal battle on a gate. She sees Aman to her right, leaning against the base of a statue of Achilles. An elderly Chinese woman sways gracefully on the grass near him, guiding her body through the slow, fluid motions of Tai Chi. Aman is watching young men in white helmets ride magnificent chestnut horses up and down Rotten Row, and doesn't notice Uzma until she flings her arms around him.

"My parents send their love," she says. "They said they're sorry they tried to kill you and it's all right about the furniture."

"Then I have absolutely nothing to worry about," Aman says, grinning. They link arms and start walking, two lovers taking in the morning air. Aman moves with the fluid grace of a couch potato who has just spent a week training with the Territorial Army. They choose a long, straight path flanked by tall, slender birches on either side. Apart from the occasional cyclist or jogger, Hyde Park is calm and green, London's traffic a distant growl to the east.

"So," Uzma says. "Question time."

"Yeah," Aman says. "Who was he? The man in my armour? The Illusionist?"

"Good question. That was Jai."

Aman jerks his arm away and takes a step back.

"What?"

"That was Jai. Don't be mad. We couldn't think of what else do with him."

"I don't understand," Aman says, rubbing his head. "What do you... Who was that in the big white bubble, then?"

"That was Shankar the Illusionist. Or, like he says, Shankar the Great Illusionist. Well, not him physically, of course – he was standing near the building with the big ads. His work. Vir and Anima just flew around it. The explosion was his as well."

Aman crosses the path, shaking his head, and sits down carefully on a green bench.

"Just tell me everything," he said. "I heard you coming up the escalator at Hamleys. I tried to warn you. Jai knocked me out. And then?"

Uzma sits beside him, feet on the bench, a hand on his arm.

"It wasn't me," she says. "I was a few steps below, completely petrified, trying not to bolt. Tia volunteered to walk in front so I'd have enough time to speak if Jai attacked. There were lots of her – she kept a circle all around me while we went from floor to floor, looking for you. When Jai charged, he killed a few Tias, but I told him to stop. He looked so angry, but he froze. I couldn't believe it. He just stood there, waiting for orders. And I told him what I wanted him to do, and he did it."

"What did you tell him?"

"I told him he was my slave now. That he belonged to me, and he also had to obey you and Vir. He had to protect us from all harm, and help us fix the world. I told him he could never harm anyone again unless we asked him to. That he wasn't even to think of doing anything that would make me unhappy. And that he could never let anyone see his face again. Except us."

She falters, and they look at each other in silence. A jogger passes, ghost music trickling out of his iPod.

"Good command list," Aman says.

"Thanks. I thought it up on the helicopter. There was one more thing on the list, but I've forgotten what it is."

"You should tell him he has to obey commands from you even when you're not physically with him. You know, over the phone, in writing, that sort of thing."

"Nice. Yeah, I'll do that. What else?"

"I'll make a list. I'm having a little difficulty wrapping my mind around it. So what are you going to do with him? Is he going to be your sidekick? Your bodyguard? Your dog?"

"Don't say that," Uzma says, looking away. "I don't know. Maybe I should send him away. To meditate on a beach forever and think happy thoughts. We had a team meeting last night, before I came over to your hotel, and it was terrible. He was in there with us, and we couldn't look at him. He just kept staring at me with this blank smile, this adoring face. I had to ask him to wait outside."

"Team meeting, huh? That's good to know."

"Look, Aman, we all wanted you to be there. You know we did. But Tia said you were too tired. It was bad enough you weren't there when we were trying to figure out what to do with Jai, how to stage his death, how to hide him."

"Whose idea was that anyway?"

"Mine. Shankar wasn't even with us at that point – it was just Tia and me, and then Sher and Anima brought Vir. We had to put a lot of makeup on him. Zothanpuii and Shankar weren't even with us – they'd gone back to the hotel. Zothanpuii's not wearing a white vest anywhere near a river again. She had to change. I don't believe the whole show came together in the end."

"It was a great show, though. Especially you. You're a born con artist."

"I'm an actor."

"And a damned fine one. Where are the others now?"

"Hotel. Though I think Vir might have gone off with some groupies. Last night was very crazy. Premalata's left, by the way."

"What do you mean, left?"

"Yeah. She fainted, and then when they woke her up she said she was scared and she quit. They let her go."

"Good. She was crazy anyway."

"And after you left there was the press conference, and then we went to a few parties, and Tia had to drop me home. There were some paparazzi who tried to follow me but I told them to jump into the river and they did. Tia got the others back safe too. We're meeting today for lunch. You're coming, obviously."

"Is that an order?"

Uzma turns towards him sharply. Something in her eyes sends a shiver up Aman's spine.

"No, it's bloody well not an order," she snaps. "Don't make this difficult, Aman. I didn't know what my power was. But I can control it now. People only have to obey me when – I can't explain. It's a different voice. I have to mean it more."

"I'm sorry," he says. "But it's just... did you order me to come to London? I didn't want to. Did you make me?"

"No!" Uzma jumps off the bench and stands, hands on hips, eyes blazing in fury. "Stop making me question everything I ever did! How on earth am I supposed to know? Do you think I planned all this?"

"That's not what I said," Aman says. "Your powers were growing. You didn't know what they were – it's just a possibility, that's all. I'm not saying you're an evil supervillain mastermind."

"That's just lovely, isn't it? It's also a possibility that you're not really in love with me. That it's just my powers hypnotising you. Have you thought about that?"

"Yes. I have," Aman says. "Sit down, won't you? My neck hurts. I think a Skeletor doll tried to have sex with it."

She laughs, a full, deep laugh that echoes across the park. A passing cyclist falls in love with her and off his bike. She helps him get up and tells him to move on and lose five kilos. When he's gone, she huddles up next to Aman, head on his shoulder.

"I've thought about this a lot, and I have a speech to make," he says.

"Make it," Uzma says.

"I love you," says Aman. "Maybe it's your powers, maybe it's because you're cleverer and wiser than I am, maybe it's your smile, maybe it's your body. Probably your body – have you seen it? Anyway, my point is, I love all of you and wondering whether I'd have loved you if you didn't have your powers is like wondering whether I'd have loved you if you had elephant ears and only spoke Mandarin. And I probably would have. The end."

"That's a good speech," she says. "Did you practise it?"

"Some of it. It was a lot better in my head, and I went off the rails a bit. But I meant well. Thought I'd say my piece before you met a lot of poets and they all fell in love with you."

"Kiss me," she says. It's an order. He does.

A short while later, she leans back with a satisfied expression.

"Now, as future leaders of the world, we should talk work," she says.

"Look at you, all enthusiastic superhero."

"Can't really be an actress now, can I? All character conflict would be resolved five minutes in."

"Or you'd tell Aamir Khan to take a hike, and they'd find him in Switzerland four days later. But maybe with really careful screenwriters..."

Uzma smirks. "It's all your fault, you know. 'The world needs to be saved, it's irresponsible to not use your powers,' all those reproachful looks whenever I said I didn't want to do it. But you were right. And it's all going to happen now, Aman. We're going to make everything better. We could go and fix the Middle East this evening, if you're free. Once you've told me who to talk to and what to say, that is."

"And you'd trust me to know what was best for everyone? That's not what you said in Goa. I decided to quit because of what you told me."

"You wanted out because you saw you'd made mistakes, Aman. I had nothing to do with that. Yes, I thought you'd got it wrong, but I wanted you to find a better way to use your powers. I never asked you to do nothing."

Aman heaves a sigh.

"You're right," he says. "Yeah. Can't blame you for any of that. And... I just agreed with you again."

"So we helped each other work things out, right? You showed me that I needed to think about more than myself, and I showed you what you were doing wrong. Sorted. And now we'll have the whole team to back us up."

"What's this team called, by the way?"

"We thought of lots of names, but they're all taken. Bloody comics. We thought we'd let you decide. Getting our team name is the first order of business at today's meeting."

"But I'm not in the team."

"Of course you are. We'd have to keep your identity secret anyway. You started this team, Aman. Don't even think of not being in it. Besides, you're our research guy, our strategist, our publicist, our administrator."

"Your supplies guy. Your accountant and financier. Your tech support. Got it."

"No, Aman. You're team leader. And yes, you'll support us, just like you have from the start. But you don't have to handle it all alone. You'll have far more important things to do. Which is why our second order of business at today's meeting is hiring a manager."

"I saw your first press conference after I called you," Aman says. "Good speech. Who wrote it?"

"I did. It was mostly the speech from Vir's video anyway."

"Why didn't Vir make it, then?"

"Well, I asked him to, obviously. But the journalists said I should do it. I'm, well, prettier, plus I'm a British Muslim woman and they didn't get Vir's accent. You know how it is."

"I do."

"Are you... are you saying I'm trying to control this team, Aman? Because that would be really unfair."

Aman reaches out to embrace her, but she pulls away.

"Uzma, you'd be the last person in the world to make a power bid of any kind," Aman says. "I know you didn't want any of this. I know it was thrust upon you, and you're trying to deal with it."

"I didn't even know how my power worked until yesterday," Uzma says, blinking back tears. "Give me some time!"

"I'm sorry. Really."

"Then help me instead of doubting me," Uzma says. She gets up and stalks off. Aman runs after her and grabs her hand.

"I'm sorry," he says. "Uzma, I don't doubt your intentions at all. Really."

"Good," she says. "Because you'd have felt like an utter

idiot. Because I'm going to do a fantastic job."

"I know," he says. "And the whole world will love you. Even the ones who only get to watch you on TV."

"You think my power might grow enough for it to work on camera?" she asks.

"We'll know soon enough. Whether or not that happens, you'll still be huge. Biggest star in the world. Bigger than the Beatles."

"All right, all right," she says. "I have done one thing I shouldn't have, though."

She reaches into a pocket and pulls something big and sparkly out of her jeans. Aman's eyes widen.

"Is that the Koh-i-noor?" he asks. The diamond catches the sun and Uzma's face glows. She grins widely and her eyes are full of mischief as they meet Aman's.

"I think I'm going to keep it," she says.

"You do that," he says. "It didn't belong to them anyway. Besides, you're going to rule the world, and you're a woman so the curse won't get you."

"Or I could sell it and buy my brother a table," she says.

"Or you could spend the money to buy off the leaders of the anti-superhuman movement. Which began yesterday, by the way."

"There's an anti-us movement?"

"Yeah. Humans Against Super Humans. They're going to need a better acronym."

"That was quick," Uzma says. "Well, I could always talk to them."

"There'll be more," Aman says. "All over the world. People will hate us. We make them obsolete."

"We should send Sher back to India then. Maybe Vir. We've got to protect the others."

"Well, that's something I want to talk to you about," Aman says. "We might not be the only ones."

Uzma's eyes shine. "Did they find the missing British passengers?"

"No," Aman replies. "But I was looking at the emails we got after I uploaded Vir's video – and there are a lot of people who wrote in saying they had superpowers too. Most of them are crazy or just lying, of course, but there are clusters of people – in Prague, Tokyo, a few other cities – whose stories sound like ours. They all say it happened a week ago. They were all travelling. They all found out they had powers later. They all want help."

Uzma stuffs the Koh-i-noor back into her pocket.

"You think they might be telling the truth?"

"It's possible. We have no idea why this happened to us, or who or what was responsible. We've barely had time to breathe since it started. But whatever did this to us is still out there. We need to find out so much. We need to learn what else is going to change. If this isn't some giant hoax, it happened all over the world. Rio. Istanbul. Abuja. Shanghai. Wellington. Kabul. New York – which I suppose was inevitable. Maybe we were only the first wave."

"Well, we need to get these people together!" Uzma covers her mouth with her hands and starts walking in no direction in particular, the enormity of Aman's revelation threatening to swallow her up.

"I don't know," Aman says. "Maybe we should let them sort things out for themselves."

"Aman, they'll need help. There'll be more Jais. There'll be more people like Bob. This needs to be the first case we look into. Write to them! Bring them to... wherever our headquarters will be?"

"Yes, headquarters. Third order of business in today's team meeting."

Uzma stops pacing about and looks Aman in the eye.

"What's wrong now? Why don't you want to talk to them?"

"They could be lying."

"What if they're not?"

"Then they'll find their own answers. They have superpowers, that's a start. We need to help humans first. Lots of them. Soon."

"That's not it, is it?" Uzma crosses her arms and smiles grimly. "Come on, out with it."

"I don't think they should meet you," Aman says. "Don't be angry."

"I'm not," she says. "You're right, maybe they shouldn't. But let's take a vote on this at the meeting. It was Vir they thought they were talking to, you know. He should decide."

Aman takes a deep breath. "Uzma," he says.

"Yes?"

"We both know I'm not going to that meeting."

Two children, a boy and a girl, run down the path towards them. Uzma pulls out the Koh-i-noor and hands it to the girl. The new ruler of the world grabs the diamond and runs away from the crazy adults and their staring contest.

"Why won't you trust me?" Uzma asks. "I can control it now. I'd never make you do anything you didn't want to."

"I trust you," Aman says. "I don't trust your power. I'd want to please you even if you weren't trying."

"You just said my power was a part of me and you loved all of me."

"I do," Aman says. "But like you said to me once, you have really creepy powers."

"But I trust you," Uzma says. "When you told me you wouldn't listen to my calls or go into my mailbox, I believed you."

"Well, you shouldn't have,"

Uzma's face turns white.

"You looked at my mail?"

"Yes. And listened in on a few phonecalls. Before I met you. And the day you arrived. I was afraid you might be working for whoever was killing people like us. You would have been perfect for the job – we'd all have loved you on sight and gone anywhere you wanted us to. Anyway, I haven't looked since then, of course. And I hated myself for doing it even then, but lives were at stake. Whatever the reason, I did it. And you shouldn't have trusted me."

"Well, I forgive you," Uzma says. "Don't leave us, Aman. Don't leave me. I don't want to do this without you."

"I don't either," Aman says. "But it's not just about us, is it?"

Uzma stares at the ground. Aman takes a step towards her, reaches out, but doesn't touch her. When she looks up again, her face is composed. He has never loved her more, but he watches her eyes harden and knows he's lost her.

"I like how you assume that everything I might want to do with the world is somehow not good enough," she says. "And that you'd always have a better plan. And I'd not let you do it."

"I didn't –"

"You're right. We can't work together, Aman."

"I should go," he says.

"What are you going to do?"

"I'm going to take my armour and wander around the world beating bad people up and giving away their money. I want to go off to some small island and build a lair. And build a robot army and hatch plots to change the world. You want to come with me?"

"No," Uzma replies. "I like it here. I think I'll try being superhero team leader for a bit. The world needs changing, I've heard. And I think I have a better chance of actually getting things done than anyone else."

She watches Aman's face crumple.

"Don't be an idiot," she says. "I love you. And when you come back and beg me to let you join my team, I'll probably say yes. I might even take you back if I don't hook up with Johnny Depp. That's *might*, not *will*."

Aman's eyes light up.

"Maybe I could be your arch-nemesis," he says. "When I mess up the global economy again, you could all come smash my den. And when you people end up becoming the pawns of large companies and other people who want to keep things exactly the way they are – and you will – I'll be around to introduce a little chaos. We can keep each other in check."

"Sure. Of course, we could have stayed together and fought like normal couples, but I suppose this is nobler. More self-sacrifice. Good for you. Too bad you still only get to be the villain."

He's smiling now. "You want to meet up sometimes in luxury holiday resorts for dirty weekends?"

"No. I'm very busy. You can keep asking, though. Are you going to send the new superheroes to me?"

"No. Are you going to give me my armour?"

"No."

"I just deleted all your new emails."

"Harsh. Slap yourself."

He does, hard, and rubs his cheek afterwards, looking wounded.

"That was mean," he says.

"Arch-nemesis, remember?" She steps forward, grabs him and they kiss.

"Take care of yourself, all right?" she whispers. "Now get out of here."

He nods, and takes a few steps back down the path, trying to persuade himself to leave, not wanting to stop looking at her.

"I could make you stay," she says. "I could make you forget you ever wanted to leave."

"I know," he says. "But will you?"

He turns and walks away.

Uzma watches him go, words poised on the tip of her tongue, a small smile playing over her perfect lips.

ACKNOWLEDGEMENTS

The world of *Turbulence* could not have been saved, or even created, without the dashing deeds of the following super-squadrons:

The Daily Saviours: Cleo Omega and Josh the Bold

Titans of Industry: Cathwoman and The Grand Sophie

The Zeno Agency: Trusty John and Zesty John

Home Base: Grasshopper Girl, Sister Sinister and Zombie R

The Arthouse Horrors: Brutal Banerjee and the Karachi Killer

Assorted Toughs: The Tadpole Mafia, iBultu, Mr Thames, The Not-so-Old Brewer, Pu the Pugilist, Earthlight

Wren and Martin Private Investigations: Eagle Eye Sarkar

ABOUT THE **AUTHOR**

Samit Basu is one of India's most talented and prolific young writers. He is the author of *The Simoqin Prophecies*, *The Manticore's Secret* and *The Unwaba Revelations*, the three parts of The GameWorld Trilogy, published by Penguin Books India, and *Terror on the Titanic*, a YA novel published by Scholastic India. *Turbulence* was published in the UK to rave reviews and won *Wired*'s Goldenbot Award as one of the books of 2012. The sequel, *Resistance*, is coming soon from Titan Books.

Basu's work in comics ranges from historical romance to zombie comedy, and includes diverse collaborators, from X-Men/ Felix Castor writer Mike Carey to Terry Gilliam and Duran Duran. His next GN, *Local Monsters*, is to be published in 2013.

Samit was born in Calcutta, and currently divides his time between Delhi and Mumbai. He can be found on Twitter, @samitbasu, and at samitbasu.com.

ECKO RISING
Danie Ware

Ecko is an unlikely saviour: a savage, gleefully cynical rebel/assassin, he operates out of hi-tech London, making his own rules in a repressed and subdued society, When the biggest job of his life goes horribly wrong, Ecko awakes in a world he doesn't recognise: a world without tech, weapons, cams, cables – anything that makes sense to him. Can this be his own creation, a virtual Roschach designed just for him, or is it something much more? Ecko finds himself immersed in a world just as troubled as his own, striving to conquer his deepest fears and save it from extinction.

If Ecko can win though, then he might just learn to care – or break the program and get home.

"With action aplenty, this sf/fantasy mash-up is a thrilling, genre-defying roller coaster ride." *Library Journal*

"Wickedly entertaining." *Publishers Weekly*

TITANBOOKS.COM

THE COMPANY OF THE DEAD

David J. Kowalski

March 1912. A mysterious man appears aboard the
Titanic on its doomed voyage. His mission? To save the ship.
The result? A world where the United States never entered
World War I, thus launching the secret history
of the twentieth century.

"Time travel, airships, the *Titanic*, Roswell ... Kowalski
builds a decidedly original creature that blends military
science fiction, conspiracy theory, alternate history, and
even a dash of romance." *Publishers Weekly*

For more fantastic fiction from Titan Books in the
areas of sci-fi, fantasy, steampunk, alternate history,
mystery and crime, as well as tie-ins to hit movies,
TV shows and video games:

VISIT OUR WEBSITE

TITANBOOKS.COM

FOLLOW US ON TWITTER

@TITANBOOKS